LIMELIGHT

ARCANE CASEBOOK 5

DAN WILLIS

Print Edition – 2020

Initial Edits by Barbara Davis
Edited by Stephanie Osborn

Cover by Mihaela Voicu

Published by

Dan Willis
Spanish Fork, Utah.

1

DOG DAYS

It was after three in the afternoon when Alex Lockerby entered his modest, mid-ring office. The door opened onto a waiting room with two rather battered couches opposite and a single desk to the left in front of a large window. Alex had seen the room and the desk almost every day for six years and it never failed to make him smile.

"Hi ya, boss," the woman behind the desk said, looking up at him with a grin. "Any luck?"

The smile tried to run away from Alex's face, but he held it tight. The girl was slim and pretty with blue eyes and thick black hair that spilled down over her shoulders. Papers and notes were arranged on the desk in front of her, and Alex knew from experience they held the names of potential clients along with their information, all neatly laid out. As secretaries went, Sherry Knox was a great one, but she wasn't Leslie.

Leslie Tompkins had been Alex's secretary, confidante, and friend for over a decade, and Alex owed much of his success to her business skills. She'd been with him from the days of his basement office in Harlem when he was so broke he couldn't afford cigarettes, all the way up to the good times. All that had ended four months ago when Leslie married Randall Walker, the assessor for Suffolk County, and moved out of the city. Leslie had been the beating heart of his business, and the office just wasn't the same without her.

Keeping his smile in place, Alex nodded in answer to Sherry's question.

"I recovered Dr. Coville's notebook," he said, pulling a slim notebook bound in blue leather from his coat pocket. "A rival company paid off his lab assistant to steal it for them. I found it under the false bottom of a desk drawer in his apartment."

"What will the assistant do when he discovers it's gone?"

"I called Coville and told him to call Danny," Alex said. "His assistant will be in handcuffs soon, and Coville will be by to pay his bill and pick up his notebook." Alex laid the book on the table, then pulled some folded bills from his trouser pocket. "I also stopped by the Zimmermans' and got paid," he said, setting the money next to the notebook. "Add that to the cashbox."

Sherry's smile slipped a bit.

"Can you do it?" she asked. "It doesn't like me."

Alex resisted the urge to roll his eyes.

"It's a box, Sherry," he said. "It doesn't have opinions."

She fixed him with a cool stare that reminded him more than a little of Leslie, then pulled open the bottom drawer of her desk. Leaning down, she extracted a heavy steel box with a complex rune etched into the surface of its lid.

"Then you explain why it won't open for me half the time," she said, setting it on top of the desk. She knocked on the lid with her knuckles, then leaned close.

"It's me," she said.

The knock activated the engraved rune and it pulsed for a moment with purple light, but there was no click from inside the box. Sherry looked up at him with her most *I told you so* expression.

Furrowing his brow, Alex knocked on the lid.

"It's me," he said. The rune pulsed purple again and with a smart click, the lid popped up.

Sherry opened the box and began counting the stack of bills, adding it to the rubber-banded roll in the box. Alex smiled at the size of the roll, remembering when it took him a whole month just to make rent and Leslie's salary. It was early May and he already had more than enough to cover the month's expenses.

The pass rune, on the other hand, vexed him. Lifting the lid halfway, he checked the rune on the top. It was perfect, the same rune he'd been putting on his cashbox since he first got one. He pulled the lid fully open and examined the latch on the underside. When the pass rune activated, the spring-loaded pin would retract long enough for the lid to pop open. He pushed the pin with his finger, and it moved freely against its spring. There was no reason the cashbox shouldn't work for Sherry.

Unless she's right and it just doesn't like her.

Alex pushed that thought from his mind; runes didn't think, so they couldn't like or dislike people. He'd just wait until it faded and make sure he took extra care engraving the next one.

Sherry finished counting, noting the total on a pad of paper in the bottom of the cashbox before returning the roll of bills and closing the lid. She moved the cashbox to the desk's bottom drawer as Alex took a cigarette from his silver case.

"So what's next on the docket?" he asked, offering a cigarette to Sherry. She selected one, then lit it with the touch tip on the desk while Alex lit his with his lighter.

"I've got three good cases," she said, picking up one stack of papers and handing them over. "There are a half dozen more I need to get more information about." She nodded at the other stacks.

Alex thumbed through the pages she'd given him and sighed. He'd thought that with success would come a better class of case. His business used to be following cheating husbands and finding lost dogs. Now he found hidden assets for rich people mired in contentious divorce cases and located tchotchkes that people had lost or had been stolen. Only once in a great while did he get a fun case, like locating Dr. Coville's stolen notebook and exposing an industrial espionage scheme.

"All right," Alex sighed, standing up from the desk. He was about to move to his office to review the potential clients when the waiting room door closed.

"Wow," a familiar voice cut in. "Things must have gotten boring around here without me."

Alex whirled to the door where a striking older woman with chestnut brown hair and hazel eyes stood.

"Leslie!" he cried, crossing the room in two bounding steps to embrace her.

"Good to see you, kid," she said, as she squeezed him tight.

Alex stepped back, grinning.

"You haven't changed a bit," he said.

"It's only been five months," she said, beaming from the compliment. "You remember Randall." She gestured over her shoulder to the tall, slim man behind her.

Alex stuck out his hand and Randall took it. He had a long face with a narrow nose and brown eyes made larger by a pair of spectacles. A short handlebar mustache angled slightly upward, giving Randall a jovial appearance, tempered only a little by the distinguished gray creeping into his temples.

"I remember," Alex said, shaking his hand. "I oughta slug you for stealing her away." His voice was menacing but he wore a smile on his face.

"I regret nothing," Randal said, his mustache exaggerating his own grin.

"So what are you doing in the city?" Alex asked, turning back to Leslie.

"Randall has some friends here, and we were visiting," Leslie said, still beaming.

When Leslie first met Randall, Alex had assumed he was just a normal public servant, but he'd been the County Assessor for one of the most expensive pieces of ground in the state right at the time it became valuable. His family grew up there and he had quite a bit of family land that he'd inherited. Once the land values spiked, Randall had parceled up the family land and sold it off bit by bit, making a small fortune in the process. Since he married Leslie, Randall had retired to enjoy his new life.

Alex was happy for her, despite her being gone. If anyone deserved the proverbial fairy-tale ending, it was Leslie.

"Well I'm glad you decided to come by," Alex said.

For the first time Leslie's expression slipped. She recovered instantly and her expression turned sheepish.

"I — need a favor," she said, drawing out the first word with a wheedling tone.

"Oh, let me guess," Alex said. "You almost blushed when you said that. One of your new friends has misplaced their prized hound?"

"You're right, Lizzie," Randall said with a chuckle. "He is quick."

"Sorry," Leslie said with a shrug.

Alex laughed. He hadn't gone looking for a lost dog in years. Mostly his current rates were too high for people with such a simple request, and dog catching could be a time-consuming task.

"Well," he said in a skeptical voice. "Since it's you."

Leslie broke out her million-dollar smile and the room seemed brighter.

"Her name is Wilhelmina," she said, opening her handbag and taking out a red leather band decorated with silver studs. "My friend is worried because she slipped her collar. If the pound gets her, they won't know who to call."

Alex took the collar and turned it over. The leather was excellent quality and the silver studs had only a hint of tarnish.

"This will do fine," he said. "Follow me."

He turned and headed back out into the hall.

"Where are you going?" Leslie asked, hurrying along behind him. "Since when don't you do finding runes in your office?"

Alex reached into his trousers and pulled out a key ring with three keys on it. One was his oversized, skeleton type vault key, the others were for his office. He stopped at the next door down the hall from his and inserted the key.

"I've made a few changes since you left," he said, winking at Leslie. He turned the key and pushed the door open.

Inside was an office very similar to Alex's, though it was a bit smaller. The front area was wider than it was long, with a door in the far wall just opposite the hall. Beyond that door was a small office with a window against the outside of the building. The front space was furnished sparsely, with a large table occupying the center of the room.

An enormous map of Manhattan was stretched over the top, held in place by four pins attached to the table at the corners. Against the right-hand wall stood a small sideboard with a cigar box on it, and there was a coat rack in the corner. The wood floor was bare, revealing a large focusing rune Alex had painstakingly painted in the center, directly beneath the table. He had a similar one in his office but that was covered by his rug.

"Welcome to my finding room," he said, stepping aside so that Leslie and Randall could enter.

Leslie whistled, looking around.

"Fancy," she said, giving him a wink.

"I do a lot of finding work these days, so it's just easier to have a dedicated room," he said, closing the door behind them. Walking over to the sideboard, he opened the cigar box. It was like the one he used in the field, but unlike that one, this one only held a half-dozen cheap tin compasses.

Extracting one, he moved to the table and set it down, placing Wilhelmina's collar over it, making sure they touched. Next, Alex took out his red-backed rune book and tore out a finding rune, adding it atop the collar.

Leslie took Randall's arm and grinned. She'd seen Alex do this many times, but for her husband it was a new experience. Alex touched his cigarette to the flash paper and the rune erupted in flame. A few seconds later the orange construct left behind by the fire burst into tiny sparks and vanished.

"Oh," Randall exclaimed, sounding a bit disappointed. "I thought it would point somewhere on your map."

"It did," Alex said, picking up the dog collar and indicating the tin compass. "Just not the way you thought it would."

He sighted down the compass, whose needle was pointing in the direction of the core. Moving it slowly, Alex slid it along the surface of the map until it passed the core and headed out toward the west side docks. Abruptly the needle wavered and spun around, pointing back the way it had come.

"Looks like Wilhelmina's got herself arrested," Alex said, picking up the compass and indicating the spot beneath it. "The west side pound is right there."

Leslie nudged Randall in the ribs and nodded in Alex's direction. The look on her face was as proud as a mother whose favored son had just won a grade school spelling contest.

"Very impressive, Alex," he said with an approving nod, then he turned to Leslie. "I'll go call Clair and have her meet us over there," he said.

"Use the phone in my office," Alex said as Randall headed for the door.

When he was gone, Leslie looked around the room, lighting it up with her smile.

"Looks like things are working out," she said. Her face grew cloudy and she looked in the direction of the office. "How's *she* working out?" Leslie put emphasis on the word 'she.' "Do you know who sent her yet?"

Alex's jovial mood dimmed, and he shook his head.

"She hasn't asked me anything about the Archimedean Monograph or Sorsha or even Andrew Barton, apart from wanting to know if he's handsome."

"Every girl wants to know that," Leslie said with a sly look.

"I'm starting to think she might have been sent by Moriarty," Alex said, admitting something he hadn't told anyone yet, even Iggy.

"Why?" Leslie asked. "To keep an eye on you?"

Alex shrugged.

"I don't know. What I do know is that she's a damn good secretary."

Leslie stuck out her lower lip and pouted outrageously at that remark.

"Not as good as you, of course," he amended.

"It's all arranged," Randall said, coming back into the room. "Clair will meet us over there, then we'll all go out for some supper."

Alex picked up the tin compass and handed it to Leslie.

"Take this in case dear Wilhelmina has managed to escape doggy jail," he said.

Leslie accepted the compass, but her face fell.

"You're not coming?" she said.

She looked absolutely distraught — then a thought struck Alex.

"Your dear friend Clair wouldn't be single and in her thirties, would she?" he asked.

Leslie's expression grew mocking.

"Why Alex, how could you even say such a thing?"

Her manner was dismissivc, but Alex detected a faint blush in his former secretary's cheeks.

"I have a client coming in to retrieve some stolen property," he said. "I have to be here in case he has questions."

Leslie cast an appraising eye over him, trying to detect any trace of deceit.

"All right," she said at last. "But next time we're in the city you are having lunch with us."

"It's a date," Alex said.

"Looks like that went well," Sherry said once Alex returned from walking Leslie and Randall out.

Alex just shrugged.

"Finding dogs is easy work," he said.

"Why don't you do it any more, then?"

"It's too time-consuming," he said. "I can send Leslie out with a compass to track down wayward Wilhelmina, but most people want me to find the pooch myself. If they haven't already been collared by the dog catcher, that can take hours. It just isn't worth my time."

Sherry thought about that for a moment. Alex could tell she was thinking because of the way her nose wrinkled up.

"I get a couple of calls a day from people who've lost pets," she said. "Why don't you hire someone to do the legwork for you? I mean all you need is someone who can follow a compass, right?"

Alex considered that. Sherry had a point; once the rune had been cast, finding the missing pooch was just a matter of following the compass needle. No special training or deduction was required.

"I'd still have to be here to cast the rune," he said. "These days, I'm out of the office more than I'm here."

Sherry's nose wrinkled again.

"But that's not true either," she said after a moment. "The only thing you have to do is actually write the finding runes. Once they're written, anyone can use them, right? You could teach me. Then when someone calls in, I could have them bring in a focus for the rune, cast it, and then give the compass to someone else to actually find the missing pet."

It wasn't a bad idea. Alex charged forty dollars for his finding runes these days, but he could go back to twenty for pets. That would still leave more than enough to pay for an assistant to do the finding. He wondered if this was Sherry finally making a play to learn his runes, but discarded that idea immediately. Everybody knew that once written, all you had to do was burn the paper to activate them. He'd have to teach her how to focus on the missing animal to help form the link, but that wasn't exactly top-secret information either.

"All right," he said after a minute. "I'll give it some thought."

Sherry beamed at him. She seemed very proud of her idea.

Dr. Coville came by right at five, paid his bill, picked up his notebook, and left quietly. Alex didn't even know he'd been by until he came out of his office at five minutes past.

"I'm sorry," Sherry said in response to his inquiry. "I didn't know you wanted to talk to him."

"It's all right," Alex said, picking up the evening edition of the paper from Sherry's desk. "I thought he might have some questions for me."

Sherry stood up and locked the desk with a key from her own ring. She tamped out her cigarette in the ashtray on her desk and retrieved her hat from atop the file cabinet on the wall.

"If there's nothing else, boss, I'm going home," she said. "Alex?"

Alex looked up from the paper, realizing that he hadn't been paying attention to her.

"Is something wrong?" she asked.

Alex nodded at the paper.

"Margaret LaSalle died," he said, looking over the headline. "It says she was shot in her apartment."

"Who's Margaret LaSalle?"

Alex looked up again, focusing this time.

"She's a mystery writer," he explained. "My landlord, Dr. Bell, is very fond of her work. This will come as a shock to him."

"Oh, I'm so sorry," Sherry said, clearly meaning it. "Did he know her?"

Alex shook his head.

"Not as far as I know."

"Well, tell him I'm sorry; that's a shame."

Alex promised that he would, and Sherry walked out to catch the crosstown crawler.

Moving to the window, Alex looked out until he saw Sherry exit the building and turn west toward the crawler station. Satisfied that she was gone, he folded the newspaper under his arm, put on his hat, and exited the office, locking the door with his key.

He walked down to the next door and unlocked his map room. Once he was inside with the outer door locked, he moved to the inside door that separated the map room from the back office. This room wasn't locked, and it was entirely empty except for another door on the right-hand wall.

Alex shut the inner door and took out his pocket-watch, flipping it open. The new door had the same protections on it as the front door of the brownstone, and Alex felt the construct in his watch releasing the magic that kept the door closed.

With the protection temporarily nullified, Alex pushed the door open and stepped inside a narrow hallway. Snapping his watch closed, he shut the door and felt the protection constructs lock it down tight. Moving along the hallway, he passed into a large room with a vaulted ceiling. His workshop occupied one side of the space with a library and hearth on the far side. Across the space was another hall that led to the kitchen and bedroom he'd made for himself here in his vault. On the left-hand wall was an open space where his heavy vault door would appear when he opened the vault with his runic key, but since he hadn't done that this time, the wall was blank.

He crossed the main room and entered the hallway on the opposite side. Passing the bedroom and the kitchen, he came to the end of the hall where another door stood, just like the one in his spare office. Taking out his pocket-watch again, he unlocked the door and pulled it open. This time when he stepped through, he was in his own bedroom on the third floor of Iggy's brownstone.

"It's good to be home," he said to no one, then shut the door behind him.

2

LICHTENBERG

Alex hung up his hat and suit coat before heading downstairs. At this time of day, Iggy would usually be indulging his passion for cooking by making dinner, but there wasn't any smell of food in the house. When he reached the foyer, Alex turned into the library and found Iggy, sitting in his usual reading chair with an open book in his lap. A lit cigar sat in an ashtray on the little table between Iggy's chair and Alex's, with a glass of brandy nearby. Alex recognized the book; it was Margaret LaSalle's first big mystery, *The Poison Pen Letters*.

"I see you've read the paper," he said, moving to the liquor cabinet and pouring himself a Scotch.

Iggy sighed and closed the book in his lap.

"I can't believe she's gone," he said, setting the book aside and picking up his brandy.

Alex sat down in the empty chair and sipped his drink.

"Did you know her?"

Iggy shook his head sadly.

"Not personally," he said. "I just appreciated her work. Most writers these days tell fanciful tales of adventure. They're fine, of course, enjoyable even, but Margaret," he paused with a wistful smile fluffing his bottle-brush mustache. "Margaret wrote real mysteries. The kind with devious plots, interesting characters, and satisfying resolutions." He leaned back in his chair and puffed his cigar. "She was a singular talent."

"I'm sorry," Alex said.

"She was supposed to have a new book out next month," Iggy said. "The world is a poorer place for Margaret's loss."

"The police are calling it murder," Alex said. "According to the paper, she was shot in her apartment."

Iggy's face hardened and he nodded.

"I was thinking I'd go around to the Central Office on Monday and see what I can find out," Alex continued.

"Good lad," he said. "Find out everything you can. Get yourself on the case if possible. I want to know what happened to Margaret LaSalle. If someone did murder her, I want them to hang for it."

Alex held his mentor's gaze for a long moment, then nodded. Iggy set his brandy aside and picked up the book.

"Why don't you run down and see Mary?" he said, opening it reverently. "I don't feel like eating tonight."

"Sure thing, Iggy," Alex said.

The incessant droning of a bell dragged Alex from blissful unconsciousness into groggy awareness. He fumbled for the lamp on his bedside table, finally locating the pull cord and blinding himself with the light when it snapped on. The alarm clock read three twenty-eight when he grabbed the receiver off the telephone and pressed it to his ear.

"Hello?" he mumbled.

"Lockerby?" a familiar voice replied. "I can hardly hear you, talk into the mouthpiece."

Alex pried his bleary eyes open and focused on the body of the candlestick-style phone still sitting on the table. Picking it up, he held the mouthpiece in front of his face and tried again.

"Is that you, Lieutenant?" he said, his brain finally identifying the voice of Danny's boss, Lieutenant Frank Callahan.

"Yeah," came the reply. "I need you to meet me on the north side of St. Patrick's Cathedral as soon as you can. I've got a dead guy here and I'm pretty sure he was killed by magic."

"Right," Alex said, sitting up. "I'll be dressed in a few minutes, but the cabs have stopped running, so you'll have to send a car for me."

"It's already on the way," Callahan said.

Alex hung up and dressed quickly. Using his pocket-watch, he opened the door to his vault and retrieved his investigation kit. Having a more-or-less permanent door to his vault in his room and one in his office had revolutionized his commute. It was all thanks to his growing understanding of linking runes. He'd reasoned that if the rune that created the vault were engraved on something durable, like a steel plate, then he could link as many individual keys to the plate as he wanted. Each key would open its own individual door into the vault created by the primary rune carved into the plate.

One vault, many doors.

It had taken a few months, but he'd figured it out. He had to completely empty his old vault and make a new one to test it, but it had been worth the effort. The best part was that he could open a vault door from anywhere, using a vault rune and his key, go into his vault, and close the door behind him. As long as some other door was open, like the ones to his room or office, he wouldn't be trapped inside. He still couldn't open a door with just the key like he'd seen Moriarty do, but it was a work in progress.

Alex left the vault, shutting the simple door behind him and headed downstairs. The plain door in his bedroom and the one in his second office were closed and secured, but they weren't actually vault doors, so the vault still counted as open, even when they were closed.

"Lad?" Iggy's voice came from the library where the reading lamp still burned.

"Got a call from Lieutenant Callahan," he said, leaning into the library. "He wants me at an inner ring crime scene."

Iggy had a stack of books on the reading table and was about halfway through *Murder at Blackwater Falls*, his favorite of Margaret LaSalle's books.

"You going to read all night?" Alex asked, trying to keep the concern out of his voice.

"I just want to finish this one," Iggy said.

Alex nodded as if he understood. He'd never been that attached to someone he'd never even met, but before meeting Iggy and becoming a detective, his life had been fairly sheltered.

"Let me know if it's something interesting," Iggy called as Alex headed for the door.

The patrol car Callahan sent for him dropped Alex off in front of St. Patrick's Cathedral at just after four in the morning. At this time of night, the lights were off and the building was a dark hulk against the night sky. Five patrol cars were parked on the opposite side of the street along with the truck used by the coroner's office.

"It's about time," Callahan growled, motioning Alex over to where several bored looking cops were standing underneath a dark street lamp. The Lieutenant was almost as tall as Alex with a square jaw and the kind of face women described as ruggedly handsome. He wore a gray suit with his badge clipped to the breast pocket of his jacket.

As Alex approached, he saw a man lying on the grass that surrounded the cathedral. His eyes were open, but he was clearly dead.

"Okay, Lieutenant," Alex said, joining the big man next to the body. "What have you got?"

Callahan pointed down at the body.

"You tell me," he said.

Alex reached into his kit and pulled out a battery-operated flashlight, snapping it on and running the beam over the dead man. He was younger than Alex had thought at first, still in his twenties if Alex had to guess. His clothes were good quality and his jacket was tailored. The only thing amiss was two burn marks, one on his left hand and one in the center of his chest.

Taking a pencil from his pocket, Alex lifted the shirt fabric around the burned hole, shining the light onto the blackened skin beneath. Returning the pencil to his pocket, he pushed up the coat sleeve on the man's left arm, then unbuttoned his cuff, rolling the shirt up to his elbow.

"Okay," he said after shining his light on the dead man's arm. "He was struck by lightning."

"That's what I told you an hour ago, Lieutenant," an annoyingly familiar voice cut in.

Alex turned to find Dr. Daniel Wagner, the new coroner, standing outside the ring of policemen with his arms crossed across his chest. Unlike the policemen, the coroner's clothes were rumpled, and he looked fairly disheveled.

"Now, if you're done wasting my time," Wagner said, motioning for one of his orderlies. "I'd like to take charge of this body and go home."

"Just a minute," Callahan said, waving the orderly back. "Both of you are wrong," he looked from Wagner to Alex. "There's no way this man was hit by lightning."

"Of course he was," Wagner said before Alex could speak. "Your trained monkey there," he indicated Alex, "is just about to point to the scarring on the man's arms."

Callahan peered down and Alex pointed his flashlight on the exposed left arm where a series of vein-like scars could be seen. They reminded Alex of roots.

"Those are Lichtenberg Figures," Wagner continued. "They're scars that form along the path that lightning takes when it passes through the body. The monkey," he pointed to Alex again, "noticed the burn on the dead man's left hand, obviously where he was touching that lamp post." Wagner pointed to the burned-out street lamp behind them. "Lightning hit the post, transferred through our victim to the ground, killing him in the process. Now, if you don't mind, I have a job to do."

He glared at Callahan and Alex in turn.

"Well?" Callahan said, turning to Alex. "Is he right?"

"You both are," Alex said.

"I'm surrounded by idiots," Wagner growled.

"You were right about the evidence," Alex admitted to the fuming

Coroner. "But the Lieutenant here is right, this couldn't have been a lightning strike."

Wagner threw up his hands and started to protest but Alex went on before he could speak.

"Because these buildings," he pointed to the cathedral and Rockefeller center, "were required to install lightning rods on their roofs five years ago by state law. Before that, lightning deaths in the city were much more common and the Lieutenant knows that. Nowadays they only happen in residential areas."

Warner looked like he wanted to reply but clamped his mouth shut instead. He might be an ass, but he wasn't stupid. He knew when to give up on a losing hand.

"If you know this wasn't a lightning strike," Callahan said to Alex, "then why did you say it was?"

"I said he was hit by lightning," Alex said, indicating the dead man. "But instead of lightning hitting that street lamp and electrocuting our victim, it happened the other way around. Lightning hit him, here in the chest, then traveled up his left arm and down to ground through the lamp post, melting the wires inside. That's why the light's out."

"How is that possible?" Wagner sneered. "Or do you think Andrew Barton killed this man?"

Callahan gave Alex a furtive look and Alex realized that's exactly what the Lieutenant thought. Of course New York's resident electrical sorcerer, the Lightning Lord himself, could have killed the dead man; that's why Callahan wanted Alex to see the body. He'd need witnesses if he wanted to have a chance of arresting a sorcerer.

"No," Alex said, answering Wagner's question. "If a sorcerer wanted to kill this guy they'd just turn him into a slug and step on him. Barton's far too smart to kill someone in a way that could only lead back to him."

"You think one of the other sorcerers did this?" Callahan asked, lowering his voice. "Is someone trying to frame Barton?"

Alex shrugged.

"It's possible," he admitted, "but it seems a bit obvious. A sorcerer would have a better plan, don't you think?"

"You still haven't explained how the victim got hit by lightning," Wagner jeered. "Since you don't think Barton did it."

"I don't like to offer an answer before I investigate," Alex said, setting his kit bag down and opening it up.

"How long do you need?" Callahan asked as Alex extracted his oculus and multi-lamp.

Alex looked around at the scene. Aside from the body, there wasn't really anything else to look at. Besides, the police officers had been over the scene and would have destroyed any evidence of footprints.

"Ten minutes," he said. "Maybe fifteen."

Wagner swore, storming off toward the coroner's truck, and Alex grinned.

"I miss Anderson," Callahan growled.

"Me too."

He lit the ghostlight burner he'd clipped into the base of the lamp, then closed the shutter, causing a pale greenish light to shine out through the cut glass lens. Strapping on his oculus, he played the beam over the body of the dead man. The Lichtenberg Figures on his arms and chest lit up, glowing brightly under the light. Alex could even see them running across his chest, shining out from beneath the white shirt. It looked like drawings of blood vessels Alex had seen in Iggy's medical textbooks.

Alex expected the scars made by the magical lightning to glow, but as he passed the light over the rest of the dead man, the body glowed as well. The glow wasn't as bright as the scars, but it was there.

"I think our dead man drank a potion of some kind in the hours before he died," Alex told Callahan. "The lightning was definitely magical, but his body shows signs of residual magic."

The Lieutenant scribbled the details in his notebook and Alex blew out his lamp. He was about to take off his oculus but decided that, since Wagner was in such a big hurry, he ought to be thorough. Replacing the ghostlight burner with the silverlight one, he played the lamp over the body again. Several things jumped out immediately. There was a stain on the man's jacket near the sleeve. Alex couldn't tell what had made it but from the volume of the liquid and its position, he guessed it represented a spilled drink. There was also smearing on his lips, cheeks, and neck.

"Lieutenant," Alex called. "I don't think this man was alone tonight." He ran through the evidence, pointing at the marks only he could see.

"So," Callahan summarized. "Our boy here was at a bar or a nightclub where he spilled his drink, kissed a woman, and then he makes his way out here. There are a half dozen clubs near the core, that's only a few blocks from here. Maybe someone at one of them can tell us who he is."

Alex stood up and started walking toward the cathedral where rows of decorative shrubs and flowers had been planted. After a minute of searching, he found what he was looking for.

"Look here," he said, waving Callahan over. "See how the grass here is trampled and some of these flowers have been stepped on?"

Callahan pointed his flashlight at a patch of bare ground between the flowers where a small hole had been pressed into the dirt.

"I don't think our dead man was alone," Alex said. "Judging from the footprints, he and a lady friend stopped here, behind this bush, and had...relations." He pointed to a spot in the grass that lit up under the silverlight, indicating the presence of bodily fluids.

"So Romeo brings his girl back here for a little fun up against a church," Callahan said with a look of disgust. "He'll spend some time in Purgatory for that one. What happened to the girl?"

Alex played his light around again, but there wasn't any more evidence to be seen.

"Maybe she's the one who killed him," Alex offered, gesturing at the dead man.

"Or she left before that part happened," Callahan said. "We need to know how he was killed and where the woman went."

"I suspect if you canvass those nightclubs you mentioned, you can find someone who saw the woman leave with him," Alex said, gesturing to the dead man. "As for the method of his electrocution," he shrugged. "I don't know of any rune powerful enough to do it."

"So that only leaves sorcery," Callahan said. "Which brings us back to Andrew Barton. Or Sorsha Kincaid if you're right about the woman."

Alex laughed at that, eliciting a glare from the Lieutenant.

"You think sorcerers aren't prone to...indiscretions?" he asked.

"No." Alex shook his head. "But the Ice Queen has a private flying castle. Why would she bring someone here, of all places?"

Callahan seemed to consider this for a long moment, then he shrugged.

"I suppose," he admitted at last. "That just leaves the Lightning Lord."

"I still don't think he had anything to do with this," Alex said.

"When was the last time you talked to your pal, Barton?"

"A few months ago."

"Good," Callahan said. "I want you with me when I talk to him."

"Okay," Alex said, stowing his lamp and oculus in his bag. "Just don't make it too early, I have a feeling I'll be sleeping in a bit tomorrow."

"We're not doing it tomorrow," Callahan said, waving Wagner and his orderly over.

"I know a few sorcerers, Callahan," Alex said. "None of them are the kind of person I want to roust out of their beds in the middle of the night. Count me out."

Alex started to step away, but Callahan grabbed his arm.

"Someone who can shoot lightning is running loose in the city and they've already killed one person, maybe two if you're right about the woman. I need answers and I need them right now."

Alex sighed. With his new vault, he could just step around behind the cathedral, open a door, and be back in his nice warm bed in minutes.

"Fine," he growled as his sense of duty overrode the vision of sleep. "But you are definitely paying my rate on this one."

3

POWER

The uniformed security guard stationed in the lobby of Empire Tower was surprised to see anyone storm into the building at four-thirty in the morning. He had been sitting at his station with his feet up on the mahogany counter reading the paper when Alex and Callahan entered with half a dozen uniformed officers in tow. Startled, he jumped to his feet before they reached him. That surprise, however, was dwarfed by his shock at Callahan's demand that he wake up no less a person than Andrew Barton.

The guard flatly refused until Callahan threatened to have him arrested. Even then the guard was only willing to telephone upstairs and pass the buck to his boss. While Alex watched the guard's animated phone conversation, Callahan walked over to the phone booths along the wall.

With nothing to do but wait, Alex lit a cigarette and leaned against a pillar. After a few minutes, Callahan returned.

"Any luck?" he asked.

"He's still arguing with the guy upstairs," Alex supplied. "Where did you go?"

"I had one of my boys check the hospitals near St. Patrick's,"

Callahan said. "One of them located a woman that showed up with burns on her arms. She also has those lichen-whatever markings on the palms of her hands. Five'll get you ten she's our missing girl."

"Great," Alex said. "Let's go ask her what happened."

"Can't," Callahan whispered. "She died right after she showed up, some kind of seizure."

Alex ground his teeth. A live witness to the death of the electrocuted man would have saved the police a lot of time. Maybe he could find a clue in her belongings.

"I'll want you to come by the Central Office to look through her belongings," the Lieutenant said, anticipating him.

Tomorrow was Sunday, but since Callahan was willing to wake up a sorcerer to chase this case, Alex doubted he'd wait 'til Monday.

"I'll come by right after Mass," he said. Thinking of church made Alex think of Iggy. "Can I ask you a favor, Lieutenant?" he whispered as the security guard continued his discussion with his superiors.

Callahan raised an eyebrow and shot Alex a challenging look.

"What kind of favor?"

"Do you know anything about the death of Margaret LaSalle? She's a mystery writer who was shot in her apartment the day before yesterday."

"I heard about it," Callahan hedged. "It's not my division's case. Why?"

"LaSalle was a friend of Dr. Bell's and..."

"And he wants you to poke around and make sure her case gets solved," Callahan guessed. "Nice to see your mentor holds the department in such high esteem."

"Lieutenant," Alex said in a wounded voice. "It's not like that."

In point of fact, LaSalle and Iggy had never met, but Callahan would understand Iggy's interest if he thought they knew each other.

"What is it like, then?" the Lieutenant growled.

"He just wants me to poke around and give him some peace of mind," Alex said. "You know the Doc, he's a good guy and he's helped you guys loads of times."

Callahan glared at him, holding his eyes for a long moment.

"You're pouring it on awful thick," he said. "Fine, I'll pull some strings and get the case transferred to Danny. He won't mind you working it, but you'd better damn sure close that case."

"Not to worry, Lieutenant," Alex said, suppressing his desire to grin. "You know what a sharp detective Danny is. He'll probably have it wrapped up before I even get there."

"Yeah, well don't show up until Monday," Callahan said. "I'll have to get the Captain to sign off on this and he won't be in 'til then."

Alex promised that he wouldn't jump the gun just as the security guard hung up the phone. Before he had a chance to speak, the main elevator opened and another uniformed guard motioned Alex, Callahan, and the policemen all into the car.

"This way, officers," he said.

When the elevator arrived at the offices of Barton Electric a minute and a half later, a tall, heavyset man stood waiting for them. He wore an expensive, tailored suit and had a cigar clenched in his teeth. Alex recognized the man as Adam Duncan, Barton's chief of security. There wasn't time for Duncan to have been roused from sleep and get dressed, so Alex surmised that he was already awake for some reason.

"Alex," he said as the policemen got off the elevator. "They didn't tell me you were here. What's all this about?"

"You know this guy?" Callahan asked, stepping up beside Alex.

"Lieutenant Callahan," Alex said. "Meet Adam Duncan; he runs the security detail for Empire Tower."

"Lieutenant," Duncan said, putting out his hand. "I understand you'd like a word with Mr. Barton."

Callahan hesitated and Alex could almost see the wheels turning in his head. As a high-ranking police detective, Callahan was used to telling people what he wanted in no uncertain terms. With one of the New York Six, however, he had to be diplomatic. Alex knew all too well that diplomacy ran against the Lieutenant's basic nature.

"Yes," Callahan said, taking the offered hand and shaking it.

"Well don't be all day about it, then."

Alex turned to find Barton himself approaching. He was dressed in a grease-stained work shirt with heavy trousers and his dark hair looked a bit unkempt. Since the last time Alex saw him, he'd grown a pencil mustache that made him look like Clark Gable. Clearly he'd been awake for some time and based on his harried look, Alex would bet he hadn't been to bed.

"Mr. Barton," Callahan said, turning to the sorcerer.

"You're that policeman," Barton said as he approached. "From that museum heist — Calloway?"

"Callahan," Alex supplied. Andrew Barton had met the Lieutenant when he'd tagged along to recover his stolen train motor from a gang of thieves.

Barton's eyes shot to Alex and his eyebrows rose in surprise as he recognized him.

"Figures I find you interrupting my work, Lockerby," he said, changing course to shake Alex's hand. "What's this about?"

Alex shook his hand, then let Callahan explain.

"So you think I'm going around murdering amorous couples in the dead of night?" Barton said with a mocking grin.

Callahan coughed nervously and shook his head.

"Nothing like that," he assured the sorcerer. "But someone is."

"Oh, obviously," Barton agreed, cutting Callahan off. "There's no way someone standing next to the cathedral could have been struck by natural lightning. If I had to guess, I'd say they have a charm of some kind, infused with electrical power."

In addition to their flying castles, icebox disks, and crawling buses, sorcerers could imbue common objects with temporary spells that anyone could use. The only downside of charms is that they were time-consuming to make and therefore expensive. Most sorcerers had better things to do with their time and their magic. Shield charms were common among presidents and other heads of state, keeping them safe from an assassin's bullet.

"Where would someone get a charm like that?" Callahan asked in a diplomatically neutral voice.

"If you're asking if I make them, the answer is no," Barton said. "Nor do any of the New York Six. We have an agreement not to make charms that can be easily used to kill."

"Is there any other use for a lightning charm?" Alex asked, genuinely curious.

Barton shook his head.

"No," he declared flatly. "It's too unstable to use as a power source. All you can really do with something like that is throw lightning bolts around."

Callahan chewed on that for a moment.

"Is there any way to track this charm, or the person using it?"

"Nothing special that I can do," Barton said, then he thumped Alex on the arm. "But your friend here is a wiz at finding things. Sorry I can't be more help."

"All right," Callahan said with a sigh. "Thank you for seeing me."

"Not at all, Lieutenant," Barton said with a smile. "I'm always happy to help the police."

Callahan turned to go, but Barton called him back.

"You mind if I chat with Alex for a few minutes?"

"Take your time," Callahan said, then he turned to Alex. "I'm going to make sure the woman from the hospital makes it to the morgue, then I'm going home. See you tomorrow afternoon?"

Alex nodded, then Callahan and his men boarded the waiting elevator.

"See what working for the police gets you?" Barton said once they were gone. "Dragged out of bed at all hours. You should work for me and you'd at least get a good night's sleep."

"You're up at all hours," Alex pointed out.

Barton looked shocked at that observation, then chuckled.

"I suppose I am," he admitted. "But there's just so much to do. You know I'm starting on my third relay tower next month, down in Brooklyn, and my new tower in the Bronx is already up to half of its full capacity."

Alex looked carefully at Barton. The careworn look he'd had the last time they spoke was gone, as were the strands of gray that had crept into his hair.

"I take it you solved your power problem?" Alex guessed.

A cloud of irritation crossed the sorcerer's face.

"No thanks to you," he muttered, giving Alex an exaggerated look of displeasure.

Barton had theorized that rune constructs could be used to connect his electricity spells to the many etherium generators housed within Empire Tower. He'd been right, of course. Alex had seen it almost instantly. Linking runes could have connected the master spell with the generators allowing them to all work off one spell instead of each one having to have a separate spell of its own. The more spells Barton was forced to cast, the more toll it took on him physically. Alex's linking idea would reduce the load of his generators to almost nothing. It was such a good idea that Alex had used it as the basis for redesigning his vault to accept multiple doors. It was also an idea Alex didn't want out in the wild. The more he thought about what could be done with linking runes, the more dangerous they seemed. Best to keep that knowledge to himself.

Still, Barton had apparently figured something out on his own, so no harm done.

"I told you that you didn't need me," Alex said, with all the false modesty he could muster. "How did you manage it?"

Barton got an enigmatic grin and raised an eyebrow theatrically.

"Would you like to see?"

It was late and Alex was tired, but his curiosity was piqued, so he nodded.

Barton's face split into a wide grin and he led Alex toward the private elevator that went from the corporate lobby up to Barton's private office. Alex had taken this elevator before, but this time once he was inside and closed the door, Barton took out a key ring from his pocket. He selected one of the keys and slipped it into what looked like a small gap in the decorative plate that encircled the buttons. Turning the key smartly, Barton pulled the plate open, revealing three additional buttons. Pushing the one in the middle, he snapped the plate closed and replaced the key ring in his pocket.

Instead of going up, the elevator went down for what felt like half a minute. When it opened, Barton led him out onto a small landing with a railing running around it. Looking over the edge, Alex saw that they were several stories above the floor. Barton's giant etherium generators rose up from below, passing the platform and reaching up several more stories. The air smelled of ozone and crackled with so much power that Alex felt the hair on his arms stand up.

"Impressive, aren't they?" Barton said, standing with his hands on his hips and looking up at the huge machines. "I've been powering Manhattan with these for years and now they're sending energy all the way up to the Bronx."

"I thought you were going to replace these with smaller ones," Alex said.

"That was before I got permission to build my relay towers," Barton said, motioning for Alex to follow him to the end of the platform, where a catwalk ran along the outside wall of the building. "I'm putting the new generators in the towers instead. With what I'm about to show you I can channel almost ten times the power as before in a single generator. What you see here will be enough for Manhattan for years to come."

The catwalk ended at a heavy metal door that reminded Alex of the original door to his vault, except this door had no keyhole or mechanism to open it. Barton reached out and placed his hand on the door, palm first. Alex felt a shift in the magical energy of the generator room and then the door swung inward.

Beyond it was a bright yellow spell, spinning slowly like a tiny galaxy.

Alex had seen spells like this once before when he'd been in Sorsha Kincaid's flying castle. Sorcerer's spells were made up of complex webs of magical energy that turned in place. The motion tended to flatten them out, giving them the look of galactic disks full of millions of stars.

"What is this?" Alex asked, leaning close to examine the spell. As he drew near, he could feel the energy within it.

"This is what is powering all my etherium generators," Barton said as the vault door shut behind them. The room was suddenly quiet. Alex hadn't realized that the generators made a deep, thrumming sound until the thick door was again sealed.

"I thought each generator needed its own spell," Alex said, recalling their conversation of a few months ago.

"They did," Barton said with a mischievous grin, then he turned and swept his arm at the wall. "Until I found someone to make those."

Alex looked up from the spell and saw what he had missed on walking into the room. Along the walls, running from floor to ceiling were dozens of linking runes, maybe as many as a hundred. Alex didn't need to be told what they connected to. Each rune joined this spell with one of Barton's etherium generators, allowing them to draw power from the realm of magic and convert it to electricity.

It was exactly the solution Alex would have proposed himself. It was also a solution that very few runewrights were capable of making. As far as Alex knew, only the shadowy organization known as the Legion knew about using them in this way.

Don't forget Moriarty, he reminded himself.

Either of those sources was bad.

Alex looked at Barton and found him watching with an expectant look.

"Linking runes," Alex said with an approving nod. "You don't need a new spell for each new generator, you just link them back to this one."

Barton nodded with a wicked grin.

"I knew you were smart enough to figure it out," he said. "Would you like to meet the man who did it?"

Alex tried not to sound eager.

"Very much."

Barton walked around to the back side of the spell and opened a plain wooden door. As Alex followed, he examined the linking runes. They weren't as sophisticated or as well drawn as his, but they would get the job done.

Beyond the door was a balcony that ran around the upper floor of a runewright's workshop. Down below, Alex could see writing tables, bottles of ink, stacks of paper, shelves of exotic ingredients, and a thin man who looked far too young to be a master runewright.

"Brad," Barton called, leading Alex down to the workshop floor via a spiral staircase. "There's someone I want you to meet."

The young man looked up and blinked as if he hadn't heard anyone come in. He appeared to be in his mid-twenties with longish hair the color of dirty straw and brown eyes. His face was thin and pockmarked and a few days of stubble clung to his chin. When he saw Alex, his eyes widened and his hand twitched.

"You said this was my job," he protested to Barton, coming over to meet him in the middle of the floor. "I solved your problem and now you bring him in."

He jabbed an ink-stained finger at Alex. For someone Alex had never before met, he seemed quite hostile, casting furtive glances between Alex and Barton.

"Relax, Brad," Barton said, putting his hands on the young man's shoulders. "Alex isn't here for your job."

Brad seemed to relax a bit, but his fingers were still twitching and his eyes kept darting in Alex's direction.

"How long has it been since you slept?" Barton asked, still holding the young man by the shoulders.

"What day is it?" he asked.

"Sunday," Alex supplied.

Brad's eyes focused on Alex, but he didn't say anything.

"Alex, this is Bradley Elder," Barton said. "He's responsible for the work you've seen."

"Where did you learn to use linking runes like that?" Alex jerked his thumb in the direction of the spell room.

"From my father," Brad said. "I used to work for a chemical company, but when my father died," he shrugged and a sly smile played across his face. "I got his rune book."

That made sense; sometimes runewrights wouldn't train their children in the art, preferring them to find some other employment. It also probably meant that Brad wasn't a member of the Legion. His father might have been, but that was by no means a certainty.

"It's nice to meet you, Brad," Alex said, putting out his hand.

Brad just stared at him. Clearly Barton had spoken about Alex, and the man thought of him as a rival.

"I have to get back to work," he said, ignoring Alex's hand and heading back to his writing table.

"Don't mind him," Barton said, clapping Alex on the shoulder. "He's a bit...eccentric."

"To say the least," Alex muttered. "But if you don't want to offer me his job, why did you show me all this?"

Barton gave him an excited smile and pointed to a map of the eastern seaboard on the wall.

"Construction has already begun on the Brooklyn tower," he said, pointing to the area. "And the mayor of Jersey City is practically begging me to put the next one across the river." He looked back at Brad who was busily working at his table, then to Alex. "Brad is good, but he isn't fast enough by himself," he explained. "He's still working on the runes to complete the Bronx tower. At that rate, the Brooklyn tower won't be up to full capacity for months after it's finished." He gave Alex an intense look. "You knew what those runes were the moment you saw them, and how they worked," he said. "And you've got a few ideas on how to improve them."

Alex started to object, but Barton stuck a finger in his face.

"Don't deny it," he said. "I saw it in your face when you looked at them. I need you, Alex. Truth be told, I need you and Brad and three more like you."

Alex thought about Barton's situation. Brad had solved the spell problem, but based on what Alex could see, it looked like his solution was clumsy. He was using a separate linking rune for each generator. If Alex showed him how to link the spell to an anchor at the site of each tower, he could link the generators to the anchor, instead of linking them individually back to Empire Tower. It was technically the same number of runes, but he wouldn't have to travel back and forth to complete each rune. That alone would save weeks.

"Come on," Barton said, sensing Alex's hesitation. "I need you. The people of New York need you. It'll take me years to put up my towers without your help."

The problem with Andrew Barton was that he was a dreamer and he had the uncanny ability to carry people along with his vision.

"Give me a week to think about it," he said at last.

Barton gave him a big, genuine smile.

"All right," he said. "But I'll tell you right now, you won't regret coming to work here. My team and I are going to change the world, Alex, and you can be a part of that. All you have to do is say yes."

Ever since Alex had become a detective, he'd never wanted to be anything else. But if he was honest with himself, Barton's offer tempted him. The sorcerer was right, his vision was big enough to change the world, and he wanted Alex to be a part of it.

It was a singular honor and Alex would have to give it some serious thought.

4

THE NOTEBOOK

Alex pushed through the vault door into his bedroom, then dropped heavily on his bed. He hadn't bothered to take off his hat, and it fell off and rolled across the floor on its brim before falling onto its top. He pried an eye open and tried to focus on it, but his eyes didn't want to obey.

It was well after dawn when Alex got home from the electrocution case and he'd slept clear through to mid-afternoon. After attending a late Mass, he'd gone to the Central Office to pick up Callahan and then on to the city morgue to look over the bodies of the dead man and woman for clues. He'd spent hours and had been very thorough, but beyond both bodies showing residual signs of magic, there just wasn't anything to go on.

It had been a grueling day and now that he was home, all he wanted to do was sleep.

His stomach rumbled, reminding him that he hadn't actually eaten, and he groaned in protest.

"I thought I heard you," Iggy's voice came from the open bedroom door. "I take it your day was not as productive as you hoped?"

Alex groaned again and forced himself to sit up.

"Callahan was later than me, so I had to wait around in the lobby of the Central Office for almost an hour," he said, leaning down to retrieve his hat. "Then we went through the dead woman's effects, which amounted to a handbag."

"Any identification?" Iggy asked.

"No," he said with a sigh. "All she had was a folding makeup mirror, a tube of lipstick, a coin purse with a dollar thirty-four in change, a key ring, a tin of aspirin, and a folded paper with the word *Limelight* printed on it."

"What about the body?"

Alex stood and hung up his hat.

"She glowed with magical residue like the man," Alex said, taking off his suit coat. "There were Lichtenberg Figures on the palms of her hands, along with second degree burns. Her clothes were nice but not too expensive, although she was missing her shoes. Based on the condition of her feet, she walked barefoot for some distance."

"She probably had heels on," Iggy said. "Dropped them along the way."

"Is there any food?" Alex asked as his stomach rumbled again.

Iggy grinned and motioned for Alex to follow.

"I'm sure I can find you something," he said. "Come on."

They went downstairs, past the second floor, then into the brownstone's kitchen. The large oak table sat in the center of the room under an elaborate wrought iron chandelier. To the right was the preparation counter with its heavy gas stove, oven, sink, and an oversized icebox.

"Get a plate and the carving knife," Iggy said, as he headed for the icebox.

Alex went to the decorative hutch that contained the dinnerware, retrieving enough plates, forks, knives, and napkins for both of them. As he set them out on the table, Iggy came back with a rough loaf of brown bread, a wedge of cheese, and a beef roast under a cover.

"So, what does Lieutenant Callahan think about the case?" Iggy asked as Alex retrieved a long, gleaming carving knife from one of the hutch's drawers.

"He thinks we're at a dead end," Alex said, passing over the knife.

Alex could cut bread himself, of course, but Iggy had been a doctor, so he was much better with a knife.

"What about the paper?" Iggy said, deftly cutting the bread into slices. "I've never heard of anything called limelight, outside of the theater of course."

Alex shrugged.

"Don't know," he said. "The paper looked like it had been folded into a packet, like the kind that holds quinine powder for your gin." Some people added other powders to drinks, usually things like aspirin or bicarbonate, but he'd never heard of a brand called Limelight.

"It's probably nothing," Iggy said, cutting the roast into thin slices. "But that paper looks to be to be the only clue you've got. If you can find out what limelight is, you might be able to figure out where she bought it."

"That's pretty thin," Alex said as he piled slices of beef on his bread. Iggy looked irritated until he realized Alex was talking about the lead and not the beef.

"Someone may come looking for them," Iggy suggested.

That was possible, but many New Yorkers didn't even know their neighbors. In the end it was possible that the only ones who would miss the dead couple would be their landlords.

"Did you talk to Callahan about Margaret?" Iggy continued as Alex took a bite of his sandwich.

Alex nodded, still chewing.

"He's going to talk to the chief and get Danny put on the case in the morning," he said, once he'd finished his bite. "I've got his okay to work it, but they won't be paying me, not that that matters," he added hastily.

"Good," Iggy said. "I want to know what you find out."

Alex promised that he would call with an update as soon as he learned anything, and they lapsed into silence. When they finished eating, Iggy went back to his reading chair, but Alex excused himself and returned to his bed, though he did take off his clothes before getting in it this time.

When Alex arrived at the Central Office the following morning, he expected Danny to be excited to see him. Instead his friend sat behind his desk, glaring at him with his arms crossed.

"Good morning?" Alex ventured when he caught Danny's icy stare.

"No thanks to you," Danny said, picking up a folder from his desk. "Do you know what this is?"

Alex admitted that he did not.

"Some lunatic blew up a hardware store yesterday," he said. "I got the case this morning."

"Congratulations," Alex said. "Sound like an interesting case."

"Oh, it is," Danny said, opening the file. "Whoever did it stole guns and ammunition, so they're clearly up to something big. The man who brings them in is going to be the next Elliot Ness."

"You're up to it."

"Of course I'm up to it," Danny hissed through clenched teeth, keeping his voice low. "But this isn't my case anymore because my lieutenant just informed me that I have to help you solve a break-in where some writer got murdered."

"Oh," Alex said, chagrined. "Sorry about that."

"You know what the worst part is? This belongs to Derrick Nicholson now."

Danny said that like he expected Alex to know who Nicholson was.

"He's Detweiler's stooge," Danny went on without a pause. "I'd be amazed if he can find his own desk without a map."

Alex had worked with Lieutenant James Detweiler before and the man seemed competent.

"Why would Detweiler assign a case like this to a bad detective?"

"Because he wants to solve it himself," Danny fumed. "Nicholson is such a lost cause that Detweiler will have to be there holding his hand the whole way. And when it's over, he'll be the one everyone remembers. I could have made lieutenant off this, now Detweiler is likely to be the next Captain."

Alex didn't know what to say to that. Danny was a great detective in his own right, and he deserved a case like this. He hadn't meant to spike his friend's chances for advancement, but he'd done it nonetheless. He felt like a heel.

"I'm sorry," he said. "I promise I'll try to rope you into the next big case I get."

Danny glared at him and tossed the folder down on his desk.

"Here," he said, picking up another thin folder and handing it to Alex. "This is everything on your murdered writer."

Alex took the folder and paged through it. According to the report of the investigating officer, Margaret LaSalle was shot in her kitchen by an intruder sometime last Friday afternoon. The case was handed off to Detweiler's man, Detective Nicholson, who determined that the motive was robbery since whoever killed her ransacked her brownstone.

"There's no list of what the intruder took," Alex said, paging through the folder again in case he missed it.

"Since the owner was dead, there wasn't any way to know," a Jersey accented voice cut in.

Alex looked up to find a paunchy man with unkempt black hair and a broad face standing nearby. He wore a rumpled blue suit and had a gold detective's shield clipped to his jacket pocket, just like Danny.

"This is Detective Nicholson," Danny said, jerking his thumb at the man.

"Did you do an inventory of the house?" Alex asked, looking over the report again. "I don't see a list of the areas that were ransacked."

"The whole place was wrecked," Nicholson said, reaching past Danny to pick up the folder on the hardware store robbery. "Thanks for switching with me, Pak," he said, hoisting the folder like a prize. "This one looks like a lot of fun."

He turned and strode away with a chuckle and Danny ground his teeth as he watched the man go.

Alex apologized again as Danny turned back to him with a murderous stare.

"I suppose you're going to want to go over the scene," he said, picking up his suit coat from the back of his chair. It wasn't really a question, so Alex just closed Nicholson's unhelpful report and tucked the folder under his arm.

Margaret LaSalle lived in a west-side brownstone that looked almost identical to Iggy's, though its bricks were more of a rust color instead of tan. The entrance had a pair of doors, each with a large stained-glass panel bearing an intricate art nouveau pattern.

Mounting the stoop, Danny pulled a ring of keys from his pocket and selected one that had been marked with a bit of painter's tape. Inserting it in the lock, he opened the door, admitting them into a small vestibule and then into an elegant parlor.

"This doesn't look ransacked," Alex said, looking around. The front room occupied the same space as Iggy's library with a marble fireplace, a Persian rug, and several elegant couches and chairs. "Did Nicholson have the cops clean the place?"

"No chance," Danny said. "But it doesn't look like there's much of value here."

"Let's split up," Alex said. "You check here and the basement, I'll take the upper floors."

Danny agreed and they went their separate ways.

Alex found Margaret's bedroom on the second floor. Like Nicholson predicted, it had been thoroughly ransacked. Drawers were pulled out, their contents scattered on the floor, and the jewelry box on the dresser was empty. Alex made notes on what he found, then pressed on.

The bedroom on the third floor had been converted into an office. It was obviously where LaSalle did her writing. A large desk of light-colored wood stood in the middle of the room with shelves lining the walls. Books of all description packed the shelves, though there were empty spaces where books had been pulled down and dumped on the floor. A filing cabinet stood against the back wall, its drawers pulled open and much of their contents littering the floor. A glass-fronted liquor cabinet stood beside it, but its doors were closed.

Alex spent the next hour going over the office. He drew a vault door on the wall and retrieved his kit bag, then used amberlight to rebuild the scattered files. They consisted mostly of correspondence between LaSalle and her fans, publishing contracts, and letters from her publisher. None of it seemed particularly valuable or interesting.

Remembering his own book safe in Iggy's library, Alex checked the books that had been thrown on the floor. None of them contained hidden compartments, so he returned them to their shelves.

He was about to check the attic when something caught his eye. Most of the books on the shelves were either reference books or crime novels. All of them looked read, but in relatively good condition.

Except for one.

A simple book bound in black leather was placed on the third shelf of one of the bookcases. It stood out because there was no name on the spine, as if it had been worn off through use. When Alex looked closer, he saw that the surface of the shelf in front of the book was scratched. Clearly the book had been taken down and put back repeatedly.

"Well, well," he said, pulling the book from the shelf. "Now we're getting somewhere."

Alex sat at Margaret LaSalle's desk reading when he heard the sound of footsteps on the stairs.

"You have any luck up here?" Danny said, entering the room.

"I've been through Margaret's desk," Alex said, sitting behind the simple wooden structure. He opened a drawer and pulled out a simple ledger, placing it on the desk. "This is her account book; according to what I read, she's got about two thousand dollars in a bank account, her brownstone is paid off, and she has no debt."

"Any unusual transactions?" Danny asked, picking up the book and flipping through it.

"Not that I can see," Alex said. "It's fairly basic, and she doesn't even have an investment account." He picked up a thin, leather-bound notebook from the desk and held it up.

"Then there's this," he said.

Danny put the ledger down and gave Alex a quizzical look.

"It appears to be Margaret LaSalle's idea book," he explained.

"Her what?"

Alex held the book out and Danny took it.

"Whenever she thought up an idea for a book, she wrote it here," he explained. "Here's Death at Dawn," he turned a few pages. "And this is the plot for the Doom Clock." Alex kept turning pages. "Some are just rough ideas." He pointed to a page with just a single line of text.

A politician frames his mistress for the murder of his wife.

"Okay," Danny said after reading some of the entries. "So what? Are you saying our burglar was looking for this?"

Alex shook his head.

"I don't think the burglar knew this existed," Alex said. "I think all of this," he waved his hand around at the partially reassembled room, "was done to throw us off the track."

"I think you're right," Danny said.

Alex had been prepared for his friend to object, so he was caught off guard.

"I checked the main floor and the basement, and I can tell you that whoever robbed this place didn't do a very good job," Danny explained. "I found a case of silverware on the bottom shelf in the pantry and a lock box full of stock certificates in a trunk under the basement stairs. Neither of those were well hidden, and that means our thief didn't spend much time searching, not as long as this mess would lead us to believe. So, what do you think he was after?"

Alex pointed to a bookcase that sat right behind the desk. The upper shelves held knick-knacks and several plaques given to LaSalle as awards. The next shelf, however, held a row of thick books, and the one below was packed with thick folios.

"These," Alex said, indicating the row of books, "are copies of all of Margaret LaSalle's books. These," he indicated the folios, "contain all the research notes she made when writing those books."

Danny examined the shelf, then looked confused.

"It doesn't look like anything is missing," Danny said, doing a quick count. "There are twelve books and twelve folios."

"That's where this comes in," Alex said, putting the black notebook down on the desk. He flipped a few pages, indicating the idea notes for several of LaSalle's books. "Each entry for a book she wrote has a page full of notes, sometimes more."

"That makes sense," Danny said. "She wrote the ones she had the most ideas for."

"I agree," Alex said, giving him a sly grin as he turned another page. "So where's this one?"

Danny looked down at the page full of notes.

"The Rooster Crowed at Sundown," he read.

"It's the story of a movie actress who's killed on the set of her latest film," Alex explained. "There are multiple suspects that have motives but also alibis. It's also the most detailed idea in this notebook that hasn't already been written."

"So your theory is that someone broke in, killed Margaret LaSalle, and stole her latest book?" Danny asked.

"No," Alex said. "You remember those fancy glass panels in the front doors? Well, they weren't even cracked, and the lock hadn't been forced. If it had, the key you brought wouldn't have worked."

"You think she knew her attacker," Danny said, nodding. "She let him in and then he killed her."

"She might have left her door unlocked, of course," Alex said. "But that wouldn't explain why her manuscript is missing along with all her research."

"Don't you think that's a bit of a reach?" Danny asked. "We don't know that she wrote that story in the first place."

"True," Alex said, opening the middle drawer of the desk. He took out a thick stack of receipts that had been paper clipped together. Pulling the clip off, he thumbed through them until he'd pulled two out. "These are for a ream of typewriter paper, and a box of ribbons," he said. "They're dated two months ago."

Danny looked around the room and then at Alex.

"I'm going to assume you didn't find a bunch of blank paper or typewriter ribbons when you searched this place."

Alex shook his head.

"All right," Danny said. "Let's say you're right. Why steal a manuscript?"

"Could be any number of things," Alex said with a shrug. "Maybe it was a rival who wanted to publish it as his own."

"It's as good a theory as anything else, I suppose," Danny said. "So how do we prove it?"

"First we have to find out if Margaret LaSalle actually wrote this Rooster book," Alex said. "Can you find out who her publisher was?"

Danny nodded.

"As soon as you do, we'll go see them," Alex continued.

"Why don't I just call and ask him if LaSalle was writing a book?" Danny said.

"Books have to be approved by the publisher," Alex said, remembering Iggy's description of how publishing worked. "They have to be edited. It's possible the publisher has a copy of the manuscript. If we can get that, maybe we can figure out why our murderer wanted it so badly."

Danny nodded.

"Okay," he said. "I'll call your secretary as soon as I have an address."

"In the meantime, I'll hang on to this," Alex said, picking up the black notebook. "Maybe there's something useful in it."

Danny looked like he might object but just then the front door downstairs opened.

"Detective Pak?" a familiar voice called. "You here?"

"Upstairs," Danny called, moving out into the hall.

Alex followed and found the short, stocky form of Lieutenant Detweiler coming up toward them.

"What can I do for you, Lieutenant?" Danny said as they met on the second-floor landing.

"I'm looking for...there you are," he growled when he caught sight of Alex behind Danny. "How did you do it, Lockerby?" he shouted. "How did you know?"

Alex and Danny exchanged confused looks.

"Ease off, Detweiler," Alex said. "You're not making any sense."

"You knew that hardware bombing case was poison and you managed to bail your friend out of it," he jerked his thumb at Danny, "and you landed me with a case that's going to make me look like a laughingstock."

"What?" Alex protested.

"Don't give me that innocent look," the Lieutenant said. "You got me into this and you're going to damn well get me out of it! Now pack your little bag of tricks, because you're coming with me."

5

HARDWARE

A sign in the front of the Milton Brothers Hardware store boasted that they carried the best selection of fixtures on the east side. A sign on the door said they were closed, but Alex knew for a fact that their selection had markedly decreased. A thick-necked man with a bushy mustache and an Italian accent stood in front of the store arguing loudly with a uniformed officer.

"Not that way," Detweiler said as Alex made for the door.

The Lieutenant turned and headed up the street toward the corner, leading Alex around behind the building. The back of the hardware store was a blank brick wall. As far as Alex could see, there wasn't even a rear door.

Which explained the hole.

About chest high was a circular hole in the wall about two feet in diameter. Below the hole, a section of the bricks had been torn out, leaving a gap just large enough for a man to pass through sideways. A bored-looking policeman stood leaning against the wall beside the hole, but he straightened up as Detweiler approached. If the Lieutenant noticed, he didn't comment.

Alex looked the scene over then turned to Detweiler and Nicholson.

"Seems pretty straightforward," he said. "Your burglars tried to blow a hole in this wall, but they didn't use enough explosive."

"How do you know that?" Detective Nicholson asked.

Alex pointed to the hole in the wall.

"The bricks here were pulverized by the explosion," he said. "You'll find what's left of them inside the store. But these," Alex pointed to the bricks on the ground. "These they had to pull out one by one."

"Is that important?" Detweiler asked.

Alex picked up one of the bricks and held it up.

"Notice how most of these are intact? They've been pulled out one at a time, by hand. If they knew they'd have to make their hole bigger, your thieves would have brought a crowbar or a sledgehammer."

"You can't know that they didn't," Nicholson said.

"And how do you know there was more than one thief?" Detweiler added.

Alex turned the brick in his hand over, showing all the sides.

"If they'd used a crowbar there would be tool marks on the bricks," he said, tossing it back on the pile. "And an explosion big enough to make even that little hole would have made a lot of noise. There's an apartment building two blocks that way, and that would give the thieves just a few minutes to get in and conduct their robbery before some curious citizen came looking."

"And it would take one guy at least five minutes to tear out that many bricks," Detweiler said with a nod. "So at least two guys."

"Who didn't use enough dynamite," Alex finished.

Detweiler smiled at that.

"Well I guess you don't know everything, now, do you?" he said.

Alex raised an eyebrow.

"What do you mean?"

Detweiler pointed to the round opening where the brick had been blasted away, indicating the edges.

"An explosive like gunpowder or dynamite would leave burn marks on the stone."

Alex wasn't an expert on blasting, but the remaining bricks and mortar showed no signs of being scorched, much less burned.

"And how—"

"I worked a mortar in the war," Detweiler supplied. "I've seen what explosives do to brickwork."

He didn't look old enough for that, but many people lied about their age to enlist.

"Nitroglycerin?" Alex asked.

"Not a chance," Detweiler said. "It'd take an expert just to transport that stuff and you made a compelling case that whoever did this wasn't an expert."

"Well, this seems to be your area of expertise," Alex said. "What did they use?"

Detweiler turned to Nicholson.

"You got that thing?"

The detective reached into the inside pocket of his jacket and pulled out a folded piece of paper.

"When I got here this morning," Nicholson said, passing it to Alex, "one of the uniforms found this. It was sticking out from under one of those bricks."

"Do you know what that is?" Detweiler asked as Alex accepted it from Nicholson.

The paper was cream-colored and thin. Alex knew that coloring came from the chemical process it had undergone when it was made. He'd used hundreds of sheets of the stuff in his career.

"It's flash paper," he said. "Runewrights use it to make rune constructs easy to activate."

"So I'd say this is your area of expertise," Detweiler said, throwing Alex's line back at him.

Alex unfolded the paper and found a basic rune scrawled on it. The line work was sloppy and the runic symbols were barely recognizable.

"This is a mending rune," Alex said, handing it back to Nicholson. "And not a very good one."

"I don't care what it is," Detweiler said. "I want you to explain this hole." He jerked his thumb at the wall. "Since the thieves didn't use regular explosives, what did they use?"

"If you're implying they used a rune to do that," Alex said, "I hate to be the bearer of bad news, but there's no such thing as a blasting rune."

Detweiler and Nicholson exchanged a disbelieving look.

"From what I hear," Nicholson said, "you've got dozens of little papers like that one that are all manner of useful. Are you saying you can't blow a hole in a wall?"

"That's what I'm saying," Alex pushed back. "There is something called a popper or sometimes a bang rune, but it's more like a firecracker. It couldn't dent this wall, much less blow a hole in it."

"Then what about this?" the detective asked, holding up the rune paper.

"Doubtless one of your thieves dropped it when they were pulling down the wall," Alex said. "If it was on the ground when the blast went off, it would have blown away."

"So," Detweiler chimed in, "at least one of the thieves was a runewright."

Alex could only shrug at that.

"It's possible," he said. "They may have written this rune or they may have bought it on the street, I don't know. What I do know is that they didn't buy or make a rune to blow that hole, because one doesn't exist."

"I thought you runewrights kept your magic to yourselves," Nicholson said.

"That's true," Alex admitted. "But a blasting rune would be useful in mining and railroad construction. If someone had invented one, it would be common knowledge."

"Unless whoever invented it wanted to rob businesses," Nicholson said.

Alex scoffed at that.

"Anyone smart enough to figure out a blasting rune would be smart enough to sell them to the railroad," he said. "They'd make a fortune."

"Well what other explanation is there?" Detweiler asked.

"What difference does it make how they got in?" Alex asked. "Shouldn't you be more concerned with the fact that they stole weapons and ammunition?"

"How—d" Detweiler began but Alex cut him off.

"Detective Pak told me."

"It matters because dynamite isn't easy to come by," Nicholson said.

"If these guys can just whip up a magic boom whenever they want, it makes them much more dangerous than just a couple guys with guns."

Detweiler nodded along with his detective's explanation, which was more intelligent than Danny had given the man credit for.

"And," the Lieutenant added, "if these guys have that ability, I have to warn the Captain."

"So he can handle the press?" Alex guessed.

"That's exactly why," Detweiler fumed. "If these lunatics start blowing up things in the city, the press is going to be howling for action."

"And," Alex said, finally understanding, "if you don't catch them quickly, it will be your head the Captain gives to the press."

"So you see how you got me neatly boxed in by switching this case for the murder of that writer."

"That was just a coincidence," Alex protested. "My landlord knew the dead writer and he wanted me to poke around, that's it. I didn't know anything about this 'til you brought me here."

The Lieutenant and the Detective exchanged a long, calculating look.

"Well, you are here," Detweiler said. "Do that thing you do with the mask and the lamp."

Alex thought about that. It was already after noon and he didn't want to waste any more time on fairly straightforward theft. Still, if Detweiler was right, and the thieves had used something new to blow a hole in the hardware store wall, he wanted to know about it.

"All right," he sighed, setting down his kit. "But I'd better be getting paid for this."

Detective Nicholson grunted something non-committal but the Lieutenant nodded.

"Find something I can use and I'll make sure they cut you a check."

Detweiler might be a schemer and a bit of an ass, but he was honest, so Alex started unpacking his gear. He started with silverlight but all it revealed was old stains of urine and vomit on the brick wall and surrounding ground.

"Looks like your thieves wore gloves," Alex said, replacing the silverlight burner in his lamp with the ghostlight one.

"Yeah," Detweiler said, his voice dripping with sarcasm. "I figured that when you said they pulled this wall apart with their hands."

Alex didn't waste a response on that. Lighting his lamp, he played the greenish beam of light over the wall. The edges of the hole lit up like a display window at Macy's. Shining the light inside the store, Alex could see the rubble from the explosion glowing as well.

"Okay, Lieutenant," Alex said, blowing out his lamp. "I owe you an apology. Whoever blew this hole in the wall used magic to do it."

"I thought you said that wasn't possible," Nicholson said.

"It shouldn't be," Alex said. "But as a friend of mine is fond of saying, if you eliminate the impossible and nothing remains, then some part of the impossible must be possible."

"Well that's just great," Detweiler growled. "Some nutcase is running around the city blowing holes in things with a new kind of magic."

Alex was reminded of the dead couple, hit by impossible magical lightning.

"Seems to be a lot of that going around," he said.

It was almost five when Alex climbed the steps to the brownstone. Detweiler had gone back to the Central Office after an hour, but Detective Nicholson had kept Alex at the hardware store going over everything. All the time he was there, Alex had wanted to get back to Margaret LaSalle's notebook. So when Nicholson finally let him go, he called Sherry and told her he was going home.

"You're home early," Iggy said from a distance, when Alex let himself in.

"Long day," he said, hanging up his hat. He put down his kit bag and extracted Margaret LaSalle's notebook from inside.

Alex moved into the library, expecting Iggy to be there, but found it empty.

"Iggy?"

"I'm in the greenhouse," came the explanation.

Alex headed into the kitchen and then through to the brownstone's back doors. The one on the left went out into the tiny, walled back yard, the one on the right stood open and led into the small, glassed-in greenhouse. Rows of flowers and herbs lined the sides, with the end reserved for Iggy's passion — orchids.

Behind the heat lamps that kept the orchids at a proper temperature sat Iggy in a padded chair. During the spring and summer, Iggy liked to sit in the greenhouse and read. This time, however, he was just sitting with a snifter of brandy and a cigar.

"I figured you'd be reading," Alex said, turning around one of the heavy kitchen chairs and pulling it near the greenhouse door.

Iggy puffed out a plume of cigar smoke.

"I finished *The Pressed Rose* an hour ago," he said, setting his cigar aside. "It was Margaret's last book."

"Maybe not," Alex said, sitting down. He held up the black notebook.

"What's that?"

Alex opened the notebook and flipped through it.

"This is Margaret LaSalle's idea book," he said. "There are pages of notes on her previous books and tons of not fully formed ideas. Then there's this."

Alex held up the book, showing double facing pages full of notes. Iggy sat up eagerly in his chair.

"According to this, Lasalle was working on a new book called *The Rooster Crowed at Sundown*," he said.

Iggy chuckled at that. When Alex raised an eyebrow, he explained.

"The title is meant to convey that something is amiss," he said, "but roosters can crow at any time."

"Well, it scared someone," Alex said. "LaSalle's house was ransacked like a thief was looking for valuables, but there were plenty of obvious things they missed."

"You think it was cover for something else," Iggy said with a sage nod.

"I found several receipts in her desk. According to them, she bought a large quantity of loose paper and typewriter ribbon a couple of months ago. There wasn't any of that in her office today."

"So the reports were right," Iggy said. "She was writing something new."

Alex nodded.

"There was an empty space on the shelf where LaSalle kept her manuscripts, and on the shelf below, where she kept folios full of her story notes."

"If Margaret LaSalle was writing a new book, she'd have lots of notes," Iggy said. "She was famous for basing her books on real events. *The Poison Pen Letters*, for example, was based on the case of Amy Gilligan, who murdered 48 people in her convalescent home after convincing them to name her as the beneficiary of their life insurance policies."

"How close were the books to the events they were based on?" Alex asked.

"The crimes were real, but she would fictionalize the details. Still, she did strive to get the details of the crimes correct. It gave her work a real feeling of authenticity."

"It sounds like she did a lot of research," Alex concluded. "When I searched her office, there wasn't anything relating to a new book there, just this." He held up the idea book.

"So whoever killed her stole her notes and her manuscript," Iggy said.

"Do you think whoever did it wanted to publish it as their own?" Alex asked. "A rival perhaps?"

Iggy shook his head.

"I doubt it," he said. "How would they have known she had finished her book?"

"How would anyone?"

Iggy stroked his mustache for a moment.

"What if her book was about a recent crime?" he said. "She would have interviewed people who were involved, police, survivors, maybe even the perpetrator, assuming they're still alive."

"You think she found something while she was doing her research?" Alex asked. "Something that someone involved was afraid would get out?"

Iggy didn't answer, still stroking his mustache. After a moment he nodded at the notebook in Alex's hands.

"What's this rooster book about?"

Alex glanced over the page, then shrugged.

"Well, from what I can piece together, it's about a movie actress who is murdered on the set of her latest project," he said. "There are a bunch of suspects — her manager, her understudy, her lover, and so on. All of them have motive, but they also have alibis."

Iggy stood up quickly and moved to the kitchen.

"What?" Alex demanded, following Iggy to the library.

Iggy went straight to the liquor cabinet and poured Scotch into his empty snifter. Downing it, he poured himself another one.

"I take it you've heard of this case?" Alex asked.

"Yes," he said. "And so have you. It's the Dolly Anderson case."

Alex racked his brain, but the name simply had no meaning.

"It was about fifteen years ago," Iggy said, staring out the window at the sidewalk. "Right before you and I met. Dolly Anderson was the darling of Broadway. Everyone loved her, the tabloids couldn't get enough of her, and she could sing like a nightingale."

"What happened?"

"She was electrocuted," Iggy said. "On stage during the opening performance of a play called *The Rogue's Gallery*."

"That doesn't sound like murder," Alex said, when Iggy didn't go on.

"Officially, it was ruled an accident, but no one believes that," Iggy said. "She was electrocuted when she picked up a prop telephone. It had a bell inside that could be rung off stage but there had to be a power wire to ring the bell. If I remember the papers right, the death was chalked up to a loose wire. They charged the theater's electrician with negligent homicide, but at his trial he was able to prove that he wasn't even in the theater that day and the phone prop worked perfectly during the rehearsal."

"So if *The Rooster Crowed at Sunset* is about the death of Dolly Anderson, maybe Margaret LaSalle discovered something new about it. Maybe she could prove it really was murder."

Iggy looked back at him with a somber face.

"Maybe more than that," he said. "What if Margaret found out that Dolly was murdered and then figured out who did it?"

"Wouldn't she go to the police if she'd done that?"

"Probably," Iggy said. "But remember, Margaret was writing a novel, a work of fiction."

"So?"

"So she might have just made up the ending," Iggy said. "Guessed at who really killed Dolly."

"Then why kill her?" Alex asked.

"Because, as you so astutely pointed out earlier, how would anyone know that she was writing a book in the first place?"

"You said she would have conducted interviews with the people involved," Alex said, following Iggy's train of thought. "So maybe she asked questions that spooked the real killer, made them think that she'd solved the case."

"In that case," Iggy continued, "they'd move heaven and earth to prevent the book from ever being published."

"And they'd have to take the research about the book, in case it revealed anything about the killer," Alex finished. "And to cover it up, they'd make the whole thing look like a robbery."

Iggy sighed and nodded, returning his gaze to the street outside.

"So now what?" Alex asked. "If Dolly Anderson's killer took LaSalle's manuscript and her notes, he would have burned them by now. Danny's trying to run down her publisher, but beyond that, we don't have any solid leads."

"Of course you do," Iggy said. "You know this has something to do with the death of Dolly Anderson. Margaret LaSalle was an excellent writer and she had good investigative instincts, but she was no detective."

"What are you saying?" Alex asked with the uncomfortable feeling that he already knew.

"If she can do it, I have every faith in you, lad," Iggy said. "If you want to know who killed Margaret LaSalle, you're going to have to solve Dolly Anderson's murder."

6

THE INFERNO ROOM

Alex was at the office early the next morning. In former days that would have been quite an accomplishment, but since all he had to do was walk though his vault from his bedroom to his second office, the commute was extremely short.

After he shut his office-side vault door, he quietly let himself out of the map room into the hall, then strode confidently down to his main office. When he reached the door, the light in the waiting room was on. Alex grabbed the handle and turned it. Instead of being locked, it turned easily.

"How do you do it?" he asked, pushing the door open.

"Hi ya, boss," Sherry said, looking up for her desk as Alex came in. There was a notepad on the desk along with several client folders. "How do I do what?"

Alex shut the door behind him and pulled out his watch.

"It's seven seventeen," he said after consulting it. "I didn't expect you to be here."

Sherry smiled at that and indicated the files on her desk.

"I had to catch up on some paperwork," she said.

"Why not do that during the day?"

"You're working two different cases for the police," she said as if that explained everything. "When you work with the cops, you often send me to the library or the Times to do research. I didn't want to fall behind."

"Uh-huh," Alex said, unconvinced. "You know I've been thinking about it and I'm pretty sure you've beat me into the office every day since I gave you your own key. It doesn't matter when I come in, you're already here." He gave her a penetrating look. "You're not sleeping under your desk, are you?"

Sherry laughed at that.

"Are you really getting after me for being early?" she asked. "I didn't realize it bothered you so much. If you'd like, I'll come in eighteen and a half minutes late tomorrow."

"You're only allowed to do that the day after Christmas," Alex said, catching her reference. "And only if your name is Bob." In Charles Dickens' *A Christmas Carol*, Scrooge's clerk, Bob Cratchit, was eighteen and a half minutes late getting in to work the day after the momentous events of the story.

"I'll make a note of it," Sherry said, still grinning. "I'm sure I can endure being called Bob for one day out of the year."

Alex gave her a penetrating look, then walked over to the desk.

"As it turns out," he said, offering her a cigarette from his silver case, "you were right. I do need you to do some research over at the Times this morning."

Sherry raised an eyebrow questioningly as she selected a cigarette.

"I need to know everything you can find out about the death of a Broadway starlet named Dolly Anderson," Alex said. "Focus on the people the press thought might be involved. The agony columns love to print any wild theory they come across."

Sherry picked up a clean notepad and scribbled down Alex's instructions.

"Take as much time as you need," Alex said, heading for his office. "I've got to meet Danny at a publishers' today, so I'll be here until he calls."

"Your friend will just have to go without you," a silky voice interjected. "I have more important work for you."

Alex heard the door open. His back was to it, but he recognized the voice.

"When it rains, it pours," Alex said, turning around. "It's awfully early. What brings you here, Sorceress?"

Sorsha Kincaid stood in the open doorway, one hand on the doorknob and one on her hip. She was dressed immaculately, as usual, in a loose white blouse with a form-fitting blue vest and dark pencil skirt. Usually she wore slacks when she was working, favoring the fashion of modern women who wore men's-style clothes. Today her only concession to that style was a gold watch chain running from the third button of her vest to the right-hand pocket.

Alex looked past the sorceress, into the hall, and saw her two FBI agents, Redhorn and Mendes, waiting there.

"I just got one of your cases dropped in my lap," Sorsha said, swaying into the room. "Along with a half dozen others."

"One of my cases?" Alex asked, looking to Sherry who just shrugged.

"The death of James Cooper and Paulette Burns," Sorsha supplied, leaning on Sherry's desk. She reached across the desk and lit the match from the touch tip lighter, then produced a cigarette from thin air and lit it.

"Who?" Alex asked, taking the match from her and returning it to the lighter.

"They were electrocuted over by St. Patrick's," she said, puffing on her cigarette. "Saturday night."

"Ah," Alex said. "The last I heard about it, Lieutenant Callahan didn't know their names. Why did the police give that case to you?"

Sorsha held up her hand and snapped her fingers. Alex expected something to appear in her hand just as the cigarette had done, but instead agent Mendes handed the sorceress a stack of brown police case folders.

"Your electrocution case," she said, pulling a folder off the top and dropping it onto Sherry's desk. "A woman who supposedly dissolved into a pile of sand," she dropped another folder on the desk. "Witnesses claim that two men who had a fight in an alley were throwing glowing balls of acid at each other; only one of them survived," she dropped a folder. "Three women reported an invisible man in the ladies changing room at Bloomingdales. And this one," Sorsha said, holding up the last folder. "People at the *Inferno Room* say that several dancers were on fire."

"You mean they were dancing well?" Alex asked as she dropped the last folder onto the stack.

"No," Sorsha said with a sardonic smile. "Literally. If it wasn't for the quick response of the fire department, the entire place would have burned to the ground Saturday night. Seven people are dead and a dozen more are in the hospital. I need you to come with me to go over the scene. Then I want your input on all of these cases." She put her hand down on the stack of folders.

Alex raised an eyebrow but didn't say anything.

"Well?" she said, obviously expecting some protestation.

"I'd tell you people you were drinking moonshine if I hadn't seen James Cooper with my own eyes," he said. "Andrew Barton told us that you sorcerers have an agreement not to make potentially lethal charms, so that's not it either."

Sorsha cast a furtive glance at Sherry then leaned close enough to Alex for him to smell her perfume.

"Could our new friends be behind it?" she said in a low voice.

Alex hadn't really thought about the Legion, but he considered it.

"No," he said at last. "First, this is a bit brazen for them. From what we've seen, they like to operate in the shadows."

"And secondly?"

"They're runewrights," Alex said. "There wasn't any evidence of rune activity at the electrocution crime scene. These cases sound more like sorcery."

"Except there weren't any sorcerers at the scene of James Cooper's electrocution."

"None that he or Paulette Burns saw," Alex challenged.

"You found evidence that they were, how did you put it?" She picked up the bottom-most folder and flipped it open. "'Romantically involved' right before James' death. Hard to imagine they got up to that sort of thing with a sorcerer just standing around watching."

Alex admitted that it did seem unlikely.

"What are we left with, then?" he asked.

Sorsha bit her lip, something she did when she was thinking.

"Alchemy?" she suggested.

"Not likely," Alex said. "The lightning that electrocuted Cooper and Burns was powerful. Most Alchemical solutions don't produce that kind of external magic."

Sorsha bit her lip again, this time in frustration.

"Well, we're not going to figure it out standing here arguing," he said. "Let me get my kit and we'll go down to the *Inferno Room* and see if we can get some useful clues."

The *Inferno Room* was a nightclub in the middle ring, frequented by working class people looking for a meal, a drink, or to unwind after work. It wasn't as fancy as *Northern Lights* or the *Emerald Room*, but you didn't have to wear a tuxedo to get in, so it had its virtues.

From the outside, the nightclub was just a plain structure. Only the presence of a large red awning with the name of the place indicated the presence of a nightclub, though Alex expected their band could be heard playing on most nights.

Now the building stood empty. Alex could see smoke damage above the broken windows, staining the awning above. An exhausted-looking man in a dark suit stood talking to a man Alex presumed to be the fire chief, with a uniformed policeman standing nearby, keeping curious onlookers moving along the sidewalk.

"Are you Captain Tisdale?" Sorsha said, striding confidently up to the man in the fireman's uniform.

Tisdale gave her a disapproving look until he saw Agent Redhorn, then he put two and two together.

"Miss Kincaid," he said, suddenly all deference. "I was informed you'd be coming. They said to keep everyone out of the building."

"Is it safe to go in?" she asked.

Tisdale nodded.

"The fire burned a hole in the roof, but it should be sound as long as you don't go walking on it."

"You got it out pretty quickly," Alex observed.

"We did," Tisdale said. "But how do you know that?"

"Your station's only a block away," Alex explained. "And the roof would be a total loss if the fire had gotten big. Good work."

Tisdale nodded his appreciation of the compliment, then turned to the man in the suit.

"This is Milton Fry," Tisdale said. "He owns the *Inferno Room*."

"And I'd like to know when I can get inside my club," Fry said. He had a harried, unkempt look about him and his patience was clearly at an end.

"We need to investigate the scene," Sorsha said in a calm, even voice. "As soon as we're done, you'll be informed."

Alex watched a shadow move across Fry's countenance. He clearly didn't like being told what he could and couldn't do in his own club, but he'd heard Sorsha's name when Tisdale greeted her, and he had no wish to tangle with a sorceress.

"Where are the witnesses?" Sorsha asked Tisdale.

"You'll want Officer Cranston for that," he said, pointing at the uniformed policeman.

"The ones we thought knew something are over there," Cranston said, pointing to a diner on the far side of the street. "We also sent a bunch to the hospital."

Sorsha turned to Agent Redhorn.

"Go get statements," she said. "Then go over to the hospital and do the same."

If Redhorn had a problem with being dispatched to statement duty, it didn't show. He nodded and motioned for Mendes to follow. Alex hadn't seen much of Agent Mendes since she'd been shot during an attempt on his life. She didn't seem to be holding any grudges, and gave Alex a smile and a wink as she headed down the sidewalk after her partner.

"Stop staring," Sorsha admonished as Alex admired the retreating form of Agent Mendes. "We have work to do."

Alex followed her into the dark interior of the nightclub. The area near the door had tables for diners. Some had been overturned as panicked patrons rushed the door to get away from the fire. Others stood as if they were just waiting for a busboy to clean them, with plates of partially-eaten food sitting undisturbed.

Beyond the tables was a wide dance floor with a bandstand at the far end. A long bar ran the length of the left-hand wall. In the center of the dance floor was a large burned area. The wooden pillars that held up the ceiling were blackened and charred, and the chandeliers full of magelights that hung from the ceiling were bent and twisted from the heat. Everything here was wet, a testament to the efforts of the firefighters, and a pile of debris from the missing roof lay scattered around, having been dragged apart and saturated to extinguish burning embers.

Sorsha stopped and surveyed the destruction with her arms crossed. Most of the dance floor had been destroyed, as well as part of the bar and the bandstand.

"Do you think you can get anything out of this mess?" she asked.

Alex put down his kit bag and moved to the circle of debris under the missing roof. He circled it twice before looking back to Sorsha.

"How many people died here?"

Sorsha did the trick where she pulled her notebook out of thin air, then flipped a few pages.

"Six," she said. "A bartender also died on the way to the hospital, probably overcome by the smoke."

Alex nodded, then went to the bar. After a few minutes he returned.

Sorsha raised an eyebrow once he arrived.

"Well?"

"Now we know why the fire didn't destroy the whole building," Alex said, leading Sorsha across to the debris.

He pulled out his handkerchief and used it to pick up a piece of broken glass.

"The barman," he said, holding up the curved fragment. "He tried to put the fire out."

"That looks like a piece of a magelight," Sorsha said, leaning in to examine the charred fragment.

Alex used his handkerchief to wipe away some of the smoke residue from the glass, revealing a red color.

"This is a piece of a fire grenade," he said. "A rack behind the bar is designed to hold them, but four are missing."

Sorsha looked to the bar and back to the debris.

"So the fire starts and the barman rushes to put it out, carrying a grenade in each hand."

"That's what I figure," Alex said.

"He made two trips before the smoke overcame him," Sorsha said.

"No," Alex said. "Fire grenades were made illegal a decade ago because they contain carbon tetrachloride. It's supposed to displace the oxygen so a fire smothers, but unfortunately it also creates a toxic gas. I suspect that's what overcame our hero barman."

"Okay," Sorsha said. "But that doesn't answer the question of how this fire began."

Alex bent down and opened his kit, extracting his oculus and multi lamp. He swept the scene with silverlight first. The room lit up with residue from vomit, blood, alcohol, and many other unidentifiable things. The bar was covered in arm marks and fingerprints, but nothing seemed out of place for a nightclub.

Satisfied that he'd found everything that could be found, Alex switched to ghostlight. First he played the light over the floor where the debris pile was. That was the most likely place since the initial report was that some dancers had actually caught fire.

"Anything?" Sorsha asked.

"No," Alex said, checking to make sure the burner in his lamp hadn't gone out.

Sorsha walked out onto the floor and held out her hand.

"Don't," Alex warned her.

"I'm just going to move the soot," she said. "It's blocking the floor beneath."

"Yes," Alex admitted, realizing she was right. "But you'll contaminate everything with magic."

Sorsha blushed slightly and lowered her hand.

"Sorry," she said. "I didn't think of that."

Alex pulled his handkerchief out of his pocket and used it to clean the soot off a section of the floor. When he pointed his light at it again, it bloomed into brilliant green.

"There's definitely magic here," he reported.

"Let's assume the police report is correct," Sorsha said. "Several dancers on the floor literally caught fire and just...kept dancing?"

"If the fire was magical, maybe they didn't even know they were on fire until it was too late."

Sorsha crossed her arms and sighed, staring around intently.

Alex held up his lamp to blow it out, but before he could, something glimmered from the bar. He stood and walked closer, sweeping the length of the bar with the greenish light beam.

Down at the unburned end, a stain on the bar glowed brightly. It looked like a spilled potion from the pattern.

"Did you find something?" Sorsha asked, crossing the floor after him.

"There's residue from a potion here," he said, indicating the spot on the bar. He raised the lantern, sweeping it over the shelves of bottles behind the bar. Many of them had been knocked over, but some remained where they had been the night before. None of them glowed back at him.

"I don't see any potions in the liquor," he said, moving to the end of the bar and around to the back.

The bar had a small lip along the outside edge, so the spilled potion had run across the bar and down behind it. Alex found the spot and trained his lantern on the ground. The floor was still wet from the water the firemen had used to put out the fire, but there were a few greenish streaks to be seen.

"I don't think the presence of a potion is going to help us," Sorsha said, running her fingers across the spot Alex had indicated. She raised her fingers to her nose. "Whatever it was couldn't have been very strong," she said. "All I smell is bourbon."

Alex looked around the floor with his lamp, but didn't see anything glowing. As he stood up, however, he caught a flash of green from the shelf under the bar where glasses were stored.

"Besides," Sorsha continued from the other side of the bar. "Alchemy can do amazing things, but it can't give people magical powers."

"You're assuming that's what it did," Alex said, standing up and laying a piece of wet paper on the bar. “What if the potion changed a person’s body chemistry? Made them temporarily immune to fire while their sweat became flammable.”

“Why would anyone brew something like that?” Sorsha asked.

“I don’t know,” Alex said. “But Paulette Burns had a piece of paper just like this one in her purse.”

Sorsha picked up the sodden paper carefully. It was about four inches long and three wide, without any markings on it.

“It’s paper, Alex,” she said, holding up her notebook next to it. “I’ve got lots.”

“Do yours glow with magic?” Alex asked, pulling off his oculus.

Sorsha set down the paper and put on the offered lens.

“It glows,” she confirmed.

“That means it’s been exposed to magic,” Alex said. “And the only magic I can find is the potion stain on the bar.”

“So the paper was on the bar when the potion spilled,” Sorsha said, passing the oculus back. “How is that important?”

“Because the one Paulette had was folded, like you use to keep medicinal powders.”

Sorsha nodded slowly.

“So you think it contained something magical meant to be added to a drink. Do you have any idea what?”

“This paper is blank,” Alex said, pointing to the bar. “But the other one had the word Limelight written on it.”

“I’ve never heard of that,” Sorsha admitted. “What is it?”

Alex grinned and shrugged.

“I have no idea,” he admitted.

7

BODIES OF EVIDENCE

"That cab was filthy," Sorsha said as Alex held the door for her to step out on the sidewalk in front of the city morgue.

They'd finished up at the *Inferno Room*, but Redhorn and Mendes had taken Sorsha's personal floater to get the witness statements at the hospital, so she and Alex had to travel by cab.

"I'm sure he appreciates you traveling down here on the streets with the little people," Alex said with a smirk. To the cabbie he said, "Keep the change," as he handed the man a ten spot.

He turned back to Sorsha as the cab drove away, and found her glaring at him with her arms crossed.

"I've taken cabs before," she said in an even voice. "That one smelled like a fish market. I'm going to have to burn these clothes when I get home."

"Let me know if you need any help with that," Alex said, doing a poor job of hiding a smirk.

Sorsha's eyes dropped to slits.

"You know this is the morgue, right?" she asked. "I can always leave you here when I go." Her stern look faded into a sly smile. "I'm sure Dr. Wagner would love to have you as a customer."

Alex was sure she was right; Dr. Wagner would love to have him as a customer. Wagner took over for Dr. Anderson when the former coroner retired and he hadn't liked Alex from the start. Alex hadn't helped matters when he'd had to blackmail Wagner to get access to the morgue on the very first occasion they met.

Maybe he's gotten over that, Alex thought as they rode the elevator down to the morgue.

"What are you doing here, Lockerby?" Wagner's voice assaulted him the moment he got off the elevator. "You have a death wish?"

"He's with me," Sorsha said, moving around Alex.

Wagner's face soured and he stretched his lips into an unconvincing smile.

"Sorceress Kincaid," he said. "I wasn't told you'd be coming. How can I help you?"

"We're here to see the bodies from the fire at the *Inferno Room*," she said, sweeping past Wagner. "I assume they're in the cooler."

"Of course," Wagner said, hurrying forward to catch up with her.

"I know the way," Sorsha said, waving him off. "We won't keep you from your work."

Wagner looked as if he didn't know whether to be relieved or upset at the sorceress' dismissal, but his face clouded over when Alex passed. Alex made sure to give him a big grin.

"Why do you antagonize him?" Sorsha asked, once they reached the cooler.

"Might as well," Alex said, pulling out his rune book. "He hates me anyway."

Alex tore a climate rune from the book, touched it to his tongue, and then stuck it to his hat.

"I won't always be here to get you in," she said, pulling the heavy door open and releasing a blast of arctic air.

Alex used his brass lighter on the rune and it blazed turquoise for a moment, then a bubble of warmth drove the chill away. Sorsha was right, of course. Thanks to Wagner he had to have a chaperone any time he wanted to examine a body. It was inconvenient, but so far, he hadn't been able to get any new leverage over the new coroner.

"That reminds me," he said, hesitating. "I need to make a phone call. Why don't you get started without me?"

Sorsha gave him a hard look, then entered the cooler.

"Don't bother Dr. Wagner," she cautioned. "We might need him later."

Alex promised to be good, then headed down the hall to the secondary office used by the several orderlies who worked for Wagner. It was usually empty, so Alex went in and picked up the phone on the desk.

"Detective Pak," he told the police operator when she answered.

"Where have you been?" Danny chided him once the call connected. "I found Margaret LaSalle's publisher. I was waiting to hear from you so we could go by together."

"Sorry, I got pulled into an FBI matter by Sorsha. We're down at the morgue looking at some burn victims."

"There usually isn't much to look at with burn victims," Danny said.

"So why don't you come by and get me and we'll go see the publisher together?"

"All right," Danny said after a long moment. "But lunch is on you for making me wait."

Alex chuckled and agreed. Trust Danny to be thinking of food.

"Hey," Alex interjected before the line went dead. "I need you to pull a police file."

There was a tense pause. Danny had gotten files for Alex before and he'd landed in trouble for it before.

"Why?"

"I told Iggy about LaSalle's missing book," Alex explained. "Apparently she based her books on real cases and Iggy recognized the bits from the notebook. It's the case of a Broadway star named Dolly Anderson who died fifteen years ago. Apparently it was a big deal at the time."

"All right," Danny said. "I'll put a call in to the records office, then come over."

Alex hung up, then called his office, but the phone just rang. Sherry was probably still at the Times archives looking up the details of Dolly Anderson's death.

When he returned to the cooler, Alex found Agents Redhorn and

Mendes had arrived. Redhorn stood by Sorsha, who was examining one of the charred corpses, and neither he nor the sorceress seemed affected by the deep chill of the cooler. Mendes, on the other hand, stood shivering behind them.

"Here," Alex said, passing her a climate rune as he passed. "Stick this to your jacket."

Mendes did as she was told and Alex produced his squeeze lighter, igniting the rune.

"That's amazing," Mendes said as the magic took hold. She gave him a big smile.

"Stop flirting with my Agents," Sorsha said, motioning him over.

"Don't worry, Sorceress, Agent Redhorn's not my type."

Redhorn gave Alex an unamused look but that was par for the course with the blocky man. Alex had never seen him be anything but cordial, but something about Redhorn's presence gave Alex the impression that he understood violence and wasn't afraid to use it.

"These are the bodies from the nightclub," Sorsha said, indicating seven gurneys against the left wall. "If you're right about the alchemy, at least two of them should show residual magic under your green light."

"Ghostlight," Alex said, opening his kit.

"Did you make that up or was that Dr. Bell?" she asked.

"That's Iggy," Alex chuckled. "He's got a way with words."

As Alex got out his gear, Redhorn brought them up to speed on the witness statements.

"Of the people who actually saw the fire start, they all said pretty much the same thing," he said, reading from a flip notebook. "A man and woman on the dance floor suddenly began bouncing flaming globes back and forth as they danced. Some said they were juggling, other said the globes were just floating along with them."

"And that didn't bother anyone?" Sorsha asked.

"Most of them thought it was a floor show," Mendes supplied.

"After a few minutes, the dancers seemed to drop the fireballs," Redhorn continued. "That's when the fire started."

"Everyone said that the dancers burst into flame," Mendes said. "They died almost immediately."

"Several dancers nearby were caught up when the fireballs exploded. The rest," Redhorn shrugged, "is self-explanatory."

Sorsha looked at the charred bodies on the gurney and shivered. Alex knew she wasn't affected by the cold, but he understood. The idea of burning to death made his stomach turn.

"This is sounding less and less like alchemy," Sorsha said, turning to Alex. "How are you doing?"

"Do you have a map of where these bodies were found in the police file?" he asked.

Mendes handed the file to Sorsha and she flipped through it before nodding.

"These bodies show residual magic," Alex said, indicating two of the corpses. "This one and this one."

Sorsha checked their toe tags then compared the numbers to the chart in the file.

"These are our dancers," she said. "They were found at the source of the fire."

"No one else showed any signs of magic," Alex said, blowing out his lantern. "It's not any alchemy I ever heard of, but unless these two were latent sorcerers—"

"Don't be absurd," Sorsha interrupted.

"Unless these two were latent sorcerers," Alex repeated, "this is alchemy of some kind."

Sorsha chewed her lip, then turned to Alex.

"You're sure it's not some kind of rune?" She gave her agents a sidling look. "Something our *marked* friends would use?"

She put emphasis on the word 'marked.' Alex knew she meant the Legion. Ever since he'd discovered their name, they'd agreed to keep it to themselves, which meant the FBI didn't know.

"No," Alex said. "If a rune had been involved, they would have had to have been written on the dancers, and that would leave an after image. Plus, their whole bodies wouldn't glow, just the place where the rune was written."

Sorsha nodded. It was clear from her expression that she was thinking along the same lines, she just wanted to be sure.

"You said you found a paper with the word 'Limelight' on it. Could that be what we're looking for?"

"I hope so," Alex said. "It's the only clue we've got."

"Do you think any of your alchemist friends would know what it is?"

Alex shrugged.

"I can ask."

"Do it," she said, handing the police folder back to Agent Mendes. "Today. Before someone takes this potion and burns down an apartment building."

Sorsha swept out of the room with her federal agents trailing in her wake. Alex watched them go before packing up his equipment and pulling the sheets up over the dead. Since Danny hadn't arrived yet, Alex searched the other shrouded bodies until he found a woman in her fifties. Her body didn't tell him much, and he had to roll her up on her side to see her wound. She had a single gunshot wound in her back just a bit left of center. Clearly it hit her heart, and she would have been dead before her body hit the floor. The only other things he learned were that Margaret was right handed, based on the pencil impressions on her fingers, and she was a fairly heavy drinker.

"What are you still doing in here?" Danny's voice snapped him out of his thoughts.

Alex looked up from the body and found his friend standing in the doorway of the cooler.

"I saw the sorceress and her flunkies leaving when I arrived."

"Sorry," Alex said, pulling the sheet up over Margaret LaSalle. "Just checking our murder victim."

"Let me guess," Danny said. "A single shot in the back that hit the heart. She was killed instantly."

"How did you know?" Alex asked, picking up his bag.

Danny grinned and held up a brown police folder.

"I picked up the file from Wagner on my way in."

"Well, she probably knew her attacker," Alex said.

Danny nodded.

"Shot in the back in the front room of her apartment," he said. "It's likely she let her murderer in. Did you find anything else?"

"Nope," Alex said, as he moved out into the hall.

"Good," Danny said, shutting the heavy cooler door. "I'm starving."

The offices of Broadstreet Publishing were on the south side of the inner ring, so Danny stopped at an upscale diner near it to grab lunch. Alex ate his eggs and toast quickly, then excused himself to use the phone.

He called Linda Kellin, Andrea's daughter, but she didn't know of any potion or compound called Limelight. Alex thanked her and dialed the number of *The Philosopher's Stone*, an alchemy shop on the other side of town.

"It's Alex Lockerby," he said when the proprietor, Charles Grier, picked up the phone.

"It's been a while, Alex, how are you?" Grier asked.

Alex had helped the late Dr. Kellin save Grier's life a few years ago and they'd stayed in touch.

"I've got a problem I could use your help on," Alex said. "Have you ever heard of an alchemical powder called Limelight?"

Grier hesitated for a moment.

"No," he finally said. "Do you know what it's used for?"

"As far as I can tell you add it to alcohol and it...gives you magic-like abilities?" It sounded stupid when Alex said it out loud, but he couldn't think of any other way to say it.

"It sounds like Pixie Powder," Grier said.

Alex had never heard of that and he said so.

"It was also known as Speakeasy Sawdust," Grier explained. "As you might imagine, it was popular during prohibition. It was a powder you'd put in beer and when you drank it, you'd be able to make little magical lights appear. It was a big hit with large groups and most speakeasies were like big parties. It fell out of favor once the bars opened up again."

"How have I never heard of this?" Alex asked. He'd never really gone to speakeasies; mostly he'd been too young and too broke.

"I cooked some up back in the day," Grier admitted, "but it was expensive to make and all it did was make a few glowing lights so it lost its demand after a people started drinking alone again. Making Pixie Powder just isn't worth the cost."

"But the magic lights weren't dangerous, were they?"

"No, you couldn't even touch them. Are you saying that this Limelight stuff is giving people real magical abilities?"

Alex explained the events of the electrocuted couple and the fire at the *Inferno Room*. When he was done, Grier whistled.

"That's something I've never heard of," he admitted.

"Can you ask around, maybe see if someone knows about it?"

"I doubt anyone would tell me if they did know," Grier said. "We alchemists are just as secretive with our recipes as you runewrights are with yours. If you could bring me a sample of this Limelight powder, I could run some tests and try to figure out what it's made of."

"I'll see what I can do," Alex said. "But keep your ear to the ground and let me know if you hear anything."

Grier promised that he would, and Alex hung up.

"What was all that?" Danny asked from behind him.

"Sorsha's case," Alex said. "What's this?"

"The bill," Danny said, handing over a slip of paper with a grin.

"Four bucks?" Alex protested. "For lunch? You really took me for a ride, didn't you?"

"You owe me," Danny said. "I've been getting you police files and getting you into the morgue for months. The only time I see you anymore is when you need a favor."

Alex was going to object, but Danny had a point. He dug a fiver out of his wallet, dropping it on the counter as he put on his hat.

"Well, let's solve this case, then," he said. "You can take all the credit and then you can buy lunch."

The office of Broadstreet Publishing was an unimpressive space on the first floor of a converted brownstone. The lettering on the door read, *Broadstreet Publishing, Paul Baxter - Editor*. Beyond the door was a small front room with several couches crammed into the space and a secretary's desk piled with stacks of papers bound in string, and packages wrapped in heavy paper. From the look of the desk, it was a cinch that no secretary worked there.

"No phone," Danny observed, pointing at the desk. "It's just for show."

To the right as they entered was a plain wooden door with a posted sign that instructed visitors to leave manuscripts on the desk unless they had an appointment.

"Do you suppose you get an appointment by calling the secretary?" Alex asked.

Danny polished his gold detective badge with his sleeve.

"Time to make our own appointment."

He grabbed the doorknob, but before he could turn it, the door pushed open. Danny started to go inside but Alex grabbed his arm, pointing to the door jamb. The strike plate had been torn out as if someone had kicked the door in.

"Step back," Danny whispered, reaching into his jacket for his .38 police special.

Alex hadn't prepared for trouble; his 1911 and his knuckleduster were both in the gun cabinet in his vault, so he moved away from the door. Holding his gun at the ready, Danny shouldered the door open and stepped around it quickly, lowering his weapon.

"Police," he shouted. "Don't move."

Someone inside shouted in alarm as Danny stepped into the room.

"What are you doing?" a man's voice said.

Alex followed into the room and found Danny standing in front of a little balding man in a rumpled suit. He wore spectacles that made his eyes look comically large and his dark hair was combed over a wide bald spot. Ink stains covered his fingers and he held a fountain pen in one hand.

"Who are you?" Danny demanded of the man. He lowered his pistol but didn't put it away.

"I'm Paul Baxter," the man shouted. "I'm the one who called you."

Alex and Danny exchanged glances as Danny holstered his weapon.

"We're here because you're Margaret LaSalle's publisher," Danny said. "We're investigating her murder."

Paul Baxter looked surprised.

"Why did you call the police, Mr. Baxter?" Alex asked.

"That's just it," he said. "It's about poor Margaret."

"What about her?" Danny said.

"I got a package in the mail this morning," he said. "Margaret sent it last week, obviously before she died. It was the manuscript for her new book, *The Rooster Crowed at Sunset*."

Alex felt the hair rise on his arms and he grinned.

"We'd like to see that," he said. "It might have something to do with why she was murdered."

"I'd love to help you, but that's why I called the police," Baxter said. "While I was at lunch, someone broke in here and stole it."

8

SUSPECTS

Alex pushed open his office door at ten after five. He'd spent the afternoon going over the offices of *Broadstreet Publishing* with a fine-toothed comb and had come away empty. The front office was the dumping ground for all the manuscripts Paul Baxter didn't ask for, so the whole room was covered in fingerprints with no way to tell one set from another.

The inner office had been a bust as well. Alex checked over Baxter's desk, but found only the publisher's prints. Whoever had absconded with Margaret LaSalle's manuscript must have worn gloves.

"That bad, boss?" Sherry asked, reading Alex's face as he came in. She stood by the short filing cabinet, pouring herself a cup of coffee from the pot.

"Worse," Alex said, tossing his hat so it landed on the coat rack. "I've got two cases with no suspects and precious little clues."

Sherry smiled at him as she walked her full coffee cup back to her desk.

"I might be able to help you with that," she said. Sitting down, she took a sip from the cup and immediately made a face. "When are you going by Empire Tower again?" she demanded, giving Alex a hard look. "I've been digging through old newspapers all day, and I'm covered in dust." She brushed at her blouse for emphasis. "I need a good cup of coffee."

"I'll go and see Marnie in the morning," he promised. "I'll even take an extra thermos so there'll be plenty."

Sherry beamed and set the offending coffee down.

"Now what have you got for me?" Alex said, sitting on the corner of her desk.

She pulled out a notepad with lots of tightly written script and began flipping pages.

"So," she said, gathering her thoughts. "Dolly Anderson was the biggest star Broadway had a few years ago, and she was in a play called *The Rogue's Gallery*. On opening night, she went to pick up a prop telephone on stage, and in front of God and everyone, she was electrocuted by a faulty wire."

"I didn't think they used live props in plays," Alex said, making a mental note to look into it.

"It wasn't a real phone," Sherry said, flipping a few pages. "According to the reports, it just had a bell in it so they could ring it, but that required power. Anyway, it was eventually ruled an accident, but for months the papers were full of wild theories."

"Like what, for example?"

Sherry flipped a few more pages.

"Well first off, the play was written by a guy named Benny Harrington," she said. "His career was on the skids because his last couple of plays flopped."

"How did he land the biggest actress on Broadway then?" Alex asked.

"Apparently they were friends," Sherry supplied. "But there were theories that she was going to back out at the last minute, which would ruin Harrington."

"So he kills her on stage?" Alex said. "That can't have been good for business."

"It wasn't. The play closed that same night and Harrington was ruined. He died a year later from pneumonia."

"Doesn't sound like he had a great motive," Alex said. "Still, if

Dolly was going to quit, he might have killed her out of spite. Who else have you got?"

"There's lots," Sherry said. "Dolly was dating Claude McClintock at the time and they were always fighting in public, it was all over the papers."

"Claude McClintock the movie actor?"

Sherry got a far-away look and sighed.

"Yeah," she said. "That was before he was in pictures."

"Who else?" Alex prodded when Sherry didn't go on.

"Then there was the understudy, Regina Darling. When Dolly died, she got her chance to take lead roles."

Alex had heard that name; she was a big star on Broadway now. If she'd killed Dolly to get her out of the way, it had certainly worked out for her.

"There's also Maybelle Leone," Sherry said.

"The fashion designer?" Alex asked. "How does she fit into this?"

"She provided all of Dolly's dresses for the play."

"The failing play?" Alex said. "Her designs are worn by actresses and rich ladies. I think Sorsha even has some of her stuff. Why was she providing costumes for a low rent play?"

"According to papers, her designs weren't getting noticed at the time. Harrington's play was all the work she could get. Apparently she hated Dolly, though no one seems to know why."

"What about the owner of the theater?" Alex asked. "It was his equipment that electrocuted Dolly, so was he a suspect?"

Sherry nodded.

"Since Harrington's past two plays had flopped, he'd taken out an insurance policy on the theater. If the play didn't last at least three weeks he stood to get a sizable payout."

Alex didn't know much about how insurance worked for show business, but that didn't sound kosher.

"Did it say why they ruled him out?" he asked.

Sherry shook her head.

"All I know is his name, Ethan Nelson." She closed her notepad and handed it to him. "There's a few other people who were suspects; you'll find them in there. As far as I can tell, though, Dolly Anderson's death was just a tragic accident."

Alex sighed as he flipped through the notes. It was a lot to take in, and he'd have to go over it thoroughly. There was also whatever the police had on the case, that would probably have more detail and list the various suspects' alibis.

Assuming they have alibis, he reminded himself.

If Iggy was right about Margaret LaSalle, she must have found something out of the ordinary in this case. Something worth killing to keep quiet.

"All right," Alex said, flipping the pages closed on the notepad. "You did great, but it's been a long day, so why don't you head home? I've got to go over this, so I'll lock up."

Sherry didn't have to be told twice. She put on a broad-brimmed hat, picked up her handbag, and wished Alex a good night. He watched her go, listening to the sounds of her shoes on the stairs as she headed to the street. When he was satisfied that she was gone, he dropped the notepad into his kit bag, picked up his hat, and headed for his second office and the door to his vault.

"This is quite a list of suspects," Iggy said. He sat at the kitchen table paging through Sherry's notes while Alex cleaned the dinner dishes. "The way I remember it, the police focused on the theater's electrician. He was eventually acquitted. They just didn't have enough solid evidence against him."

"Which doesn't mean he didn't do it," Alex chimed in, "just that the state's attorney couldn't prove it."

Iggy made a non-committal noise and Alex looked over his shoulder to see him puffing on his after-dinner cigar, deep in thought.

"I think if the electrician was the killer, this case would have been too simple to appeal to the likes of Margaret LaSalle," he said at last. "If I had to guess, I'd say she'd write it so one of these others did it. Someone with a less obvious motive would have appealed to her."

Alex nodded as he scrubbed the silverware. He and Iggy had

discussed Sherry's notes all during dinner and he was no closer to having a solid suspect than he was before. That wasn't terribly surprising, but it would have been nice to have someone to focus on.

"I'll have Sherry run down everyone on the list tomorrow," he said. "Once she finds them, I'll interview them, see if Margaret LaSalle talked with them."

"Two things," Iggy said, still paging through the notepad. "First, just because Margaret didn't talk to one of the suspects doesn't rule them out."

"If she didn't talk to them, how would they know about her book?" Alex asked.

"It would be easy if they were still in contact with any of the people Margaret did talk to," Iggy pointed out. "All the people on that list knew Dolly Anderson, so it stands to reason they know each other."

"Good point," Alex admitted. "What's the second thing?"

"Secondly," Iggy continued, recapturing his original train of thought. "I wouldn't do too much until you see that police report. They will have already done a lot of the legwork for you. Once you get a look at it, you'll know better who to focus your attention on."

"Danny already requested it," Alex said. "I don't know how long—"

The chime of the doorbell interrupted him, and he looked back over his shoulder in the direction of the front door.

"Are you expecting anyone?" Iggy asked as Alex dried his hands.

"No, but the way my week has been going, they probably want me to go with them to the scene of a disaster." He set aside the dish towel and headed for the front hall. "Be right back."

"Let me know if you leave," Iggy said, turning his attention back to the notepad.

Alex passed out of the kitchen and into the library, then through the vestibule to the front door.

"Sorceress," he said, pulling the door open to reveal Sorsha standing on the stoop. She wore an elegant evening gown with a long string of pearls around her neck that were so white they almost glowed in the light from the house. Her long cigarette holder was in her hand while the other hand rested on her hip in an impatient manner.

"When I said I wanted you to talk to your alchemist friends today," she said, giving him a cold stare, "did you imagine that I wanted to wait until tomorrow for a report?"

"Why yes, it is a pleasant evening," Alex said, stepping back and holding the door open. "Won't you come in?"

She glared at him for a long moment, then sauntered past him and into the library.

"Well?" she said, the impatience that had been in her body language now creeping into her voice.

"Neither of my contacts had ever heard of Limelight," Alex said. "Charles Grier, you remember him?"

Sorsha nodded. She had met the man after Alex had rescued him from kidnappers.

"Well he mentioned something called Pixie Powder that used to be popular during prohibition. It would let people create glowing lights, but they weren't dangerous."

"So Limelight is Pixie Powder, just stronger," she said.

Alex shrugged.

"Maybe," he said. "Grier said he might be able to figure out what it is if we brought him a sample."

"Great," Sorsha said, puffing on her cigarette. "Where can we get some?"

Alex thought about that, then smiled.

"I know a place that deals in, shall we say, questionably legal potions," he said.

"Why am I unsurprised?" Sorsha said with an amused smirk.

"Are you up for some field work tonight?"

"Is this place still open?"

"Of course," Alex said, reaching for his hat, hanging on a peg in the hall. He put it on and offered Sorsha his arm. After a pause, she took it.

"Iggy," he called back to the kitchen. "I'm going out. Don't wait up."

Sorsha's driver dropped them off on a side street in Chinatown. Most of the shops lining the road were shuttered and dark, but a few places were open, most selling food of one kind or another. There weren't many street lights and several of the buildings seemed to loom ominously over the street.

"This is a nice part of town," Sorsha sneered as the other people on the street gawked at her obvious wealth. "Are you concerned?"

"Not at all," Alex said, lighting a cigarette. "I've got a sorceress to protect me."

Sorsha rolled her eyes. Alex offered her his arm again, and after a moment she took it.

"Just where are we going?" she asked, as he steered them down toward the darker end of the street. "I'm concerned," she went on when he didn't answer.

"Do I need to open my vault and get my pistol?" Alex asked with mock sincerity.

"That's not what I mean," Sorsha said, lowering her voice. "I didn't tell the FBI about the Legion or their mind control rune."

"I thought we were in agreement that telling the government about the existence of mind runes would be a monumentally bad idea," Alex said under his breath.

"We are," Sorsha said. "But this Limelight sounds like something the Legion would be involved in. The only people who know about them are you, me, and Dr. Bell."

"And you're worried that there aren't enough of us to stop whatever the Legion is up to," Alex guessed.

"There could be hundreds of them," Sorsha said. "And whatever they're up to, they've got a head start on us."

Alex was tempted to tell her about Moriarty, but he wasn't sure he wanted anyone else knowing about his mysterious benefactor. Even if he told Sorsha, it wasn't like Moriarty could help. Alex didn't have any idea how to contact him. If he was honest with himself, he didn't know if Moriarty was even an ally.

"Are you going somewhere with this, Sorceress?" he asked at last.

"I don't know," she said. "But I'm worried about what will happen if we get in over our heads. The Legion is dangerous and we know next to nothing about them."

"We know they got some of their members from the Whalers," Alex said.

"The British military runewrights who are looking for the Archimedean Monograph?" Sorsha said. "I asked around about them, and no one's heard anything about them for a decade."

Alex shrugged.

"It's a place to start," he said.

"Let's figure this Limelight business out first," she responded. "Where *are* you taking me?"

"Here," Alex said, steering Sorsha to a metal stair that ran down below street level. A yellow light bulb hung from a fixture in front of an elaborately painted sign that read *The Lotus Garden*.

"Alex," Sorsha said, rounding on him with a cross expression. "This is an opium den."

"What better place to buy mind altering substances?" Alex pointed out, heading down the stairs.

"And just how do you know about this place?" she asked, following him to a single, sturdy-looking door on the landing below.

"From a case," he said. "A woman's husband disappeared and I traced him here."

He took hold of the door and pulled it open.

"I was only here once and that was a long time ago."

The interior of *The Lotus Garden* was dark, and garish paper lanterns hung in the corners of the foyer, illuminating a narrow hallway to one side. Across from the door was a podium like the ones where a maître d' would stand at in fine restaurants. This one was occupied by a small Chinese woman in her early thirties with jet black hair styled to be wavy, a broad face, and dark eyes. She wore a silver, Chinese-style dress that hugged her figure as if it had been painted on. A keyhole cutout started below the collar, showing a generous amount of her upper chest. On a better-endowed woman it would have been scandalous, but on her it was tasteful. Embroidered kanji ran from her shoulder down each side of the dress, and a long slit ran up from the hem almost to the woman's hip. It revealed a tantalizing amount of athletic leg that looked perfectly sculpted, thanks to a pair of very high heels.

The woman looked up as Alex and Sorsha came in. When she saw Alex, her face split into a wide smile.

"Alex!" she cooed, coming around the wooden podium to embrace him. "It's been forever. Why haven't you come back to see me?"

"Only once, huh?" Sorsha said with a raised eyebrow.

"Wendy," Alex said, doing his best to extricate himself from the young woman's grasp.

"I should be very cross with you," Wendy said. She had no accent to speak of, but she had been born and raised in the city so that wasn't terribly surprising. Her smile at seeing Alex faded when she noticed Sorsha.

"Who's your friend?" she asked, looking up at Alex with a sour expression.

"Wendy Xin, this is my friend Sorsha," he introduced them. He left off the Sorceress' last name. There was no need for anyone to know who she really was, and the presence of sorcerers around ordinary people had a tendency to cause problems.

"You didn't say girlfriend," Wendy said hopefully. "Or wife."

"Sorsha's just a friend," Alex said. "She's looking for something and I'm helping her find it."

"Oh," Wendy cooed, leaning against Alex. "How can I help? Maybe once you're done, you and I can talk for a while."

Wendy was the face of *The Lotus Garden* and had been for at least five years. Her father ran the place and was, Alex suspected, well connected with the Chinese mob. Apart from being a wanton and a shameless flirt, Wendy was the person to ask about any kind of drug or narcotic.

"Do you have a powder called Limelight?" Sorsha asked, exasperation clear in her voice.

Wendy put a finger to her lips and cocked her head to one side.

"No," she said at last. "I don't think I've ever heard of anything called Limelight. What does it do?"

"It's an alchemical powder," Alex said. "You mix it with alcohol and it's supposed to give you some kind of magic powers for a few minutes."

Wendy whistled at the thought.

"We don't have anything like that," she said. "If my father knew it existed, he'd have some, so that means it's either really expensive or it doesn't exist."

"Let's assume it's expensive," Alex said.

"Then you'd have to go to a swanky club," Wendy said. "Some place where people have lots of money. Probably in the core."

"How would you get something like that at a nightclub?" Sorsha asked.

"You'd have to know somebody with connections," Wendy replied.

That meant anyone who might have Limelight would be tied to the criminal underworld, probably to the mob.

Sorsha turned her cool gaze on Alex.

"Well I don't travel in those circles," she said. "Do you know someone that fits Miss Xin's description?"

Alex took a deep breath and let it out slowly.

"Yeah," he said, dreading what came next. "I do."

9

ACQUAINTANCES

"How do I look?" Alex asked, coming out from the bedroom in his vault. He wore his tuxedo, except for the tie, which was giving him trouble. Sorsha looked up from the bookshelf in his little library where she'd been perusing the books.

"Let me help with that," she said, holding out her hand for the tie.

A nightclub in the core would require better attire than his suit, so after Sorsha's driver had flown them to the core, Alex had opened a door to his vault in the side of a convenient building.

"You've changed your vault since the last time I was in here," Sorsha observed as she focused on Alex's tie.

She was so close he could smell her delicate floral perfume.

"Keep your head up," she said as he looked down at her.

"Just a few improvements," he said. He'd had the foresight to put the door to his map room and the one to his bedroom down new hallways and out of sight from the main room.

"I'd like to see what you've done," Sorsha said as her hands worked the ends of the tie into a knot. "Can I have a tour?"

Alex wondered if she was suspicious about his work or if she was just making small talk.

"Maybe later," he said as she smoothed the ends of the tie and stepped back. "Right now we've got a lowlife to deal with."

"So who is it we're seeing?"

"His name is Jeremy Brewer," Alex explained, "but his clients call him the Broker."

Sorsha cocked her head at him.

"He's some kind of trader?"

"No," Alex chuckled. "He's more of a facilitator. People who want something stolen come to him and he finds criminals to do the job."

"Really?" Sorsha said, a sly smile creeping onto her face.

"None of that," Alex said in a firm voice. "We need him to help us and from what I've heard he can be...temperamental."

"I thought you knew him."

"No," Alex lied. "We've never met, but I've heard his name."

Alex had met the Broker a few years ago and he'd threatened to drop him into the East River to get a name out of the man. He wouldn't recognize Alex, since he'd been wearing a disguise rune at the time, but he didn't want Sorsha to slip and say something that might give him away. After all, she couldn't reveal what she didn't know.

"Are you sure you can get us in to see him?" Sorsha asked. "If he's as well connected as you say, he probably knows I work with the FBI."

"I doubt he'll see me at all," Alex said, checking his reflection in the mirror over his fake hearth. The knot was perfect. "I suspect, however, that he'll be more than willing to see you."

The nightclub known as the Emerald Room looked exactly as Alex remembered. It was built like a bowl with a circular dance floor a full story below the entrance. Concentric rings ran around the dance floor in a semi-circle with tables on each level. A long mahogany bar was located on the far side of the floor with a bandstand next to it. A woman in a flowing gown was standing in front of the band, crooning into a microphone as the band played. Couples filled the floor, moving to the music, and a haze of cigarette smoke hung in the air.

"How do we find this broker?" Sorsha said, holding on to Alex's arm as they stood at the top of the stairs.

A second set of stairs led up from the dance floor to a door in the back wall of the building. Several openings ran along the wall, indicating the presence of private rooms.

"Up there," Alex said, indicating the door at the top of the other stairs. He led her down to the floor, then around to the other stairs.

"How should I play this?" Sorsha asked as they approached the door at the top of the stairs.

"He's bound to know you work with the FBI, so act like you don't know what he really does."

Sorsha nodded.

"So the story is that we're looking for Limelight and someone told us he could supply it," she said.

Alex nodded, then grabbed the doorknob and pulled it open so Sorsha could enter. Beyond the door a wide hallway ran off to the right in a curve, following the contour of the curved main room. As he followed her, Alex flashed back to the first time he'd been in this hallway. Back then a bent-nosed man in a black suit had stood watch beside the door at the end of the hall. The only thing that had changed was the man with the black suit and slicked-back hair looked a bit older. He was still a plain thug and he gave Alex and Sorsha the once-over as they approached.

"You lost?" he sneered in a thick Jersey accent.

Sorsha gave him her iciest stare, and he stood up a bit straighter. Alex grinned as he realized that the move had the effect of putting distance between the man and Sorsha. She held his gaze for a long moment, then reached into empty air and pulled out one of her pale blue business cards.

"Tell Mr. Brewer that I'd like a quick word," she said, pressing the card against the thug's lapel.

"Uh, yes miss," he said, fumbling to take the card. He gave Alex a penetrating look, but seemed not to think him a danger at all compared to the Ice Queen, so he turned and entered the private room.

"Good so far?" Sorsha hissed.

"Perfect," Alex replied.

A moment later the door opened again, only this time it wasn't the bent nosed thug. The man at the door this time was tall and handsome, with perfectly straight teeth, slicked-back hair, and a crooked smile. He wore an expensive suit and several gold rings on each of his hands. Alex recognized him as Jeremy Brewer, the Broker himself.

"Miss Kincaid," he said with an ingratiating smile. "What an honor to receive you. Won't you please come in."

Brewer made a sweeping gesture with his hand and Sorsha nodded politely before stepping inside.

"And who is your friend?" he asked when Alex followed.

"This is Mr. Lockerby," she said.

Alex gave the room the once-over before Brewer shut the door. It looked much like it had the last time he'd been in it. A couch and an easy chair sat in an 'L' shape in the center of the space with a door leading to a washroom behind and a liquor cabinet on the back wall. Brewer's bodyguard, a tall, bald man with bushy eyebrows was standing at the cabinet pouring drinks, but his eyes never left Sorsha.

"Won't you sit down, Miss Kincaid?" the Broker said, indicating the couch.

Sorsha sat, crossing her legs and pulling her cigarette holder out of thin air. Alex thought she was pouring it on a bit thick, but her actions definitely validated who and what she was.

"Do you have a light, Mr. Brewer?" she asked.

Brewer produced a gold plated lighter and flicked it to life.

"Before you tell me why you're here, Miss Kincaid," he said, holding the flame under her cigarette. "I have a question for your friend."

Alex tried not to react. He remembered the last time he'd been in this room, the thug guard had grabbed him from behind. Alex had used a flash rune to get out of that situation and he touched the tip of his thumb to his flash ring in case he had to make a similarly fast escape.

Brewer's gaze shifted to Alex.

"Your name is Lockerby?" he asked.

Alex nodded.

"Alexander Lockerby," he said. "But you can call me Alex."

"I believe you're also known as the Runewright Detective," Brewer said, tucking his lighter into his jacket pocket.

"That's me," Alex admitted.

When Brewer's hand came out of his jacket pocket, it held a small .22 semi-automatic pistol which he leveled at Alex.

"Mr. Brewer," Sorsha protested.

"I'm sorry, Miss Kincaid, but I must ask you not to interfere."

"Interfere in what?" Alex asked, keeping his voice even and his expression neutral. Normally his suit had shield runes written in the coat, but since they tended to become corrupted when multiple runes were in close proximity, his tuxedo didn't have them.

"I must confess that I don't have a very good opinion of runewrights Mr. Lockerby," Brewer said. "Would you do me the courtesy of showing me your teeth, please."

"My teeth?" Alex had a moment of confusion, but then he remembered the last time he'd been in this room. Brewer's bald bodyguard had knocked out one of his teeth.

Alex opened his mouth and leaned his head back.

"Check him," Brewer said to the bodyguard.

The big man crossed the floor and peered into Alex's mouth for a long minute.

"He has all his teeth," the bodyguard reported.

"Is that all?" Sorsha asked, an amused smile ghosting her lips.

"I apologize for the necessity," Brewer said, returning the gun to his pocket. "Some time ago I was visited by another runewright who behaved rather badly. He lost a tooth during an altercation. I must confess it's put me off your profession entirely."

Alex gave him a look of mild interest meant to convey boredom with the topic. He had, in fact, lost a tooth the last time he was here, but with Iggy's medical runes, he'd regrown that tooth in a matter of days.

"Sorry to hear that," he said.

Brewer gave him a patronizing look, then returned his attention to Sorsha.

"And what brings one of the New York Six to me?" he asked.

Sorsha blew smoke from her cigarette before answering.

"I need to acquire an alchemical substance," she said simply. "It's relatively new, as far as I can tell. I have it on good authority that you are the person to ask."

Brewer showed no sign that the question surprised him.

"And what is this alchemical substance you seek?" he asked.

"I believe it's called Limelight," Sorsha said. "It's mixed with alcohol and it's rumored to grant the drinker some kind of magical abilities."

Brewer raised an eyebrow at that. He made a show of thinking about the name, though Alex was sure he knew it all along.

"I might know where I can get some Limelight for you," he said. "Does it really grant magical abilities?"

Alex looked to Sorsha, but her expression was unreadable. If Brewer thought the Limelight worked, he might decide to keep whatever supply he could acquire for himself.

"It seems to," Sorsha said, taking another drag on her cigarette. "So far the FBI has confirmed that four people have died from using it. There are a dozen more potential cases, all ending in serious injury and death."

"I had heard that you consulted with the government," Brewer said in an easy, unperturbed voice. "Is this an official visit then?"

Alex knew that was the question Brewer had been wanting to ask since the moment they arrived. He was probably planning how to set up shop somewhere else as they spoke. Sorsha gave him a predatory smile, then shook her head.

"I'm just here as a concerned citizen," she said. "Now, can you get me Limelight or not?"

Brewer flashed a genuine smile. Sorsha's declaration of indifference appeared to have convinced him. Now he was focused on how much money he could extract from the wealthy sorceress.

"I might know someone I could ask," he said. "I can't promise anything, you understand. Alchemical products aren't my usual business."

"I understand," Sorsha said. "How long would these inquiries take?"

Brewer rubbed his jaw, then checked his watch.

"Maybe half an hour," he said. "If I can find a supply, how much would you like?"

Sorsha's predatory smile returned.

"As much as you can get me, Mr. Brewer," she said.

The Emerald Room's band was playing something fast and brassy that Alex didn't recognize as he escorted Sorsha back down to the bar on the bottom level. Brewer had wanted privacy to make his inquiries, so Alex and Sorsha had to wait at the bar.

"That went better than expected," Alex called over the music.

"I'm not so sure," Sorsha said. "Did you see that pistol Brewer pointed at you?"

Alex had seen it, of course. It was a small caliber, maybe a .22, but that was enough to do the job.

"What about it?"

"It had a spellbreaker rune on it," Sorsha said.

Alex felt a chill go up his spine. Since his tux didn't have shield runes, he'd figured on Sorsha's protection covering him. He knew she maintained a barrier spell. With the spellbreaker, the longest her barrier would last would be the first shot, and after that they'd both be vulnerable.

"That's a problem," he said.

"I wanted you to know," Sorsha said as they reached the floor. "If things go south, I'll need you to cover me while I take out Brewer and his bodyguard."

Alex looked around at the other patrons. It didn't look like any of them had overheard Sorsha, but with the music, she'd been forced to yell.

"This way," he said, leading her out onto the dance floor as the band struck up a slower number.

He took her in his arms and pulled her close, so his mouth was near her ear.

"Now we can talk without being overheard," he said. Due to their proximity he didn't even have to raise his voice.

"Uh-huh," Sorsha said in a voice that clearly communicated that she thought Alex had other motives.

"About your plan," he said, ignoring her tone. He explained about his tuxedo and why if he put runes on it, they would disrupt the ones on his suit.

"But you keep your tuxedo in your vault," Sorsha said once he'd finished. "Why don't you just keep your suit in your bedroom at Dr. Bell's house? Do you sleep in your vault now?"

"More often than you'd think," he lied.

Sorsha fixed him with a dangerous stare, and for a moment he thought she'd detected the lie.

"Then keep your tux in one of the other rooms in your vault," she said, exasperation in her voice.

Alex bit his tongue to keep from blushing. In truth he kept his tux in the wardrobe in his bedroom at the brownstone with all his other clothes. Now that he was using his vault more it would be easy to keep the tux there so any shield runes wouldn't interfere with the ones on his suit coat. It was obvious and he should have thought of it himself.

Sorsha rolled her eyes and shook her head.

"Just when I start thinking you're smart," she growled.

"If Brewer pulls that gun again, I'll use a flash rune to blind him," Alex said. "Be sure to cover your eyes or it'll blind you too, and I want you to take care of his bodyguard. That guy hits like a runaway train."

Sorsha suddenly smiled, leaning even closer to him.

"The only way you could know that," she whispered, "is if you'd been here before. Was it you who lost that tooth? I know Dr. Bell could have easily grown you a new one."

Alex grinned back at her as he led her around the floor and the husky-voiced singer began crooning again.

"I'll never tell," he said.

Her smile morphed into a grin.

Five hours later Alex's phone rang. He groped for it in the dark of his bedroom and knocked it over.

"Uh, hello?" he said once he managed to find the receiver.

"Figures you'd be sleeping, Lockerby," Detweiler's voice assaulted him.

"Lieutenant?" Alex managed, turning on his bedside lamp. Picking up his alarm clock he focused his bleary eyes on it. "It's four thirty in the morning."

Alex had only been in bed for three hours. After his dance with Sorsha, Brewer had managed to get them five packets of alchemical powder that he claimed was Limelight. Sorsha paid an exorbitant price for it and had given Alex two of the packets to give to Charles Grier. By the time Alex finally got home it was after one in the morning.

It felt like he hadn't slept at all.

"Yeah," Detweiler growled over the line. "Bad things happen in the middle of the night. Get dressed and grab your bag of tricks. I need you at Midtown Central Bank as soon as you can get here."

"What happened?" Alex asked, swinging his legs out of bed. He shivered as his bare feet hit the cold floor.

"Our friends with the boom rune are back," he said. "And this time they killed someone."

10

BOXES

Despite its name, Midtown Bank had branches all over the city. Midtown Central Bank was located on the west side in the seventies. By the time Alex arrived, the sun was beginning to lighten the sky and the chill of the spring night was fading.

Seven police cars lined the curb in front of the imposing edifice of the bank. It was made in the Greek style with steps leading up from street level to a large set of double doors flanked by marble columns. Alex imagined that the doors would be equally decorative. He had to imagine since there was no sign of them. A gaping, door-shaped hole between the columns was all that remained of the entrance. The stone façade around the hole was fractured in a spiderweb pattern, and chunks of the stone had fallen out.

Alex spotted Detective Nicholson talking with a uniformed officer and an agitated man who appeared to have dressed in a hurry. From his animated discussion, Alex guessed him to be an officer of the bank.

"About time you got here, scribbler," Detective Nicholson muttered when Alex walked up.

Alex pasted a wide grin on his face and doffed his hat.

"Late but worth the wait," he said.

Nicholson snarled at him; clearly he wasn't having a good morning.

The bank officer muttered something about police incompetence and stalked away without another word.

"So what have you got here, Detective?" Alex asked.

"Your buddies blew the doors to smithereens," Nicholson said, mounting the stairs up to the gaping hole.

Alex let the comment slide about the robbers being buddies just because they were runewrights.

"The bank had a night watchman," Nicholson continued, "but he was near the door when the explosion went off, so it knocked him out cold. From there, they went straight to the vault and blew the door off that as well."

"Your Lieutenant said someone was killed?" Alex prompted as they reached the non-existent front door.

Nicholson passed inside with Alex in tow, then pointed toward the side of the bank where the offices were. A body lay on the floor with a sheet covering all of it but the man's shoes.

"I thought you said the night watchman was just knocked out," Alex said.

Nicholson gave him an appraising look.

"What makes you think that's the watchman?"

"He's got quality shoes, but the heels are worn," Alex said, nodding in the body's direction. "Means he had to look presentable, but his job kept him on his feet."

"Cute," Nicholson said. "When he came to, the thieves were in the vault. He took a shot at one when they came back out and they shot back. He lived long enough to tell us that there are two thieves and they're brothers."

That information didn't seem terribly useful, but Alex made a note in his flip book just the same. Iggy had taught him that you never knew which details would end up being important.

"How much did they get?" Alex asked.

"Pretty much everything," Nicholson said. "According to the bank manager, they had a quarter of a million dollars on hand. Our thieves even blew the locks out on a bunch of the deposit boxes."

The bank's vault was in a back room, protected by a steel cage. As they entered, Alex noted that the lock mechanism in the cage door had been blasted away by a small but powerful explosion. It left a rough, circular hole in the metal and would have made it easy to manually extract whatever was left of the bolt to release the door.

That was troubling. Alex didn't know how the runewright burglars had managed to turn a bang rune into something much more powerful, but being able to focus the blast down to such a small area took an incredible level of precision. Iggy could probably do it, but Alex doubted that he could, not yet anyway.

Then there was the crude mending rune he'd found at the first crime scene. The runewright who made these new blasting runes would be far too skilled to produce such crude work. Now that Alex knew there were two thieves, however, it stood to reason that one was the expert while the other didn't have much skill.

The thick steel door that had protected the vault had five holes blown in it. Each one was over the spot where heavy metal rods extended out from the door to keep it closed when it was locked. The holes let the thieves simply reach in and slide the remaining bits of the bars out, allowing them to open the door.

Alex whistled as they looked completely through the door. The rune that made that hole was extremely potent.

"You got that right," Detweiler said, stepping around the door.

"Hello, Lieutenant," Alex said. "Those brothers made quite a mess, didn't they?"

Detweiler's face soured, but then he nodded.

"Wait until you see in here," he said in the voice of a man running on only a few hours of sleep. "Did you bring your bag?"

Alex held up his kit so the lieutenant could see it and Detweiler waved him forward around the open vault door.

Several metal carts stood in the interior of the vault. Alex didn't spend much time in bank vaults, but he knew that those carts would hold the coins and bills the bank used in their teller windows. The coins had been dumped on the floor, but the bills were gone. A shelving unit stood against the back of the vault, but it was similarly empty. Rows of deposit boxes ran down each side of the vault, many of them open. Round holes had been blasted in each of the open doors, right over their locks. Most of the boxes had also been dropped on the floor along with any of their contents the thieves deemed unworthy of taking.

"What a mess," Alex observed.

"You think this is a mess, Lockerby?" Detweiler said, anger edging into his voice. "Just imagine what the morning papers are going to say about this. Two guys just walked up to this bank, blasted their way inside, and made off with everything but the kitchen sink. Add that to the hardware store and we're going to look like idiots."

Alex wasn't particularly worried whether Detweiler or Nicholson looked foolish in the papers, but something the lieutenant said tickled his memory.

"These shelves," he said, picking his way carefully to the back of the vault. "What was on them?"

"Two hundred grand in cash," Detweiler said. "Once that little tidbit gets out, the bank is going to have to shut down. There'll be a run by lunchtime. I need to find that money, Lockerby."

"How much would you say all that cash weighs?" Alex pressed.

Detweiler looked at the shelves and shrugged.

"I don't know," he admitted. "A lot."

"Then how did two guys get it out of here?" Nicholson said, catching Alex's line of thinking. "They would have had to make a bunch of trips to whatever they were driving."

Alex turned in place, looking intently at the walls of the vault. After a moment, he went back out into the cage room.

"Where are you going?" Detweiler demanded, following him out. "I need you to use that finding rune you're always so proud of and find the guys that did this before there's a panic."

Alex reached out and rubbed his finger on the wall, then touched his finger to his tongue.

"Here," Alex said, pointing to the wall. "This is how they got so much money out so quickly." The walls were made of brick and painted white with a row of pegs for visitors to hang their coats before accessing their deposit boxes. There was also a barely discernible line of chalk running up from the floor, then over and back down in the shape of a door. "One of them opened a vault right here. After that, all they had to do was carry the money into it and shut it before they left."

"Why didn't they just open it inside?" Nicholson asked. "That would have been an even shorter trip."

"It also would have interfered with the deposit box doors," Alex pointed out. "The one with the blasting runes opened the vault, then the other one grabbed the money while his partner blasted his way into the boxes."

"So that's it?" Detweiler growled. "Is that all you can tell me?"

"Of course not," Alex said, hanging his hat on one of the pegs in the wall. "You're right about my finding rune, though. If our thieves left anything behind, I can use it to track them."

"Can't you just use the money?" Nicholson asked.

"It doesn't have any ties to anything or anyone here," Alex said. "It's just money, it comes in and goes out every day. A tracking rune requires something with history, something with meaning."

Detweiler nodded at that.

"Like the stuff in the deposit boxes," he said. "If we can find out what they took and who they took it from, you can use the owners to find their missing property."

"And that will lead us right to our thieves," Alex said.

"Fine," the lieutenant said. "Get to it then. The sooner we can wrap this up the better I'll like it." He turned and headed out into the bank proper. "Let me know as soon as you have something."

"Of course, Lieutenant," Alex said with a grin. "Shouldn't take too long."

"You've been in here for three hours, Lockerby," Detweiler's voice pulled Alex's attention from sorting the debris on the vault floor. "Have you found anything?"

Alex sighed and stood up. He'd inspected the vault with his lantern and oculus and had come up empty. The rest of his time was spent trying to make sense of the things the thieves had dropped on the floor when they rifled through the deposit boxes.

"Not as much as I'd hoped," he said. "I do think I know what our thieves were looking for, though."

"You mean besides money?"

Alex left the vault, motioning for the lieutenant to follow. Outside the cage was a small table where people wanting to access their deposit boxes had to sign in. Alex had been using it to sort through the things dropped from the deposit boxes. He had a pile for legal documents and other papers, one for journals and account books, and one for everything else, mostly watches, lighters, and knick-knacks of sentimental value. Below that, he had several things laid out in a row.

"Recognize this?" he said pointing to a pad of what looked like tissue paper.

Detweiler ran his finger over the paper and nodded.

"It's that stuff you runewrights use," he said.

"Flash paper," Alex confirmed with a nod.

He picked up a thin book and handed it over. The lieutenant flipped through it quickly, then nodded.

"Is this some kind of instruction book for writing runes?" he asked, handing it back.

"It's a lore book," Alex said. "Every runewright has one. It's where we keep the runes handed down to us from our teachers. Some lore books are dozens, even hundreds of years old, containing all the rune knowledge of their various owners."

"Okay," Detweiler said. "So what?"

"So I also found these," Alex said, picking up a stack of loose pages, each with a rune diagram written on it.

"I get it, some of the boxes had runewright stuff in them. Why do you think that's important?"

"Because I think that's what the thieves were looking for," Alex explained. "One of the things that limits runewrights is that we keep our knowledge to ourselves. Lore books are family secrets, passed down from parent to child or from master to student. Once you've learned everything in your lore book, it's very difficult to get any better. All you can do is try to figure out new constructs on your own."

"So you think they were here looking for other people's lore books," Detweiler said, "to learn more runes?"

Alex set down the stack of runes and nodded.

"That's exactly what I think."

"Well if these lore books are so important, then you should be able to use them with your finding rune," Detweiler said. "Right?"

Alex sighed.

"Maybe," he said.

The lieutenant's face reddened and his eyebrows tried to move together.

"Are you pulling my leg?" he demanded. "You said that you could use the owners of the missing stuff to find what's missing so long as it was important to them."

"That's exactly how it works," Alex said. "But a working runewright wouldn't keep his lore book in a deposit box, he'd keep it close so he could refer to it. The books in here are probably owned by people who inherited them. They're valuable as family heirlooms, but the owners might not have a firm attachment to them."

"But they might," Detweiler countered.

Alex admitted it was a possibility.

"You need to have Detective Nicholson track down everyone whose box was broken into, then find out if they had a lore book in there. If they did, there's a good chance I can track it."

"What about missing jewelry? That's the kind of thing someone might be very attached to."

"That should work as well, but I think the lore book is a better option."

Detweiler rolled his eyes at that.

"Whatever works is a good option, don't you think?"

"Yes, but we know they put the money in their vault," Alex said. "There's a good chance they'll keep it in there rather than leaving it lying around wherever they're staying. If the cash and valuables are in their vault, I won't be able to track them."

"And you think the lore books won't be in the vault?"

"If I'm right, and that's what they were after all along, then they'll have those on them. That's the only way to study them. You find someone with a missing lore book that belonged to their favorite uncle or their grandfather — and I'll find your missing brothers for you."

Detweiler sighed and rubbed the back of his neck.

"All right," he said at last. "I'll tell Nicholson to focus on the lore books, but if he finds someone missing their mother's wedding ring, I'm calling you."

"Looking forward to it," Alex said, retrieving his hat and coat from the pegs on the wall. "The sooner you catch these boys, the better I'll sleep."

Alex took a cab from the bank and headed south, past the core, to *The Philosopher's Stone*, the little alchemy shop owned by Charles Grier. Alex had broken into the shop on a previous occasion, when Grier had gone missing and Dr. Kellin asked Alex to find him. This time Alex simply went in through the front door.

"Alex," Grier said, coming out from the back when the bell over the door rang. "How are you?" Grier was a thin, balding man in his fifties. He was in his shirtsleeves and wearing a heavy apron to protect his clothes. The store, much like the man, was clean and orderly with shelves of potions and ingredients lining the walls with the more valuable stuff under the glass top of the counter.

You look tired," Grier said as Alex approached.

"It's been one of those weeks," he said. "I brought you a present."

Alex took the two packets of paper-wrapped powder that Sorsha had given him from his pocket and laid them down in front of Grier.

"Is this what you were asking me about?" he asked, picking up one of the packets and examining it.

"As far as I can tell," Alex said.

"And does it really give ordinary people magical abilities?"

"I don't know," Alex admitted. "Sorsha Kincaid and I were able to get a few packs of the stuff, but apparently it's rare as hen's teeth. We didn't want to waste any."

Grier dropped the packet back on the counter.

"Well, it's not much, but I can work with it," he said. "Give me a couple of days and I'll be able to tell you more about it."

"Thanks, Charles." Alex pointed to the back wall of the shop. "Do you mind if I use your phone?" he asked.

"Be my guest," Grier said, taking out a small cardboard container and placing the packets of Limelight inside. "You know, since you told me about this stuff, I can't shake the feeling that I've heard about something..."

"Something like what?" Alex asked with his hand on the phone.

"I could swear I remember someone talking about using potions to instill magical abilities."

"Do you remember where you heard it?" Alex asked, paying close attention.

Grier stroked his chin in thought, then shook his head.

"Maybe it was an article," he said, "or an academic paper." He shook his head and growled in frustration. "I can't remember, but there aren't that many places I would have read about theoretical alchemy. I'll see if I can figure out where I ran across it while I'm conducting the tests on these." He held up the box with the Limelight in it.

"Well, if you figure it out, call my office and leave word with my secretary."

Grier promised that he would, then hurried into the back, heading for the stairs down to his lab in the basement.

Alex picked up the phone and called Sherry, telling her where he'd been and promising that he hadn't forgotten about seeing Marnie for coffee. His next call was to the Central Office of Police.

"You need to get down here," Danny said as soon as Alex greeted him.

"Did you find out who stole Margaret LaSalle's manuscript?" Alex asked.

"No," Danny said. "It's about that file you had me pull, on the death of Dolly Anderson."

"You got it?"

"About that," Danny said in a tone that implied he didn't want to go into it on the phone. "Apparently that file is restricted, and Callahan has to get special permission from the Captain to get it. He wants you to explain why we want it before he'll do that."

"And he wouldn't take your word that we need it?"

"Well," Danny said, hedging again. "The last time you had me request a file for a case I wasn't working, Callahan got suspicious. He thinks you want the file for some other case and he's not going to stick his neck out for that."

"Danny," Alex said, "we need that file."

"Well then you'd better get over here and explain it to Callahan."

Alex pinched the bridge of his nose and sighed.

"All right," he said. "I'll be there as soon as I can."

11

FILES

The detectives who served Manhattan all had their offices on the fifth floor of the Central Office of Police. Each detective had a desk in a large open area called the bullpen and the lieutenants who oversaw them each had an office along one wall. Lieutenant Frank Callahan's office was the third from the end, and Alex had been there a few times before. The first time, Danny hadn't been a detective, just a plucky beat cop with big dreams who'd gotten himself targeted by the mob. Alex had threatened Callahan that day, told him right to his face that if he let anything happen to Danny, it would be war between them.

It wasn't the smartest thing he'd ever done. He had an inch on Callahan's six feet, but the Lieutenant had him by at least twenty pounds of muscle and Alex knew for a fact that Callahan was as tough as they come. But Danny was Alex's friend, one of the few, and Alex was willing to go to war for a friend.

"What's this about, Callahan?" Alex demanded when he stormed into the glassed-in office. He might have sounded a bit more belligerent than he felt.

"Shut up, Lockerby," Callahan snapped at him from behind his paper-strewn desk.

Definitely too belligerent.

Danny sat in one of the two wooden chairs that faced the Lieutenant's desk and he gave Alex a subtle shake of his head when they made eye contact.

"Close the door and sit down," Callahan said.

"All right," Alex said. He shut the door and took the chair next to Danny. "Now if it's not too much trouble, how come Detective Pak here can't get access to a fifteen-year-old file?"

Callahan considered them both for a moment, then sighed.

"Danny tells me you think the murder of Margaret LaSalle has something to do with the death of Dolly Anderson."

Alex nodded. "That's right," he said.

Callahan held his gaze for a long moment, then sat back in his chair.

"Convince me."

Alex's first impulse was to argue that Danny believed it and that ought to be good enough for Callahan. Instead he opened his kit bag and took out Margaret LaSalle's notebook and dropped it on the desk. He flipped to the page of notes regarding LaSalle's new book, then recited Iggy's interpretation of them as Callahan read along. After that, he explained Margaret's habit of using real cases as the basis for her stories.

"That's a nice theory," Callahan said once Alex finished, "but it's pretty thin from where I'm sitting. She could have been killed over a bad debt and the thief only took what he thought he was owed."

That wasn't very likely. Alex could tell the lieutenant was reaching, he just had no idea why.

"I suppose that's possible," Danny said. "Except for the manuscript. Someone stole that right out of her publisher's office. If Margaret LaSalle's death isn't about what's in her book, then why do that?"

Callahan thought about that for a moment, then nodded. "I have to admit, that does fit the facts."

"So you'll get the file," Danny said.

"No."

"Why not?" Alex demanded, resisting the urge to leap to his feet in outrage.

"Because if I do, you two are through with this case," Callahan said. "Dolly Anderson is one of the most famous unsolved cases the department has. I know it was officially ruled an accident, but nobody here buys that. The reason that case file is restricted is because for the last fifteen years hundreds of cops and detectives have been wasting department time trying to solve it. The Chief finally had enough."

"Why does that matter?" Alex asked. "Danny's not going off on some wild goose chase, there's a legitimate connection here."

"I get it," Danny said, looking at Alex. "He means that if anyone higher up learns that there's something new in the Anderson case, they'll take the case away from us."

"That's exactly what I mean," Callahan said. "You wanted this case for your friend the Doc, right Lockerby? Well if I get you that case file you can kiss it goodbye."

Alex leaned forward in his chair and rubbed his temples. One of the many reasons he was glad not to be a cop was dealing with political nonsense like this.

"Does that mean you're taking over?" Danny asked. There was no note of challenge in his voice and Alex felt a note of tension suddenly spring up in the room.

"Is that what you think, Pak?" Callahan said, a dangerous tone creeping into his voice. "That I'd horn in on your case to grab some cheap headlines? Maybe a commendation from the Chief?"

Danny held his gaze for a moment, then shrugged.

"Just checking," he said with a grin.

"Well, if you're both satisfied," Callahan said. "I suggest you figure out what Margaret LaSalle knew that got her killed, and if that leads to Dolly Anderson's killer so much the better."

It sounded like a dismissal and they both stood.

"And whatever you do, not a word about the Anderson case around here."

"Yes, sir," Danny promised.

"Good," Callahan said, leaning back in his chair again. "Danny, why don't you go grab some lunch. I need a quick word with your friend."

He nodded in Alex's direction and Alex and Danny exchanged a confused look.

"I'll be at the diner then," Danny said, squeezing by Alex on his way to the door. As he did he whispered, "Play nice."

Danny let himself out of the office and once the door was shut, Alex sat back down.

"Okay," he said when Callahan didn't immediately speak. "What's this about?"

"You asked me for this case, Lockerby," Callahan said. "Did you know about the connection to Dolly Anderson?"

Alex shook his head.

"It was just like I told you," he said. "Iggy was a fan."

Callahan nodded and sighed.

"All right," he said, more to himself than Alex. "I think this will work out fine, better than fine if we play our cards right."

"I'm sure it will," Alex said, having no idea what the lieutenant was talking about. "Care to let me in on it?"

Callahan leaned forward and glanced at the door to be sure it was, in fact, closed.

"For months now, somebody higher up in the department has been messing with Danny. He's been transferred off high-profile cases and given grunt work. Now there's always a bit of that going on in the department with the lieutenants trying to make sure their boys look good, but this seems to be specifically directed at Danny."

"Somebody doesn't like the fact that he's Oriental," Alex said. "And if they're higher up, that could only mean Captain Rooney or Chief Montgomery."

"No," Callahan said. "Any order I get goes through half-a-dozen aides, desk officers, and paper pushers before it gets to me. Besides, if the Chief or Captain Rooney had it out for Danny they would have stopped his advancement to detective, in the first place. This is someone else."

Alex gave a moment's thought to breaking into the police file room and trying to ferret out the problem, but the most likely outcome of that idea would be him going to jail.

"It's nothing Danny hasn't dealt with before," Alex said. "He can handle it."

Callahan sighed and shook his head. "I'm afraid that doesn't work for me," he said.

"Well you are his lieutenant," Alex said. "If you can't take care of it, I don't know what I can do."

"You can shut up and listen," Callahan said, anger creeping into his voice. "Do you know Senator Andrew Barkley?"

The question came out of nowhere and Alex was forced to shrug.

"He represented the core and a piece of the inner ring," Callahan explained. "Well, he dropped dead of a heart attack last week."

Now that Callahan reminded him, Alex remembered seeing that story in the paper.

"That means," Callahan went on, "that there will be a special election this fall to replace him, and I happen to know that the Captain has aspirations of following in his father's footsteps."

Captain Rooney was the son of a US Senator and the New York State Senate would be a good place to start a political career.

"So," Alex said, picking up the thread of Callahan's thought. "If Captain Rooney wants to win that election, he's going to have to start campaigning soon."

"Which means he has to retire from the force," Callahan said.

"And let me guess," Alex continued. "You're going to be replacing him?"

Callahan smiled and shrugged.

"I'm on the short list," he said. "Me, Detweiler, and McClarin from Sixth Division, but I've got the edge."

"So why are you worried about Danny? If you're Captain, no one will dare to mess with him."

"I want Danny to replace me as the Lieutenant over Division Five," Callahan said. "He's definitely good enough, but since I don't know who's got it out for him, I need something ironclad that proves it."

Alex began nodding.

"Like solving a decade old, high profile case?"

"Exactly," Callahan said. "A case like that is a career maker. No one would dare object to his becoming Lieutenant if Danny solved the Anderson case."

"All right, Lieutenant," Alex said, standing up. "I'll make sure he gets it done, you can count on me."

"That's what I'm worried about," Callahan said. "You are the one who asked me to assign this case to Danny, and everyone knows that you help him out from time to time. For this to work, Danny has to be seen as the one who solved this case. That means none of your grandstanding, no getting your name in the papers, and definitely none of your little show-and-tell sessions where you walk everyone through a crime and then point out the culprit. Got me?"

Alex nodded. He didn't usually take the credit for cases he helped the police solve, but Callahan was right, he had managed to show up in the tabloids a few times in the past. And even though he didn't take public credit for most of the cases he worked on, the cops still knew about his involvement. If he wanted to make sure Danny got the credit for solving the Dolly Anderson case, he had to make sure everyone saw his friend doing it.

"Don't worry, Lieutenant," he said. "I'll make sure the only people who know I'm involved are you, Danny, and Dr. Bell."

"Good," Callahan said, picking up a folder on his desk. "Now get out of here and get to work. Oh, and don't tell Danny about the Lieutenant thing. That's just between you and me."

Alex promised that he wouldn't say anything to Danny and then opened the office door. Before he left, however, he turned back for a moment.

"You know, I'm working with Detweiler on this bank bombing thing," he said.

"I heard," Callahan said, not looking up from the open file on his desk.

"You said he's in the running for the Captain's job. If you want, I could spike his wheel on this case."

Alex was almost certain that offer would enrage Callahan. The big lieutenant had certain ideas about justice that Alex usually approved. Instead he chuckled.

"Don't bother," he said. "Detweiler's a good cop, but he doesn't have a chance."

"Isn't he married to Captain Rooney's niece?" Alex asked.

Callahan looked up at him, and the grin on his face spread into a wide smile.

"He is. But how do you think it would look if the guy running for Senator appointed his nephew-in-law to succeed him?"

Alex hadn't considered that. If Rooney just retired, he could appoint Detweiler and no one could object, but Rooney had to win an election in November. He would have to pass Detweiler over or be accused of nepotism by his opponent.

"Right," Alex said, then he stepped out into the hall and shut the door behind him.

"What did Callahan want?" Danny asked through a mouth full of ham sandwich.

Alex dropped his hat on the counter next to Danny and sat down, waving off the waitress who started heading in his direction.

"Not much," he said. "He was just worried I'd steal the spotlight on this case."

"You don't do that," Danny said. "Not even when you should. And why does he care?"

"It's like he said, this case is a big deal. You solve this, it makes the department look good. It makes Callahan look good."

Danny put down his sandwich and glared at Alex.

"Don't feed me that line," he said, though his tone was amused. "Callahan's like you when it comes to getting his name in the papers. He doesn't care."

"About himself, no," Alex said with a chuckle. "But he does like to see his detectives get ahead."

"I can take care of myself," Danny said with only a small note of indignance.

"Sure you can," Alex said. "But somebody is going to make a name for themselves if we manage to figure out what happened to Dolly, so Callahan and I decided that's going to be you."

Danny looked as though he might object, but then shrugged.

"So how are we supposed to figure out what really happened to Dolly without access to the police file?" he asked before taking another bite of his sandwich.

Alex gave him the smuggest smile he could manage.

"Just tell me," Danny said, rolling his eyes.

"Well, I had Sherry dig into the Times archives, so I've already got a list of people we should talk to."

Danny sighed and shook his head.

"If we had the police files, we'd know who had alibis and whether or not they were verified," he said. "It's not going to be easy to recreate all that work, even if everyone involved is still alive and in the city."

"I've got an idea about that," Alex said. "After all, the police aren't the only people who maintain files on high profile cases."

The offices of *The Midnight Sun* were in an industrial building in the east side mid ring. The building had a front section with their offices and archives and a warehouse section behind that held their printing press and shipping dock.

"You've got to be kidding me," Danny said when he pulled up to the curb. "I thought Callahan specifically told you to keep this story out of the papers, even a tabloid like this."

Alex put his hand on his chest in a display of wounded pride.

"Trust me," he said. "You know I'd never go against Lieutenant Callahan's explicit instructions."

"Uh-huh," Danny said, looking profoundly unconvinced.

"Well, if you want to go with what Sherry gleaned from the Times, we can leave."

Danny switched his gaze between Alex and the building and then sighed.

"All right," he said.

Alex clapped his friend on the shoulder and headed for the front door.

"Just follow my lead," he said.

The Midnight Sun's front office had a few battered-looking couches and a desk with a bored-looking secretary who sat filing her nails as Alex entered. She looked up and gave Alex a sneer before going back to her nails. Her name was Laura and she'd flirted with Alex outrageously when he first came to the office. He'd been dating Jessica at the time, so he paid her no mind.

Apparently she took that rejection badly, because she hadn't given him the time of day since.

"I'm just here to see Billy," he said, walking past her.

"Did I hear my name?" a man with a boyish face and a dimple in his left cheek said, leaning out of an office at the end of a short hallway.

Alex waved and Billy Tasker grinned back.

"What brings you here?" he said, waving Alex and Danny back to his office.

Tasker had been a crack reporter before he'd taken the job at the Sun and his office showed it. Rows of file cabinets lined one wall with a desk in the center of the room loaded down with files, papers, and stacks of photographs. A well-used typewriter sat in the middle of the desk flanked by two telephones. A worn couch was against the front wall, facing the desk, but it was the only seat in the room beyond the desk chair.

"Thanks for the tip on those counterfeit paintings," Tasker said to Alex as he and Danny headed for the worn couch. "It almost makes up for you stiffing me on that vote fraud story last year."

"Sorry," Alex said. "Turned out to be nothing."

That was miles from the truth, but Alex wasn't about to tell Billy that Mayoral Candidate William Ashford was using mind control runes in an effort to get elected and presumably take over the city. Billy gave Alex a penetrating look, as if he were trying to detect deceit, but gave up after a few moments. Alex had gotten very good at lying to people to protect his secrets. Not that he was happy about it.

"I take it you have something for me now?" Billy said adding a big smile to his boyish face.

"Have you heard about the murder of Margaret LaSalle, the writer?"

Tasker thought a moment, then nodded.

"Sure," he said. "But I heard that was a robbery."

"It was meant to look that way," Alex confirmed.

Tasker's smile got bigger and he picked up his notebook and pencil. "Go on."

"I need a favor," Alex said.

Tasker raised an eyebrow and gave Alex a withering look. With his boyish face it wasn't the rebuke he obviously meant it to be.

"The last time you needed my help, your story turned out to be nothing," he said.

"That's not my fault," Alex said. "But I'll throw you a bone here. What I need is your file on the death of Dolly Anderson."

Billy almost dropped his pencil and Danny hid a grin.

"Are you onto something about Dolly's death?" Taker asked. "Are you saying it's tied to the death of that writer?"

Alex explained about LaSalle's missing manuscript and what the subject of the book was. While he talked, Tasker practically salivated, scribbling like mad on his notepad.

"I can sell five thousand papers with just that," Tasker said once Alex finished.

"You could," Alex said, putting an instant damper on the young man's enthusiasm.

"You want me to hold this?" he said incredulously. "Why?"

Alex leaned forward and lowered his voice.

"Which would you rather have, a story about a possible connection between a current crime and the death of Dolly Anderson..."

"Or?" Tasker prompted.

"Or being there with a cameraman when Dolly's killer is arrested."

"I don't see why I can't have both," Tasker said.

"Because," Danny said, "if word gets out that the police are working the Dolly Anderson case again there'll be a feeding frenzy in the media. Much bigger fish than you will lean on my superiors to assign the case to someone who will give them access and freeze you out."

"He's right," Alex confirmed. "You run with this now and this is all you'll get."

Tasker looked from Danny to Alex and back again.

"I'll be there for the arrest," Tasker said.

"If we make an arrest, I promise you'll be there," Alex said.

"With my cameraman," he pressed. "Who can take all the pictures he wants."

"Within reason," Danny said, "but yes."

Tasker hesitated so Alex pressed.

"You can always run the story about LaSalle's murder being connected to Dolly later if we don't find anything," he said. "No one else is going to scoop you because we're the only people who know."

"If it gets out, all bets are off," Tasker said, reaching for one of the phones on his desk. "Deal?"

"One more thing," Alex said. "All credit for any arrests goes to Detective Danny Pak." He nodded at Danny. "Keep my name out of it."

Billy considered that for a moment, then shrugged and nodded.

"Deal," he said, putting the phone receiver to his ear. "Research? Bring me everything we have on the death of Dolly Anderson."

12

THE EXHIBIT

Alex hefted his heavy kit bag, rolling his sore shoulder as he reached the fourth-floor landing of the building that housed his office. The bag wasn't usually very heavy, and he used his handkerchief to wipe the sweat from his forehead.

"Do you mind?" Danny said, stopping behind him on the top step.

"Sorry," Alex said, turning left and heading toward his office at the far end of the hall. "This thing is heavy."

"Yeah, well it wouldn't be if you didn't make me stop at Empire Tower so you could get two Thermos bottles full of coffee," Danny said, leafing through The Midnight Sun's file as he followed. "Hey, did you know that Dolly Anderson was dating Claude McClintock, the movie actor?"

"Yeah, Sherry found a couple of stories about that in the Times archives," Alex said.

"How is the new secretary working out?" Danny said as Alex approached the office door.

"Well enough that I went to Empire Tower just to get coffee for her," Alex said, pushing the door open.

"You did?" Sherry cooed as he came in. "I was sure you'd forgotten."

She held out her hands eagerly and Alex chuckled.

"I should start paying you in this stuff," he said, opening his kit and pulling out a full Thermos. Sherry got up from her desk and came around to get it as Alex pulled the second Thermos from his bag, setting it on the desk.

"Who's your friend?" Sherry said as she filled the office pot with Marnie's coffee.

It took Alex a moment to realize what she meant. Danny had been by his office before, just not in the nearly six months that Sherry had been his secretary. He wondered if Danny was right, did he only see his friend when he needed something?

You hardly see anyone anymore, he reminded himself. *Too many secrets to keep*.

"This is Danny," he said. Sherry may not have met him, but Danny had called the office many times looking for Alex.

Sherry's smile brightened.

"Nice to finally meet you, Detective Pak," she said. "Would you like a cup of coffee?"

"Yes, please," Danny said.

Alex did a double-take but Danny wasn't looking at him. His eyes were fixed on Sherry as she poured coffee into a paper cup for him.

"Be careful," she said, passing over the cup. "It's hot."

Danny thanked her and immediately set the hot cup down on her desk — all without breaking eye contact.

Alex cleared his throat and picked up the tabloid folder that Danny had put down.

"Danny and I are going over the Anderson case," he said.

"Is that the police file?" Sherry asked, giving Danny a warm smile, then heading back to her desk.

"No..." Alex began.

"My boss wouldn't give us the police file," Danny jumped in. "Apparently lots of detectives have tried to solve it in the past so the file is restricted."

"So you and Alex are going to do what all those other policeman couldn't?"

"We're going to try," Danny said, sitting on the corner of her desk.

"So we'll be in my office," Alex said, a bit more loudly than was strictly necessary.

"Right," Danny said, hopping up. "Duty calls." He gave Sherry a wink and headed for Alex's private office.

"Don't forget your coffee," Alex said, giving Danny a disapproving look. The man was shameless when it came to women.

Danny went back for the paper cup of coffee.

"If anyone calls, tell them I'm out and take a message," Alex said as Danny passed him and entered his office.

Sherry nodded, but her eyes suddenly went wide, and she stood up.

"What is it?" Alex asked.

She blushed and sat back down.

"Nothing," she said. "I just remembered I need to make a call."

Alex could tell that she wasn't telling him everything. He thought about pressing the issue, but Danny was waiting, and he had a case to solve.

"If anything comes up, let me know," he said.

"That's a lot of suspects," Danny said after they'd gone through Sherry's notes and the tabloid file.

It had taken an hour and now Alex understood why the Anderson case had gone unsolved. Initially there had been two dozen suspects, people with motive and potential access to the phone that electrocuted Dolly. After weeks of investigation, the police seemed to have focused on six people: Regina Darling, Dolly's understudy; Ethan Nelson, the owner of the *Royale* theater; Maybelle Leone, fashion designer; Claude McClintock, Dolly's on-again, off-again beau; Benjamin Harrington, the author of the ill-fated play, and Gregory Dubois, the set electrician at the *Royale*.

In the end, the police focused on Dubois, the electrician. All the evidence seemed to point to him, but at his trial his attorney was able to prove that he hadn't been in the theater the day of the murder. Add to that the fact that the phone functioned perfectly during a rehearsal the afternoon before the deadly performance and Dubois was acquitted. That didn't automatically put him off Alex's list, but since he died three years ago, it was very unlikely he was Margaret's killer.

"Where do you want to start?" Alex asked, sitting back in his chair and opening his right-hand desk drawer. He'd drunk all of his coffee and now he needed something stronger.

"We could divide them up and interview each of them," Danny said. "I mean Margaret LaSalle didn't have access to the police file either so she would have had to do her own interviews, right?"

Alex nodded, pouring two fingers of Scotch into a glass and passing it to Danny.

"I think we should take them together," Alex said, pouring a glass for himself. "It'll take longer but we're less likely to miss something."

"You're assuming there's something to find," Danny said, downing the scotch.

"Margaret LaSalle found something," Alex said. "We just have to follow the same path."

"Okay," Danny said, rubbing his temples. "So I ask again, where do we start?"

As he asked the question, the door to Alex's office burst open.

"At the museum," Sherry said, an excited smile on her face.

Danny looked questioningly at Alex, but he just shrugged and looked back at Sherry.

"My first job as a secretary was working for Weldon Swain," she explained. "He's the curator over at the American Museum of Natural History. Anyway, one of the exhibits he was really proud of was one about famous New York mysteries."

"And he has something to do with Dolly Anderson?" Danny asked.

Sherry gave him an absolutely glowing smile.

"He has the telephone that electrocuted her."

Alex and Danny just looked at her for a stunned minute, then they looked at each other.

"Well, you wanted to know where to start," Alex said, standing up. "Grab your hat."

Alex used to enjoy going to the museum, but he hadn't been in several years. The last time he'd been there was with Jessica, and the curator had given them the run of the place. It was one of his fondest memories. It was also the reason he hadn't been back.

He'd known that one of Sherry's previous jobs had been as a secretary at the museum; in fact, that was as far back as he could trace her. Before that, it was as if she hadn't existed. Maybe that was just when she had moved to the city, but it bothered him that no one seemed to know where she'd come from. With the number of dangerous enemies he was amassing, Alex really wanted to know where Sherry had come from — and who might have sent her.

Until he could figure that out, he resolved to keep her where he could keep an eye on her.

The office of Weldon Swain was in a small basement space in the museum with a simple glass door and a bored-looking secretary. Swain himself was a short, thin, well-groomed man with a pinstriped suit and a pencil mustache.

"Oh, no," Swain said when he saw Alex. "I don't want to hear it. You need to leave."

Danny gave Alex a confused look, but he could only shrug.

"Mr. Swain, it's me, Alex Lockerby."

"I remember," he said with a sneer. "The last time you were here we had to rebuild our vault and then a security guard stole a mummy out of our storage room. You're bad luck and I've got all of that I can handle. You need to go."

"Mr. Swain," Danny said, taking his badge out of his pocket. "This is a police matter and we need your cooperation."

Swain hesitated and a look of uncertainty washed over his face. He'd met Danny before, but only as part of the police contingent that had hid out in their vault waiting for thieves to break in. Clearly he didn't remember.

"Uh," he said, looking from Alex to Danny. The expression on his face said that he thought this might be some kind of trick. Another look at Danny's badge convinced him.

"Who are you?" he asked, politely. "And how may I assist the New York Police?"

Danny introduced himself, then took out his notebook.

"Do you know a woman named Margaret LaSalle?" he asked.

Swain's face grew suspicious again.

"If you're implying that I'm involved in some salacious—" he began.

"She's a novelist," Danny cut in. "And she was murdered in her apartment last week."

Swain looked alarmed and then confused.

"How is it you think I can help?" he asked. "I assure you I've never heard of this LaSalle woman."

"We found a notebook in her house," Alex explained. "According to what she wrote, she was researching famous mysteries of New York as the basis of her book. There's a strong possibility that whoever killed her didn't want her looking into one or more of those mysteries."

"We were told that you have an exhibit like that here," Danny continued. It was the story they agreed on since they didn't want Swain to figure out that they were looking into the Anderson case specifically.

Swain seemed visibly relieved and he smiled.

"Yes, we have quite a few artifacts that are from unsolved mysteries and famous accidents. Would you like to see them?"

"We'd appreciate that." Danny nodded.

Swain led them up two floors and into the back where they had a room dedicated to New York history. In the corner was a glass case about the size of a Macy's window display. Inside were a collection of strange objects along with photographs and printed cards that explained the story of each.

"You see," Swain said excitedly, pointing to an elaborate flapper dress. "That's the dress Isabel Cassidy was wearing when she died mysteriously in her room. The door was locked from the inside, but the police always suspected foul play."

Alex hadn't heard of Isabel Cassidy but if the dress was any indication, she was someone wealthy. Some of the decorative strands of the dress were silver wire.

"And that's the letter opener that killed Hilton Powell, the textile magnate," he said, indicating a slim, silver stiletto. "The police initially thought he tripped and fell on it." Swain pointed to a photograph of an elegant office where a bloodstain could clearly be seen on the carpet. The edge of the carpet was pulled up as if someone had caught their toe on it and tripped.

"The coroner disagreed," Swain went on excitedly. "He said the wound wasn't consistent with a fall. The police looked into the family since Powell had threatened to disinherit them all at one time or another. He was quite the puritan if the stories are to be believed. Anyway, it turned out the old man was broke. He'd put his wife on the board of all his companies and she'd transferred control to the children before he could make good on his threat."

"So they had no motive," Danny said.

"Right," Swain said, practically shaking with excitement. "The only clue the police had was a fingerprint on the letter opener that didn't belong to Powell, but it didn't match any of his children either. The case was never solved."

"What's this?" Alex said, indicating the black candlestick telephone sitting in the very center of the display. He knew it was what they were looking for, but if he let Swain go on, they'd be there all afternoon listening to the provenance of each object in his collection.

Swain clapped his hands together with an expression of bliss.

"That's my crown jewel," he said. "That, gentlemen, is the telephone that electrocuted Dolly Anderson."

"The Broadway star?" Danny asked, feigning ignorance.

"Yes," Swain confirmed. "A faulty wire in the phone electrocuted her on stage during the opening performance of Benny Henderson's play, *The Rogue's Gallery*."

"No kidding?" Alex said, then he turned to Danny. "That seems like as good a place to start as any."

"What do you mean, start?" Swain said, a note of fear creeping into his voice.

"We need to take a look at some of these things," Danny said. "See if they match up with notes in the murdered woman's notebook. If they do, that might tell us what the killer was interested in."

"These are priceless artifacts, gentlemen," Swain objected.

"Take it easy, Mr. Swain," Danny said, putting on a reassuring smile. "We just need to examine them. We'll be careful."

Alex could sense that the man was wavering, so he decided to give him one more push.

"Whoever killed Margaret LaSalle broke into her house and shot her in the back as she tried to get away," he said, embellishing a bit for effect. "We need to find this guy."

"All right," Swain said, taking a heavy ring of keys from his pocket. He thumbed through them until he found the one he wanted, then he opened the lock on the display's glass door. "I need to go tell my secretary that I'll be up here," he said, putting the keys away. "Don't touch anything delicate till I get back."

"We'll start with the phone," Danny said, picking it up gently. "They're pretty sturdy."

Swain gave him a hesitant look, then hurried away.

"He'll be gone for five minutes at most," Alex said, opening his kit.

As Alex took out his lamp and oculus, Danny turned the phone over. On the bottom was a heavy cardboard circle that kept the user from touching anything inside the phone.

"Do you have a screwdriver in your bag?" he asked.

Alex kept a little tool kit in his bag in case he had to make repairs to any of his equipment in the field and he passed it to Danny. Working carefully, Danny loosened the set screw on the bottom of the phone and removed the cardboard divider. Inside there was a bracket where the wires from the wall attached to the inside of the phone. Above it sat an electric motor and a bell.

"Look at this," Danny said, using the screwdriver as a pointer. Above the bell were two screws that held wires. "This one goes to the earpiece, and this one to the mouthpiece."

"How do you know that?" Alex asked. He'd used a telephone most every day for the past fifteen years and he wouldn't have known how the inside of one would look.

"I helped set up the campus switchboard when I was at college," he said. "I've seen hundreds of these things and I can tell you that these wires," he indicated the two wires running up into the phone from where the screws held them, "are much heavier than they need to be."

"So?" Alex asked, still not sure where Danny was going.

"The microphone and speaker in a phone don't need much current to run," he explained. "These wires could carry a lot more current."

"Could having more current have electrocuted Dolly when she held the phone to her ear?" Alex asked.

"No," Danny said, turning the phone over and examining the body of the base. "She would have had to touch the wires directly, one in each hand."

"Why in each hand?"

"Because, in order for the current from a wall outlet to kill her, it would need to go across her heart. That means entering from the body of the phone and exiting through the earpiece."

Alex lit his silverlight and pulled his oculus down over his right eye. Closing his left, he pointed the lamp at the phone.

"Turn it over," he said.

Danny began rotating the base of the phone so that Alex could see all sides.

"Now the earpiece."

Danny repeated the process with the earpiece. As it turned, Alex could see his friend's fresh fingerprints on the little wooden cone, and a shining dot.

"That's it," he said, taking the handset from Danny and putting his finger next to the disk. He took off the oculus and passed it to Danny. "Take a look."

"What is that?" Danny asked once he had the oculus on.

"It's metal," he said. "Probably the head of a nail or tack that someone drove into the earpiece, then sanded smooth."

Danny took off the oculus and squinted at the handset where Alex's finger was.

"I can't even see it," he said. "So someone attached the heavy wires to the back of this pin and then when Dolly picked up the earpiece it made contact with her hand."

Alex nodded and Danny grinned.

"This means that Margaret was right," he said. "Dolly Anderson was murdered."

Alex grinned back as his friend.

"Now all we have to do is prove it."

"Should we take this?" Danny wondered, holding up the phone. "It's evidence."

Alex thought about that. Danny had a good point. If whoever killed Margaret thought the phone would tie them to Dolly's murder, it would be easy for them to smash the display case and steal it.

"No," he said finally. "If this phone could be tied to the killer, they'd have stolen it long ago. Let's not tip our hand just yet. We'd have to come clean with Swain if we want to take the phone and he'd be on the phone to the Times before we got out of the building, bragging about how his exhibit was helping the police reopen the Dolly Anderson case."

It was clear that Danny didn't like that answer, but he didn't try to refute it.

"All right," he said after a long minute. "Pack up while I put the phone back together."

"How come the police didn't notice those weird wires?" Alex asked as he put away his gear.

"I doubt anyone would think twice about them if they hadn't taken dozens of these things apart," he said.

"What are you doing?" Swain's voice called out as Danny replaced the phone in the display.

"Don't worry, Mr. Swain," he said, his reassuring smile back in place. "Turns out the notes Miss LaSalle made refer to different things than you have here. The New York Police Department appreciates your cooperation, though."

"Oh,"Swain said, looking both disappointed and relieved. "Well I wish you luck with your investigation."

Alex picked up his bag as Swain relocked the glass door of the display. When he finished, he gave Alex a sour look, then headed out of the room.

"We need to start interviewing those suspects." Danny said. "Where do you want to start?"

"Give me a minute," he said, looking after the curator.

Alex left the room and hurried down the stairs to the main floor.

"Curator Swain," he called, jogging over to the little man.

"What now, Mr. Lockerby?" Swain said. "Disappointed nothing was destroyed this time?"

"I'm really not sure what's got your goat," Alex said. "I mean, I'm the guy who stopped a bunch of thieves from stealing several fortunes from right under your nose. I didn't expect a parade or anything, but I'm not sure why you're so angry?"

Swain sighed and pinched the bridge of his nose.

"You may recall, Mr. Lockerby, that your friend Dr. Bell asked to be allowed to tour our exhibits after closing along with you and your girlfriend."

Alex remembered. It had been one of the most enjoyable dates he'd had with Jessica. That was also the reason he tried not to think about it.

"Well that was the only time in all my years here that I've ever allowed such a thing, and what did I get for my trouble?"

"Someone stole a mummy?" Alex offered, remembering his earlier comment.

"Yes,"Swain fumed. "One of our security guards, a man who had been here for years, took the mummy and smashed the Canopic jars that went with it. Priceless historical artifacts were destroyed and a mummy stolen, all because I let you and your friends go traipsing through the museum after hours."

Alex was confused as to the cause and effect that Swain was suggesting.

"How did my being here make a security guard steal a mummy?" he demanded.

"Because," Swain growled. "I had to change up the security routine for you. Obviously the guard saw his chance and he took it."

Alex clenched his teeth. That actually made sense. Worse, something about Swain's description of the crime jogged his memory.

"The missing mummy," he said. "Where was it being displayed?"

"It wasn't on display," Swain said. "We had to move some of our Egypt display into storage to make room for the artifacts from the Almiranta. You know that, you asked me to show you the mummy, it was in our basement storage area."

A shiver ran up Alex's spine as several bits of Swain's story fell into place. The mummy in question had been an ordinary mummy, not a king or anything, but the jars that were smashed were the same ones Alex and Iggy had found ancient hieroglyphic runes on. He'd been assuming that the theft of the mummy was just a coincidence, or like Swain thought, maybe it was a crime of opportunity.

But what if it wasn't?

He didn't know about the Legion then, but clearly they'd been watching him for some time, probably others too. What if he'd stumbled on one of their plots, something that they'd had to put on hold because the jars got moved? They could have easily hidden something in the mummy's wrappings, something set to trigger when the runes on the jars were activated.

Alex believed that coincidences happened, but to have the jars smashed just hours after he and Iggy had discovered runes on them? That stretched the bounds of credulity. Someone stole that mummy to keep him from discovering what it was hiding. All he had to do now was find it, and maybe he could find out what plot he'd unwittingly foiled.

Maybe he'd find a solid link to the Legion.

"Curator Swain," Alex said, putting his hand on the man's shoulder. "I can't tell you how sorry I am about your mummy. And I just couldn't sleep well if I thought that me being here had anything to do with that."

"Well, uh, thank you," Swain said, his angry expression softening a bit.

"I'll tell you what," Alex went on. "Since I am a detective after all, I'll look into your missing mummy and see if I can find it for you, no charge."

Swain grew suspicious again but eventually he nodded.

"I have a file on the theft in my office," he said. "It's everything I gave to the police."

"That will be just fine," Alex said, following the curator toward his office.

13

HIDE AND SEEK

"Hi ya, boss," Sherry said when Alex pushed open the door to his office. "I see you brought the detective back."

Alex stepped in and Danny came in behind him. She shouldn't have been able to see him while he was still out in the hall, but she might have heard more than one person and assumed. Still, Sherry never seemed surprised when he arrived at the office, and from the look of her, she'd recently reapplied her makeup.

"Good to see you again, Miss Knox," Danny said with his smoothest smile.

"Did you have any luck at the museum?"

Alex nodded and offered her a cigarette.

"The telephone was rigged," he said. "No doubt about it."

"So you were right," Sherry said as Danny offered her a light.

"Yep," Alex confirmed. "We'll need to start interviewing those suspects right away. Did you manage to find any of them?"

Sherry tore the top page off one of her notebooks and handed it to Alex.

"Maybelle Leone has an office in the garment district," Sherry said as Alex scanned down the paper. "Regina Darling lives in a posh apartment building in the core and she's starring in a play at the *Schubert*

Theater. The *Royale Theater* is still owned by Ethan Nelson and they are open every night but Sunday."

"That means they'll both be in the theater district tonight," Danny said. "We should go."

"About that," Sherry said, tearing another page from a different note pad. "A Lieutenant Detweiler called two...five...maybe ten times. He seemed quite insistent that you call him as soon as you got in."

Alex took the paper but hesitated. Sherry would cover for him if he wanted to go help Danny, and the Anderson case was starting to get interesting. Even as he had the thought, however, he remembered the dead guard at the bank. If Detweiler was calling, he must have tracked down one of the owners of the missing lore books. He needed to help find the blast-happy runewrights before they killed again.

"I'd better take a rain check," he told Danny. He explained about the bombing at the bank and Danny nodded in agreement.

"You call Detweiler and we'll reconvene in the morning," he said.

"You want me to meet you at the precinct?" Alex asked as Danny headed for the door.

"I can meet you here," he said, his eyes darting to Sherry. "Nine okay?"

Alex rolled his eyes, but agreed, and Danny left.

"Anything else I need to know?" he asked Sherry as he headed for his office.

"Miss Kincaid called wanting an update on that alchemical powder," Sherry said. "I told her that you said it would be a few days."

"Do me a favor and call Charles Grier in the morning," he said. "Let me know if he's learned anything yet."

"Will do, boss."

Half an hour later, Lieutenant Detweiler and Detective Nicholson escorted two people into Alex's second office.

"All right, Lockerby," the Lieutenant said. "We're here. You want to tell me why your finding rune won't work down at the Central Office?"

"It'll work just fine anywhere," Alex said, ushering them over to his enormous map table. "But it's much easier to get an exact reading with a bigger map."

"So your rune will pinpoint one of the missing books on this?" Nicholson asked, a note of awe in his voice.

"That's the plan," Alex said, turning to the people who had come in with Detweiler and Nicholson. One was a short man with bushy hair and an expensive suit, the other a young woman with a pretty face and a plain dress. "Who wants to go first?"

The bushy-haired man seemed annoyed to be there, but the woman raised her hand excitedly. Alex took her to the map table and explained how the rune worked, then he asked her about the missing rune book. It had belonged to her grandfather, whom she dearly loved, and it was an important memento of their relationship.

Alex had her place her hand on the brass compass he'd already laid out on the map, then put a finding rune on her hand and ignited it. When the flash and the rune disappeared, the compass stubbornly pointed north.

"What does that mean?" Nicholson asked.

"It means he didn't find it," Detweiler growled.

"We knew there was a chance the missing rune book was being kept in a vault," Alex said a bit defensively. "Let's try the other one."

The bushy-haired man was the owner of his missing rune book. He'd written it himself, but he never really had any talent for runes. He kept the book when he gave up rune magic, but he didn't consider it a cherished possession.

"Well, you did write it yourself," Alex pointed out. "That means it should have a strong connection to you."

"Or you're just trying to pad your bill," Detweiler said. He had a look of profound impatience and he kept pacing back and forth while Alex was talking.

"Don't worry, Lieutenant," Alex said as he set up for the next rune. "If this doesn't work, I'll leave it off the bill."

Detweiler grunted an acceptance but his posture and bearing didn't change. Alex guessed he was under a great deal of pressure to solve this case. That also explained why he wasn't letting Detective Nicholson work it alone.

This time when Alex ignited the finding rune, the compass needle swung around and pointed to a location on the south side. He slid the compass along the line it indicated until he was almost to the docks. At that point the needle swung around as he passed the spot it was seeking.

Moving carefully, Alex circled the spot, making sure the needle kept pointing inward.

"Right there," Alex said, pointing to an outer ring block. "That's where the missing rune book is. Five will get you ten that's where your bank robbers are too."

"Can't you nail it down more?" Nicholson asked.

"Sure," Alex said, tossing him the brass compass. "Just follow that and it will lead you right to it."

"Get your hat, scribbler," Detweiler said. "You're coming too."

Alex rode in the back seat of Detweiler's car as they had dropped off the bushy-haired man and pretty young woman at the Central Office. The lieutenant had called ahead and two patrol cars full of uniformed officers joined them on their trip to the south side. To Alex, it felt like a parade.

After almost an hour they pulled into a dingy side street full of run-down buildings. Alex pulled out the brass compass and found it pointing right to a ramshackle rooming house in the middle of the block. A faded sign in the window advertised rooms to let and claimed reasonable rates.

"Right on the button," Alex said, showing the compass to Detweiler and Nicholson. "That's why you use a big map."

"They'd have to pay me to stay here," Nicholson said as they piled out of the car.

"Shut up," Detweiler growled, waving the other cars to pull up beside him.

"Let's do this quietly if we can," Detweiler said. "I don't want to tip them off and start a shoot-out. Remember, they took guns and ammo from the hardware store, so we know they're armed."

Alex had actually forgotten that.

"You want me to knock on the door and pretend to be looking for a room?" Alex asked as Detweiler sent half his men around to the back, in case the bank robber tried to make a run for it.

"No one in this neighborhood would believe you," Nicholson said. "Not in that fancy suit."

Alex had grown up poor and had only recently become successful. As a result, he often forgot that his circumstances were fundamentally different now. In the old days, he'd only had one good suit for work, but now he owned five and they were all of good quality.

"That's not a bad idea though," Detweiler said, nodding at the detective. "You give it a shot."

Nicholson took the shiny detective badge off his lapel and concealed it in his hand, then he mounted the steps up to the front door and knocked. Alex, Detweiler, and the rest stood off to the side where the person opening the door wouldn't be able to see them.

The door opened and, after a short conversation, Nicholson showed the person inside his badge. A moment later he stepped back and motioned for the lieutenant.

"This is Mrs. Marinos," Detective Nicholson said when they reached the door. She was a heavyset, no-nonsense sort of woman with iron gray hair and thick spectacles. "According to her, she rented a room to two brothers from Georgia. They were quiet and respectful, but they suddenly packed up and left about an hour ago."

"Is that strange?" Alex asked.

"Their room was paid up till Friday," the woman said.

"Show me the room," Detweiler said, then turned to the officers at his back. "Search the place, make sure they're not here."

Mrs. Marinos protested at the intrusion, but she was only playing to her renters. She had no desire to make an enemy of Detweiler and his cadre of policemen. The room she rented to the brothers was on the second floor. There were two beds inside along with a closet, dresser, and a table with two chairs. A threadbare rug lay in the center of the floor and a metal wastebasket sat beside the table, but that was all.

"You sure this is it?" Nicholson asked Alex.

The needle of the compass was pointing to the table.

"Here," Alex said, moving to the trash can. Reaching in he pulled out the burned remnants of a rune book. "Looks like this is definitely the place."

"The landlady said they packed up and rushed out of here an hour ago," Detweiler said. "That's about the same time as you used your finding rune. And before they left, they burned the rune book. How did they know we were coming?"

Alex had been wondering about that himself. As far as he knew, there wasn't any way to detect a finding rune, but he couldn't think of any other explanation.

"Let me take a look," he said, setting his kit on the table and opening it up.

He didn't even bother with the silverlight; a room like this that rented by the week would be lousy with blood, food, and bodily fluids. If runes were used, however, there would be magical residue, and that he could see with the ghostlight.

"What's that?" Nicholson said, leaning over to peer into Alex's bag.

"This puts out special light," Alex said, clipping the ghostlight burner into his lamp. "And I can see it here." He put his oculus on the table while he lit the lamp.

"What are all the lenses for?" the detective asked.

"I have to use different ones to see different colors of light," Alex explained as he took the covers off the sides of the multi lamp. Usually he just used one side to project a single tight beam, but in a small room like this, having all four sides of the lamp open would be faster.

When he got the oculus on and dropped the right lens into the field of view, the entire room lit up. There were several lines of runes running down the wall between the two beds. Alex recognized some of them, but others were unfamiliar. On the wall next to the table was a chalk line for a vault door and a line of glowing liquid residue ran in a staggering arc from the table to the vault.

"What are you seeing?" Nicholson asked.

Alex took out his notebook and began sketching the runes as quickly as he could. Magical residue could remain for hours and sometimes days, but exposure to ghostlight had a tendency to make the residue fade faster.

"There's a privacy rune here," he said, indicating the highest spot on the wall. "That obviously didn't work very well."

"Why not?"

"Because if it had, my finding rune wouldn't have been able to locate the book," Alex answered.

The next rune down didn't make much sense, but Alex recognized a linking rune as part of the construct. Below that was a bang rune, but not the overpowered one the robbers had used at the bank. This one would barely have made a sound when it went off.

"Why would they put that on their wall?" Nicholson asked when Alex revealed its presence.

"No idea."

"Have you figured out how they knew we were coming?" Detweiler's voice broke in.

Alex took off his oculus and set it on the table.

"Best I can figure is that they were using a privacy rune," Alex said. "It's supposed to prevent people from listening at doors, but it also does a good job at stopping finding runes and other location magic from working. They had one on the wall there."

"But your rune worked," Nicholson pointed out.

Alex nodded. "Either my rune was too powerful for the privacy rune to stop, or this rune wasn't done properly. In either case, I think it failed when my finding rune located the book and that alerted the runewright brother."

Detweiler looked like he wanted to swear but he kept his temper in check.

"Anything else?" he asked.

"They opened a vault here," Alex said, pointing to the wall. "And they spilled something magical on the floor."

"Any idea what?"

Alex shrugged. "There are lots of magical inks used in rune magic," he said. "Could be anything."

"You aren't exactly a big help," Detweiler growled.

"Did you learn anything from the other tenants?"

Detweiler ground his teeth and shook his head.

"Just that our brothers have a southern drawl," he said.

'That should help," Nicholson said, somewhat eagerly.

"There's three million people in this city, Detective," Detweiler said. "Two hillbillies from Georgia might stick out a bit, but it's not like they're going to be easy to find."

Alex packed up his bag and left the lieutenant and his men to finish their work. Nicholson offered to give him a lift home, but Alex didn't want to wait for a car to become available, so he decided to take a cab instead. There was a drug store two blocks down and he headed for it. When he reached it, he didn't go inside to call a cab, but rather went around to the back and opened a door into his vault. Checking to make sure no one was watching, he passed inside and shut the door behind him.

Alex found Iggy cooking dinner in the kitchen once he'd returned to the brownstone from his vault. He wore a heavy cloth apron over his button up shirt as he seasoned a pot of some orange sauce that bubbled away on the stove.

"So," he said when Alex entered the kitchen. "Tell me what you've learned about Margaret's murder. I've been anxious for news and the papers have moved on to other stories."

Alex had to take a minute to gather his thoughts. He'd been so focused on the bombing robberies he had quite forgotten about Margaret.

"You were right," he said. "Danny and I confirmed that Dolly Anderson was murdered, so it's likely Margaret figured it out." He walked Iggy through their trip to the museum, though he didn't mention the missing mummy. The files from Curator Swain were still in his kit bag, and he'd look at them later if he had the time.

"Why take Danny?" Iggy asked. "You could have handled that on your own and had him start doing interviews."

Alex explained the conversation he'd had with Lieutenant Callahan and why it necessitated keeping Danny close. When he finished, Iggy stroked his mustache and nodded.

"Callahan's a good man," he said. "The detectives should do well with him at the helm."

"Danny too," Alex said, somewhat defensively.

"Of course," Iggy said with a dismissive waive of his hand. "I was thinking, though, you might want to back off and let Danny handle this by himself. A lot of folks still have prejudice against Orientals and if word got out that you helped him, someone might use that to hurt his chances."

Alex thought about that for a long moment. Iggy had a point. It was the same point Callahan made, but Callahan wanted Alex to help.

"Maybe," he said. "But I think Callahan's right. Danny needs a big, splashy case that no one can argue with."

Iggy raised an eyebrow and gave Alex an amused grin.

"And you think Danny won't be able to solve it without you?" he said.

"No, Danny's sharp," Alex said. "But Dolly Anderson's murder has gone unsolved for fifteen years. If I were in Danny's shoes, I'd want all the help I could get."

Iggy stroked his mustache and nodded slowly.

"Probably wise," he said at last. "I take it you'll be doing the interviews together then."

Alex explained their plans as he set the table.

"You seem distracted," Iggy said once Alex finished laying out the silverware with the forks on the right side.

"Sorry," he said, moving the forks. "It's just this other case that Lieutenant Detweiler's got me working on. These bank robbers detected my finding rune and made a run for it before the cops got there."

"I don't think that's possible, lad," Iggy said. "Someone must have tipped them off."

Alex thought about that. The only people who even knew that the rune had worked were Detweiler, Nicholson, and the two victims who had their lore books stolen. It was possible that one of the victims was secretly working with the brothers, but it didn't seem very likely that one of the two people the police brought in were also in on the robbery.

"I found a privacy rune on their wall along with a couple of others," Alex said. "I think it failed when my rune located the lore book. The runewright who cast it must have noticed that it stopped working and got spooked."

Iggy didn't look convinced.

"Did you make a copy of the rune?"

Alex took out his notepad and flipped to the appropriate page.

"It's pretty rough," he said. "Whoever wrote it didn't have a very steady hand."

Iggy took the note pad and studied it carefully. After a minute he got up and went to the library to fetch his magnifying glass from the drawer in the reading table.

"I can't explain the poor writing," he said, tapping the notebook. "But this rune isn't a privacy rune, at least not in the way you mean. This also isn't three separate runes, they're all part of the same larger construct. You saw the linking rune?"

Alex nodded.

"It didn't look like it tied to the other constructs," he said.

Iggy shrugged.

"I'm just guessing, but if I'm right, this is actually a very advanced construct. Look here," he pointed at the privacy rune. "See how several of the symbols are missing."

"Sure," Alex admitted. "But that might just be all the guy knew."

"I don't think so," Iggy said. "The symbols that are missing are the ones that would make the construct stable. If he'd added in even one of the missing bits, the construct would have worked as a privacy rune."

"Are you suggesting he wanted it to fail?"

"I think that's exactly what he wanted," Iggy said. "This middle part links to the bang rune. If someone is searching for them with a basic finding rune, then the privacy rune is enough to handle it. If, however, someone is using a strong finding rune, like yours, the privacy rune will fail and activate the bang rune." He pointed to the third construct on the paper. "Note how this bang rune is also underpowered."

"Loud enough to get their attention but not so loud that it would disturb the other tenants in the house," Alex said, nodding. "That's clever."

"It's more than clever," Iggy said. "Whoever did this is extremely dangerous Alex. They've already shown that they're willing to kill. You need to help the police find them before they kill again."

"Right," Alex sighed.

Iggy grabbed his hand and Alex looked up into the old man's eyes.

"I'd appreciate it if you'd stop these fellows without getting yourself blown up in the process."

Alex chuckled and nodded.

"Right," he said again.

14

SEALED

Alex was up early the next morning. He told Danny to meet him at the office at nine, but his friend was clearly taken with Sherry and she wasn't discouraging him. While Alex didn't really care who Danny dated, Sherry was still an unknown and he wanted to warn Danny off.

Most Orientals couldn't get very far with women of other races, but Danny had a compelling amount of charisma and charm. He did pretty well for himself. Now that Alex thought about it, he wasn't really sure what Sherry's background was. Her skin tone and hair appeared Mediterranean, but she had no trace of an accent and Knox was an English name. Her facial features were strangely mixed as well. As he considered it, Alex doubted her heritage mattered very much, but the fact that he couldn't place it bothered him nonetheless.

His thoughts were interrupted by a knock at his bedroom door.

"You up, lad?" Iggy's voice asked.

"Yeah," Alex called as he finished tying his tie in the bathroom mirror. "Come in."

He heard the door open and Iggy's footsteps as he crossed the room.

"I was wondering if I might use your vault this morning?" he asked, appearing at the open bathroom door.

"Sure," Alex said as he ensured his tie was straight and his hair had been properly slicked back. "But what do I have that your vault doesn't?"

"An exit in your office building," Iggy said with a chuckle. "I need to visit a few friends on the upper west side and I want to pick up some alchemy supplies."

Alex smiled at that. Iggy was very wealthy thanks to his previous career as a worldwide bestselling author, but he was very frugal nonetheless. A cab ride from Alex's office would cost less than one from the brownstone.

"I also thought you might like to see this," Iggy said, holding out a copy of the morning paper as Alex exited the bathroom.

He turned the paper over and read the enormous headline.

The Brothers Boom, it read. *Bombastic Bandidos Break the Bank!*

"Uh oh," he said, scanning the story. It had pretty much all the details about the bombing case except for the amount stolen from the bank. Whoever wrote it even knew more than Alex. According to the story the brothers were named Roy and Arlo Harper. Worst of all, however, was that Alex was mentioned by name to be working with the police on the case. "Detweiler is not going to be happy about this."

"I suggest you call him as soon as you get to your office," Iggy said, handing Alex his coat.

They emerged a few minutes later in the back room of Alex's second office and, after making sure no one was outside the door or coming up the stairs, they stepped out into the hall. Iggy wished Alex luck and headed off down the stairs to take the nearby crawler or catch a cab.

When Alex reached his door, it was about twenty after eight but the light inside his office was on and he could smell coffee brewing.

"Good morning, boss," Sherry greeted him when he came in. Her normally cheerful smile was absent, and she nodded toward his office with a shrug.

Alex ground his teeth and hung up his hat.

Cops? he mouthed at her and she nodded.

"Well, that will save me the call," he muttered.

He pushed open the door and found Detweiler, Nicholson, and two uniformed officers waiting for him. The lieutenant was seated behind Alex's desk, drinking his whisky with Detective Nicholson in one of his chairs and the two officers standing on the opposite side of the room.

"I'm surprised at you, Lockerby," Detweiler said, holding up a tumbler of scotch. "I figured you were too cheap to buy the good stuff." He drank it in one go and set the glass on the desk. "Of course, being a snitch to the papers probably pays better than chasing cheating husbands and finding lost dogs."

"If you're referring to that piece in the *Times* this morning, I had nothing to do with it," Alex said.

"Don't lie to me," Detweiler said, slamming his fist down on Alex's desk so hard that the window in his door rattled. "Nobody knew about the bombers being from the south except you and the cops from last night."

"And none of them would sell a story to the papers," Alex said with a smirk.

"Your name was in the article," Detweiler shouted. "No cop would give you any credit if they snitched to the papers, the only person who would do that is you."

Alex hadn't thought about that, but the lieutenant was right. If a cop had sold the story, they would have made the cops look better and they certainly wouldn't have mentioned Alex.

"I couldn't have given them the story," Alex said. "It mentioned the brother's names. Until I read it in the paper, I didn't even know their names."

"That doesn't prove anything," Detweiler growled. "We got the names from the old lady at the boarding house, you could have picked them up on your way out last night."

"But I didn't," Alex insisted. "I would never talk to the press about a case I was still working on."

Detweiler's mouth dropped open in a look of profound disbelief.

"You brought a tabloid reporter to the arrest of the Ghost Killer," he said. "He's the one that started calling you the Runewright Detective. It's on your God-damned window! You two," he gestured to the uniformed officers. "Arrest this punk."

"Really, Lieutenant," a new voice interrupted. "Must you shout and swear at this hour of the morning?"

All eyes turned to Alex's office door as Sorsha Kincaid pulled it open. As usual she was immaculate in a pair of black, high-waisted pants with pinstripes and a short-sleeved white shirt. The pants had a double row of buttons that ran up the front and suspenders that went over her shoulders. Her usually burgundy lipstick was darker, almost black to match the slacks, and her platinum blonde hair glowed with reflected light. Alex never cared for the fashion of working women dressing in men's clothes, but Sorsha made it work.

"Miss Kincaid," Detweiler said as Nicholson rose from his chair. "I apologize for my language, but I assure you it was warranted." He nodded at Alex. "Lockerby here has been leaking details of my ongoing case to the press."

Sorsha gave him a cold look, then shifted her gaze to Alex. He'd seen that look before, many times, so it didn't have the same effect on him. Sorsha seemed to realize this and her pale blue eyes flashed for a moment as if lit from within. An icy chill enveloped Alex and he shivered before it vanished.

"Alex is many things, Lieutenant," Sorsha said, grinning slightly at Alex's discomfort. "But he isn't the kind of man to jeopardize an ongoing case for some cheap headlines. Alex only leaks details to the press once a case is wrapped up and then he always uses a Mr. William Tasker of the tabloid, *The Midnight Sun*. I believe he was the reporter you mentioned who was present when the Ghost was arrested."

"I don't know about that," Detweiler said. "What I do know is that Alex is the only one who could have leaked the story."

"I do apologize, Lieutenant," Sorsha said, sweeping into the room and sitting down in the empty chair. "But I have a bad habit of listening at keyholes. I heard you mention that Alex was with you last night when you almost caught the bombers."

"That's right," Detweiler said, sitting back down in Alex's chair. "That's where we learned their names."

"From the landlady where they had been staying?"

"You think she called the papers?" Detective Nicholson offered.

Sorsha turned to look at Nicholson and nodded.

"She, or one of her other tenants would have a better motive than Alex, don't you think?"

"But Alex's name was in the story," Nicholson said. "How would they know who he was?"

"You mentioned it yourself," Sorsha said, turning back to Detweiler. "Alex's name is known thanks to Mr. Tasker. If they heard one of you call him by name, it would have been easy to put two and two together."

"I didn't call the *Times*, Detweiler," Alex said. "I want these guys caught as much as you do, and I don't want to cause a panic."

Detweiler's eyebrows furrowed so deeply that they appeared to merge.

"Fine," he growled, standing up. "But I'd better be able to reach you if I need you."

"I'll be around," Alex said as Detweiler motioned for his men to withdraw. "And Lieutenant, be careful when you find these guys. I was looking at the runes they used last night, and I think they might be more dangerous than we first thought."

"Well, that's just great," Detweiler said giving Alex the once-over to make sure he was serious. Finally he nodded. "Thanks for the warning," he said, then followed his men out.

"What is it with you?" Sorsha said once the Lieutenant had gone. "You seem to attract trouble."

"What can I say," Alex said, putting away his scotch bottle. "I've got the luck of the Irish."

"Lockerby is a Scottish name," Sorsha corrected him.

"Not that I don't appreciate your timely intervention, Sorceress," Alex said, sitting down across from her. "But to what do I owe the pleasure?"

Her perfect features darkened and she sighed.

"I need you and your bag of tricks at a crime scene," she said. "There's been another magical death. Two this time."

Alex checked his watch. Danny would be arriving at any minute.

"All right," he said, standing up. "Let me get my kit and leave some instructions with my secretary and we can go."

Sorsha's floater dropped them off in front of an outer ring apartment building that had seen much better days. The brickwork was crumbling and several of the windows were cracked or boarded up. A uniformed policeman stood on the curb out front and directed them up to the second floor where another uniform stood outside an apartment door.

Chunks of wood and splinters littered the hallway and the door looked like instead of being opened it had been chopped down. When Alex got close, he could see why. The door and the frame appeared to have fused together into a single piece of wood. In the space where the door met the jamb, the wood looked as if it had simply grown together, like a tree that had come up through a fence over the course of decades. As Alex ran his finger along the edge, he couldn't tell where the door ended and the jamb began.

In the center of the door was a hole that had obviously been made with an axe. Chunks of the door had been hacked out and broken off, leaving a jagged opening just big enough for a grown man to squeeze through.

Beyond the hole, the light in the apartment was on. Alex peered in and saw two people, a man and a woman on the floor, obviously dead. Even at this distance, he could see their faces were blue as if they'd been asphyxiated.

"What happened here?" he muttered as Sorsha peered around him.

"That's what I need you for," Sorsha said. "According to the police who were first on the scene, neighbors heard these two arguing and then it suddenly stopped."

"Did they argue a lot?" Alex asked, mostly out of habit.

"I don't know but it makes sense," Sorsha said. "When someone came to check on them, they found the door like this and no one answered from inside. They called the police and the police called the fire brigade who had to chop down the door."

"All right," Alex said, reaching in through the hole to set his bag down. "I'll take a look." He followed, stepping carefully over the broken and splintered bits of the door, then turned to help Sorsha through.

The two bodies were those of a man and a woman. The man lay on his back next to a small table that was covered in writing supplies while the woman lay a few feet away. Both were on their backs, but Alex assumed the policemen moved them in order to take their vitals.

"How much has been moved?" Alex asked.

"I just got here too," Sorsha said in a mildly sarcastic voice. "But from what I was told, it wouldn't be much. The police were only in here for a few minutes."

Alex was about to ask why, but as he approached the prone bodies, he saw why. The man's face was blue, but that wasn't the only peculiar thing. At first glance, his eyes and mouth appeared to be closed, but as Alex looked closer, he realized that the flesh of his eyelids and lips had grown together like the door. He knelt by the body and turned the head toward him, revealing that the man's nostrils had disappeared as well. It was as if he'd never had openings in his head.

"Dear God," Sorsha said as she realized what she was seeing.

Alex stood up and examined the woman's body. Her face was similarly without any openings. His stomach churned as he realized that whatever magic had sealed the apartment door had also sealed these people, leaving them unable to breathe. They'd suffocated where they fell.

"What could do something like that?" Sorsha wondered. Alex could tell from her voice that she was trying not to be sick.

That gave him an idea.

Standing, he moved to the kitchen sink, just beyond where the woman lay. Looking into it, he nodded.

"Come take a look," he said, motioning to Sorsha.

"What happened?" she gasped when she reached the sink.

The porcelain bottom of the sink had formed together completely closing up the drain.

"Whatever happened in here sealed up every opening," Alex said, reaching beyond the sink to tap on the tiny window in the wall. "Look how the glass and the frame have fused. I'll bet you won't be able to find an opening anywhere in this room."

Sorsha ran her finger under the cold water faucet and it came away dry.

"I don't think I could do this if I wanted to," Sorsha said.

Alex moved to the table and examined its contents. There was a pot of ink, several pens, flash paper, a pack of matches, and a large quantity of threadbare fabric rectangles. A notebook stood open with lots of scribbles in it next to a bottle of cheap bourbon and two glasses. One glass had a tiny amount of liquor in the bottom, the other held five folded paper packets.

"Well?" Sorsha said.

"Let me have a look with the oculus," he said, retrieving his kit.

He set the oculus lenses for ghostlight and lit the burner, but as soon as he put the lens over his eye the glow of residual magic nearly blinded him.

"Okay," he said, taking it off. "The whole room was exposed to powerful magic, but that's no surprise."

"No," Sorsha agreed.

Alex picked up the notebook and flipped through it for a few moments, then he nodded.

"Poor bastard," he said, looking down at the dead man.

"Did you know him?" Sorsha asked.

Alex shook his head.

"No," he said. "But I know plenty of runewrights just like him." He turned and indicated the table, but Sorsha spoke before he could explain.

"Yes, I see the flash paper and the matches," she said. "He was a runewright."

"A poor one," Alex elaborated. "That's why he was working with these."

He held up one of the fabric rectangles.

"What are those?"

"I think they used to be socks with holes in them," Alex said. He held up the notebook in his other hand. "According to this he was working on a new kind of mending rune, one that could mend multiple things at once."

"Like a pile of socks that need darning," Sorsha said, catching on.

Alex nodded.

"If he figured it out, it would have made him a fortune," Alex said, looking around at the meager apartment. "It was his ticket out of here."

"What happened?" the Sorceress asked. "How could a better mending rune do all of this?"

Alex picked up the cup with the powder packets in it and handed it to Sorsha.

"Limelight?" she asked, looking at the contents of the cup.

"There's a few empty wrappers on the table with the flash paper," he said. "I think our dead runewright was using it to give himself direct magical power."

"To enhance the rune? Would it do that?"

"Based on the fact that there isn't an opening in anything in this room," Alex admitted, "I'd say it worked a little too well."

"Yes, but how?" Sorsha pressed.

Alex just shook his head.

"There's no precedent for this. Maybe if I study his notes, I'll have a better idea, but from what I've seen, they're pretty scattered. I'll probably have to show it to Iggy. I think I'm going to need his help figuring it out. He's out today, but we can look at it tonight."

Sorsha looked around at the room and shivered.

"Study quickly, Alex," she said. "This Limelight business is getting bad and if we don't put a stop to it, there's no telling how much worse it's going to get."

"What I want to know is how he knew about Limelight in the first place." Alex nodded at the dead man.

Sorsha shook her head.

"The FBI has been looking into where this stuff might have come from, but so far we don't have any leads."

Alex reached into the cup and took out two of the packets.

"I've got to go meet Danny about a case," he said, dropping the packets into his jacket pocket. "But I'll stop off at Runewright Row and show these around. Maybe someone there will know where they came from."

"Don't forget to talk to Mr. Grier," she said. "See if he's figured out what this stuff is or who is making it."

"I'll do that too," Alex promised.

15

FASHION

An hour later, Alex got off the sky crawler from the east side at Empire Station. From the upper deck of the crawler, he could see the Central Office of Police, but he'd arranged for Danny to meet him here instead. He'd told his friend that he needed to ask his runewright friend Marnie about the Limelight powder, but in reality he just needed a good cup of coffee — badly.

After he left Sorsha's crime scene, he'd stopped at Runewright Row to ask around about the strange alchemical powder. He'd spent half an hour going up and down the row and no one had ever heard of it, to say nothing of knowing where it came from. The whole trip had been a massive waste of time and given him a headache.

"You look like hell," Marnie said as he approached the fancy bar that Andrew Barton had set up for her. Like everything else in Empire Station, it was made of dark wood, with a marble top, and brass accents all around. In place of her old, battered coffee pot, Marnie now had a tall brass percolator that gleamed in the mid-morning light.

There were three counters on the long coffee bar and a young, fresh-faced man and woman each worked to help the small line of waiting customers. It seemed that word had gotten around about Marnie's coffee, which didn't surprise Alex in the least.

"You look prettier," Alex said, walking around the side of the bar to give Marnie a hug.

"Here you are, Mr. Lockerby," the young man said as he brought a cup to Alex. Marnie had given standing orders to make sure he didn't have to wait for his coffee.

Alex thanked the young man and took a grateful sip.

"I needed that," he said, blowing on the steaming liquid.

"Bad day?" Marnie asked.

"You could say that," he said, suppressing a shudder as he remembered the unfortunate runewright and his wife.

Marnie put her arm around his waist and hugged him to her side.

"You should take your own advice and come work here," she said. "Mr. Barton mentions you at least once a week when he comes to check on the station."

Alex grinned at Marnie. He had to admit, she looked ten years younger now that she didn't have to stand at a pushcart in the outdoors every day. Being the queen of coffee in Barton's showcase station clearly agreed with her.

"He doesn't need me," Alex said, giving her a squeeze back before she released him. "I met his new runewright," Alex searched his memory for the young man's name. "Bradley Elder."

Marnie's face closed over and she snorted.

"You don't like him?"

"I don't," she declared, crossing her arms. "You should see him walk around here like he owns the place."

"He did solve a big problem for Mr. Barton," Alex said, trying to be diplomatic.

"Well he's got no use for other runewrights," she said. "I broke one of those special pitchers you made for me and I asked him if he could put a rune on another one, just until you came by and I could get the broken one replaced. He looked at me like something he found on the bottom of his shoe."

Alex didn't like that, but he wasn't surprised. Enchanting the brewing glass for Marnie was tricky and took time to learn. He'd spent a year getting good at it while he and Jessica were dating. It was something that the young Mr. Elder wasn't likely to know. Still, he shouldn't have been an ass to Marnie.

"Don't worry about him," Alex said, pushing the matter from his already cluttered mind. "He's just young. Do you have a list for me?"

Marnie ducked under her counter and came up with a folded sheet of paper that contained all the rune glass she needed. Runes could do a lot of things, but they weren't permanent, and with the amount of people Marnie served every day, the rune-glass Alex made for her had to be replaced every couple of weeks.

"You be careful of that one," Marnie said, hanging on to the list when Alex tried to take it from her. "He hates you."

That got Alex's attention. He'd only met Bradley Elder once and as far as he knew he hadn't given the young man any reason to think twice about him.

Marnie could see the thoughts playing out on Alex's face and her mouth turned up in a sly grin.

"He's terrified that Mr. Barton will convince you to work for him, then he won't need that little scab. When he found out that you were the one putting runes on my brewing pots, he changed his tune quick. Offered to do it for free. I just told him you'd be by later and he hurried off."

Alex sighed. He understood basic jealousy, but he'd never really had much time to indulge in it. For most of his life he'd never really been anybody special. It wasn't till he met Iggy that he really started to learn his craft, both as a detective and a runewright. Even now when he had a fair amount of success and even some notoriety, there were plenty of people more learned and more powerful than him, Iggy and Sorsha just to name two.

"Well I hate to say it, but Mr. Elder's job is safe," Alex said, taking the list from Marnie. "I like my job."

He expected her to protest, but she just gave him an affectionate jab on the arm and smiled.

"Won't stop me from trying to convince you," she said.

"I might have known I'd find you here," Danny's voice interrupted.

Alex turned to find his friend crossing the marble floor of Empire Station with a smile on his face and a spring in his step.

"Do you know how hard it is to park around this building?" Danny went on.

"Hello, Danny," Marnie said without missing a beat. "I'll get your usual."

"Usual?" Alex said, raising an eyebrow. As long as he'd known Danny, his friend hadn't been much of a coffee drinker.

"That's your fault," Danny said, fishing his change purse out of his pocket. "You introduced me to Marnie here and now I can't hardly stomach the stuff at the Central Office. Even diner coffee tastes like mop water."

Alex understood that. He'd had pretty much the same reaction when he first discovered Marnie and her magic coffee. Back then it was necessary fuel to keep him going, since his life energy had been all but spent. Now, with that particular problem solved, he found he didn't need it as much, though he still came by at least once a week just to check on Marnie.

"Thanks," Danny said as Marnie handed him a steaming cup.

Between the perpetual grin and the sunny attitude, Alex guessed that Sherry hadn't managed to catch him before he left the Central Office. He wondered how long his friend had waited at his office under the pretense that Alex might get done with Sorsha quickly. If Danny's attitude was any gauge, he'd enjoyed his time with Sherry quite a bit. Alex needed to wave him off before he fell for her.

"So where to first?" Danny said, once he'd paid for his coffee.

"The Garment District," Alex said, waving goodbye to Marnie. "After that we'll hit the theater and then see if we can talk to Regina Darling."

The storefront of Leone Fashions sat on the corner of a block with large glass display windows running all the way around the corner in a graceful arc. They showcased the kinds of dresses people usually only saw in the movies or on newsreels. Alex had seen some on women in high end nightclubs, and he knew Sorsha had a couple of Leone dresses. All he really knew about them was that they were very in demand, and very expensive.

An attractive salesgirl directed Alex and Danny to an elevator in the back of the shop that led up to the offices and manufacturing floors above. They got off on the third floor where an irritable receptionist tried to give them the brush off until Danny jammed his badge in her face and threatened to have her arrested.

Finally they were ushered into an elegant art nouveau office with an Oriental theme. Large, elegantly carved frames stood in front of the plain walls, draped with rich, embroidered fabric. A desk made from ash or white oak sat in the middle of the room holding only a blotter, a desk calendar, an inkwell and pen stand, a nickel-plated telephone, and a large table lighter in the shape of an elegant vase. The side panels of the desk had relief carved scenes of samurai fighting battles and each of the legs had a Chinese dragon running up from the floor so that their open jaws seemed to hold up the table-top. Two chairs sat in front of the overdone desk. They were made of cherry wood but the upholstery was white leather to match the desk.

"Are you the young men who've been causing trouble in my office?" a stern voice demanded as the white double doors at the back of the office opened. They revealed a tall, almost emaciated woman in her sixties, clad in an elegant, cream-colored dress that hung to her knees. Her iron-gray hair was bound up in a large bun on top of her head, held in place by two lacquered chopsticks, and a long string of pearls dangled down from her neck to her waist. She carried a black cigarette holder that reminded Alex of Sorsha's, and it trailed smoke as she moved.

Alex and Danny rose as she swept into the room with a nervous and harried looking young woman in her wake. She made a show of moving to her desk, then she sat with all the elegance and grace of a queen taking the throne.

"Now," she said as Alex and Danny sat down. "I am Maybelle Leone. You will be good enough, please, to tell me what this intrusion is about. I have a very busy day ahead of me."

"We're here about the death of Margaret LaSalle," Danny said. He went on to introduce himself and Alex, but Maybelle wasn't paying attention.

"Margaret's dead?" she said in a dumbstruck voice. She took a breath and steadied herself. "I...I didn't know."

"It's been in the papers," Alex said.

Maybelle Leone looked at him with an imperious gaze.

"Fashion is a harsh mistress," she said. "I barely have time to read the trades. I am sorry about poor Margaret, though. She was an important woman. Do you know that only a handful of women write mysteries, and Margaret was one of the best."

Alex did know that, but he held his tongue.

"Her killer simply must be brought to justice," Maybelle went on. "How can I assist the New York Police?"

"We believe she came to see you recently," Danny said, flipping open his notebook.

"I wouldn't say recently," she turned to the frazzled young woman standing behind her chair. "Agatha, be a dear and look in my calendar. Find out when it was that Margaret came to see me."

"Yes, Mrs. Leone," the girl said, then she scurried away.

"Why did Miss LaSalle come to see you?" Danny asked.

They both knew why, of course, but Danny was fishing to see if the fashion icon would lie about it.

"She wanted to ask me about my relationship with Dolly Anderson, the famous actress," she said without a pause.

"What did she want to know?" Danny said.

"She was writing a new mystery and she wanted to base it on Dolly's death," Maybelle said with a wistful smile. "It was all terribly exciting."

"If I remember that case," Alex said, "the press seemed to think you had a feud with Dolly."

Maybelle's austere expression slipped for a moment, replaced by one of irritation.

"The papers do love their drama," she said. "Dolly and I were dear friends. I explained all this to Margaret."

"Whoever killed Margaret stole her notes," Danny said. "So we'd like to know what you talked about in case it has something to do with her death."

"Fine," Maybelle sighed. "But I'm going to save time and just start at the beginning."

"That's fine," Danny said.

"I met Dolly right after I launched my fashion business," she said. "Dolly was an up and coming actress and I needed exposure. I had been approached by Benny Harrington to provide a gown for one of his plays. Benny was the biggest playwright on Broadway back then."

"Didn't he write the play Dolly was in when she died?" Alex asked.

Maybelle nodded.

"Yes, that was later though, when his fortunes had fallen. But when Dolly and I were starting out, everyone wanted to be in a Harrington play. So I provided the dress for Dolly and we both went on to fame and fortune."

"So why did the papers think you were enemies?" Alex asked.

"My husband and I were supposed to meet Dolly in Hollywood to dress her for a movie she was going to do. I got sick, so he went without me and some muckraker took a picture of them together."

"They claimed he was having an affair?" Danny said.

"Dolly called me in tears," Maybelle said. "She swore they weren't, and I believed her."

"So you didn't hate Dolly?" Alex asked.

"Of course not," she said with an indignant look. "Dolly and I remained friends until her tragic death."

Something about her voice made Alex think that Maybelle had some lingering doubts, but he didn't press the issue.

"Is that why you provided the dress for her to wear that night?" Alex asked. "As you said, Benny Harrington's fortunes had fallen by then. Wasn't that play his last chance to save his career?"

Maybelle gave Alex a hard look and she thought for a minute, then nodded.

"Benny had several bad plays in a row," she said. "*The Rogue's Gallery* was his last attempt to get back on top. He called in every favor he could—that's how he got Dolly to star in it."

"So Harrington approached you too?" Danny asked.

"No," Maybelle said. "Dolly insisted he use me. She wouldn't take the part if he didn't."

"Why did she have to insist?" Alex asked as mildly as he could.

Maybelle sighed and a look of profound displeasure crossed her face.

"My fortunes weren't doing well then either," she admitted. "I had filed for bankruptcy. Dolly insisted Harrington use me as a way to help."

"I guess it worked," Danny said. "You're one of the top designers in the city."

"You're sweet to say that," Maybelle said, giving Danny a smile. "But that success came at the cost of Dolly's life."

She paused and sighed.

"How do you mean?" Danny pressed.

"After Dolly's death, all the papers obsessed over her for months. The picture they used was the promotional image from the play."

"And she was wearing your dress," Alex guessed. "Tens of thousands of people obsessing over Dolly, wanting to be close to her and all they had to do was buy a dress from you."

She took a long drag on her cigarette and nodded.

"Suddenly my designs were all the rage again," she said. "It gave the House of Leone new life."

"Did Margaret LaSalle tell you why she was using Dolly Anderson's death as the basis for her story?" Danny asked.

"No," Maybelle said in a lazy drawl. "But I can guess. She thought Dolly was murdered. I can tell that you think it too. You're wondering if I killed her to get my brand back on top?"

"The thought crossed our minds," Alex admitted.

"I didn't," she declared, giving Alex a hard stare. "Dolly was my dear friend. She put her reputation on the line to try to help me and it worked. I only wish it didn't cost her life."

Alex gave Danny a slight shrug. He felt like Maybelle was being honest and it didn't seem like she had a strong motive. This looked like a dead end.

"Is there anything else you can remember about your meeting with Margaret LaSalle?" Danny asked. "Anyone she might have asked about?"

"No," she said, blowing out a cloud of smoke. "But if you ask me, the person you should be looking at is Dolly's understudy."

"Regina Darling?" Alex said. "Why?"

"That talentless bitch rode Dolly's coattails for years," Maybelle said, her face twisted into a sneer. "Dolly is the one who discovered her, and she was under an exclusive contract. She had to keep being Dolly's understudy for two more years but with Dolly out of the way, Regina suddenly got leading roles. She became a big star almost overnight." Maybelle turned to Danny. "I believe that's what you policemen call a motive."

Alex had to admit, it was a motive — and a pretty good one.

"If you ask me, Regina Darling killed Dolly to get her out of the way," Maybelle concluded.

Danny waited for her to go on, but when she didn't, he flipped his notebook closed and took out one of his business cards.

"If there's anything else you remember about your conversation with Margaret LaSalle, please call me."

She accepted the card and then Danny and Alex showed themselves out.

"What do you think?" Danny asked once they were back on the street outside.

"I don't think she's our murderer," Alex said. "Dolly's death benefitted her but there's no way she could have known that it would happen."

"She might have done it out of spite," Danny said. "If she was lying about the affair with her husband, then she might have wanted to kill Dolly over that. The windfall to her business wasn't part of the plan, just a twist of fate."

Alex thought about that. He felt like Maybelle really did care about Dolly, but she might just be an exceptional liar. If that were true, her emphatic declaration that her husband wasn't cheating on her might be false as well.

"I guess we can't cross her off the list just yet," he admitted.

"So, who's next?" Danny asked as they got into his green Ford.

"Now we go to the theater district," Alex said, checking the address Sherry had written out for him. "Time to see Ethan Nelson, owner of the *Royale* theater."

16

BROADWAY

The Royale Theater had been a staple of the Theater District for over a decade. It stood right on the famous boulevard, in the middle of a block with its massive marquee hanging almost over the street. The façade was done in the art deco style with towering stone figures on each corner of the building and polished metal accents running up from the street level. Banks of magelights covered the marquee and ran up along the vertical sign that displayed the name, Royale.

Since it was only early afternoon, the street in front of the theater was empty and Danny parked right in front. Standing sandwich boards stood out in front of the ticket window advertising a play called *Murder in the Cathedral* along with photographs of the major stars. A sign in the ticket window proclaimed that cast members and deliveries should enter though the back. Alex hesitated when he saw it, but Danny just walked right by, pulling open the heavy front door.

"Police go in the front," he said with a wry grin.

Alex followed into the theater's dark lobby, then up a wide staircase with a sign pointing upward that read, Office.

"Who is this guy, again?" Danny asked as they climbed.

"Ethan Nelson," Alex said, pulling out his notebook. "His father,

Martin Nelson, built the theater back in 1887. When he died in 1912, Ethan took over. He's managed it ever since."

Danny made a non-committal noise that indicated he'd heard and pressed on to the upper landing. A hallway ran along the left side of the theater with doors at regular intervals that led to private boxes. To the right was a door with a frosted glass panel. The words, Royale Theater Offices had been painted in gold on the white surface of the glass.

The door opened on a large, cluttered office with a desk in the center of the room surrounded by file cabinets, tables filled with posters, and handbills advertising various plays. Two couches sat against the near wall opposite a wooden staircase that ran up to the third floor.

A skinny man with bushy black hair sat behind the desk reading through a thick pack of papers that had been stapled together. He had blocky features with a wide nose, thick eyebrows, and a look of intense concentration. Alex figured he was in his late forties or early fifties. A full glass of dark liquid sat next to a half empty bourbon bottle on the desk along with a lit cigarette in a glass ashtray, and an empty plate next to a salt and pepper shaker. He'd thrown his suit coat over the back of the chair where he sat.

The man looked up as Alex and Danny came in, his face taking on a slightly worried look.

"Something I can do for you boys?" he asked.

"Are you Ethan Nelson?" Danny asked, pulling his badge out of his pocket and holding it up.

"That's me," he said, setting down the papers and sitting up straight. "Is there a problem I don't know about?"

"I'm Detective Pak, this is Alex Lockerby," Danny said, as he clipped his badge to his coat lapel. "We're looking into the murder of Margaret LaSalle."

Nelson sat waiting for more, then he shook his head.

"Is she an actress?" he asked. "I just run the theater; if she's an actress, you'll have to check with the producer, he does the hiring."

"Margaret LaSalle is a writer," Alex explained. "She might have come to see you about the death of Dolly Anderson a few years back."

Recognition dawned in Nelson's eyes and he stroked his chin and nodded.

"This is the theater where Dolly died," Danny added, "correct?"

Ethan blew out a breath of air and sat back in his chair.

"Dolly Anderson," he said, somewhat wistfully. "That takes me back. Yes, Dolly was killed in an accident back in twenty-two. Terrible thing. I've met some of the biggest names in the business, but Dolly..." he shrugged. "She was one in a million."

"Do you remember talking to Miss LaSalle?" Alex pressed. "Older woman, was writing a mystery based on Dolly's death?"

"I remember," Nelson said, his fond smile disappearing. "She came by around last Thanksgiving, asked a bunch of questions about Dolly's death." He shook his head.

"Sounds like you didn't approve," Alex said.

"No," he said. "Every few years someone comes around wanting the real story of Dolly's death. Ghouls," he sneered. "They should let Dolly rest in peace."

"We're not here about that," Danny assured him. "We just want to know what the two of you talked about."

Nelson sighed and took a drag on his cigarette.

"She wanted to know about the accident," he said. "Everyone always does."

"And what did you tell her?" Danny asked, his pencil poised over his notebook.

"Same thing I tell everyone else," Nelson said. "Dolly Anderson was electrocuted on stage in front of a packed house by a faulty prop. The police investigated for months, they accused my electrician of negligent homicide, there was a trial, and he was acquitted. In the end the whole sad affair was ruled a tragic accident."

"That sounds like the standard story," Alex said. "What do you think happened?"

Nelson chuckled, but there was no humor in his voice.

"You sound just like that LaSalle woman," he said. "She thought that Dolly had been murdered, that there was some dark secret that the police and the papers never found. Nonsense!" he growled. "The idea that anyone murdered Dolly is ridiculous! Everyone loved her. Dolly was a force of nature. It was impossible not to love her."

Clearly Nelson believed what he was saying and just as clearly, he'd told this story many times.

"Margaret wasn't the only one who believed Dolly was murdered, though," Alex asked. "Didn't the police consider you a suspect?"

Nelson rolled his eyes and shook his head.

"Yeah," he admitted. "I suppose they did. They didn't have any evidence, mind you. It was all because of the insurance policy."

"Insurance?" Danny said. "Was there a fire that night as well?"

Nelson laughed, but this time it was genuine.

"Not that kind of insurance," he said. "I had insurance on the play through Lloyds of London. If it closed in under four weeks, the policy would pay me for my losses."

Alex exchanged a questioning look with Danny.

"You can insure your box office?" Alex said.

"You can insure anything," Nelson said. "You just have to find the right agent. Dolly had a policy on her face that would pay out if she ever got in an accident or something like that."

"So if the play closed early, you'd still get paid?" Alex asked.

Nelson nodded.

"Got it in one," he said, taking another drag on his cigarette. "You see old Benny Harrington was on the ropes. He'd had four bum plays in a row, and the last two closed on opening night."

"So, you took out the insurance policy in case his play flopped," Alex said.

"That's why the police thought you had motive to kill Dolly," Danny said. "If she died, you'd get paid."

"That's no motive," Nelson said. "If the play was a hit, I get my fee plus a cut of the box office, and that'd be far more than the insurance policy. If the play flopped, the policy would pay out anyway. Either way, I win."

"Maybe," Alex said. "But if you force the play to close the first night, then you can hire out the theater right away. You get paid twice."

"Well, that would be a pretty good plan," Nelson admitted. "Except for the fact that after Dolly's death I had to close down the whole theater. It took me over a month to convince anyone to work here again. I almost went broke."

"But you didn't," Danny said. "Because of the insurance policy."

"But I almost did," he said. "I had to borrow money against the theater, and even then it was touch and go for months. The cops went through my books with a fine-toothed comb; I'm sure there's a record. Dolly Anderson's death wasn't a benefit to me. If Benny's play had succeeded, it would have made me a fortune. *The Royale* would have been booked for months. If I wanted money, the safe bet would be to let the play open."

"But Harrington had four flops," Alex pointed out.

"Which is why I had the insurance policy," Nelson said. "Any way you look at it, fellas, I didn't have any motive to kill Dolly Anderson."

It made sense. Alex wasn't sure how a person would go about getting play insurance, but he knew people who would. If Nelson was telling the truth, though, he didn't have any visible motive.

Nelson reached for his cigarette again but bumped the salt shaker, tipping it over. He jumped in his chair, stifling a curse and picked up some of the spilled salt, tossing it over his shoulder. Alex had seen people do that before, ostensibly to ward off evil spirits.

"Does that help?" he asked.

Nelson shrugged.

"Couldn't hurt," he said. "Sorry, but you need to understand there isn't a more superstitious group of people on the planet than actors."

"I thought you just ran the theater," Alex said.

Nelson laughed and pointed to a faded poster on the wall in an ornate frame. The image was of a solitary lighthouse rendered in silhouette. *The Lighthouse Keeper*, was written across the bottom in gold letters.

"My one and only play," he said, then he looked around the office sadly. "Guess I was better suited running theaters than starring in plays."

"Can you think of anyone who did have a motive to kill Dolly?" Danny asked, dragging the conversation back to the topic at hand.

Nelson sighed and ran his fingers through his bushy hair.

"Dolly was the goose that laid the golden egg," he said. "Benny Harrington knew having her in his show would make the critics and the public pay attention, even if he did have four previous flops. Having her here, at *The Royale,* said that we were the kind of theater that could cater to the biggest stars. She was good for everyone."

"Not everyone," Alex said. "A woman that successful, that powerful. Someone hated her, maybe enough to kill."

Nelson just sat for a moment, then he took a drink.

"There was her understudy," he said at last. "Regina Darling. She played second banana to Dolly for years, then right after Dolly died, she was offered a starring role. She's been on top ever since."

"She wasn't a slave," Danny said. "If she wanted to strike out on her own, she could just do it."

Nelson laughed at that, a loud sound of genuine amusement.

"You don't understand the theater, Detective. If Dolly didn't want Regina to leave, she could spike her wheel with every producer in town. No one would work with Regina if Dolly didn't like it. They'd be cutting their own throats the next time they wanted to hire Dolly."

"Was Dolly stopping Regina from having her own career?" Alex asked.

"No idea," Nelson said with a shrug. "You'd have to ask one of the producers who worked with her. I just run the theater."

"Anything else you can tell us, Mr. Nelson?" Danny asked. "Maybe something strange that Margaret LaSalle might have asked you?"

"Not really," he said. "Sorry."

Danny thanked him and they withdrew.

"What do you think?" he asked once Alex followed him down to the dark lobby.

"I want to talk to a friend of mine," Alex said. "He's in the insurance business. I want to know more about this policy Mr. Nelson took out."

"You think he lied about that?"

Alex shrugged.

"I don't know," he admitted. "But if Nelson is telling the truth about that, I don't see how he had any motive."

"That's the way I see it," Danny said. "Who's next on our list?"

"Regina Darling," Alex said. "The understudy." He pulled out his notebook where a core apartment building address was written.

"Let me call in first," Danny said, heading for the steel and glass phone booth by the lobby door.

Alex leaned against the painted banister of the stairs while Danny made his phone call. So far, he had two non-suspects, one who claimed to have loved Dolly Anderson and one who had motive to keep her alive. Neither struck him as a bad sort, but Iggy had often impressed him that murder wasn't the exclusive purview of bad people. Plenty of murderers thought of themselves as good.

Still, nothing shone the light of truth on a killer like a solid motive.

"And so far we don't have a hint of motive," he muttered.

"Maybe we'll get lucky," Danny said, crossing the lobby to where he stood. "And the understudy will confess."

Alex shook his head and chuckled. "You ever been that lucky?" he said.

Danny shook his head. "Nope," he said. "You'll have to tell my how it goes with Regina. Callahan wants me back at the Central Office."

"Trouble?"

"Sounded like it," Danny said. "He didn't say what, but something's up."

"Okay," Alex said with a long-suffering look. "You go do the cop thing with your lieutenant and I'll go see the most beautiful woman on Broadway."

Danny rolled his eyes.

"What would I do without you to do all the hard work for me?" he said, sarcasm practically dripping from every syllable.

Alex put his hand over his heart with a look of absolute piety.

"It's my cross to bear." He clapped his hand on Danny's shoulder. "But I'll do it for you, my friend."

"You're real funny," Danny said, rolling his eyes again. "You want me to give you a lift?"

"Regina lives south of Empire Tower," Alex said. "I'll get a cab."

"Take good notes," Danny said as they headed for the door.

"I don't know if you'll want me to write down everything."

"Shut up," Danny groused.

The apartment building where Regina Darling lived was a tower of white brick reaching twenty stories into the Manhattan sky. The lower floors were sheathed in white marble that made the whole edifice glow in the afternoon light. A set of bronze doors separated the sidewalk from the lobby, each ten feet high. The scale was deliberately designed to make the residents of the building feel grand — and to make any visitors feel small.

Like the building outside, the lobby of the apartment tower was white, with tiled floors laid out in mosaic patterns of white, blue, and pale purple. Elegant furniture filled the open spaces, set out in small groupings to keep conversation intimate in the cavernous space. Two elevators stood against the back wall, framed in bronze like the outer doors.

Regina lived on the eighteenth floor, not the penthouse level, but still well beyond anything Alex could afford. The elevator opened on a wide hallway with cream-colored carpet and white oak tables holding flowers. Alex turned right and looked for number seven. It turned out to be at the end of the other hall on the corner of the building.

He knocked and waited.

There was no sound from inside, so he knocked again.

"Just a minute," a woman's voice came from inside.

Nearly two minutes later, the lock scraped, and someone pulled on the door. The door rattled and the person beyond cursed.

Alex smiled as the lock scraped and clicked again. The door had been left unlocked and the person inside had locked it by accident. A moment later the door cracked open and a bloodshot green eye peered out at him.

"What is it?" a woman's voice asked. "Do you have any idea what time it is?"

Alex pulled out his watch and flipped it open.

"It's ten after three," he said.

"I don't have first call till five," she said. "Go away for at least an hour."

The door shut before Alex could say anything more. He stood

there for a moment, wondering what to do, then he raised his hand to knock again. The door opened again before his hand could fall and the green eye returned.

"You're not my driver," she declared.

"Regina Darling?"

"Who are you?"

"My name is Alex Lockerby. I'm a private detective."

"Did I hire you for something?" she asked, a note of genuine confusion in her voice. At first Alex thought she might be drunk but she seemed more tired than inebriated.

"No," Alex said. "I actually need to talk to you about Margaret LaSalle."

"The writer?" she said, starting to sound more awake.

"Yes, she was murdered, and I'm trying to get to the bottom of it," Alex explained.

"Margaret's dead?" Regina gasped. She started to pull the door open but stopped herself almost immediately.

In the brief second it was partially open, Alex saw a strong jaw that tapered to a pointed chin with a pert, narrow nose and dirty blonde hair the color of freshly harvested wheat. It was clear she wasn't wearing makeup, and her eyes had dark circles, but she was still breathtaking.

"I'm afraid so," Alex confirmed. "I believe she came to talk to you a few months ago. I'd like to ask you some questions regarding what you talked about."

The green eye darted up and down, taking Alex in, then the lid drooped down, into a half-closed position.

"I remember," she said. "I liked her. I even started reading some of her books."

"Would it be okay if I came in?"

The skin at the corner of the eye contracted and Alex caught the hint of a dimple in the cheek below.

"I'm afraid I can't receive you right now, Mr. Lockerby, but I do want to help you find Margaret's killer. I'm in a play over at the *Shubert Theater* and I have to get ready for work. Why don't you come to my dressing room after the late performance and I can answer your questions then?"

Alex hesitated. He wasn't interested in waiting around for Miss Darling to finish her play.

"Tell you what," Regina said when he didn't answer immediately. "The late performance starts at 9, I'll leave a ticket for you at the box office. You can watch the show, then we can meet afterward. Just come to my dressing room and I'll answer your questions then, deal?"

Alex nodded.

"All right, Miss Darling," he said. "Until tonight."

Alex stopped on his way out of the building to call his office. He should have done it when Danny called in, but *The Royale* theater only had one phone booth.

"How are things there?" Alex asked when Sherry picked up the phone.

"I got three calls already this week to find lost dogs," she said. "I could be taking that work if you'd show me how to use a finding rune."

Alex had forgotten about Leslie's visit and his brief foray back into the dog finding business. He still didn't know who had sent Sherry to be his secretary and he had a gut reaction to keep her at arm's length from his magic. That said, he needed her to trust him if he was ever going to find out what she was doing in his office and teaching her how to use a finding rune wouldn't really give her any new information. After all, writing a rune and using it were two completely different things.

"It's not a bad idea," he said. "Let me get this LaSalle business taken care of and then I'll have time to teach you."

"You won't regret it, boss," she said with a gleeful tone in her voice.

"So, any messages?"

"Yes," she said. "Charles Grier called a few hours ago. He wants you to call when you can."

"All right," he said. "I'll give him a—"

"Hang on, Boss," Sherry interrupted, a note of tension in her voice.

Alex could her hear her talking to someone in the office but couldn't hear what she was saying.

"Boss," Sherry came back on. "There's an Officer Gibbons from the Central Office here, and he wants to talk to you."

Alex felt a wave of annoyance start to rise. Gibbons was probably sent by Detweiler or Nicholson, wanting him to hold their hands again. He wanted to tell Sherry to have Officer Gibbons wait while he made his way back to the office, but making the man wait wouldn't affect his superiors and they were the ones Alex was irritated with. He ground his teeth, but then remembered Danny's sudden, unexplained recall to the Central Office. Something big was afoot.

"All right," he said. "Put Gibbons on."

17

BLOOD TIES

Two uniformed policemen stood on the corner of an ordinary-looking block in the west side inner ring. Rows of shops lined one side of the street with well-kept apartments opposite. Because this was the inner ring, everything was neat, orderly, and clean, even the street itself.

The only things out of place were the knot of people at the corner with the policemen, and the fact that both of the policemen carried billy clubs. The crowd was made up of men, women, and children of all descriptions and it spilled out into the street, blocking a good deal of traffic. Normally the two policemen would have taken to the street to disperse the mob and get traffic going again, but they just stood on the corner, clubs in hand, not moving.

Because of the traffic problems, Alex had to abandon his grid-locked taxi a block away and walk to where the stone-faced officers stood their vigil. As he reached the corner, he could see what the fuss was about. He'd known that the Empire Bank and Trust had been robbed by the Brothers Boom but he wasn't prepared for the sight. The bank stood in the middle of the block, a sturdy looking brick building that stretched up four stories. It had a glass front, with double glass doors, but Alex only knew that because of the bits of shattered glass that littered the sidewalk and street. The metal frames of the doors hung, twisted from their hinges, and the curtains that had been inside the offices were protruding from the openings where windows had been.

Dozens of police cars lined the street on both sides and a small army of uniformed officers were moving up and down the block taking statements from groups of people that huddled together as if they were cold, despite the late spring warmth. The black coroner's van was parked in front of the bank and, as Alex came around the corner, two white jacketed orderlies opened the rear door to load a body wrapped in a white covering inside. As they opened the door, Alex counted at least three similarly wrapped bodies already inside.

"That's far enough, you," one of the officers said as Alex drew near. He was a large man with very little neck, dark, beady eyes, and shoulders like an ox. As Alex looked the man over it was plain why he'd been put on this duty. There were scars from fighting on his knuckles and his nose had been broken at some point, so badly it hadn't healed properly. The officer's nameplate read, *McIntyre*.

Reaching into his shirt pocket, behind his flip notebook, Alex found one of his business cards.

"Lieutenant Detweiler asked for me," he said, handing the card to Officer McIntyre. "Show this to him or to Detective Nicholson and they'll vouch for me."

McIntyre scrutinized the card thoroughly before giving Alex a penetrating look.

"Wait here," he said.

"Wait a minute," his companion said, looking at Alex. "You're that guy, the Runewright Detective."

Alex didn't want to grin at that, but apparently he couldn't help it.

"Yeah," he said. "That's me."

"It's okay, McIntyre," he said. "The Sergeant said to let him through."

McIntyre held on to the card for a long moment, then he handed it back with a bland expression. He stepped to the side and let Alex pass, watching him out of the corner of his eye as he went. Alex was used to that; most cops didn't have any use for private detectives.

Tucking the business card back into his shirt pocket, Alex crossed the street as he headed up the block. Bits of masonry and glass crunched under his feet as he reached the building. The two white-coated coroner's orderlies came out of the bank building carrying another body, and Alex waited for them to pass before heading inside. By his count that was five dead.

Stepping inside, Alex paused to take in the scene. The bank was a long, fairly narrow building. A counter full of teller stations occupied a long counter along the left-hand wall with a staircase running up to the second floor opposite. At the back of the room stood a gaping hole that showed a narrow alley between the bank and the building behind it.

Chunks of the brick that had made up the back wall littered the floor, and masonry dust covered every surface. Clearly the Brothers Boom had come in that way and if they'd used their explosive rune to escape, the debris would be out back instead of inside. Several uniformed officers were sifting through the debris of what had once been a glassed-in office. Someone had clearly been inside when the back wall blew. Alex could see blood spatter covering the wall by the now-empty windows.

The orderlies came in again and headed behind the teller's counter. Curious, Alex followed and found three more covered bodies laid out.

"It's bad this time," Detective Nicholson's voice reached him.

Alex looked up to find the man descending the stairs. He looked haggard and worn. Alex doubted the captain or the chief were being patient with the situation, to say nothing of the mayor.

"Why did they attack in the middle of the day?" Alex asked as the detective approached.

"We had extra patrol cars outside every bank on the island last night," Nicholson said.

"So they figured it would be easier during the day?"

Nicholson nodded.

"Looks like they were right," he said. "According to the eyewitnesses, the Brothers blew up the back wall, walked in, went upstairs to the vault, stole all the cash, and then just left."

Alex considered that. Even with the use of a vault to hold the cash, the Brothers wouldn't have had much time before a crowd formed.

"Did they open any of the deposit boxes this time?" he asked.

"No," Nicholson said. "They only took the cash."

That explained how the Brothers had gotten away before a big crowd gathered. With wounded people in the bank, no one would question people running out, especially if they weren't carrying piles of cash.

"The Captain is all over us, Lockerby," Detective Nicholson said, looking around at the devastation as if it would reveal some hidden clue. "Seven people were killed, including the bank manager, and eight more were taken to the hospital. The Lieutenant and I need you to find something, anything that will help us find these animals."

Alex nodded in agreement.

"I'll check the vault," he said. "If they left any clues, that's the most likely place."

"It's upstairs," Nicholson said.

That was odd. Vaults were usually lined with steel which made them heavy, and the upstairs seemed like an odd choice.

"Did they take any cash from the tellers?" Alex asked.

"Nope, just from the vault."

Alex nodded and hefted his kit bag.

"I'll start there, then" he said, heading for the stairs.

An hour later, Alex had gone over the vault with silverlight, ghostlight, and even amberlight for good measure. He found nothing useful. There were plenty of fingerprints but no way to tell which, if any, belonged to the Brothers. He could see where they'd opened their vault door in the wall, but the chalk they'd used was ordinary and, of course, he had no way of re-opening their vault, even if he had their key.

"Tell me you've got good news, Lockerby," Detweiler's voice interrupted him as he packed up his kit bag.

"I'm sorry, Lieutenant," he said. "They just didn't spend enough time here."

"Damn it," Detweiler growled. He looked as haggard as Nicholson had. "We need to find these boys. Right now we've got every officer we can get our hands on keeping watch on the rest of the banks in Manhattan. We've even got detectives standing watch."

That explained the reason Danny had been called away.

"We can't keep this up," Detweiler said. "Sooner or later we're going to have to stand down and then these brothers will have the run of the city. Hell, they've got enough cash now they'll probably hole up in the Waldorf Astoria eating caviar and drinking champagne until we give up."

He didn't say that the papers would blame him, but he didn't have to. Alex knew the score. Detweiler could try to push the blame off onto Detective Nicholson, but that wasn't his style. The lieutenant might be a hard-ass, but he was a fair hard-ass.

"Do we know if the brothers went out the front when they left?" Alex asked.

"Eyewitnesses say they went out the way they came in."

Alex picked up his bag.

"Well, I'll check the alley, then. Maybe I'll find something there."

Alex considered the hole in the back of the bank. It was much larger than the first one had been and had blown away the bank's brickwork cleanly. Whoever had developed this rune had refined it quite a bit in a very short amount of time. Whoever had ignited the rune had put it a little too low on the wall and he would have to duck to get out, but other than that, it was perfect.

Grabbing the bare brickwork on top of the hole, Alex ducked out through it. The alley beyond showed almost no sign of the explosion that had taken place there. Most of the debris from the wall had been blown inside the bank, but there were a few stray chunks of masonry and dust to be seen.

The bank was closer to the end of the block where Officer McIntyre and his partner were busy keeping the public at bay, so it stood to reason that the brothers would head that way. The alley between the bank and the buildings behind it was narrow and consisted of hard-packed dirt with a few of the heartier weeds growing up through it.

Moving carefully, Alex hugged the side of the bank as he moved. After a few yards he found a fairly distinct boot print heading away from the hole in the bank wall. He set down his kit and extracted a magnifying glass from it.

"Find something?" Detective Nicholson said, leaning out of the hole in the wall.

"Maybe." Alex leaned close to the print and examined it through the magnifier. "There's bits of plaster and masonry dust in this print," he said. "That means that whoever made this print came from the bank, and since we know that only the Brothers exited this way, this print must be one of theirs.

"Let me take a—ow!"

Nicholson emerged from the hole clutching his hand.

"What happened?" Alex asked, shinnying along the wall to where the debris started.

Nicholson leaned close to the edge of the wall, then looked down at his hand.

"There's a bit of metal sticking out of the wall here, probably a bracket for hanging the plaster. It cut me."

"Wrap your handkerchief around it and help me look for anything I can use to find our robbers," Alex said, turning back to the alley. "Hey," he said, turning back. "Show me where you grabbed the wall."

Alex stepped around Nicholson as the detective pointed at the broken brickwork. When he'd come out, Alex grabbed the top of the hole and ducked under. Nicholson had grabbed the side, and sure enough, there was a bright bit of metal sticking out from the broken brick. As Alex looked, he saw more strips of metal running along the inside of the brickwork. They were exactly what the Detective had guessed them to be, metal mounts to hold the plaster on the inner wall.

Holding the magnifier in over the spot Nicholson indicated, he examined the metal. A stain of bright blood clung to the end, evidence of where it had cut the Detective's hand.

"You grabbed the wall when you came through the hole," Alex said.

"Of course," Nicholson said. "Some detective you are."

"I grabbed it too because the hole is too low," Alex went on, ignoring the dig.

He opened his kit bag and pulled out his oculus, then loaded his multi-lamp with the silverlight burner. The shimmering light quickly showed Alex where the detective's blood covered the sharp metal edge. From there, Alex ran it up and down the wall until he found what he was looking for.

"What is it?" Nicholson asked, holding his handkerchief to his wounded hand.

"Right here," Alex indicated a spot on the wall. Nicholson would see it as just another bit of broken wall, a bit lower than the one that had cut him. To Alex, however, it was the lighthouse at Alexandria. Under the silverlight, it glowed a bright bluish color.

"It looks like our Boom Brothers—"

"Brothers Boom," Nicholson corrected.

Alex gave him a withering look and continued.

"It looks like one of them grabbed this wall," Alex explained. "There's blood right here." He indicated the spot. "And since this was the inside of a wall this morning, it has to be their blood."

"Does that mean you can track them?" Nicholson asked, hope blooming on his face.

Alex swung his lamp back toward the alley.

"There's not enough," he said, sweeping the lantern side to side as he went. "But since we know one of them got cut, it stands to reason that sooner or later we'll find a..."

He stopped and pointed to the ground.

"Blood trail," he finished. On the hard ground of the alley a single drop of blood had hit the dirt and dried. It wasn't much, but it would be enough.

Alex took out his rune book and opened it to the section where he kept finding runes. In former days he only stocked a few in his book, because of the expense. It cost about five dollars to make a finding rune, due to the expensive ruby- and silver-infused inks needed to write them. These days, however, Alex kept a half a dozen in his book at all times. Tearing one out, he placed it on the ground next to the dried blood.

Opening his bag, Alex took out a rolled-up tool pouch and quickly untied the string that kept it closed. Setting it on the ground as well, he unrolled it with a flick of his wrist. Inside were many sewn-in pockets that held various implements Alex might need for collecting evidence and making simple repairs in the field. He ran his fingers along the tools until he came to a folded jackknife occupying a slot between a screwdriver and an adjustable wrench. Taking it out and opening it, Alex used the blade to cut into the dirt next to the bloodstain. Once he'd loosened the soil, he carefully scooped the stained bits onto the rune paper using the flat of the knife blade.

Returning the knife to his tool pack, Alex rolled it back up and dropped it into his bag without bothering to tie it. He carefully picked up the fragile rune paper and folded it into a packet with the bloodstained dirt inside.

It reminded him of the packets of Limelight he had in his pocket.

The dirt thus secured, Alex picked up his kit and went back into the bank.

"Sweep off that table," Alex said to Nicholson.

The detective brushed the dirt and masonry dust from a small, decorative table, and Alex set the rune paper down.

"Go get Detweiler," Alex said, reaching into his kit for his rolled-up map and the cigar box that contained his compass and weights. "Tell him to be ready to move; I should know the exact position of the Brothers Boom in just a minute."

"What if they have one of those warning runes?" Detective Nicholson asked. "Won't they just disappear like last time?"

"Last time my rune still found the missing rune book," Alex said. "This time it will be linked to one of the brothers. Once my rune makes a connection, Detective, we'll have them."

18

THE THEORETICIAN

The needle of Alex's battered brass compass pointed squarely at the *Carlton*, a modest hotel in the east side mid-ring. It was a plain, four-story structure of the same earth-colored brick that gave the brownstone its name. A striped awning stretched out from the entrance to the street and it had a round-topped wooden door atop a short stoop.

"You're sure about this," Lieutenant Detweiler said from the driver's seat of his car. "If your rune didn't tip them off already, I don't want to give them any more warning."

"If you want to go around the block again, Lieutenant, we can," Alex answered. "But the answer's not going to change."

"All right," Detweiler said, pulling over on the opposite side of the street from the *Carlton*. Once he killed the ignition, he nodded at Detective Nicholson in the passenger seat. "Call 'em."

Nicholson picked up the radio mic that hung on the dash and pressed the button on the side with his thumb.

"This is Detective Nicholson to standby cars," he said. "Suspects are at the Carlton hotel, move in. Repeat, move in."

Detweiler and Nicholson got out but when Alex opened his door, the lieutenant pushed it closed again.

"You stay here," he said, leaning down to look through the open window. "I don't want you getting shot."

"Aw, Lieutenant," Alex said, putting on his widest smile. "You do care."

Detweiler rolled his eyes and sneered.

"If they're not inside, I might still need you to find them," he growled.

Alex reached through the window, handing him the battered compass.

"Turn it on its side when you get in there," he said, passing it to Detweiler. "You'll be able to tell if they're above or below you. It'll take you right to them."

The lieutenant accepted the compass without comment, then hurried across the street after Nicholson. As the men reached the opposite sidewalk in front of the hotel, four police cars full of officers arrived. Detweiler led the way into the hotel, holding the compass out in his hand.

Alex sat back in his seat and tried to calm the butterflies in his stomach. The Brothers Boom had already proved that they had no scruples about killing, and there was no way to know what Detweiler, Nicholson, and the policemen were walking into. If they took the room where the brothers were holed up quickly, it might be fine, but if the brothers knew they were coming, it could be an ambush. If they thought they couldn't get away, would they set off one of their empowered blasting runes?

Alex shuddered at the thought.

Based on what he'd seen, Alex knew that rune was capable of destroying the wooden walls and floor of the *Carlton* with ease. Detweiler wouldn't have time to clear the other rooms without alerting the brothers, so there could be innocent bystanders just a few feet away.

He lit a cigarette to calm his nerves and sat watching the hotel. The minutes seemed to stretch out forever. Alex had almost decided that the brothers had skipped out again, somehow tricking his finding rune to another empty hideout when he heard gunshots ring out. Glass from a third story window shattered outward and Alex saw it fall to the sidewalk below. More shots rang out, but he lost count when multiple weapons were brought to bear at once. After an explosive volley, the sounds stopped, and an eerie silence hung in the air.

Orders or no, Alex got out of Detweiler's car and picked up his kit. He crossed the street, reaching the sidewalk just as Detective Nicholson exited the hotel.

"Did you get them?" Alex demanded, a bit more urgently than he probably intended.

"One of them," Nicholson said. "He's hurt pretty bad and unconscious."

Alex turned, looking at the street. A crowd of onlookers had gathered, attracted by the sound of the gunshots. He saw lots of surprised and curious faces, but no one looked angry or frightened.

"If the other brother was out somewhere, he's going to disappear once he sees this," Alex said.

Nicholson nodded in agreement.

"We're searching the rest of the hotel in case he hid inside but we took the room by surprise, so I don't expect we'll find him."

"He wouldn't have any reason to hide if he didn't know you were coming," Alex confirmed. "Do you think the one you have will talk?"

"Even if he will, we won't know for a while," Nicholson said. "He's shot up pretty bad. We've got an ambulance coming for him right now."

"Think he'll make it?"

Nicholson shrugged.

"Captain's on the way over," he said. "Probably the press too. The Lieutenant wants you to take a look at the room before they get here."

Detweiler would want Alex gone before Captain Rooney arrived. He wasn't Alex's biggest fan.

"All right, we'd better get going then."

The room the Brothers Boom had holed up in was about the size of Alex's bedroom at the brownstone. There were two beds, a small desk, and a tiny bathroom. Papers and what appeared to be some of the missing rune books were strewn across the top of the desk and there were several bullet holes in the drawers.

A large bloodstain marred the throw rug in the center of the room and based on the pattern of the bullet holes in the back wall, the unfortunate brother had taken refuge behind one of the beds when the police broke down the door. The officers had hauled the wounded man down to the lobby to await the ambulance, so Alex had the room to himself.

"Work fast, Lockerby," Detweiler said, then stood beside the door to watch.

Alex quickly opened his kit and swept the room with ghostlight. There was magical residue where the brothers opened a vault door, and a place where another alarm rune had been put on the wall. Like the one from before, this one had gone off.

Satisfied there was nothing else, Alex blew out his lamp and checked the room the old-fashioned way. He looked into the bathroom, which consisted of a sink, toilet, and bathtub. The top of the mirror was damp, as was the tub, but the bathroom was otherwise empty.

Two suitcases sat at the foot of each of the beds and Alex opened each. They both contained clothing and toiletries but nothing else. Lastly, Alex checked the desk. The drawers were empty but the books on top were a wealth of information.

"Step it up, Lockerby," Detweiler growled. "The chief just pulled up."

"He'll be a minute talking to the press," Alex said, setting the rune book he'd been examining into a pile on the corner of the desk. "Besides, I think I've got everything I can."

"Well?" Detweiler said, a note of impatience in his voice.

"Our two brothers are Roy and Arlo Harper," he began. "So this is the right room."

"The one we shot didn't have an identity card," Detweiler interrupted. "And at least some of those rune books were stolen. How can you be sure you got the right names?"

Alex pointed to the suitcases.

"They're written on the inside," he said. "They had an alarm rune on the wall here," he indicated the spot. "And it went off, but we got lucky."

"How so?"

"Roy was in the bathtub when it went off. He didn't hear it."

"How do you know the one we shot was Roy?"

"Easy," Alex said with a grin. "Arlo's suitcase smells like silver ink. He spilled some in there and that makes him the runewright. Since the man you shot didn't have a rune book on him and there isn't one here with the name Harper in it, that makes him Roy. Arlo is the one at large and he has his rune book with him."

Detweiler swore as Detective Nicholson stood behind him taking notes.

"I was hoping we had the dangerous one," he said. "Anything else?"

Alex shrugged and pointed to the notebooks and papers on the desk.

"I'd need to study these notes to tell you any more," he said. "What I can tell you is that it looks like Arlo was teaching Roy about runes." He picked up a thick, black notebook and opened it so Detweiler could see. "This has simple runes in the beginning, but they get much more complicated as it goes along. I can tell you from experience it usually takes years to improve that much."

"What makes you think he didn't spend years on it?" the Lieutenant asked.

Alex paged through the book.

"Look how in the beginning the runes are neat and orderly, but look here," he flipped further on. "Back here they're sloppy, almost crude, like he isn't used to writing them."

Detweiler scanned the page and then shrugged.

"I'll take your word for it," he said. "What about the rest of it?"

"Arlo was working on these," Alex said, pointing to the rune papers. "I might be able to use them to anchor a finding rune."

"I thought it just had to be something the person owned," Nicholson said. "If those belong to Roy, won't they work?"

Alex shrugged.

"It depends on whether or not they were important to him," he said. "There has to be an emotional bond between the person and the object in order for the finding rune to establish a connection."

"Give it a try," Detweiler said. "We need a break."

Alex quickly set up his finding rune map and compass, taking care to use one of the rune designs that wasn't done on flash paper. When he activated his own rune, however, the compass didn't even spin.

"What about the rest of this stuff," the Lieutenant asked, pointing to the clothing and the suitcase.

Alex shook his head.

"Nothing in there looks special. If you let me take the notebook, I'll go over it tonight and see if I can learn anything."

Detweiler weighed that idea, then shook his head.

"Better not with the Captain coming up," he said. "Come by in the morning and you can go over it in my office."

Alex promised that he would, then picked up his bag and headed down the back stairs just ahead of the Captain.

Rather than going home, Alex caught a cab over to the west side shop of Charles Grier.

"You have something for me?" he asked, once he'd let himself in.

"Alex," Grier said with a wide smile. He was wearing his heavy apron as he poured powder from a large can into several small jars. "Yes, I found something very interesting," he said, setting the can aside. "You remember I said I remembered something about using alchemy to induce spontaneous magical powers in people?"

"I remember," Alex said as Grier screwed the lids on the jars.

"Well, I thought that I'd read it, so I went back through my old copies of the AAC journal."

"The what?" Alex asked.

"The American Alchemical Conclave," Grier explained as he moved the jars to an empty spot on one of his shelves. "Any licensed alchemist can join. Anyway, they put out a magazine every month with information on different uses for potions or better brewing processes, that sort of thing. It's mostly just junk but every month they solicit an article by someone important in the field."

"What kind of articles do they write?"

"Mostly theoretical," he said. "They all try to one-up each other to prove they're the smartest."

"And that's where you read about Limelight?"

Grier went behind his counter and took out two magazines.

"In this one," he said, opening the first. "An alchemist named Guy Rushton suggested that Pixie Powder wasn't just making people's thoughts into colored lights, but that it was actually granting them magical powers, albeit weak ones. He theorized that if the powder could be brewed down into a concentrate, it might be able to grant people real power."

Alex didn't know what to make of that.

"That makes sense, I guess," he said.

"You're the only one who thinks so," Grier said. "Rushton was practically laughed out of the conclave for the very idea."

"Well if that made him a laughing stock, then why did they let him write another article?"

"Guy Rushton worked for Standard Oil," Grier said. "He has dozens of patents in his name and developed some of the alchemical solutions that turn oil into gasoline and make synthetic rubber possible. He's a legend."

"So his reputation was damaged but he earned it back."

Grier nodded, then opened the second magazine.

"It was this one that really finished Rushton," he explained. "In here, he wrote that a distillation of Pixie Powder might have additional applications for people who already possessed magical power."

"Why would someone who already has magical ability need that?"

Grier's smile became conspiratorial.

"Because, if Rushton was right, drinking the enhanced powder would grant the practitioner enhanced insight. Make them capable of great leaps of magical thought."

"You mean the kinds of leaps that might lead someone to have several dozen patents for their work?" Alex asked, a shiver of excitement running down his back.

"No one realized it at the time," Grier said. "They threw him out of the AAC, but looking back now? The article doesn't sound very theoretical, it sounds like Rushton was speaking from experience."

Alex stood there just trying to get his head around the idea. If Rushton was right, Limelight would do more than give average people magic, it would allow runewrights, alchemists, and sorcerers to make intuitive leaps, design new spells or potions.

Like a new kind of mending rune, one well beyond the abilities of its creator.

Another shiver rand down Alex's back, but this time it was accompanied by a cold knot of fear in his gut. He remembered the dead runewright, how his notebook showed rapid leaps from a basic mending rune to something that had sealed every opening in the room. The spell had been crude and poorly drawn, but it had worked to a degree Alex wouldn't have thought possible.

Crude.

That knot in Alex's stomach clenched harder as he realized where he'd seen that kind of crudely rendered yet advanced rune work before.

"Arlo Harper," he gasped. The rune paper he'd found at the first robbery was crudely drawn, just like the ones in the notebook on the desk had been. Alex had assumed that Arlo was trying to teach Roy to be a runewright, but if Roy had the talent, they would have come up together, taught by the same person. Those notes weren't Roy's, they were Arlo's.

"Pardon?" Grier asked.

Alex's mind reeled at the realization. When he finally focused, he grabbed Grier by the arm.

"Is Guy Rushton still alive?" he gasped.

"I should think so," Grier said.

"Where?"

Grier shook his head.

"I wouldn't know," he said. "Why don't you ask around at Standard Oil, that's where he used to work."

"Do you mind if I take these?" Alex said, pointing to the trade magazines.

"Help yourself."

Alex thanked Grier, dropped the magazines into his kit bag, and headed out into the street. He needed to talk to Iggy right away, and probably Sorsha too. Making up his mind, Alex went around to the alley behind Grier's shop. It was empty and out of sight of the street, so Alex took out the piece of chalk he always kept in his jacket pocket and drew a door on the wall with trembling hands. He tore a vault rune out of his book and opened the door with the oversized key from his ring. With one final check to make sure he was unobserved, Alex stepped inside and closed the door behind him.

The clock on the wall read five eighteen when Alex entered his office. As he expected, Sherry was still there, sitting behind her desk, and she greeted him with a smile.

"I was just about to head home," she admitted. "Three potential clients came in today. I put the folders on your desk."

"I'll have to look at them later," Alex said, somewhat flustered. He tossed his hat on the coat rack then turned to the desk. "I need you to find out where I can find a man named Guy Rushton; he works for Standard Oil."

Sherry wrote that down.

"They'll be closed now, but I'll call them first thing in the morning," she said. "Anything else?"

"Yeah, call Sorsha Kincaid's office and tell her secretary that I need to see her as soon as possible. Tell her I'm heading home and Sorsha can meet me there."

Sherry gave him the look she always gave him when he was forgetting something.

"This came for you," she said, picking up a heavy envelope from her desk and handing it to him. On the front it had his name and the address of his office but no stamp.

"Someone delivered this?" he said.

Sherry nodded.

"A few hours ago."

Alex flipped it over and saw that the envelope had been opened. Of course Sherry had opened it, that was her job, which explained why she knew what he was obviously forgetting. He reached inside and pulled out an ornate ticket, printed in gold ink on heavy paper. His name had been written on a blank line in the center, under the words Admit One, along with today's date. The word *Schubert Theater* had been printed across the top.

Regina Darling.

Alex shut his eyes as everything came rushing back to him. He'd met her just after noon and yet that seemed like such a long time ago.

"There's a message on the back," Sherry said with an amused look.

Flipping it over, Alex read:

Alex, I wanted to make sure you didn't forget. I'll see you after the show. Don't eat, we can go to dinner and I'll answer your questions then. Regina.

He wanted to swear. There wasn't time for this, but Iggy and Callahan were both counting on him, to say nothing of Danny.

"All right," he sighed. "Tell Sorsha's secretary that I'll see her in the morning."

"Sure thing, Boss," Sherry said with a wicked grin. "Who's Regina?"

"Someone who might be a murderess, so wipe that smile off your face," Alex's voice was stern, but he couldn't help laughing.

"Uh huh," Sherry said, her smile going even wider. "You'd better get going if you want to get to the Royale Theater by seven."

She was right and Alex ground his teeth. Even using his vault to get back to the brownstone he'd have to shower and change and then get a cab to the theater district. He wouldn't have much time to talk to Iggy, and he really needed to talk to Iggy.

"See you tomorrow," he said to Sherry, then put his hat back on and headed out the door.

19

THE UNDERSTUDY

It was quarter 'til seven when Alex stepped out of a taxi in front of the *Schubert Theater*. He'd never been to a Broadway play before. To tell the truth, the closest thing to a play he'd ever seen was the Christmas pageant Father Harry put on every year at the mission. Iggy had insisted that he wear his tuxedo and one look around told Alex it had been a good call.

Since his ticket didn't have anything on it but the name of the theater and the date, Alex approached the glass booth where a girl in a gilded uniform sold tickets. She smiled at him and turned the ticket over.

"This is for Miss Darling's private box," she said. "Go up the right-hand stair and show it to the attendant."

Alex thanked her and headed inside.

The lobby of the theater was relatively small, with a set of double doors that led into the seating area and two staircases running up each side. A woman in a pillbox hat and a braided coat gave him a program before he headed up the stairs to the balcony level. At the top, a man in the theater's uniform stood beside a velvet rope, blocking access to the hall beyond the balcony doors. After looking at the ticket, he removed the rope and directed Alex to Box C, behind the third door on the left.

The box was just a private balcony area with two rows of seats and an aisle in the middle. When Alex arrived, it was empty, so he went down to the front row and sat down. Below him, the orchestra was tuning up and well-dressed patrons were milling about, making their way to their seats.

With nothing else to do while he waited, Alex opened the program book. The inside cover had pictures of all the major actors and actresses who appeared in the play. The facing page had a picture that stopped Alex short.

It was Dolly Anderson.

He did a double take and stared at the photograph. It was the same one the papers had used after Dolly's death, the one that had revitalized Maybelle Leone's business.

His eyes darted to the printing below the picture.

Regina Darling as Annabelle Quinn, it read.

Alex looked back at the picture again. This time he could pick out subtle differences between the original picture and this one. The face was almost identical, but it wasn't Dolly, and the pose was slightly off. Whoever had taken the photograph had gone to great lengths to get it as close as possible to the original.

Wondering why, Alex turned back to the inside cover. According to the title page, the name of the play was *The Rogues' Gallery*.

It was the play Benny Harrington wrote in an effort to save his career. The one Dolly Anderson had died performing.

Alex flipped past the cast pages to the description of the play. In the beginning was a section written by Samuel Harrington, listed as Benny's son. He explained that after his father's death, *The Rogues' Gallery* wasn't performed for a decade. Sam had produced revivals of many of his father's old plays and now he was doing *The Rogues' Gallery* because he managed to get Regina Darling for the starring role of Annabelle Quinn.

The house lights dimmed before Alex could read further, and he turned his attention to the stage with renewed interest. He doubted that there were any clues in the play that would help his case, but it couldn't hurt. The play took place during the big war, and opened with the murder of a sailor just back from deployment. The second scene opened in the bedroom of a house. A wardrobe stood in the back next to a door, with a bed on the left and a dressing table on the right. A large free-standing mirror stood next to the table and in the center of the stage, was a small table with a candlestick telephone on it.

Alex got goosebumps when it began to ring.

A moment later a beautiful woman that could only be Regina entered through the door and went to the phone. She picked it up and had a one-sided conversation. From the context, the audience understood that her husband, a police detective, had been called to the scene of a murder and wouldn't be home for dinner. When Regina finally put the phone down, Alex let out a pent-up breath he didn't realize he'd been holding.

From there, the play proceeded like a standard mystery story. Annabelle Quinn was pulled into the murder of the sailor when her husband was wrongly implicated. She had several close calls with the titular rogues' gallery of the title, and in the end, she discovered the identity of the real killer and exonerated her husband. The twist was that no one believed such a beautiful and delicate woman could have found a killer, so she was forced to trick the guilty party into revealing himself.

It wasn't the best mystery story Alex had encountered, but it was entertaining. The plot was sinister, but Annabelle was plucky and there were moments of humor to offset the dark subject matter. All in all, Alex found himself enjoying it. When Regina and the other cast members came on stage for their curtain call, he stood and applauded with the rest of the audience.

Alex knew it would take Regina some time to change for dinner, so as the lights came up and the audience started to file out, he just sat in the private box. It really was a shame that Dolly had died so tragically. The Rogues' Gallery certainly would have been a hit for Benny Harrington. It could have saved his career, and ultimately his life.

That thought made Alex sit up. He'd been thinking that the death of Dolly Anderson had been about killing her, but what if it had been about killing Harrington, or at least his career? It wasn't the most likely of motives, but so far no one he'd talked to seemed to have a motive for killing Dolly.

Except maybe Regina, he reminded himself.

He stood up, anxious to get his questions answered, and headed back out to the hallway. The man in the braided uniform directed him to a back stair at the end of the hallway that led down to the dressing rooms. Regina's was easy to find; it had a giant gold star on it with her name written in silver painted script.

"Come," a woman's voice said when Alex knocked.

He entered and found himself in a smallish room, dominated by a massive dressing table along the far wall with a mirror that ran up to the ceiling. A couch stood against the right-side wall opposite a free-standing rack that held the various costumes Regina used during the play. Behind the rack was a fabric privacy screen stretched around a metal frame. Alex could see the shadow of a woman projected on it from a light on the other side.

"Miss Darling?" Alex said.

She leaned around the screen and smiled at him.

"Well, you clean up good, Alex," she said with a grin. "I'll just be a minute."

She disappeared behind the screen, but it didn't provide much privacy with the light shining from the other side. Alex could plainly see her silhouette as she pulled off some kind of undergarment, then then she shimmied into a very clingy dress.

"I'm decent now," she called. "Come zip me up."

Alex moved around the curtain and found her standing with her back to him. She wore a dress made from a shimmering silver material that clung to her like it was wet. The zipper in the back was low enough that he could see the small of her back. He was no stranger to zippers; Jessica had him zip her up on many occasions, so he knew that Regina could have easily pulled the zipper at least halfway up without his help. She meant for him to see her this way. She probably put the little lamp on the end table specifically to cast her alluring shadow on the screen.

He took hold of the zipper and gently pulled it up without comment.

"Thanks," Regina said, turning to face him.

It was the first time he'd seen more than her eye close up. She had prominent cheeks with a narrow jaw that came to a soft point. Her eyes were just as green as he remembered, with pert lips and dirty blond, shoulder-length hair that tended toward brown.

"I'm starved," she said, taking Alex's arm. "Are you ready?"

Alex nodded and allowed himself to be led out to the alley between the theater and the next building. Several cabs were there, waiting for the performers, and he headed for the first one. Regina immediately pulled him back.

"Not that one," she said, tugging Alex in the direction of the second cab in the line.

"Why are we taking this one?" Alex asked as he held the door for her.

"That one has thirteen in its cab number," she said as if it were the most normal thing in the world.

"Of course," Alex said with a chuckle. "Silly of me not to notice."

"Don't make fun," she said, elbowing him in the ribs. "Everyone knows that show people are highly superstitious."

Alex flashed back to Ethan Nelson, the theater owner throwing spilled salt over his shoulder.

"I've heard that," he said.

Regina gave the driver the address of the *Rampart Hotel* and he pulled out into traffic.

"So do you believe in ghosts too?" Alex asked, doing his best not to grin.

She gave him an impish grin.

"Of course," she said.

The *Rampart* was a twenty-story hotel tower located squarely in the core. It was also the location of one of the swankiest and most expensive restaurants in the city, *The Skyroom*. Clearly it was one of Regina's regular haunts because as soon as the taxi pulled up, a uniformed bellhop opened the door and greeted the actress by name. She swept into the sumptuous lobby and made a beeline for a lone elevator on the side wall.

At least three hotel employees greeted her as they crossed the floor, as did the elevator operator.

As its name implied, *The Skyroom* occupied the top floor of the hotel with large, angled windows on the outside edges that reached up twenty feet. Each table had a tiny lamp on it and the overall lighting was dim, giving the diners a spectacular view of the nighttime city lights. The middle of the space had a dance floor with a live band beyond it and a bar beyond that.

Several couples were waiting for tables as Alex and Regina arrived. They stood in a large waiting area by the little stand where the tuxedo clad maître d' waited with an earnest expression. The dance floor was packed with people and all the tables Alex could see were full.

"Might be a while before they can get us in," Alex observed.

Regina gave him a sly smile and waggled her eyebrows.

"Rudy?" she called, waving to the tuxedoed man.

When he saw Regina, his dour face split into a grin. Alex was certain the expression was almost unknown to the man otherwise.

"Miss Darling," he said, motioning her forward. "Your usual table is ready."

He led them toward the dance floor, then around the room to the far side. As they went, Alex was aware of other patrons staring and pointing at them. He couldn't hear what they were saying over the music, but the attention was starting to give him the creeps.

Regina squeezed his arm.

"Don't worry about it," she said. "You look great."

The table that Rudy led them to was small and intimate. It sat in the far corner, where it had an almost unobstructed view of the Empire Tower and the surrounding buildings of the core.

"Do you eat here every night?" he asked once they were seated.

"Not every night," she said with an adorable smirk.

Alex waited until the waiter had taken their order before starting in on his questions so as not to be interrupted, but Regina started pointing out the sights of the city beyond their window.

"So," Regina asked as the waiter set a cocktail in front of her. "I was sorry to hear about Margaret LaSalle. What happened?"

It was a ham-fisted attempt to turn the tables on him and he stifled a smile.

"Someone broke into her apartment and killed her," he said. "They tried to make it look like a robbery, but they weren't very good at it."

Alex watched Regina carefully as he spoke. If she were responsible for Margaret's death, she might react to being called incompetent.

"So what did they really want?" she asked with no sign of being ruffled.

"Margaret's new book," Alex said, sipping his scotch.

That got a reaction. Regina was a good actress, but Alex caught the slight widening of her eyes and her shallow gasp before she could cover them.

"The one she was going to base on Dolly's death."

It wasn't a question, just a statement.

"Did Margaret tell you that's why she came to see you?" Alex asked.

"Not at first," Regina said. "She asked me the same questions the police asked all those years ago, so I figured she was writing a book on Dolly and wanted to know if her death was really an accident."

"And what do you think?"

Regina just looked at him for a long moment, then she smiled as she realized that Alex had turned the tables back on her.

"It doesn't matter what I think," she said, sipping her drink. "You believe it, or you wouldn't be here."

Alex just shrugged.

"I'm just trying to figure out who killed Margaret LaSalle," he said.

"And you think it might be me," she said with a devious smile. For someone who had just admitted to being a murder suspect, she didn't seem perturbed.

"I think someone Margaret talked to got worried that she might figure out what really happened to Dolly Anderson," Alex said, putting his cards on the table. "So tell me, Miss Darling, did you have anything to do with Dolly's death?"

The briefest hint of irritation washed across her flawless face, then she smiled.

"It will be a while before our dinner comes," she said. "Dance with me."

When Alex didn't move, she smirked.

"I promise I'll answer any question you have once we're on the dance floor."

Alex stood and led her to the center of the room. The band was playing something slow, so he took her in his arms and they began to move slowly around the dance floor. He didn't want to admit it, but it felt good.

"I'm a woman of my word, Alex," she said, leaning close. "Ask your questions."

"Did you kill Dolly?"

"Ooh," she cooed. "Right to the point. I do love a man who doesn't beat around the bush."

"Did you?"

"No," she said.

"You were her understudy for years," Alex said. "With her connections, Dolly could have blackballed you if you left her."

"But she didn't," Regina said. "It's true my career took off after Dolly died, but that was going to happen anyway."

"Says you," Alex challenged her.

"Not just me," she said, her wry smile never slipping. "I already had a leading role when Dolly died."

"Did Dolly know you were leaving?"

She nodded.

"I loved working for Dolly," Regina said, her look turning serious. "She was always encouraging me, helping me to hone my craft. She tried to get me to strike out on my own for a year. Finally, I decided to go on a few auditions, and do you know what Dolly did?"

"Tell me."

"She wrote me a letter of recommendation, said any production would be lucky to have me. I still have that letter. It's framed on my wall."

She looked away for a moment and Alex had the distinct impression she was trying to master her emotions.

"I didn't kill Dolly Anderson, Alex," she said, looking back up into his eyes. "I loved her. Everybody loved her."

"What about her boyfriend?" Alex asked. According to the papers, he and Dolly had some very embarrassing, very public fights.

Regina snickered at that and her expression turned sly again.

"You mean Claude McClintock?" she said, then she shook her head. "No, Claude didn't kill Dolly."

"Maybe she cheated on him and he found out," Alex said. "Men have killed for less."

"Not Claude," Regina said. It was clear from her voice that she found the idea to be an impossibility.

"Why not?" Alex asked.

"Because their romance was a fiction," she said. "Their agents cooked it up for the gossip magazines. It was a way to keep their names in the papers so the theaters would sell more tickets."

Alex had trouble believing that.

"Maybe it started that way and got serious later," he suggested.

Regina shook her head again.

"There was never anything romantic between Dolly and Claude," she said, "because Claude McClintock, the big Hollywood actor, prefers the company of men."

Alex hadn't seen that coming, and he wasn't sure he was ready to take Regina's word for it.

"Ask around," she said, reading his skeptical expression. "Everyone who worked with him on Broadway knew about it."

If that were true, then it would remove any motive from McClintock. In fact, Dolly being alive to be his fake lover was good for his image. Alex ground his teeth.

"Don't let that worry you, Alex," she said. "I'm sure you've got other suspects, because Lord knows the police had a lot back in the day. Now why don't you take me back to our table? Our food should be there by now, and you can ask me all the rest of your questions."

He took her arm and they went back to the little table in the corner. Alex tried not to give in to frustration, but it was difficult. If what Regina had told him was true, then he could scratch two more suspects from his list. It was starting to look like the police had been right, no one seemed to have had a motive to kill Dolly.

Yet he knew without a doubt that someone had.

It was still possible that Regina or Claude McClintock could have killed Dolly for a less obvious reason, but the kind of emotions that drove a crime of passion were usually easy to discover.

You're assuming that Regina actually told you the truth, he reminded himself.

"What are you thinking?" Regina asked, giving him a hard look. "You've just been sitting there chewing your steak for five minutes. If I didn't know better, I'd think Angelo overcooked it. Or maybe you've just grown bored with your dinner companion."

"Hardly," Alex said, setting down his fork. "I was just going over what you told me."

"More questions?" she said, her amused smile sliding back across her lips.

"I think you've told me what I need to know," Alex said. "I would like to see that letter Dolly wrote you, though."

She raised an eyebrow and her smile became demure.

"Well then," she said. "Why don't you take me dancing for a while longer, then I'll show you Dolly's letter when you escort me home. It's hanging in my bedroom."

20

THE ALCHEMIST

Alex returned to the brownstone early the next morning through the convenience of his vault. The more he used that, the more he wondered how he'd ever lived without it. When he reached his room, he found a note on his bed from Iggy, instructing Alex to wake him the moment he got in.

As he read the note, Alex thought about it, but he was still in his tuxedo and he smelled of Regina's perfume, so he decided to shower first. When he'd finally cleaned up and changed into his regular suit, he headed downstairs to the second floor where Iggy's bedroom was located.

"I'm downstairs," his mentor's voice reached him before he could knock.

Turning, he headed down to the main floor where he found Iggy sitting at the kitchen table in his pajamas with a cigar in his hand. The two trade magazines Charles Grier had loaned Alex were on the table in front of him along with several covered plates.

"I heard the shower, so I got some eggs going," he said, indicating a plate with a silver cover. "There's bread and butter and some sausage, too. Help yourself."

As Alex filled an empty plate and dug in, Iggy turned to the two articles written by Guy Rushton.

"I assume that since you wanted me to read this, that you think there's something to Mr. Rushton's theories?" he said.

Alex had just put a large spoonful of scrambled eggs in his mouth, so he just nodded.

"A potion that could enhance a runewright's cognitive abilities sounds like something out of a Jules Verne novel," he observed.

"Submarines were just things in Verne's books until they weren't," Alex pointed out.

"I assume you have some evidence to suggest that Mr. Rushton's ideas are more than just theories?"

Alex nodded.

"I've got to go over to the Central Office first thing to get some evidence from Lieutenant Detweiler," he said. "I'll get it and meet you and Sorsha over at my office in an hour."

"Why me?" Iggy asked, puffing on his cigar.

"I may have to convince Sorsha that this is serious."

Iggy scoffed at that.

"Give the girl some credit," he said. "I just read these articles and it scared me right down to my socks. You won't have to convince her."

Alex gave him a roguish smile.

"Call it moral support then," he said. "Just be at my office at eight thirty."

"All right," Iggy agreed as Alex shoveled in the last of his breakfast and stood. "I want to know what all of this is about anyway.

Alex took a cab over to the central office, then had to wait for Detweiler to get in. He used the time to call Sorsha and advise her of their impromptu meeting. Once he hung up with her, he called Sherry to advise her.

"Someone just called for you," she reported once Alex finished. "A Gretta Morris from Lloyds of London, do you know her?"

Alex had put her on to an insurance fraud scam a few years ago and she owed him a favor. He'd asked her to look into Ethan Nelson's insurance policy and explain it to him.

"She said to call her when you get a chance," Sherry said once Alex explained.

Alex thanked her, then called Lloyds.

"Hey, Alex," Gretta said when the call connected.

"I assume you found a copy of Ethan's policy," Alex said. "Anything interesting?"

"Well theater isn't really my area," Gretta said. "But I showed it to a friend who does this kind of thing. He said that this is pretty basic stuff. We don't write very many of them, but they're not unknown."

"So what does the policy actually say?"

"Basically, Mr. Nelson paid a substantial premium to insure the play for a period of four weeks," she said. "If the play was a hit, the policy would be void, but in that case the play would run for much longer than four weeks and he'd earn back his premium with ease. If the play was a flop, the policy would pay Nelson the equivalent of six weeks' income at the theater. Since the play closed on the first night, the policy paid out."

It sounded pretty straightforward.

"Is there any reason Nelson would want the play to close?" he pressed.

"Not from the perspective of the insurance policy," Gretta said. "In fact, Nelson stood to make much more money if the play was a hit, so he had every reason to let it run."

"What if the play was just a mediocre hit?" Alex asked.

"The play would have to run at least six weeks for Nelson to earn back the premium he paid plus his regular income," Gretta said. "But my friend said that if the play made it past two weeks it would likely run for at least three months, especially with Benny Harrington's reputation. If it wasn't great, it would have closed before the third week."

"All right," Alex sighed. "Thanks, Gretta."

He hung up, chewing his lip. His list of suspects in Dolly Anderson's death was getting anemically thin. He ground his teeth as he made his way back to the benches that occupied most of the main floor of the Central office to wait for Detweiler.

When Lieutenant Detweiler finally arrived, Alex asked him for Arlo Harper's notebook and the random rune papers they'd found at the first crime scene and in the hotel room. The lieutenant didn't want to give them up, but Alex pointed out he could give them to Alex or he could be ordered to give them to Sorsha. He chose the former so long as Alex promised to keep him in the loop. Considering that eight people were dead because of the Brothers Boom, Alex agreed.

Using the janitor's closet on the fifth floor of the Central Office, Alex simply opened a door to his vault and went through to his secondary office. He arrived just a little after 8:30 and found Sorsha and Iggy sitting in his waiting room while Sherry made coffee. She cast him a dour look, then looked meaningfully at the coffee pot.

He was supposed to get coffee from Marnie on his way in on Friday, but it had escaped him in the hustle of the morning. Still, it looked like Sherry had anticipated him, probably because of Iggy and Sorsha's presence. As he turned his attention to his guests, something about his last visit to Marnie tickled his synapses, but a scowl from Sorsha drove the feeling from his mind.

"I appreciate you calling this meeting to reveal whatever it is you're onto, Mr. Lockerby."

The way she said 'Mr. Lockerby' sent a chill down Alex's back.

"But in the future, I would appreciate you telling me important news when you get it, not put it off to go out on the town with some doxy."

"How?" Alex began, but Sorsha reached into thin air and produced a copy of the morning paper, already open to the theater section. On the front page was a picture of Alex holding Regina in his arms as they danced. The picture made them look scandalously intimate. Above the picture, the headline read, *Regina Darling dating Famous Runewright Detective*.

The story below suggested that Alex was no stranger to beautiful and powerful women, having been seen in public with Sorsha Kincaid on several occasions, including at a reception for failed mayoral candidate William Ashford and recently dancing with her at the *Emerald*

Room. As Alex read, his cheeks flushed and he could see why the sorceress was angry; the article implied that Alex had dumped her in favor of Regina.

As soon as he finished reading, Sorsha opened her mouth to give him a piece of her mind, but he spoke first.

"I had nothing to do with this," he said, handing her back the paper. "I was working a case last night."

"Yes," Sorsha mocked him, holding up the picture. "I can see that."

"As for not telling you important information," he went on, trying to change the subject. "Telling you last night wouldn't have done any good, because there's nothing you could have done till this morning anyway."

She gave him an icy stare for a long moment then finally shrugged.

"Well you got us all out here," she said, standing. "Are you going to tell us what you've learned?"

Alex conducted them into his office, but caught sight of Sherry laughing behind her hand as he closed his office door. He had the sinking feeling that he wouldn't hear the end of the newspaper story for some time.

Once he got Sorsha and Iggy seated, he opened his kit and took out the notebook and papers belonging to Arlo Harper, then the ones belonging to the unfortunate runewright with the killer mending rune, and lastly he added the two articles by Guy Rushton. He explained Rushton's theories, how he believed a refined version of Pixie Powder could induce real magical powers in ordinary people and how he further theorized it could give empowered people intuitive leaps.

"That sounds fantastical," Sorsha said when Alex paused. "But that runewright who was trying to make a better mending spell..." She shivered at the memory of the sightless, mouthless man and his wife. Alex didn't blame her.

"I don't think he was the only one using Limelight," Alex went on. He opened the dead runewright's notebook and showed how the early constructs in the book were neat but simple. "The more advanced they get, the more chaotic they are. It's as if he forgot how to draw basic symbols."

"People under the influence of mind-altering drugs often lose muscle coordination," Iggy said.

"Now look at this," Alex said, putting Arlo Harper's notebook on the desk where Sorsha and Iggy could see. "Look how this barrier rune is fairly well drawn." He turned a few pages and the rune became more and more unrecognizable as the line work became wavy and imprecise.

Sorsha reached up and turned a few more pages.

"It's getting better here," she said, pointing to a much straighter line.

"But it's also simpler," Iggy said.

"It goes back to the basic barrier rune," Alex said. "I don't know why, but it doesn't matter. This is the same progression we saw with the dead runewright. I think both he and Arlo Harper are using Limelight to enhance their rune constructs."

Sorsha swore, something she almost never did.

"Harper and the other runewright seem to be less skilled examples of your craft," she said to Alex and Iggy. "What could someone like you do with this?"

"I shudder to think," Iggy said. "There's a reason you were tasked by the government to recover the Archimedean Monograph; the constructs in it are reputed to be extremely powerful, which means they are equally dangerous. This," he tapped Arlo's notebook, "this could create a dozen Monographs if it fell into the wrong hands."

Alex whistled at the thought.

"We need to find Mr. Rushton," Sorsha said. "Find out if he actually did this or if he at least knows how it was done. With any luck he's the one making Limelight."

"We'd better hope so," Alex said. "Because if he's not, I don't know how we're going to find out who is."

"I think you're wrong about something," Iggy said. As Alex and Sorsha talked, he'd been paging back and forth through Arlo's notebook.

"Oh?" Alex said, curious.

"Notice how the rune goes from simple to complex and back to simple again," he said, turning the pages for them.

"We did notice," Sorsha said.

"But also notice how the line work goes from clean to almost indistinct and then back to clean. I think that's because the drug was wearing off."

Alex hadn't considered that.

"So Limelight grants some kind of insight, but when it wears off, the insight itself is lost?"

"Exactly," Iggy said.

"That doesn't make any sense," Sorsha countered. "Why doesn't he just recopy the symbols from the one in the middle?"

"Because rune magic doesn't work that way," Iggy said, his voice changing to his professorial speech pattern. "If I gave you this rune," he said, pointing to the basic barrier rune, "I'm sure you could make a reasonable copy of it. If you practiced, you could probably make several in the space of only a few minutes. But no matter how good you got at reproducing the symbols, they would never be runes."

"But I'm not a runewright," she said as if that answered everything.

"And that's why this is important," Iggy went on. "For a runewright to turn a mass of drawn symbols into a runic construct, he must imbue the symbols with magic as he writes them. Not just magic, but intent."

"When I write a rune," Alex explained, "I have to know what each part is supposed to do and understand how that piece fits into the construct as a whole."

Sorsha nodded, understanding at last.

"So, you think that this Harper fellow could write this complicated rune when he was under the influence of Limelight, but," she paged back to the simple one, "once the drug wore off, he could only do this because he didn't understand how the complicated one works."

"Exactly," Iggy said with the broad smile he always gave Alex for learning something new.

"So how does that help?" Sorsha asked.

Alex smiled at that. Now that he knew what Iggy found, he understood why it was important. He turned to the last rune in Arlo's notebook.

"Why did Arlo Harper write this rune?" he said, pointing to it.

"If you're right," Sorsha said, "It's because the drug wore off."

"Why didn't he just take more and keep working?" Iggy asked.

"He's out of the drug," Sorsha gasped.

"Him and a lot of other people I'd bet," Alex said. "That probably means that the drug is hard to make or maybe it takes time. If it was easy, there would be more on the street."

"So," Sorsha said. "If we find Mr. Rushton, we've got a good chance to stop the supply of Limelight before more people get killed." She stood up. "What are we waiting for?"

Alex put up a restraining hand, then tapped the key on the front of his intercom with his index finger.

"Miss Knox," he said. "Have you found Hal Rushton for me?"

"I called over to Standard Oil and talked with his boss," her voice crackled over the intercom speaker. "He said that Rushton was fired but he wouldn't say why or where he went. I imagine Miss Kincaid will have more luck. His name is Stacy Miller."

She rattled off the address of the Standard Oil office and Alex jotted it down.

"Shall we go?" he asked, standing.

"Yes," Sorsha said with a predatory sneer. "I suddenly have a burning desire to meet Mr. Miller of Standard Oil."

The offices of Standard Oil were in the financial district on the south end of Manhattan and Sorsha's sleek floater dropped them off in front of the building in no time. Stacy Miller was a large man, even taller than Alex with broad shoulders, a thick neck, and a paunchy waist. When he heard that Sorsha Kincaid wanted to see him, he quickly invited her back to his office. He was less forthcoming, however, about the activities and whereabouts of Guy Rushton.

"Mr. Miller," Sorsha said, speaking slowly as one would to a child. "It is quite possible that your former employee created a very dangerous potion while he worked here. Something that appears to be loose in the city."

"I can assure you, Miss Kincaid, our policies—"

"Are of no interest to me," she snapped. "I need to know what Mr. Rushton was doing here. I understand that he no longer works here, but you were his supervisor, you must know what he was working on."

Miller fidgeted nervously at his desk.

"The problem is that the work Guy did here is a trade secret," he explained. "I can't tell you anything about it."

Sorsha sighed and rubbed her temples.

"Perhaps I should give John a call," she said, turning to Alex. "I know he doesn't run this company anymore and he hates to be bothered, but this is important."

Alex knew that the 'John' Sorsha referred to was her fellow sorcerer, John D. Rockefeller who started Standard Oil over forty years ago. Miller seemed to know it too.

"Look, Miss Kincaid I can't tell you anything about Guy's work," he insisted.

"Why did you let him go?" Alex asked. "Surely that's not a trade secret."

Miller thought for a moment, then shook his head.

"No, that's not a secret, I suppose. Guy had been getting erratic," he explained. "He was always a bit eccentric but brilliant people usually are; this was something else though."

"Go on," Sorsha prodded.

"He started keeping odd hours. Sometimes he'd hole up in his lab for days on end. He'd yell at other employees. He went through a dozen lab assistants until we found one that didn't quit after the first week."

"That's why you fired him?" Alex asked.

"No," Miller admitted. "That was just the preamble. One of our accountants was doing inventory when he noticed a large quantity of expensive chemicals and equipment were missing. Guy had been using them on some personal project. That was the last straw. We had to let him go."

Miller seemed on the verge of saying more, but he looked away instead.

"Is that everything?" Alex pressed.

Miller shook his head.

"When we fired Guy, he...he had some kind of mental break. He went mad, ranting and smashing things, said we were trying to steal his legacy."

"What did he mean by that?" Sorsha asked.

"I don't know," Miller admitted. "He hadn't been working on anything company related for weeks and the notes we found after he was removed were just gibberish."

"Removed?" Alex said, catching the word.

"We had to call in men from the hospital to restrain him," Miller said.

"And where is Mr. Rushton now?" Alex asked, pretty sure he already knew the answer.

"Bellevue," Miller said in a low voice. "He was committed by a judge a week after they hauled him out of here. According to the psychiatrist who testified at the hearing, Guy Rushton is completely insane."

21

MAD SCIENCE

Bellevue Hospital was a massive complex of light-colored brick located right up against the East River. Before Andrew Barton expanded his power capacity, it was in the outer ring, though only barely, since that part of the city was where the outer ring was the thinnest, barely a block and a half wide. It was one of many hospitals in Manhattan, but most New Yorkers knew it because of its sanatorium.

As little as three years ago, crawlers wouldn't have run to Bellevue, despite its being a major hospital, because of their inability to get reliable power in the outer ring. With sky-crawlers carrying their own power in their rails, however, Bellevue now had a large, well-used station right out front. In the old days, that's how Alex would have arrived, not in a sleek, black floater being driven by a private chauffeur. At least there wouldn't be any gossip-hungry reporters here, waiting to take his picture.

The pretty nurse at the desk outside the secure wing was polite enough, but it was clear that since neither he nor Sorsha were here to see a relative, she wasn't keen on helping. Finally Sorsha had enough and gave the girl an ultimatum complete with her echoing sorceress voice and glowing ice-blue eyes. She didn't levitate off the floor or send a howling wind blowing through the room, but she might as well have. The petite nun fled in terror to summon the doctor in charge. He turned out to be a tall man in his mid-forties with a salt and pepper mustache that reminded Alex of Iggy's, and a band of short dark hair around his bald pate.

"I would appreciate your not terrorizing the staff," he said to Sorsha, showing more pluck that Alex would have expected. "I'm Doctor Christopher, and I would be happy to assist you."

Sorsha was still angry and Alex could see her trying to mitigate her attitude based on the reasonable tone of the Doctor.

"We need to see a patient here," she said. "Mr. Guy Rushton."

"Since you've already said you aren't family, I have to ask why?" Dr. Christopher said.

"I am a consultant with the FBI," Sorsha said, firmly back in control of herself. "Mr. Rushton may have created an alchemical formula that is being used in several crimes. We need to ask him about it."

Dr. Christopher seemed to think about his response for a long moment.

"Well, I can let you see Guy, of course," he said. "But I don't know how helpful that will be."

He directed Alex and Sorsha to follow, and led them through several corridors and four locked doors until they came to a large recreation room. A dozen people or more were gathered there, sitting quietly, reading, or listening to a baseball game on the radio.

"That's Guy," the Doctor said, pointing to an emaciated looking man sitting alone at a table. He had an angular face with olive skin, black hair and a two-day growth of beard. As Alex and Sorsha watched, Rushton was writing furiously on a notepad, sending his disheveled hair flying as he moved.

"I'll wait here," Dr. Christopher said. "Guy sometimes gets agitated around the staff."

Alex wanted to ask why, but Sorsha pushed through the door and he had to hurry to keep up. Guy Rushton didn't notice their approach as they crossed the tiled floor. He didn't even look up when they sat down at his table.

"Mr. Rushton," Sorsha finally commented, to get his attention.

Rushton looked up, startled. Despite his wild appearance, Alex thought he saw a clever intelligence behind his dark eyes.

"Who are you?" he demanded in the voice of a man too busy to be interrupted.

Sorsha introduced herself and then Alex.

"We wanted to ask you about a chemical you might have developed," she continued. "It's called Limelight."

At the mention of the name, hope bloomed in Rushton's eyes and his breathing quickened.

"Are you here from the fifteenth floor?" he asked in an eager voice. "Are you my new assistants? They fired that last one, right before they sent me here. They said he violated company policy. But that's not right," he said, raising his voice. "I have access to whatever I want, that's what they said. I'm a valuable employee, after all."

Alex and Sorsha exchanged nervous glances. If they hadn't known the man's history, Rushton wouldn't be making any sense at all.

"We aren't from your former employer," Alex said. "We think someone is making Limelight and—"

"What?" Rushton demanded, outrage plain on his face. "I still have more research to do on that. I didn't sign off on production. They can't—"

"Mr. Rushton," Sorsha said, forcefully. "We're trying to find the person making Limelight and stop them."

"Good," he said, still looking indignant. "Tell those suits up on the fifteenth floor that I need my supplies. How do they expect me to work like this?" He pointed at his notebook. From what Alex could see, it was filled with disjointed scribbling and half-formed ideas.

"What can you tell us about Limelight?" Sorsha asked. "If you are the one who developed it, who else would know about it?"

"No one knows about it," he said, indignant again. "It's not ready yet. It's not..."

He trailed off and then began turning the pages of his notepad.

"Mr. Rushton?" Alex prompted.

"Here," he said, pulling a rumpled piece of paper out from between two pages. It was white instead of yellow so Alex could tell it didn't belong to this notepad. "Tell those empty suits on the fifteenth floor that I can have the chemical ready soon, I just need my equipment. Oh, and I'll need a new assistant."

Alex took the paper and looked at it. It contained a list of the various types of glassware, tubing, and burners alchemists required to do their work.

As soon as Alex took the paper, Rushton went back to scribbling on his notepad. Sorsha tried to engage him again, but he shooed them away. She clenched her fist at that, but Alex put a restraining hand on her arm.

"Let's go talk to the doctor," he said under his breath.

She sighed and nodded, and then they withdrew to the hallway again.

"Is he always like that?" Alex asked the doctor once the doors were shut again.

Dr. Christopher shrugged.

"Hal is lost in his work," he said. "That's why his former employers called us. To him nothing exists outside his research."

"I saw some of what he was writing," Alex said. "That doesn't look like research, it looks like gibberish."

"It is," Christopher confirmed.

"He used to be a brilliant man," Sorsha said. "What happened?"

"The best his employers could tell, Guy was exposed to something dangerous while he was working. It had a toxic effect on his mind, and now he can't distinguish reality from nonsense. If I didn't know better, I'd say he was suffering from addiction," Christopher went on. "But in all the time he's been here, Guy has shown no signs of withdrawal, he just seems to have a desperate need to work."

Alex didn't find that surprising. If Iggy was right about how Limelight worked, Rushton would be desperate for more, so he could continue working on whatever he'd thought up the last time he had some.

Sorsha thanked Dr. Christopher and they showed themselves out.

"What do you think?" she asked once they were back on the street.

Alex sighed and shook his head.

"I think we're no closer to finding out where the Limelight is coming from than we were before," he said.

"What about that list Rushton gave you?"

Alex pulled it out and showed it to the sorceress.

"It looks like a list of standard alchemy equipment," he said. "I guess I could show it to Grier and see if he can make anything out of it."

"Do it," she said. "I'll go pick up Redhorn and Mendes then go lean on that Broker fellow."

Alex doubted Jeremy Brewer would still be in the Emerald Room. After his encounter with Sorsha, who represented both the New York Six and the FBI, Alex suspected he would have sought a different location to do business.

"Good luck," he said as she got into her car.

"Call me the moment you learn anything," she said, then he shut her door and her car lifted up into the morning sky.

Since Charles Grier's shop was all the way on the west side, Alex decided to stop by his office instead of going straight there.

"About time you got back," Sherry greeted him when he came in. She sat behind her desk with a distinctly harried look. "Everybody's been calling for you."

Alex gave her a quizzical look. He could only think of a few people who might have called for him, and that shouldn't have kept Sherry all that busy.

"Did you forget your picture was in the paper?" Sherry said. Her eyebrows were drawn together like a scowl, but her lips formed a mocking smile. "I've had at least a dozen calls about legitimate cases, ten potential cheating spouses, eleven lost pets, and one proposal of marriage."

"For you or me?" Alex asked, stifling a chuckle. He'd only had his name in the paper a few times before, but it had always brought in business, as well as its fair share of crazy people. "Sort the legitimate work, refer the cheating spouses to other P.I.s, pick a few lost pet cases

I can train you on and have them bring in something to use as a rune link."

"What about the proposal?" Sherry said with barely contained mirth. "It was for you, by the way."

"Get a picture of her along with her financial status."

Sherry's mirth turned to scorn.

"Very funny," she said with sarcasm practically dripping from her lips.

"If that's it," Alex said, hanging up his hat and heading for his office, "I've got a call to make and then I might go out again."

"There were two other calls," Sherry said. She tore off the top two pages of one of her note pads and stood. "Danny wants to talk to you as soon as possible," she said, handing him one of the papers.

"And the other?"

Sherry's mocking smile returned.

"Miss Regina Darling called for you. She was quite irritated when I told her you were out. I'm not sure she believed me." Sherry handed him the second paper with Regina's name and a telephone number on it. "Apparently you made quite an impression."

Alex bit the inside of his lip to keep from blushing and accepted the paper.

"Thanks," was all he said before entering his office and closing the door.

He stood there for a moment, staring at the yellow paper with Regina's number on it. It had been almost two years since Jessica died, and the closest thing he'd had to a date was when he danced with Sorsha at the Emerald Room. The idea that Regina might want a relationship was something that he hadn't even considered. After all, if the gossip rags were to be believed, actresses like her fell in and out of relationships on a weekly basis.

Feeling a bit better with that thought firmly in mind, Alex sat behind his desk and called Danny.

"It's about time you got in," Danny said in a grumpy voice.

Alex figured Danny would be sore about his not calling first thing in the morning, but by his reckoning he had a good excuse. Still, something about the tone of Danny's voice was off.

"You saw the paper," he guessed.

"How'd you know?" Danny said with a laugh.

"People's voices have a warmer tone when they're smiling," Alex explained. "It's the reason some singers smile when they work."

"Really?" Danny asked, and it was Alex's turn to smile. Danny was a great detective, but he didn't have the advantage of Iggy's tutelage. "So," Danny said, the smile back in his voice. "I take it your investigation went well last night? Just how late did you stay out?"

"Miss Darling insisted she would only answer questions over dinner," Alex said in a deadpan voice.

"Sure she did," Danny said in the most insincere voice he could muster.

"Anyway," Alex said, attempting to get the conversation back on the case. "She didn't have any motive to kill Dolly Anderson."

"So Dolly wasn't holding her career back? Are you sure?"

Alex explained about the letter Regina had shown him.

"She let me hang on to it and the theater manager who hired Regina is still alive, so we can double check just to be sure."

Danny sighed.

"We're about out of suspects," he said. "The only other one I can think of is Sam Harrington."

"The playwright's son?" Alex said, remembering the blurb he'd read for the play last night. "I assume he would have known Dolly fifteen years ago, but what makes you think he would want to kill her?"

"He's been putting on revivals of his father's old plays," Danny explained. "He's made quite a bit of money at it too, but that's all recent. When his father, Benny, was alive, Sam hated him."

"Why?"

"According to the information I got, Benny Harrington's work didn't sit well with his wife, Sam's mother. She was convinced he was having affairs with the actresses from his plays, you know, making them earn the part."

"I'm familiar with the idea of a casting couch," Alex said. "Is there any evidence that Benny did anything like that?"

"No," Danny said. "In fact, the wife hired several private investigators to find out and they always came up empty, but she convinced herself Benny was paying them off to lie."

"Sounds like she was unstable."

"That's an understatement," Danny said. "When Sam was seventeen, she hung herself."

"And Sam blamed his father," Alex guessed. "So he kills Dolly to spike his father's career and ruin him."

"It's as good a motive as any," Danny said. "He's living at an inner-ring apartment building near the theater district. I was about to head over there to interview him, you want to tag along?"

Alex did, but the scrap of paper with Guy Rushton's equipment request was sitting on his desk right next to Regina's number.

"I can't," he said, then he explained about his morning with Sorsha. "I've got to follow up on this thing or the FBI will have my hide." It was a bit of an exaggeration but Sorsha would kill him if he divulged the nature of her case to anyone, even Danny.

"All right," Danny said, a bit dejected. "Call me later if you get free and I'll fill you in."

Alex promised that he would and hung up. He toyed with just skipping the yellow note but sighed and picked it up.

"Well, it's about time," Regina's voice reached him when the call connected. "Here I am with a case for you and you're not even at work."

Alex was a bit taken aback by that. If Regina wanted to ask him about a job, she could have done it easily last night.

"Sorry," he said. "I had to go out on a case first thing this morning. What can I do for you?"

"I've lost something and I need you to find it," she said. "That's what you're best at, right?"

"I am pretty good," Alex hedged. "Why don't you tell me what happened?"

"It was the strangest thing," she said in an irritable voice. "When I fell asleep last night there was a man in my bed, and when I woke up... he was gone. I can't remember that ever happening before; something bad must have happened."

"As I said, I had an early case," Alex said. "I should have left a note."

"At least," Regina's voice was almost as frosty as Sorsha could get. "I'm very upset."

She didn't sound the least bit upset, but Alex knew better than to contradict her.

"I'm sorry," he said, and meant it.

"Well," she said after a pause. "I suppose that's a decent apology. I'll let you make it up to me over dinner."

"I can't tonight," Alex said. "I've got several cases to work on and I'll be at it till late."

This time the pause was longer.

"I've got two matinee shows tomorrow," Regina said. "I'll be exhausted. I guess Monday will have to do."

"Pick you up after work or do you want to eat before?"

"After, Alex," she said in a mothering voice. "Always after. Even experienced actresses get butterflies now and then and that's never good on a full stomach. Wear a suit this time," she continued. "I know a little place where there won't be any photographers."

Alex wanted to say no, but as Regina spoke, he found himself smiling.

"All right," he said. "I'll see you Monday. Looking forward to it."

That elicited a giggle from Regina.

"I should hope so," she said, then she hung up without another word.

Alex set the phone down, then flipped open his notebook and wrote Regina's phone number in it. He wanted to take the time to think through his feelings about the actress, but Guy Rushton's list was still sitting in front of him.

"I've got something for you," Alex said once he got Grier on the phone. He explained about finding Guy Rushton and his condition.

"So you think he used the Limelight powder himself," Grier guessed when Alex finished.

"It's a good bet," Alex said. "His notes were just as nonsensical as Arlo Harper's. Do you know how to make Pixie Powder?"

"Of course," Grier said. "It's not very complicated."

"Well Rushton gave me a list of equipment he said he needs. If I get this to you, do you think you can tell me if it's for making Limelight?"

"It would almost have to be," Grier said. "But if Limelight is just enhanced Pixie Powder, I should be able to tell you once I get the recipe."

"All right, I'll come by and drop off—"

Alex's office door burst open and he looked up to find Sherry giving him a wild-eyed look.

"Sorry boss," she said, regaining her composure. "Lieutenant Detweiler is on the phone. He says it's extremely urgent."

"Tell him I'll be right there," Alex said, then he raised the phone receiver back to his ear.

"Can I read you this list over the phone, Charles?" he asked. "I don't think I'll be able to come by today and I need you to get on this as soon as you can."

Grier agreed and Alex read him Rushton's list line by line while the alchemist copied it down on the other end. When he finished, Alex said goodbye to Grier and pressed the key that would transfer the call to the front office line.

"What's the good word, Lieutenant?" he said as the line connected.

"I need you to get your ass over to the morgue right now," he said in a voice that was quiet and earnest. "And bring your bag of tricks. Hell, bring every trick you've got."

"What's happened?"

"We just heard from Arlo Harper," Detweiler said. "He's demanding that we release Roy or he's going to plant one of those rune bombs somewhere crowded and set it off."

"Are you going to do it?"

"I'd love to," Detweiler said. "But Roy Harper died last night in the hospital. Now meet me at the morgue and help me find this lunatic before he brings a building down on a crowd of people."

22

ELEMENTARY

When Alex reached the morgue, he found Detweiler, Nicholson, Dr. Wagner, and Captain Rooney all waiting in one of the operating theaters. Rooney was tall and broad-shouldered with big hands and a big nose in the center of his face. He had red hair, pale skin, and a dislike of private investigators in general and Alex specifically.

It had been a while since Alex had seen the captain, and he looked thinner and more careworn. Detweiler looked agitated, shifting from foot to foot like a racehorse in the starting gate. The only one not affected, it seemed, was Dr. Wagner, who gave Alex the impression that he was missing lunch to be here and he wasn't happy about that.

A gurney stood in the middle of the room with Roy Harper's body laid out on it, and boxes containing the evidence the police collected at the hotel were stacked in the corner.

"Finally," Captain Rooney said when Alex came in. "If you're going to work with us, you could at least get a closer office." He turned to Detweiler. "Get him up to speed, we're burning daylight."

"Arlo wants his brother back and he's going to blow up a bunch of innocent people if you don't give him up," Alex said. "So you need me to find him fast."

"Do you have any idea how to do that?" Rooney growled.

"How did he make his demand?"

"He called the Central Office," Detweiler said. "He gave us till five o'clock to release Roy."

Alex clenched his jaw at that news; it was already eleven, which only left them six hours. If Arlo had sent a note, that might be traceable. If Roy was alive, Alex could have simply planted a tracking stone in his clothing and followed him to his brother. Lots of things were possible if Roy was still alive, but he wasn't.

"Come on, Lockerby," Lieutenant Detweiler said. "There's got to be something you can use to find Arlo. We've got everything from the hotel here, there's got to be something."

"It has to be something Arlo had an emotional connection to," Alex reminded them. "There might be something like that here, but it could take all day to find it if I try casting my finding rune on things one at a time. Besides, I've only got four finding runes with me and it takes about fifteen minutes for me to write up a new one."

"What about Roy's body?" Detective Nicholson said. "I mean Roy seems to be the only thing Arlo really cares about, right? Shouldn't his body have a connection to Arlo?"

"You'd think, but no," Alex said. "Arlo is connected to Roy the person. As soon as his spirit left his body, that," he pointed at the corpse, "that stopped being Roy Harper, the connection between them is gone."

"We'll just have to try whatever we can and hope we get lucky," Rooney said.

"I do have an idea," Alex said, turning to Rooney. "You remember that case of the guy hit by lighting over by St. Patrick's."

"I passed that and a few other strange deaths on to the FBI," he said.

"Lieutenant Callahan caught that case first and he had me take a look," Alex said. "When the FBI got the case, they wanted me to look at the other cases as well."

"Where is this going, Lockerby?" Rooney asked. "We don't have a lot of time here."

Alex quickly ran through his participation in Sorsha Kincaid's case and how they believed that Arlo Harper had developed his explosive rune using Limelight.

"Are you suggesting we hand this off to the FBI?" Rooney asked. His voice was neutral, and Alex couldn't tell if he liked the idea or not. The Captain was a political animal and washing his hands of any potential deaths might just appeal to him.

"No," Alex said quickly. "I'm saying that right now Miss Kincaid is trying to find the source of the Limelight. If we're right, then Arlo is going to need some, and soon."

"So if we find the source of the drug, we might be able to pick up Arlo," Detective Nicholson said.

"That's pretty thin," Detweiler said.

"Right now, it's all I've got," Alex said. He wasn't excited about embroiling Sorsha in the Police Department's case, but there just wasn't anything else he could think of. "The good news is that I can look into that without costing you any resources."

Rooney considered it as all eyes turned to him, except for Dr. Wagner, who was leaning against an equipment table with a bored look.

"Are you absolutely sure there's no way you can track him with your rune?" the Captain asked.

"I'm sure," Alex said.

"Then get out of here and find out where Arlo Harper is getting his drug," Rooney said. "And have someone from the FBI call me with regular updates."

Alex promised that he would, and scooped up his investigation kit as he headed for the elevator.

Alex called Sorsha's office from the pay phone in the morgue's lobby. Her secretary informed Alex that she was out, and he left word for her to call his office the second she could be reached.

Frustrated, he dropped a nickel in the phone and dialed the number for The Philosopher's Stone.

"Charles," he said as soon as Grier picked up the phone. "Something's come up; have you had a chance to go over that list I gave you?"

"I was planning to look at it over lunch," he said.

"I hate to ask, but this is kind of an emergency," Alex said.

Grier sighed and told Alex to hold the line while he went to get the paper on which he'd written the list.

"All right," he said when he got back. Alex could hear the alchemist mumbling to himself as he went over the list of supplies. "So far this looks like pretty standard stuff," he said. "It's mostly the glassware you'd need for brewing and a few basic chemicals and ingredients."

Alex's heart sank.

"There are one or two odd things on the list," he said. "He's listed Whale Oil and Paraffin, along with a few exotic chemicals."

"Why are those odd?"

"Well, they aren't used in Pixie Powder, so I don't know why he would want them."

Alex felt his pulse racing and he had to keep his voice even as he spoke.

"Are any of them hard to get hold of?"

"No," Grier said. "They're unusual, but most alchemical suppliers should stock them."

It wasn't the answer Alex wanted, but if the ingredients were unusual enough, maybe one of the big suppliers would have records of who bought them.

"This one's an industrial cleaning agent," Grier said. He'd kept talking while Alex's mind wandered. "I don't even know what this one is, so it's probably not for the compound."

"What's that one?" Alex asked, his interest piqued. If Grier didn't know what an ingredient was, that one was bound to be rare.

"Ytterbium," he said. "I've never heard of that before, but Guy Rushton did work for Standard Oil, so he would have access to all kinds of unusual compounds."

Alex slapped himself in the forehead. He'd been coming at this the wrong way. Stacy Miller, Ruston's boss, had said that he'd been fired for abusing company resources. If there was a rare material involved in the making of Limelight, Miller would know about it.

"Thanks, Charles, I owe you one."

"You did save my life," Grier said with a chuckle. "So it's not like we're even."

Alex hung up, then reached for another nickel—until he realized he didn't know the number for the offices of Standard Oil. Hanging up the phone, he headed for the rest rooms, taking out a piece of chalk from his pocket as he went.

A few minutes later, Alex was back in his second office. He left quietly and made his way to his main office.

"Get me the number for Stacy Miller at Standard Oil," he said as he burst through the door into his waiting room.

"Sure thing, boss," Sherry said with a smile. "Give me a minute to find the notepad it's on."

"Also, as soon as you're done, call Miss Kincaid's secretary and tell her that Sorsha needs to teleport here, to this office, as soon as humanly possible."

Sherry's smile slipped and her brows knit with worry.

"Is something wrong, boss?"

Alex almost laughed at that. In recent years his life had become one of long, boring investigations broken up by moments of sheer terror where many lives were at stake.

"Just the usual," he said with a reassuring smile.

By the time he'd hung up his hat, Sherry had Miller's number for him, and Alex headed into his office to make the call.

Stacy Miller hadn't been excessively forthcoming when Alex and Sorsha had been there in the morning, and his secretary was even less so. Alex had to drop Sorsha's name twice to get her to take him seriously. Finally, she acquiesced and got the man himself on the phone.

"I was told that Miss Kincaid needed a brief word," he said when Alex identified himself.

"I'm calling on her behalf," Alex said, speaking quickly. "Thanks to your help this morning, we've made some progress, but I need to ask you one more thing. You said that Mr. Rushton was fired because he was using expensive chemicals and equipment?"

"That's correct," Miller said, obviously eager to be rid of Alex.

"Can you tell me what those were?"

Miller hesitated.

"Well the equipment is one of our trade secrets, but it amounts to special prepared glassware."

"You had a runewright enchant his brewing equipment," Alex guessed.

"How?" Miller stammered. "How do you know that?"

"I'm a runewright, Mr. Miller," Alex said as politely as he could. "The technique isn't unknown."

"I was assured it was," Miller said.

"I have done it myself," Alex said. "In case you ever need someone to help out. What about the chemicals? What was he using that was so costly?"

There was a pause on the line, and Alex could feel Miller weighing what to say.

"I don't suppose it matters," he said at last. "The thing that really made the brass mad was Guy using a large quantity of ytterbium."

Alex remembered that from the list Rushton had given him.

"How much?" he asked.

"Oh, about half a pound."

That didn't sound like a lot to Alex and he said so. Miller laughed.

"If it were butter it wouldn't be," he said. "But ytterbium is one of the most expensive compounds known to man. It's significantly more valuable than gold."

"Do you make that?" Alex asked.

"No, that's DuPont," Miller answered. "They came up with some new process to extract it from impure samples. Look, Mr. Lockerby, I'm really quite busy. Is that all?"

"Yes, Mr. Miller, you've been very helpful."

"I'd appreciate your passing that on to Miss Kincaid," he said, then hung up.

Alex's hands trembled as he finished writing down what Miller had told him. He looked at the clock on the wall facing his desk; it read twelve-eighteen. He needed to get moving.

What I need is Sorsha, he grumbled as he headed back out into his waiting room. Without her, he would run into bureaucratic roadblocks at every turn.

"Sherry," he said as soon as he got his door open. "I need you to get me the number for DuPont's chemical division."

Sherry held up a restraining finger and Alex realized she was already on the phone.

"Actually, he's here now," she said, then held out the receiver. "It's Miss Kincaid," she said.

"Sorsha," Alex said almost before he got the receiver to his ear. "I need—"

"What is it, Alex," she interrupted in an exasperated voice. "We're very busy trying to track down your Broker. He seems to have moved to a new place of business."

"I know how to find the alchemist who's making Limelight," Alex said. "But that's not the problem." He took a deep breath and told her about the situation with the Brothers Boom.

"So you think if we find the alchemist making the Limelight, it will lead us to Mr. Harper before he can set off an explosive rune in a crowded building. So how do we find the alchemist?"

"One of the compounds on Guy Rushton's list was ytterbium," he said. "It's very expensive and DuPont is the only company that supplies it in any volume."

"So if someone else is making Limelight, they'll have to have that compound," Sorsha said, connecting the dots quickly. "And if it's expensive, DuPont is bound to have records of who they sold it to."

"If we find an alchemist on that list, we know who's making the Limelight," Alex finished.

"What if it's a company?"

Alex hadn't thought of that, but it didn't seem likely.

"If a company was making it, then the supply wouldn't have dried up," he said. "It's much more likely that it's an independent alchemist and the delay was because they had to save up to buy more ytterbium. I don't know how long it will take to convince DuPont to give us their records," Alex added. "Or how long it will take to find them, but we're on borrowed time. Go to the DuPont building and I'll meet you over there as soon as I can."

There was a click and the line went dead. As Alex stared at the receiver, there was a soft pop, and three people appeared in his waiting room. Sorsha stumbled forward, and Alex grabbed her before she fell over the top of Sherry's desk. She'd been holding on to Agents Redhorn and Mendes but let go when they all appeared. Agent Redhorn looked pale and was breathing heavily, but seemed otherwise unfazed. Mendes, on the other hand, dropped to all fours, gasping for breath. After a moment of that she scrambled forward, grabbed the trash can beside Sherry's desk and was violently sick in it.

As Mendes emptied her guts into the metal can, Sorsha let Alex hold her while she got control of herself. Eventually her breathing returned to normal, and she pushed away.

"Sorry," Mendes said, miserably, wiping her mouth with a handkerchief.

"The trash bins are out back," Sherry said without even a trace of a smirk. "Rinse the can out before you bring it back."

Mendes nodded and got shakily to her feet. Then she picked up the trash can and headed out into the hall.

"Give me a minute," Sorsha said, still a bit unsteady on her feet. "Then we'll go."

Alex gave her an amused look.

"Do you know where DuPont's chemical division is located?" he asked.

"You and I have both been there before," she said, referring to the affair with Dr. Burnham and his fog machine.

"That's their research lab," Alex said. "Their chemical supply business will be somewhere else."

Sherry cleared her throat, and everyone turned to her. After being sure she had everyone's attention, she tore a paper from her notepad and held it up.

"DuPont Chemical Supply is in the west side mid-ring," she announced. "Just west of Lincoln Square."

Alex reached for the paper, but it jumped out of Sherry's hand and flew to Sorsha.

"Show off," Alex said.

Sorsha ignored him, turning to Agent Redhorn.

"Agent Mendes seems particularly vulnerable to the effects of teleportation," she said. "I want you two to stay here while Alex and I go to DuPont. I may need you to communicate with your superiors or the local police, so stay by the phone."

"Yes, ma'am," Redhorn said. His voice sounded disappointed to be sidelined, but his posture showed relief at not having to teleport again. It was a feeling Alex was intimately familiar with.

"Are you ready?" she said, holding her hand out to Alex.

He sighed and went to retrieve his hat and kit. When he got back, he took Sorsha's hand, and they vanished together.

The trick to teleportation was to control your breathing when you landed. Alex leaned forward with his hands on his knees as he forced himself to take slow, deliberate breaths. He knew from experience that if you gave in to the impulse to gasp for air, it would virtually guarantee you'd vomit like Agent Mendes had. Of course, the more times you teleported in a day, the more likely you would lose your lunch.

As he felt safe to stand up, Alex became aware of his surroundings. He stood in front of a large industrial building made of dark-colored brick. Sorsha had fallen to her hands and knees and was still breathing heavily. Around them a dozen people were gawking at the sight of two people materializing out of thin air.

"You okay?" he asked, kneeling beside the sorceress.

Her platinum blonde hair bobbed up and down as she nodded, still not able to speak. After a minute she allowed Alex to help her up and brushed the dirt from the knees of her slacks.

"It's never just an average day with you, is it Alex?" she said.

Apparently, it wasn't an average day for the front office employees of DuPont Chemical Supply either. Having witnessed Sorsha's arrival, they guessed who she was and were more than eager to help with her requests.

Alex just sat in a comfortable chair in the front room while the company bookkeeper searched their recent records for purchases of ytterbium, then whittled those purchases down to the only one not bought by a large company, government, or university. It was interesting to watch.

Alex had been terrified of Sorsha when he first met her, but now he knew her rather well. He no longer thought of her as a powerful, inscrutable sorceress, one of the New York Six; now she was just Sorsha. Still beautiful and capable, but her mystique was mostly gone for him. Watching as the DuPont employees scurried around in response to her every whim reminded Alex of just who she really was. He didn't like admitting it, but he found that extremely attractive.

While Alex waited, he flirted outrageously with the receptionist, a fiery Spanish girl named Rosa who brought him a cup of coffee that was surprisingly good. Before he met Marnie, he might have been tempted to propose to a temptress that could make coffee like that.

"Are you quite finished?" Sorsha interrupted his banter with Rosa. He gave her a shameless look, then thanked Rosa for the coffee and stood.

"Do we have a name?" he asked.

Sorsha looked as though she was going to dispute the word 'we' but she let it slide.

"Our alchemist is Olivia Thatcher. She has a boutique just south of the core."

Sorsha held out her arm and Alex groaned. For the first time in his life, he regretted having a cup of coffee.

23

OLIVIA

Alex dropped to his knees, coughing and gagging as acrid smoke filled his nostrils. A taste like metal seemed to coat his tongue, and his eyes were watering so much he could barely see the ground. As he fought to keep his stomach from betraying him, he could hear Sorsha gasping in short, shallow breaths somewhere off to his right.

Forcing himself to stand, Alex became aware of yellowish smoke hanging in the air. Grabbing his handkerchief, he pressed it to his nose and mouth while he moved in the direction of Sorsha's gagging noises.

"Alex," she gasped as he reached her.

He grabbed her arm, pulling her to her feet.

"Here," he said, giving her his handkerchief as he pulled her away from the smoke.

"What is all this?" she said, coughing and trying to wave away the smoke.

"I think it's our destination," Alex said. He pointed down the block where they'd materialized, toward a brick building with smoke pouring out from the broken front window. A fire truck stood further down the block and men with hoses were spraying water in through the open window.

"What are the odds that's a coincidence?" Sorsha said in a voice that clearly indicated she didn't think so.

"Based on the broken glass on the street, I'd say Arlo Harper beat us here," Alex observed. "If the fire brigade doesn't get that fire out, we may never know."

Sorsha said something in the deep, echoing voice she used to summon her more impressive powers, and the smoke choking the street suddenly swirled upward into the sky. Alex couldn't help being impressed. He'd learned a lot of powerful and functional magic over his years as a runewright, but sorcerers had an almost casual connection to powers he could only dream of.

It was hard not to be jealous.

As the street cleared of smoke, Sorsha started forward, making a beeline for the firemen.

"Stand aside," she said when she reached them. If anyone had any doubts of her authority, the booming of her magically enhanced voice convinced them.

As the firemen scurried back, the sorceress raised her hands and her still-magnified voice boomed something in the strange magical language she used. As the sounds reverberated off the brickwork of the buildings, she brought her hands together. What should have been a clap was a boom that nearly knocked Alex off his feet. The licking flames rising up over the windowsill were blown out by the blast, vanishing in an instant.

The firemen gaped, open-mouthed, as Sorsha gathered her hands to her chest, then she flicked them forward as if she were throwing peanuts to the pigeons in Central Park. Immediately the glowing embers of the fire died as a frosty grime covered the tables, the walls, and the empty sills of the broken windows.

Alex felt a chill wind roll over him as Sorsha turned to him. She gave him a sly grin and waggled her eyebrows, before turning to the stunned firemen. Alex had always been impressed by the sorceress' magic, but this was the first time he realized that she knew that.

"Show off," he muttered to himself as she thanked the firemen. According to the man in charge, they'd heard the explosion from their station a block over and had come right away. If there was something inside that would help Alex find Arlo Harper, there was a decent chance it hadn't been completely destroyed.

At least he hoped.

He reached for the door. It was still on its hinges, but the glass panel that held the name of the shop had been shattered into tiny glittering shards. When he reached for the knob, however, Sorsha batted his hand away.

"What's the matter with you?" she said, rolling her eyes. "Metal conducts heat."

Alex licked his finger and tapped the knob, feeling the spittle flash to steam as he almost burned his finger. Sorsha gave him a patronizing smile and grabbed the knob, a plume of steam pouring up from where she touched it, then pushed the door open. Alex rolled his eyes at her and stepped inside. A chemical tang still hung in the air, and the floor was covered with broken potion vials, empty component tins, and shattered lab glass.

"This doesn't look like it's going to be useful," Sorsha said, stepping carefully to avoid messing up her expensive shoes. "Do you think you can find anything here?"

"Here?" Alex said. "I doubt it, but this looks like just the shop. There has to be a brew lab where she made her potions. They're usually in the basement."

"There." She pointed to a broken door hanging in a frame.

Alex led the way down a set of wide stairs to a large, open basement. It reminded Alex so much of the lab where he first met Jessica that he stumbled on the bottom step.

"Are you all right?" Sorsha asked from behind him.

Alex nodded, shaking off the feeling. The basement lab had been laid out just like Dr. Kellin's, though this one wasn't nearly as neat. Most of the glassware was shattered and the rubber tubing littered the floor. In the far back of the room, a single brew setup remained intact with a low flame burning under a jar filled with greenish liquid.

"That must have been some explosion," Sorsha said, looking around at the devastation.

"No," Alex said with a shake of his head. "Look at the broken glass." He indicated a large container with a small amount of liquid remaining in its broken bottom. "Whatever this liquid is, it has evaporated off everything except this little puddle here. If it had broken recently, there'd be spatter droplets everywhere."

"What happened then?"

"Remember Guy Rushton? Nothing mattered to him except the Limelight." He pointed to the lone working table.

"You think Olivia Thatcher did this?" she said, indicating the wreckage. "If you're right, then that's where she was making the Limelight."

"If she's the one making it," Alex said.

Sorsha gave him a hard look.

"If she wasn't, then why did your bomber pay her a visit?" she said.

"Just trying not to get ahead of the facts," Alex said as they made their way to the station in the back. "But I suspect you've got it right."

The brew station was a mess. Alex had watched Jessica work a dozen of them and each one had been a bastion of order. Brewing potions was just like cooking, you followed a recipe, exactly as it was written, and you got your result. It required precision. The remaining brew station was an island of chaos, laden with open jars of powder, dripping trays of liquid reagents, and a crumpled page written in a barely legible hand.

"Does this make any sense to you?" Sorsha asked, picking up the paper with the tips of her thumb and forefinger. A brownish liquid dripped from the paper and she quickly held it back over the table.

Alex cocked his head to the side and squinted at the text. Some of it was recognizable, but none of it made any sense, and he said so.

"You'd better let me hang on to that," Alex said as she started to put the paper back down.

She gave him a penetrating look and raised an eyebrow.

"Why do you want it?" she said, suspicion plain in her voice.

"Based on how Guy Rushton reacted to the chance to make more of this stuff," he waved at the brew table, "I figure that paper is very important to Olivia Thatcher. Since her body isn't here, I'm guessing she survived the blast and I can use this," he took the dripping paper, "to find her."

Somehow Sorsha's raised eyebrow went even higher and a sardonic smile spread across her lips.

Olivia Thatcher appeared to be in her late forties. She was thin to the point of appearing undernourished with unkempt brown hair and a wild look in her eyes. Alex's finding rune had led him to Manhattan General where Olivia was being kept for observation. A policeman found her wandering the streets muttering to herself with several cuts on her arms and back. He assumed that she'd been drinking because she was carrying a flask, but that wasn't too unusual for an alchemist.

"Olivia," Sorsha said, once a helpful nurse conducted them to the observation room. "Can you hear me?"

So far the woman hadn't reacted to their presence; she just sat on a chair in the corner mumbling to herself.

"Olivia?"

"Do you have it?" she said, her eyes suddenly focusing on the sorceress. "He took it. He took it!" She grabbed Sorsha's wrist and pulled her close. "I have to get it back. I have to...have to..."

"Who took it?" Alex asked.

"He offered me money," Olivia said. "He had lots of money, but I promised him, promised I wouldn't sell any more."

"You promised the man who offered you money that you wouldn't sell Limelight?" Alex asked.

"No," she said, grabbing Alex's arm as well. "He was mad when I sold it, so I promised I wouldn't do it again. Not even for all that money."

She wasn't as coherent as Alex would like but it sounded like Arlo had bought Limelight from her and then whoever gave her the recipe objected. That would explain why Limelight seemed to be readily available but then disappeared.

"Does this make any sense to you?" Sorsha asked.

Alex nodded and explained what he guessed about Olivia's rambling.

"Olivia," Sorsha said, kneeling down to look into her wild eyes.

"The man who wanted to buy the Limelight—"

"He took it," she said, her grip suddenly tightening on Alex's arm. "I told him I couldn't sell it but he took it anyway. I tried to stop him, tore his coat, but he...he..."

She drifted off and began muttering to herself again.

Sorsha extracted her hand from Olivia's grip, then stood, nodding for Alex to follow her back to the door.

"Why is she like Guy Rushton?" she asked. "I though Limelight was for runewrights."

"According to the article Rushton wrote, it would work for anyone with magical abilities," Alex said. "Even you."

"So she used it, too," Sorsha said.

"I'm guessing she needed it to understand how the Limelight recipe worked."

"That doesn't make any sense," Sorsha said. "How could she use it before she made it?"

"Clearly whoever brought her the recipe also brought her a sample," Alex said. "Once she used it, then she could make more."

"And now Arlo took the Limelight she made," Sorsha said.

"Limelight she was making for someone else," Alex reminded her.

Sorsha nodded.

"We'll deal with him later," she said, pointing to the clock on the wall. It was already after four. "We're running out of time."

Alex ground his teeth in frustration.

"Clearly the missing Limelight is important to Olivia," Sorsha said. "If you use her to find it, then we'll know where Arlo is."

It was a good idea. Alex could use people as the anchor for a finding rune, but it depended on them focusing on the missing item. That wouldn't be a problem with Olivia; he doubted she could focus on anything else.

"It's worth a try," he said, setting down his kit. The room had a small table in the corner, so Alex moved it next to where Olivia sat. The little tin flask she'd been carrying when she was found was the only thing on it, so Alex set it on the window-sill to get it out of the way. He put down his map of Manhattan and used the carved jade figurines to keep it from rolling up.

"Okay Olivia," he said, trying to get her attention. "I'm going to help you find your Limelight."

"He took it," she said, grabbing his hand again.

"I know," Alex said, pressing a folded finding rune into her hand. "I'm going to use a rune to find it for you. That'll be okay, right?"

Olivia looked nervous, but she eventually nodded.

"Just put your hand on this," he said, laying his compass on top of the map. He gently moved her hand, but she resisted, giving him a fearful look. "It's all right," he reassured her.

After a moment's hesitation, Olivia let Alex move her hand to where it was touching the battered brass compass, but when he tried to light the rune paper, she pulled her hand away.

"Put her hand back," Sorsha said. "I'll hold her in place."

"That won't work," Alex said, pulling out his cigarette case. "She'll panic and I'll lose the connection." He lit the cigarette, then dropped the lighter back in his pocket. "Let me try again."

It took almost five minutes, but Alex finally managed to get Olivia's hand back on the map. Whatever the Limelight had done to her mind had left her with the singular focus of making more. She seemed to have moments of lucidity where the competent, professional alchemist shone through, but the rest was garbled and confused, almost childlike. In order to get her hand on the compass, he had to keep her calm and distract her from what he was doing. He held her hand gently in his left hand while he clipped his cigarette between the fingers of his right hand.

When he finally got her relaxed, he rolled his hand over so the burning end of the cigarette made contact with the flash paper. The rune burst into flame far too quickly for Olivia to react. When she noticed it, the flame was gone and only the burning amber rune remained. She looked at it like she remembered, like she knew what it was, but then the fog of confusion descended on her again.

"Thank you, Olivia," Alex said, releasing her wrist. She immediately turned away, muttering to herself about ingredients and brewing.

Turning back to the rune, Alex watched it turn. It pulsed with the vital energy of the magic within but as he looked down, the compass needle was pointing stubbornly northward.

He swore, and Sorsha looked up at him sharply.

"It didn't work," he said by way of explanation.

"Why not?" she demanded, her tone implying that he'd done something wrong.

"If I had to guess, I think Arlo put the Limelight in his vault."

Sorsha looked at the clock, then back at Alex.

"What do we do now?" she asked. "Your bomber is going to kill a bunch of people if we don't do something. Think, damn it."

The rebuke didn't sting Alex. His own thoughts condemned him far worse, but Sorsha's words revealed how powerless she felt. It was a feeling he was sure she hardly ever experienced.

Alex, on the other hand, was quite used to it.

"I need a drink," he muttered.

"What?" Sorsha demanded, her voice almost a shriek.

Alex moved to the window-sill and picked up the silver flask. It probably held a potion, but it was the only possibility available, so he picked it up and unscrewed the lid.

"We have to do something," Sorsha shouted as Alex held the flask under his nose.

He turned to her and laughed.

Rage and something more flowed across the sorceress' porcelain face. She raised her hand to slap him, but he held the flask under her nose before she could land the blow.

"Smell it," he said as she started to recoil.

Sorsha hesitated, her desire to be angry with him warring with the need to do something. Finally she moved her nose over the top of the flask and sniffed. Immediately she withdrew and her nose wrinkled.

"What is that?"

"Red Eye," Alex said. "It's one of the cheapest brands of booze out there."

"So?"

Alex pointed at Olivia. She was still muttering to herself, but her clothes were those of a wealthy professional.

"Do you think she drinks Red Eye?"

Sorsha shook her head in confusion.

"It's not hers," Alex explained, almost shouting it. "She went after Arlo and tore his coat."

Sorsha looked like she'd been hit with a shovel.

"It's his flask," she gasped. "Where he keeps his liquor."

Alex nodded, cheeks hurting from the grin that had spread across his face.

"Now that's something important to a man," he said, placing the flask on his map. He quickly fumbled for his rune book and tore out his last finding rune. With trembling hands, he dropped it on the flask, then picked it up again and put the compass between the rune and the flask.

"Don't breathe," he said as he touched his cigarette to the paper. The orange rune burst to life, spinning lazily in circles as it pulsed with power. Below it the needle of the compass turned, slowly at first, then faster and faster until it matched the turning rune. The rune pulsed one final time and burst into a shower of sparks. As they faded, the needle pointed toward the north end of Manhattan.

Alex bared his teeth in a fierce grin.

"Gotcha," he growled.

"Where?" Sorsha said, leaning close.

Alex slid the compass off the flask, being careful not to lose contact with the map. As he moved it toward Central Park it swung around, pointing east first, then south. Following the needle, Alex slid it along until the needle began to spin in lazy circles.

"There," he said, picking up the compass. The map Alex carried wasn't very large, nowhere near as accurate as the one in his map room, but the location under the compass was impossible to miss. Dozens of train tracks all converged on a single location that covered an entire block.

"Grand Central Terminal," Sorsha said it out loud.

Alex didn't bother rolling his map or packing up his figurines, he just swept them all into his bag as he glanced up at the clock.

"Ten minutes to five," he said.

Sorsha reached out and grabbed his arm as her pale eyes glowed from within.

"Plenty of time," she said, then they disappeared.

24

TERMINAL

Alex and Sorsha materialized on the main floor of Grand Central Terminal, right in front of the information counter. Several people jumped back in alarm and then retreated into the crowd. At this time of day, the main floor of the terminal was packed with people, all going to or coming from trains that would take them all over the city and even out to the surrounding state. Alex had been to the terminal in less crowded hours and knew the main floor was mostly one vast, empty space. Now there had to be a couple of hundred people here.

"If your bomber sets off a blast rune here it'll be a massacre," Sorsha said in a low voice.

Remembering his compass, Alex dug it out of his trouser pocket. As he did, he felt no trace of the nausea and disorientation that usually gripped him after a teleport.

Must be the adrenalin.

"Do you see him?" Sorsha asked. She looked a little pale, but that was her normal complexion, so he couldn't tell if she felt any effects of their travel.

"I don't know what he looks like," Alex hissed, holding the compass up. It was pointing toward the back of the building where the stairs went down to the train platforms. He quickly tilted the compass on its side, but the needle stayed level with the horizon.

"He's on this floor," Alex said. As he looked toward the back, he saw a bank of phone booths. Lieutenant Detweiler hadn't told him the exact nature of Arlo's threat, but the only way the runewright would know if his brother had been released was by phone.

"There," he said, indicating the phones.

Sorsha took a step in that direction, but Alex grabbed her shoulder.

She looked up at him angrily, but Alex put a finger to his lips and leaned in close.

"We're not dressed like police, so he probably won't see us coming," Alex said. "But if he does, he might try to set off his blast rune before we can stop him." He looked at the big round clock on top of the information booth's roof. "We still have six minutes. Let's find a transit policeman and have him start ushering people out, discreetly."

Sorsha chewed her lip in thought, then nodded. Looking around, she spotted a uniformed officer standing against the wall near the ticket windows.

"I need to open my vault too," Alex said, as she started off in the policeman's direction.

"We don't have time for that," Sorsha said.

"I want to get my pistol," he insisted. "In case this goes bad."

"I'll deal with your bomber," Sorsha declared. "Having a pistol isn't going to help."

Alex understood that she was right, but the lack of the 1911's weight under his left arm made him feel vulnerable. As they headed to the ticket windows, he dug into his kit bag and pulled out his knuckle duster, dropping it into the right-hand pocket of his suit coat. It would require him to get in close to be effective, but Sorsha was probably right. She'd have Arlo wrapped up from the moment she saw him. Still, Alex felt better having a weapon than not.

"You," Sorsha said stepping up to the policeman and touching the center of his chest with the tip of her index finger. Instantly frost spread across the man's chest and he shivered. "My name is Sorsha Kincaid, I trust I don't need to prove that any further."

It wasn't a question, but the man shook his head vigorously. He was young and fit with a handsome face and dark hair and eyes. Alex noticed that his uniform was neat, with pressed seams in his trousers.

"No, Ma'am," he said.

Sorsha dropped her hand and the frost began to fade as it melted.

"Good," she said in a businesslike manner. "I am a consultant with the FBI, and this," she indicated Alex, "is Mr. Lockerby; he works with the police."

"What can I do for you?" the cop said, a nervous tremor in his voice.

"You read about the Brothers Boom," Alex said. "In the papers."

He nodded.

"Well, we've traced one of them here," Sorsha finished.

The man's eyes went wide as they darted over the packed terminal. That was good; at least he understood the potential danger.

"Easy," Alex said as the man's entire body tensed. "We need you to do two things. First, go tell your sergeant to call the Central Office and get Lieutenant Detweiler over here, 'cause this is his case. Once you've passed on that message to your sergeant, you and every other cop in this building need to start getting people out, quietly."

"Don't shout," Sorsha said. "Don't run. Don't cause a panic, and don't cause a scene. Just tell people that they need to leave and get them moving. Understand?"

When he nodded, she flicked her head in the direction of the security office.

"Go," she said.

Alex was sure they were going to have to tell him not to run, but the young man mastered himself, straightened his uniform shirt, and headed off at a brisk walk.

"Come on," Sorsha said, glancing at the clock. "We've done all we can."

There were only two minutes left as she followed Alex through the crowd following the compass.

"There's too many people," Sorsha said as they forced their way through the massive crowd. "Maybe you should get your gun."

"Firing off a shot would cause a mad rush," he said with a shake of his head. "People would get trampled. If things go bad, I'll try to grab him."

"What good would that do?"

"Well after I got chased by a mind-controlled sorceress last year, I got a new escape rune," Alex said. Sorsha blushed, but Alex didn't press that advantage. "It's not as fancy as my old one, but it will get the job done."

Sorsha looked like she wanted to argue, but the phone booths were close. Alex checked his compass and nodded at one on the end. The privacy door was open, revealing a thin man with unkempt, sandy hair wearing a tan suit. He had a cigarette in his mouth and the ashtray on the little shelf under the phone was full of butts. The worry in his posture and bearing were plain to Alex, as was the piece of crumpled paper in his left hand.

Alex turned in front of Sorsha with his back to Arlo.

"He's got the blasting rune in his hand," he whispered.

"I'll do this quick," she said, leaning around his body. As she did, her eyes flashed with the inner light of her magic. Arlo must have seen it because before Alex could turn, a shot rang out. A bullet hit Sorsha's magical shield right by Alex's right arm and he felt it shatter.

Alex reacted out of instinct, moving himself to cover Sorsha with his back. A second shot followed the first in quick succession, much faster than Alex could move, and dark blood blossomed on the front of Sorsha's vest. She gasped, her eyes wide in shock, and she sagged against Alex.

All around them, people were screaming and running. Two more shots slammed into Alex's back, but his shield rune stopped them. Arlo must have anticipated the intervention of a sorcerer, because he'd prepared spellbreaker runes on his gun.

"Alex," Sorsha gasped, looking around him. "The rune."

He didn't want to let her go but he had no choice, and she sagged to her knees as Alex turned. In the phone booth, Arlo held up the crumpled paper and touched his cigarette to it. Alex expected him to say something, some dying declaration of defiance or of love for his brother, but the young man's face was a mask of indignance and rage. Alex felt his guts tighten as the paper caught fire; he might have time to use his escape rune if he acted immediately, but that would mean leaving Sorsha behind.

He hesitated.

In the instant he did it, Alex knew that hesitation would cost him his life. The blast rune burned with an angry, yellow color. Alex could see how elegant it was, how much of a logical extension of a simple bang rune it was.

Then the rune exploded.

Alex threw his hands up in front of his face, as if that would do anything, but the ear shattering bang and the inevitable heat and force didn't come. Shocked, he peeked around his hands and found a round mass of fire just hanging in the air between Alex and the phone booth. As he watched, Alex could see the fireball slowly expanding, swelling as it went.

"Hurry," Sorsha gasped. She sat on the floor with blood running down her front and a rattling rasp in her breathing. "Cant...hold it..."

Alex didn't wait for her to finish her thought, he turned and charged Arlo Harper. His hand dipped into his pocket for the knuckle duster, but Harper already had his pistol in his hand. He raised it and fired.

Turning his shoulder toward Arlo, Alex ran at him. Two bullets hit his shoulder and his side hard enough to make Alex grunt, then one more traced a burning line of pain across his thigh. Alex didn't know how badly he'd been hit, but it didn't matter as he hit Arlo with all his speed and mass.

The bomber was slammed back into the back of the phone booth and the glass of the privacy door shattered into a shower of cutting shards. Arlo grunted with the force, but he didn't yield. Slamming his gun into Alex's head, he shoved back, managing to push Alex out of the phone booth.

"Alex!" Sorsha screamed.

He knew what was happening — the fireball was expanding faster; she was losing her control. Resisting the urge to confirm his fears by looking at her saved his life. Arlo pointed the gun right in Alex's face, but he was too close. Alex batted it away with his left hand, grabbing Arlo's wrist in the process. Forcing the gun arm upward, Alex brought his right hand up in a haymaker that slammed the knuckleduster into Arlo's gut.

Air rushed out of his lungs and Arlo gasped, trying to get his breath back. Alex didn't give him the chance. Turning with Arlo's wrist still clutched in his left hand, Alex pulled the smaller man out of the phone booth and sent him staggering across the floor. The gun went skittering away, but Arlo had landed near Sorsha's rapidly weakening form. Snarling, he lunged for her, but Alex kicked him in his hip, and he doubled up.

Heat washed over Alex and he could feel air pressure begin to push him. He looked at Sorsha and her eyes were rolling back in her head. The explosion would be loose in seconds. Bending down, Alex grabbed Arlo by the collar, then threw himself to the ground, sticking his leg out toward Sorsha. The sorceress had just enough consciousness left to grab onto him as a blast of air hit Alex like a hammer. He slapped his free hand down on his right forearm just as the heat and force picked him up off the ground.

Something very hard and immovable slammed into Alex and he fell to the ground, stunned. A blue afternoon sky hovered over him with clouds that seemed to take a long time drifting into focus. When they finally did, Alex rolled over, finding himself on a leaf-strewn slab of concrete. Beside him lay Arlo Harper, his clothes smoking, and his head bent at an unnatural angle.

Dead.

He must have hit the wall with his head instead of slamming into it like a belly-flopping diver, like Alex. The impact had broken Arlo's neck.

"Sorsha," Alex gasped. He turned around to find the sorceress slumped over against a soot-stained brick wall. He pressed a trembling hand to her neck and felt a pulse.

"Ugh," she groaned, looking up at him with unfocused eyes. "What...what happened?"

"The rune exploded," Alex said, trying to move her into a more comfortable position.

"People," she managed before grimacing in pain.

"Most of them ran when Arlo started shooting," he said.

"Where?" she gasped.

"South Brother Island in the East River," Alex said. "It's been abandoned ever since Jacob Ruppert's mansion burned down." He waved his hand, indicating the remaining walls of what had once been the mansion.

"Doctor," she gasped, tears of pain running down her cheeks. "Can't teleport..."

Alex pulled his chalk out of his pocket and stood to draw a doorway on the charred brick wall.

"When did you...become a doctor?" Sorsha managed as Alex took out a vault rune and lit it.

"As Father Harry used to say," Alex said as he pulled open the door to his vault. "Oh, ye of little faith."

Alex bent down to pick up the sorceress, but his leg screamed in agony when he took her weight. In the adrenalin rush of the fight and using his escape rune, he'd forgotten that Arlo shot him. Readjusting her weight, Alex tried again, this time with only mild agony. Staggering with the pain, he limped into his vault and made his way down past his little kitchen and bedroom. When he reached the door that led to the brownstone, he stopped.

"Watch," he grunted.

Sorsha dragged her eyes up to meet his. She looked tired, barely coherent.

"Get my watch," he said again, the throbbing in his leg burning like fire. He knew if he put Sorsha down, he wouldn't be able to pick her up again.

Sorsha reached down past her hip and tugged the watch out of Alex's vest pocket.

"Open it," he said. "Then touch it to my chest."

When she did as he instructed, he willed the runes in the watch to activate, then leaned against the door and turned the handle.

"Iggy!" he shouted as he stumbled into his room. He had a momentary thought of leaving Sorsha on his bed and having a rest on his nice, soft floor, but Iggy would need help getting her to the operating theater in his vault.

Alex called for his mentor again and a moment later, he tromped up the stairs and into Alex's room. He looked relieved, as if he'd expected bad news. When he took in the sight of Alex and Sorsha, his face hardened into a look of determination.

"Right," he said, taking chalk from his pocket and drawing a door on Alex's bedroom wall. Taking out his key and a vault rune, he opened the door, then helped Alex forward.

"She's been shot in the chest," Alex said. "Missed the heart."

"Obviously," Iggy said. "If it hit her heart, she'd have been dead long before this. Put her on the table," he said.

Alex did as he was told, reveling in the relief his leg experienced when he was rid of her extra weight. He wanted to sit down. Actually, he wanted to lie down, but Iggy might need help, so he just stood there on his throbbing leg.

Iggy returned to the table with a surgical tray and six potion vials. With no trace of hesitation, he unbuttoned Sorsha's vest, then her shirt, laying them open to reveal her brassiere and an ugly wound just right of center in her chest.

"How long has it been since she was shot?" he asked.

"Ten minutes," Alex guessed. "Maybe fifteen," he hedged, since he didn't know how long he'd been unconscious after using his escape rune. "How bad is it?"

"It's not good," Iggy said, probing the edges of the wound with his fingers. "We need to hurry." Taking out a pair of angled scissors, Iggy cut the strap that kept the two halves of her bra together. Alex turned away but Iggy grabbed his arm.

"Lift her head up," he said, pressing a bottle of something to her lips. She choked and coughed but managed to get it down. Iggy followed that potion with two more, then had Alex lower her back down.

Iggy opened the gold-backed rune book he kept in his surgery, the one with his powerful medical runes. Flipping it open, he tore a page out, then flipped further in and tore out another. Folding them up, he pressed them into Sorsha's wound, then pulled out his gold lighter and flicked it to life.

"Hold her," he said, grabbing Sorsha's arm and pressing it down onto the operating table. Alex did the same with the arm on his side as Iggy touched the flame to the bit of the flash paper that stuck up.

With a flash the runes ignited, a green one and a yellow one that appeared interlocked, each rotating along a different axis. After a moment they burst into showers of multicolored sparks.

As soon as the sparks touched her, Sorsha's eyes snapped open and she tried to lunge off the table. Fresh blood bubbled up from the open wound. The sorceress took two ragged, wheezing breaths, then her back arched and she screamed.

Alex looked at Iggy, but he was watching the wound. Sorsha's body shook as she ran out of air, her muscles so tight she literally couldn't breathe. After what seemed like an eternity, Sorsha slumped down on the table and Alex could see the glint of metal in the wound.

Iggy picked up a pair of surgical tongs and deftly grabbed the bullet from the bleeding wound.

"Good," he said, examining the little slug. "It's in one piece. Keep holding her."

He pulled the stopper from another bottle and poured a small amount of a mottled purple liquid into the open wound. Sorsha gasped and struggled weakly, but not with the raw power she'd exhibited before.

"Okay, lad," Iggy said, picking up a long probe with a bit of gauze on the end. He opened a pot of some blue cream and wiped the gauze through it. "I'll need to close each layer of tissue, but I think she'll be all right. Sit down and I'll take a look at your leg when I'm done."

Alex wanted to agree, but he had two things he needed to do.

"I'll be back in a minute," he said, heading out into his room.

25

DOCTOR'S ORDERS

"I need to get a message to Lieutenant Detweiler," he told the operator when she picked up. By now the Lieutenant and Detective Nicholson would be at Grand Central. Alex gave the police operator the message that Arlo Harper's body was on South Brother Island. When she heard the message, she asked Alex to hold, and a minute later Lieutenant Detweiler came on the line.

"Lockerby?" he demanded. He was speaking loud to be heard above of the all the noise in the background. "The officers here saw you, Sorsha Kincaid, and my suspect vaporized."

"Sorsha teleported us out at the last second," he said.

"Well I'm glad of that, the Mayor would have my hide if one of the New York Six got killed on my case."

"I'm touched," Alex chuckled, then his voice turned serious. "Did all the civilians get clear in time?"

"There were five casualties," he said. "Fifty more are on their way to hospitals with various wounds, and some are pretty serious. The number of the dead might go up before everything is done."

Alex growled but the deed was done; nothing he could do now would change any of it.

"How did you figure out where Arlo intended to set off his bomb?"

Alex outlined his search for Arlo and why he brought Sorsha in on the case.

"We got there with only minutes to spare," he concluded.

"Well good work, Lockerby," Detweiler said. "If he'd set off that explosion rune when the terminal was packed with people it would have been a massacre. As it is, the city's going to take it on the chin for this one."

Alex didn't doubt that, if the reporters thought that Sorsha had been killed in the blast, they were probably already headed back to their offices to write the story. A story that would doubtless make the police look like incompetent boobs.

"Make an announcement," Alex said. "Tell them Arlo threatened to set off a bomb in retaliation for his brother's death and say that the city brought in Sorsha to help find him. You'll look like diligent public servants desperately trying to save the citizens from a mad man."

There was a brief pause on the line.

"You know, that might just work," Detweiler said. "How do you come up with this stuff?"

"It's a gift," Alex said, with all the false modesty he could summon.

"What about Sorsha?" Detweiler asked. "I'll let the reporters know she's alive, but they're gonna want to see her before they believe it."

"Sorsha was shot," Alex said.

"How bad?"

"Bad," Alex said. "She's with her personal physician right now. He thinks she'll pull through, but it's going to be touch and go for a while. Tell the press she was wounded capturing the bomber and that you'll update them on her condition tomorrow."

"You said capturing," Detweiler observed. "Does that mean you have Arlo in custody?"

"He's dead," Alex said. "The blast went off before Sorsha got us out of there, it hit him hard and when we reappeared, he slammed into a wall. Broke his neck."

"Good riddance," Detweiler said. "Where's the body?"

"South Brother Island," Alex said.

"Why did the Ice Queen take you out there?"

"Sorsha tried to get him before he set off his rune," Alex lied. "If that had worked, the rune would have gone off as soon as we arrived, so she chose an abandoned island."

"Any chance he had a big suitcase full of money on him?"

Alex had forgotten about the cash Arlo and Roy had stolen. Between the two banks it was close to half a million dollars.

"It's probably still in his vault," Alex said.

"You runewrights use keys to open your vaults, right?" Detweiler said. "If I get you his key could you open it?"

Alex sighed. The government insured some banks but there were still plenty that weren't covered. They needed to get the stolen money back or there was a good chance both bank's depositors could be ruined.

"I'm sorry, Lieutenant," he said. "The only person who can open a runewright's vault is the runewright who created it."

Detweiler cursed, then sighed.

"All right, Lockerby," he said in a resolved tone. "I'll send some of the boys from the harbor patrol over to retrieve Arlo's body."

"Tell them it's in the ruins of the old mansion."

"Will do. Be sure to let me know as soon as Miss Kincaid is out of the woods, will you?"

Alex promised that he would, then hung up. He picked up the phone again and dialed Sorsha's office number. He had a very similar conversation with her secretary, telling her to let Agents Redhorn and Mendes know where Sorsha was and her condition. After hanging up, Alex figured he had about half an hour until the two of them came calling. He didn't want to get up out of his chair, but there was still something he needed to do.

Heading back through his vault, Alex exited out to South Brother Island through the still open vault door. Arlo Harper's body lay just as it had been when he left, which wasn't surprising considering he was dead.

Limping over to the body, Alex knelt down and searched it. He had some cash and a train ticket for Atlanta in his trouser pockets. Alex guessed he'd planned to leave the rune stuck to the wall by the phone booths, then board a train and set it off with a linking rune once he was away.

He cursed.

If he'd guessed Arlo's plan ahead of time, he would have just had to wait until he planted the rune and left for the train. It would have been child's play to retrieve the rune and tear it up. Once an unactivated rune was broken, its power was lost. No one needed to die, not even Arlo, and Sorsha wouldn't have been shot.

"Stupid," he accused himself.

He returned the cash and the ticket to Arlo's trouser pocket. When he did, the ticket separated and he saw that it wasn't a single ticket, but two.

He was planning to leave with his brother.

That's why he'd been on the phone, Alex confirmed. He was trying to figure out if his brother had been released. Since the police couldn't release Roy, Arlo's plan was a bust. If he learned that Roy was dead, he might just have set off his blasting rune right there.

"I guess it had to be this way," Alex said to Arlo as he checked Arlo's jacket pockets. Here he found what he was looking for, a little black book containing Arlo's runes. There were several blasting runes inside along with some minor runes and a few vault runes. In the opposite pocket, Alex found an ornate hotel key with a calligraphic letter F stamped into the base and a large skeleton key with runic markings on it.

The former indicated that Arlo had spent the previous night in a fancy hotel, most likely the *Fillmore*. Alex seemed to remember that their front doors had the same calligraphic letter embossed them. The latter key was Arlo's vault key. It was of absolutely no use to Alex, but he pocketed it along with the hotel key and the rune book. He knew that it wasn't possible to open another runewright's vault, but less than a year ago, he'd known that it was impossible to open more than one door in a single vault. That, of course, had turned out to be untrue. Maybe there was a way to open Arlo's vault after all.

He'd have to consult that Archimedean Monograph to see if it had any information on vaults that he might have missed. If he could get Arlo's vault open, then the banks they stole from wouldn't become insolvent. Alex didn't care about the banks so much, but the people who kept their money there would be wiped out if the banks went bankrupt.

The only other thing on Arlo's person was a battered brass pocket-watch which Alex left where he found it. Satisfied that he'd done all he could, he forced himself back up to his feet with a grunt of pain, and limped back to his vault. Giving Arlo's dead form a final glance, Alex pulled the heavy vault door closed, and locked it from the inside.

He continued back to the bedroom in the brownstone, then shut the permanent door. Iggy's vault still stood open in the back wall of Alex's bedroom, so Alex headed for it. When he reached his mentor's surgery, he found Iggy sitting beside the surgical table watching Sorsha's sleeping form. He'd removed her shirt, vest, and the remnants of her brassiere, piling them on one of the rollaway tables he used to hold potions and instruments. A white towel had been laid across the Sorceress' chest for modesty, and Alex could see a large dressing sticking out from the top of it, being held in place by a gauze wrapping.

"Where did you go?" Iggy demanded when Alex approached.

"I had to call Lieutenant Detweiler and let him know what happened," Alex said. He gave Iggy a brief overview of their conversation. "How's she doing?" he asked when he finished.

Iggy looked back at the sorceress.

"She's sleeping well enough," he said. "The bullet hit her lung. Lots of blood vessels in there. I think I got everything sealed up, but only time will tell."

"What happens if you didn't get everything?"

"She could bleed into her lungs," Iggy said. "If that happens and I don't catch it, she'll drown in her own blood."

Alex felt a cold knot of fear in his gut. He'd felt it when Sorsha had been shot, but he hadn't really had time to think about it, what with Arlo Harper trying to blow them up. Now, however, that feeling twisted his insides.

"Don't worry, lad," Iggy said, reading the look on Alex's face. "If she starts aspirating blood, we'll hear her breathing change. That's why I'm here." He stood up and motioned to his chair. "Now, take off your trousers and sit down so I can have a look at your leg."

Alex did as he was told, turning in the chair so Iggy could get a better look at his right thigh. Arlo's bullet had clipped him in the muscle but hadn't seemed to hit anything vital. Alex's sock and shoe were bloody, but the wound wasn't even leaking anymore.

"Through and through," Iggy pronounced, checking the back of Alex's thigh for an exit wound. "The hole will patch up easy enough," he said. "But you'll have a limp for a few days while the muscle heals." He went over to his potion cabinet and took out a small brown bottle with a dropper in the top and two vials. The first vial had red liquid inside that seemed to swirl with purple streaks. The second glowed with a faint greenish blue light.

"Drink this," Iggy said, handing Alex the glowing vial.

Alex pulled the cork out of the top of the little glass tube and downed the liquid. Immediately a warm, tingly feeling seemed to come over him, concentrating in his fingers and toes. He felt like he'd picked up a charge of static electricity.

"This will sting," Iggy said, taking the dropper out of the little bottle and positioning it over the entry wound. With a steady hand, Iggy squeezed the dropper bulb and three drops splattered on the bloody hole.

Alex sucked in his breath, as it felt like someone had attacked the wound with a pair of pliers. He couldn't be sure, but he felt like this hurt worse than when he'd actually been shot.

"Lean over," Iggy said, patting Alex on the leg.

Alex did as instructed, and Iggy repeated the process with the exit wound.

"What was that?" Alex asked through clenched teeth.

"Tincture of Purification," he said, screwing the lid back on the bottle. "You were caught in an explosion and then you were rolling around on South Brother Island. Who knows what kind of grime you picked up."

Smarting from both his wounds, Alex sat still as Iggy used gauze and alcohol to remove the dried blood around the wound. Once that was done, he handed Alex the vial with the red and purple liquid. This one tasted like a cocktail he'd had once, something with tropical fruit and vodka in it. It burned going down, but in a pleasant way.

Iggy got up and retrieved a small metal tray, placing it on the roll-away table he'd used to hold his equipment when he worked on Sorsha. The tray held a package of thread and several curved needles.

"I'll have to stitch up the wound," he said, pulling up another chair. Before he could sit down, however, the doorbell rang downstairs.

"That'll be Redhorn and Mendes," Alex said, still feeling a bit fuzzy from the glowing potion.

"I'll be right back," Iggy said. He made his way to the open vault door leading into Alex's bedroom, and tugged it closed. "No sense giving them the wrong idea," he said, then he crossed the room to the permanent door that opened into the brownstone's kitchen. "Don't run off," he chuckled as he left.

Alex could hear Iggy getting the door and he recognized Redhorn's voice, though he couldn't hear what was being said. A moment later Iggy returned with the Agents in tow. Iggy had an amused expression on his face, but Redhorn looked ready to explode.

"Explain yourself," he demanded, storming over to Alex. "How the Devil did Ms. Kincaid get shot?"

Alex was a bit taken aback by the usually reserved Agent's reaction. He fixed him with a neutral expression, then looked at Sorsha.

"Arlo Harper was ready for us," he said. "He had spellbreaker runes on his gun. We didn't expect that. As soon as he took out Sorsha's shield, I jumped in front of her, but she'd already been hit."

"Why weren't you killed?" Mendes asked, her dark eyebrows framing her eyes in an expression of skepticism.

"Spellbreaker runes interfere with sorcery," Iggy said, coming over to listen to Sorsha's breathing. "They don't affect rune magic like Alex's shield runes."

"Arlo set off one of his blast runes," Alex went on without waiting for either of the Agents to speak. "Sorsha contained the blast. She held it in place despite being shot, which gave me enough time to subdue Arlo. If she hadn't been shot, she would have been able to keep the rune from exploding."

"If she wasn't able to hold the blast, then how did she teleport you away?" Redhorn asked.

"I did that," Alex said. "Used an escape rune to get her out."

"And you brought her here?" Redhorn said. "A hospital not good enough?"

"Damn good thing he did," Iggy said, thumping Redhorn on the chest. "One of your fancy doctors would have killed her just getting the bullet out. That kind of delicate work is best done by a runewright."

"Is she going to be all right?" Redhorn asked, his voice subdued.

Alex tried to hide the grin he picked up at the sight of Redhorn being schooled by Iggy.

"I'm going to be up with her tonight," Iggy said, giving Redhorn a hard look. "If she makes it through the night, she should be fine."

"I guess that means we're staying too," he said, looking around for another chair.

"Bring in a couple from the kitchen," Alex said.

As Redhorn and Mendes went in search of chairs, Iggy sat down and started to work on Alex's leg. It stung a bit since the glowing potion was wearing off, but Alex was too spent to care.

"How are you coming with Margaret's murder?" Iggy asked.

"What this about a murder?" Redhorn asked, setting a chair down nearby.

"Margaret LaSalle," Alex supplied. "She was killed last week."

Redhorn shook his head with a slight shrug.

"Mystery writer," Iggy said. "Her last book sold almost forty-thousand copies and that was just the first week."

"Sorry," Redhorn said. "I'm not much of a reader."

Iggy turned away from Redhorn and rolled his eyes.

"I'm starting to think Margaret's death has nothing to do with the murder of Dolly Anderson," he said.

"The Broadway star?" Mendes asked, coming back in with one of the heavy oak chairs from the kitchen. "I was only a kid when she died, but I'm sure I remember her death being ruled an accident."

Alex explained how he and Danny found the rigged phone and went over their investigation of the various suspects.

"As far as I can tell most of them have solid alibis and the ones that don't had no discernible motive," he finished.

"That doesn't mean anything," Redhorn said from his chair next to Mendes. "They could have a motive you don't know about."

"True," Alex admitted. "But if they do, it's lost to the past. I'm not sure Margaret LaSalle could have dug them up after all these years either. It makes more sense that her murder has to do with something else."

"I disagree," Redhorn said. "If you're right about Dolly Anderson being murdered, and if the murderer found out that this LaSalle person was writing a book based on Dolly's death, they'd have to act. Even if they couldn't be sure she'd found anything. They couldn't take the risk that something in her book would tip off the authorities."

"He's got a point," Iggy said, wrapping gauze around Alex's leg.

"What about the alibis?" Alex said. "Most of them weren't even at the theater that day."

Iggy shrugged.

"Remember, uh," Iggy hesitated, glancing at the Agents. "Remember the old saying, when you eliminate the impossible and nothing remains..."

Alex nodded.

"Then some part of the impossible must be possible."

It was a paraphrase of a quote from Sherlock Holmes, but since Alex was the only one who knew Iggy's true identity, he'd disguised it as a syllogism. It wasn't any less frustrating, though.

"All right," Alex said. "I'll call Danny and we'll go over it again." He stood and picked up his trousers, shoe, and bloody sock. Agent Mendes turned away with a grin and Alex realized that he was standing there in his underwear.

26

FINANCIAL MOTIVES

Alex slept fitfully despite the sleeping drought Iggy had given him. As he rolled out of bed just before seven, he wanted to blame his throbbing leg wound, but the reality was that he'd been going over the LaSalle case in his mind and just couldn't get anywhere. Every way he came at the case, it just didn't make any sense. Anyone who might have a motive had no opportunity, and the ones who had opportunity had no motive.

Then there was Sorsha. He knew that sorcerers could heal themselves but she had been hit so close to the heart it would take time before her own healing magic kicked in. Alex didn't know how close she'd come to dying, but he suspected the answer was, pretty damn. Iggy had been up with her all night, so he was confident she was okay, but he resolved to look in on her once he dressed.

Grumbling to himself, Alex forced himself to stand up on his throbbing leg and limp to the bathroom. He showered and shaved, but the repetition of his morning ablutions offered no insight. His bloody suit was still in a pile on the tile floor of his bathroom, so he limped to his wardrobe and put on a different one. He'd use a cleaning rune and a mending rune on the other suit later, but right now he was too irritated.

"All right," he said as he used the little mirror in the bathroom. "Go back to the beginning."

It was something Iggy had drilled into him when Alex was first learning to be a detective. *If your case devolves into a rabbit warren of twisting paths, don't try to follow them all. Go back to the beginning and start again.* Alex hated that saying, but recognized its value.

And he wasn't getting anywhere.

He limped to the phone on his bedside table and called Danny's apartment.

"I need you to meet me over at Margaret LaSalle's," he said when Danny picked up.

"You know this is my day off," Danny grumbled, somewhat groggy.

"Just meet me there," Alex insisted, a bit more irritably than he should have.

Danny sighed, then told Alex to give him an hour and hung up.

Returning the phone to the table, Alex forced himself to his feet and limped downstairs to check on Sorsha. Iggy put the kibosh on that when he reached the kitchen, declaring that the sorceress needed her sleep. Alex wanted to argue, but Iggy's expression changed his mind. Instead, Alex got a cup of coffee and limped to the wall phone to call a cab.

"You're lucky I'm your friend," Danny said as he slogged up the stoop in front of Margaret's brownstone.

"Sorry," Alex said. "This case has got me on edge." He didn't say it, but between Iggy and Lieutenant Callahan, Alex was under a lot of pressure to find Margaret's killer.

Danny gave him a hard look, then shrugged.

"So why are we here?" he asked, digging out the ring that had Margaret's key on it. He inserted it in the door, unlocking it, then dropped the ring back in his pocket.

"I'm at a dead end with all our suspects in the Anderson murder," he said. "If we want to find out who killed Margaret, we're going to have to start from scratch and find some new clues."

Danny sighed again.

"Maybe if you didn't date our suspects, you'd have more time to spend on the case," he growled, pushing the door open. "Fine, where do you want to start this time?"

"Kitchen," Alex said, leading the way. He found two cups in one of the cupboards and set them out on the counter. Opening his kit, he pulled out a Thermos full of Marnie's coffee. Since he had to wait for Danny, he'd gone by Empire Station to see her. Unscrewing the lid, Alex poured two cups, passing one to his friend.

Danny eyed the cup for a long moment before he took it.

"Don't think this makes us even," he said, sipping the hot liquid carefully.

"Of course not," Alex said with a grin. "So last time I took the upstairs and you took the downstairs," he said as Danny sipped his coffee with eyes closed in rapture. "How about we switch it up?"

"Okay," Danny said. "Any idea what we're looking for this time?"

"Last time we were looking for signs of a robbery," Alex said. "Now we think the killer was involved in the murder of Dolly Anderson."

"So look for anything that might relate to Dolly or her murder," Danny said, a bit more awake for the coffee.

"Sounds good," Alex said.

They split up once the coffee was finished. Alex headed down into the basement and began going through the many boxes that made up Margaret's storage room. He found a box of photographs that showed Margaret in exotic locations. Other boxes contained clothes, various legal documents, assorted receipts, and keepsakes of all description. None of it seemed relevant to Dolly Anderson, so Alex moved on.

There was a modern boiler room with a boiler set up to use boiler stones or Sorsha's cold disks, depending on the weather. Another room was filled with covered furniture that didn't look important. Alex searched it anyway, just to make sure Margaret hadn't hidden anything there.

Defeated, he moved up to the main floor. The layout there included a kitchen, sitting room, dining room, and a small parlor. All were neat and well appointed. If it wasn't for the bloodstain on the kitchen tile, he wouldn't know anything was wrong. The last time they'd searched, Danny found a box of sterling silverware in the lower drawer of a china hutch in the kitchen and it was still there. That alone had told Alex Margaret's murder was no robbery.

As Alex searched, he found several valuable first edition books on a shelf in the sitting room, along with an antique gold pocket-watch in a drawer. No thief desperate enough to murder a woman in her kitchen would have missed all of that.

While his investigation didn't yield anything about Dolly or shed any new light on Margaret's murder, it confirmed his original hypothesis. Margaret LaSalle's murder was no robbery.

Dejected, he climbed the stairs to the second floor. Sticking his head into the bedroom, he found it in the same state of disarray as last time. Some things had been moved, undoubtedly by Danny during his search. Since it didn't look like he'd set anything special aside, Alex continued up to the office on the third floor.

"Hey," Danny called from Margaret's office when he heard Alex approaching. "What was the name of that play when Dolly Anderson died?"

Alex entered the office and found Danny standing by the bookshelf looking at the wall.

"*The Rogues' Gallery*," Alex supplied. "Why?"

Danny reached up and took a picture off the wall before turning to Alex with a grin.

"Because I think our murderer might have missed something." He held out a framed document for Alex to read.

Inside an orange oak frame was a typewritten letter. It was on two pages, mounted side by side, and the name at the bottom read Rupert Swan.

"Who's Rupert Swan?" Alex asked.

"He's a theater critic for the Times," Danny said. "This is a letter he wrote Margaret."

"What's that have to do with *The Rogues' Gallery*?" Alex asked, trying to focus on the page.

Danny turned the frame around, putting his finger on the glass at the top of the first page.

"According to this, he's responding to a letter Margaret wrote him.

He spends the first paragraph praising her storytelling, which is probably why she framed it."

"Does it say why she wrote him?" Alex asked.

"Yep," Danny said with a grin. "Apparently Rupert Swan wrote a review of *The Rogues' Gallery*."

"But it closed in the beginning of its first performance," Alex said. "How could anyone review it?"

"Swan says in here that Benny Harrington invited him to the dress rehearsal," Danny explained. "Somehow Margaret found out about that and she asked him for his opinion of the play. He actually wrote a review and he included it here." Danny held up the frame.

"What did he think?"

"According to this, he loved it," Danny said. "He called it, 'A return to form for Benny Harrington.'"

Alex could believe that; he'd seen the play with Regina filling Dolly's role and he'd thoroughly enjoyed it.

"Swan predicted it would be big," Danny went on. "Bigger once it got to a better theater. He goes on for five paragraphs."

Alex took the frame and scanned through the text. From what he could tell, Danny hadn't missed any important details.

"You realize what this means, right?" Danny said.

Alex sighed and nodded.

"The play was going to be a hit," he said. "Dolly's death hurt everyone involved."

"What about the boyfriend?" Danny asked. "Claude McClintock. Maybe he didn't want Dolly to be in a big hit play."

"No," Alex said. "First of all, Dolly was in a long string of hit plays, so this wouldn't have been any different. Second, the whole romance was a publicity stunt to hide the fact that McClintock is a homosexual."

Danny raised an eyebrow but had no comment.

"So where does that leave us?" he asked.

"Two hours down and back at square one," Alex said with a sigh.

"All right," Danny said, putting the frame back on the wall. "I'm calling it. Go home." He slapped Alex on the shoulder. "Enjoy your weekend and we'll get back to it on Monday."

Alex didn't want to lose two days, but he couldn't think of anything else to do, so he nodded in acquiescence. Iggy was still keeping an eye on Sorsha, but her natural sorceress regeneration should take over by the end of the day, and he'd be free to go over the case.

"Don't take it so hard," Danny said, pushing him toward the door. "I'll let you buy me another cup of that coffee before we go."

It took Alex an hour to get back to his office. Since Danny drank half his Thermos, he had to swing back to Empire Tower and get it refilled. He was already a day late keeping his coffee promises to Sherry.

Predictably, she was excited when he walked through the door and handed the Thermos to her.

"I knew you weren't dead," she said with a grin.

"Dead?" Alex said.

She dropped a newspaper on her desk. It was one of the minor tabloids, but it had a very big headline, *New York Power Couple Killed in Grand Central Explosion*. The article went on to say that he and Sorsha had been killed in the explosion while apprehending the Brothers Boom. Alex was really starting to hate seeing his name in the paper. Detweiler had told him that some of the reporters thought Sorsha was dead, but apparently his name had been mentioned as well.

"What is Ms. Kincaid going to say about that headline?" Sherry said with an amused smile.

Alex doubted she would care. Clearly the term 'Power Couple' was a crude pun referring to their magical ability. She wouldn't be angry.

Would she?

Alex pushed that thought out of his mind. He was at a dead end with the LaSalle case, and needed to figure out who had given Olivia Thatcher the formula for Limelight. If he didn't at least try to connect Thatcher with Guy Rushton, then Sorsha really would be angry. In keeping with his week so far, he didn't have any leads in that case either.

Dropping the paper on Sherry's desk, Alex hung up his hat.

"I'll be in my office," he said.

Before he could move, however, his door burst open.

"Alex!" a relieved voice gasped.

He turned to find Regina Darling standing in his doorway, a rumpled newspaper clutched to her chest.

"Regina," Alex said, surprised to see her. "Aren't you supposed to be on stage right now?"

"I couldn't," she said, charging into his arms. "I had to know if it was true." She stepped back and opened the paper. It was a copy of *The Midnight Sun* with the headline, *New York's Runewright Detective Killed.* The article was by Billy Tasker.

Alex wanted to swear but thought better of it.

"It's just a misunderstanding," he assured her. "But we'd better get you back to Broadway."

She smacked him playfully with the newspaper.

"Don't worry," she said with a dazzling smile. "My understudy is filling in; that's what she's for, after all."

She hugged him again.

"I was so worried about you," she said.

Alex felt like a heel. That story had made her skip a performance all because she was terrified for him.

"Well, since you're here," he said, putting his arm around her. "Why don't I take you to lunch?"

She looked up at him with her perfect green eyes and smiled demurely.

"That sounds wonderful," she said.

Alex's office was on the upper east side, nowhere near the fancy restaurants of the core. Regina had laughed at that, telling him about all the tiny diners and roadside dives she'd eaten at in her early career when shows went on the road. In the end she'd told him to take her somewhere decent, so he grabbed a cab and went across town to *The Lunch Box.*

"Alex," Doris said when he came in. "I was beginning to think you'd forgotten about us."

Doris was a fixture at The Lunch Box. She was a chubby woman with messy brown hair, too much lipstick, and a cheating husband. Alex had offered to find evidence of the husband's infidelity, but Doris always refused.

What would I do without the bastard? she'd said.

"Who's your friend?" Doris asked, looking at Regina.

Alex made introductions, leaving out Regina's last name.

"We'll just grab a booth," he said, leading Regina off to one in the corner away from the diner's few patrons.

"I thought you said you liked this place," Regina said once they were seated.

"I do."

"Then how come Doris hasn't seen you in a while?"

Alex sighed. He liked his life, how busy he'd gotten in recent years, but part of him yearned for the old simplicity.

"Too busy," he said with a shrug.

"Too busy to eat?" Regina said, giving him an amused look.

"Sometimes," he admitted.

Doris came and took their order, jotting it down on her notepad.

"So," Regina said once the waitress had gone. "Do you work a lot with Miss Kincaid?"

"We've had a few cases together over the years," Alex said, sensing danger in her question. "She's a consultant for the feds about magical crimes. Sometimes she pulls me in when a runewright's involved."

"Oh," Regina said with a look that managed to be both indignant and indifferent at the same time. "It just seems to me that your name shows up in the newspapers next to hers a lot."

"My name was next to yours the other day," he said.

"True," she admitted, "but there have been two mentions of you and the sorceress this week, and only one with me."

Alex wasn't sure how to answer that, but he had the feeling whatever answer he gave would be wrong.

"Before this week, my name has only been in the papers a couple times," he said. "You shouldn't judge by this week, it's a bit of a fluke."

She seemed to believe that, and it was mostly true.

"So what did happen at Grand Central?" she asked, changing the subject.

Alex explained as much as he could about the attempted capture of Arlo Harper and his detonation of a blast rune.

"So Sorsha teleported us away just in time," Alex said. It wasn't the truth, but it also didn't require a prolonged explanation. No one questioned magic when a sorcerer was involved.

"To your home," Regina asked with a raised eyebrow.

"I live with a retired Navy doctor," Alex said. "He took the bullet out and she's resting."

"At your home," Regina said again.

Alex wasn't sure exactly when it happened, but he'd lost control of this conversation.

"She's unconscious," he explained. "And moving her could be dangerous."

Regina held his gaze for a long moment, then shrugged.

"So, were you two an item before?"

Alex thought back to a single, fiery kiss they had shared years ago in a graveyard. She'd been injured then too, hit in the hip by a Nazi bullet. Iggy had patched her up then too.

"No," Alex admitted, somewhat wistfully. "It just never worked out. We should probably stop talking about the Ice Queen," he added, using her least flattering nickname.

"You should talk about her more often," Regina said with a knowing smile. "Especially the way your face lights up when you do."

Alex wasn't sure how to take that.

"Regina," he began but she held up her hand.

"I know you're not seeing Sorsha," she said. "I'm pretty good at reading people. It's all that being around actors. I can usually tell when someone's playing straight with me. If you'd been seeing Sorsha, you never would have agreed to have dinner with me the other night."

That much was true.

"Why did you ask me to dinner?" he asked.

She snickered at that and gave him a demure smile.

"Alex, do you have any idea how many men ask me out every week?"

Alex admitted he didn't.

"Dozens," she said. "Most of them want the prestige of being seen with me, some of them just lust after me."

She was speaking in a light flippant manner, but Alex could tell her words were personal.

"I cornered you into taking me to dinner because if I hadn't, you wouldn't have asked," she said, as if that made all the sense in the world. "When you knocked on my door, you weren't looking for a famous actress, you just needed some questions answered. It was the first time in a long time that someone wasn't a starstruck creep."

Alex shook his head.

"You asked me to dinner because I treated you like a regular person?"

"Yes," she said, her smile turning sly. "And it was lovely."

As Alex looked at her, Regina's smile faded, and her lips drooped a bit into sadness.

"I want to spend more time with you," she admitted. "But I don't want a shadow hanging over me the whole time."

"You mean Sorsha?" Alex asked, not really getting how Regina was connecting the dots in her mind. Sorsha had made it very clear right after that kiss they'd shared that she didn't want to have a relationship of any kind with him. In fact, he hadn't seen her for over a year after that.

"You need to work out how you feel about her," Regina said. "I'll wait. Just don't take too long."

Alex opened his mouth to tell her that he knew exactly how he felt about Sorsha but the words simply refused to come.

"Why don't we talk about something else," Regina said, smiling again.

Alex didn't want to talk about something else, but the detective part of his brain told him that pressing the issue would only anger Regina, and worse, it might hurt her, so he let it drop.

Their food came and they talked about Broadway and the theater while they ate. Regina told him stories of her early days, before she met Dolly. She told about her life as a big star and what work she had coming up. It was the kind of conversation Alex would have enjoyed, but try as he might to focus, his thoughts kept drifting back to Sorsha.

Sure he'd stepped in front of her when Arlo was shooting, but he'd done the same thing for Danny, hadn't he? He'd gone out of his way not to kill her when she'd been mind-controlled by Malcom Jones, but he would have done that for any of his friends.

Shaking his head to clear it, Alex focused on the conversation. Regina was telling a story about a theater that burned down before her troupe arrived in their small town. They had to do the play in the gymnasium of the local high school.

"Is there any reason a play would change theaters?" he suddenly asked.

"Uh, sure," Regina said after a moment. "I assume you mean when the theater hasn't burned down."

"Yes," Alex confirmed.

"Usually plays stay in whatever theater they open in," she said. "But sometimes if they can secure a bigger or better venue, they'll change."

"Don't they have a contract with the theater?"

"Yes, but that usually only goes for four weeks," she said. "After that, the producer can move the play if he wants. It almost never happens, though."

Alex explained about the letter from Rupert Swan they'd found in Margaret's office.

"Why would he say that the play needed to be moved from the *Royale*?" he asked.

Regina giggled at that.

"That's easy," she said. "Back then the *Royale* was a dump. Ethan's father really let it go."

"Would you excuse me for a minute," Alex said, standing up. "I need to go call my friend, Danny."

"Why?"

"Because Ethan Nelson killed Dolly Anderson, and now I know why he did it."

27

GHOSTS

Alex tried not to fidget as he sat in the almost total darkness of the *Royale Theater*. Beside him in the second story box sat Danny and next to him across the little aisle sat Lieutenant Callahan and Captain Rooney. Behind them was Billy Tasker, wearing a grin that almost spread off his face, and the young photographer he'd brought with him.

From where they sat, they had an excellent view of the stage as well as the only light in the room, a pale greenish glow that emanated from the large, free-standing mirror on the right side of the stage.

Alex slid his hands back and forth on his knees to keep them from sweating. It wasn't particularly warm in the theater, but a lot was riding on the next half hour. He took out his pocket-watch and popped open the lid. The glow of the runes and the blue ring that measured his life force was enough to read the time, eleven twenty-six.

"This had better work, Lockerby," Captain Rooney growled. His voice wasn't loud, but Alex heard it echo off the far wall of the empty theater.

"Don't look at me," Alex hissed back, keeping his voice low. "This was Danny's idea."

"Then why is he here in the first place?" Rooney asked Danny, though he kept his voice low this time.

"Because I don't know Regina Darling or Andrew Barton," Danny answered. "Alex said he'd help with that, but he wanted to see the show."

"What about him?" the Captain pressed, jerking a thumb at Tasker, who sat quietly in the second row.

"This is going to be the biggest arrest since Prohibition," Danny said with a grin. "I figured you'd want a picture or two."

Rooney was a political animal and with his upcoming campaign for Senator, pictures like that would make his career. A faint smile crossed his face and he nodded, sitting back.

"Of course if this doesn't work out, that reporter is going to make us look like jackasses," Danny whispered, just loud enough for Alex to hear.

"It will work," Alex said, checking his watch again, then showing it to Danny.

"Okay," Danny said to the occupants in the booth. "Ethan Nelson is up in his office finishing up the books for the day. His stage manager said he does a check of the theater before he goes up to his bedroom on the third floor. From now on, everyone has to be absolutely silent. If he hears anything, the jig is up."

Everyone in the booth nodded their assent, then all eyes turned to the stage. It was a perfect recreation of the scene from *The Rogues' Gallery*, the scene where Dolly died. Everything was there, the bed, the wardrobe, the dressing table, and especially the free-standing mirror and the end table with the lamp and candlestick telephone. It matched the set Alex had seen when he went to Regina's performance, but of course it would. Andrew Barton had teleported the set from the *Schubert Theater* right onto the stage at the *Royale*.

From the front of the theater, Alex could hear the door to Nelson's office close as he began his final inspection of the theater before bed. Right on cue, the greenish light emanating from the mirror vanished, plunging the theater into near total darkness, and the telephone on the stage began to ring. The sound was loud in the oppressive quiet of the empty theater.

It went on ringing incessantly for what felt like five minutes before the door to the front of the house burst open and Ethan Nelson came running in, spilling light from the foyer into the dark theater. Alex could clearly see the man from his vantage point. He looked confused but not alarmed. As the phone rang again, he ran down the aisle, heading for the stairs that led up to the stage. When he mounted the first one, the lamp on the table by the phone bloomed into radiance. It wasn't a bright light, but in the inky darkness of the stage, it illuminated the table, the phone, and the standing mirror.

Nelson froze on the stair. His back was to the box, but Alex could imagine the look on his face. The theater owner took a hesitant step up as the phone rang again. When he reached the stage, he turned all the way around, scanning the seats, the balcony, and the boxes for intruders.

Alex held his breath as Ethan Nelson's eye swept over their hiding place, but with so little light, he didn't see anything.

"Who's there?" he called.

The only answer he got was the echo of his own voice and the ringing of the telephone.

"This isn't funny," he yelled, storming across the stage. He grabbed the telephone, lifting it up as if he intended to pull the wires out, but there weren't any wires attached to it. It rang again as he held it in his hand, and Nelson dropped it with a curse.

Alex grinned. That had been his idea. Since Sorsha was out of commission, he needed someone to teleport the bedroom set, and having the Lightning Lord along had extra benefits. He could easily ring the phone from his position down in the dressing rooms, channeling electrical power right to the little electric motor that rang the bell.

As Ethan dropped the phone and took an involuntary step back, the greenish light began to emanate from the mirror again. As it brightened, the lamp on the table dimmed, also controlled by Barton.

"Hello Ethan," Dolly's voice said. A moment later she appeared in the mirror, bathed in the green light. She looked exactly as she had the day she'd died on this very stage.

Ethan gasped loud enough for Alex to hear.

"What?" Dolly said. "Nothing to say? Not even an apology for killing me? How disappointing."

Ethan made a twisting motion with his shoulders and suddenly Alex could see a gun in his hand.

"Some kind of trick," he almost shouted, then he raised the pistol and fired at the mirror.

It was all Alex could do to keep from laughing when the bullet hit the glass and bounced off, leaving the mirror unscathed. Since Margaret LaSalle had been shot, Alex knew that Ethan had a gun. A quick shield charm placed on the mirror by Barton ensured the mirror would not be broken before their little play concluded.

"Really Ethan," Dolly chided him. "I'm already dead, you saw to that."

Ethan ran to the mirror and looked behind it. Whatever he expected to find wasn't there. The mirror was just a mirror.

Except for Barton's magic that connected it to a similar mirror down in one of the dressing rooms. The first time Alex had ever seen Barton, it had been as a projection through a makeup mirror. Barton had just scaled the spell up to a larger mirror. He was also shining Alex's lantern on Regina Darling, all decked out in her costume dress. While she stood in front of the mirror, she could see and hear Ethan, and he could see her.

"What do you want?" Ethan gasped, his voice a strangled cry.

Regina laughed.

"Nothing much," she said in Dolly's voice. "I just had to find out. Did you really kill me just to save your daddy's theater?"

Alex could see Ethan's shoulders rising and falling as he breathed heavily.

"Of course not," he growled.

"I knew there must be more," Regina said, tilting her head to look at him quizzically. "Tell me."

Ethan shook his head and began to laugh.

"You don't even know," he growled, anger thick in his voice. "I hated you."

"But why?"

"*The Lighthouse Keeper*," he said.

Everything clicked into place in Alex's head. That was the missing piece Alex had been hoping to find, Ethan Nelson's true motive.

"You promised we'd always be together," Ethan went on, ranting. "And what did you do? You ran off the first chance you got and left me here."

Regina's face grew sad, as if she were truly sorry for Ethan.

"I didn't know you'd take it that way," she said. "Why didn't you tell me?"

"You never loved me," he spat. "I wish you were here so I could kill you again, you bitch!" He fired his gun into the mirror until it clicked empty.

Alex leaned over to Danny.

"I believe that's your cue," he said.

Nodding, Danny got up and headed back out into the hallway with Callahan and Rooney in tow. As soon as they were gone, Billy Tasker got up and came down to sit next to Alex. He started to ask a question, but Alex shushed him.

On the stage down below Ethan was yelling at the mirror. From what Alex could make out he was ranting about how he planned to kill Dolly during the closing performance. A moment later, Danny rushed the stage with several uniformed policemen he'd let in through the theater's back entrance. They quickly subdued Ethan, snapping cuffs on him. When they were finished, Danny gave Alex the thumbs up, then thanked Regina, who took a quick bow in the mirror, then stepped away.

"So," Billy said as the house lights came up. "This is going to be the biggest scoop in years! How did you figure it out?"

"You'll have to ask Danny that," Alex said, getting up. He'd coached Danny extensively on how to explain the case to the press. "Come on and I'll make sure you get first crack."

"You'd better," Billy said, though since he was the only reporter in sight, it wasn't much of a worry.

When they got down to the stage, Captain Rooney was all smiles. He explained to Billy how Danny had figured out that Dolly Anderson was murdered and had laid this elaborate trap to catch him.

"So how did you know it was Ethan Nelson?" Billy asked once Rooney yielded the floor to Danny.

"Mr. Nelson had a problem back in the day," Danny began with a grin that positively glowed. "His theater was a dump and he needed money to refurbish it. If he didn't, no producer would rent his theater and he'd go out of business. Benny Harrington had a problem too; his plays were flops and no decent theater would rent to him."

"So he put on his play here," Billy guessed.

Danny nodded.

"Now Mr. Nelson, being a smart businessman," Danny went on, "he took out an insurance policy so that if the play was a flop, he'd still get paid enough money for the renovations. If the play was a hit, he'd make more than enough."

"But that doesn't explain why he killed Dolly," Alex said, making sure Billy got the right information for his story. "Wouldn't it be smarter to let the play go in case it succeeded?"

"There was a problem," Danny said. "Harrington invited a critic to see the dress rehearsal. That critic loved the play, which was great news for Ethan Nelson, but he also told Harrington to move the play to a better theater as soon as his contract was up."

Billy began nodding along as he scribbled.

"And if the play moved," Danny concluded, "Nelson wouldn't make enough for his renovations."

"So he did the only thing he could," Billy said, putting the pieces together. "He stopped the play so he could get the insurance payout."

"Very good, Mr. Tasker," Danny said.

"I still don't understand why he wanted to kill Dolly," Captain Rooney said. "I took a look at that rigged telephone he made, it would have taken a week to put together."

"I think I can answer that one, Captain," Alex said. "Remember when Ethan said he hated Dolly because of *The Lighthouse Keeper*? It was a two-person play they were both in when they were young. I'm guessing they were sweet on each other, but then Dolly made it big..."

"And Ethan didn't," Rooney said with a nod.

"Makes sense," Billy said.

Alex turned away now that he was sure that tomorrow's front page would have the right headline. He was just in time to meet Regina and Barton as they came up from the dressing rooms below.

"How did I do?" Regina asked, all smiles.

"You were wonderful," Alex said. "Got him to confess to everything."

"Who knew he was carrying a torch for Dolly Anderson?" Barton said, coming up to stand beside them. "Speaking of carrying a torch," he said, handing Alex his lantern. "How did it look from this end?"

"Amazing," Alex said. "Thanks."

Barton grinned like a schoolboy.

"I'm just glad you brought me in for this," he said with a chuckle. "How did you get the idea to trick him into confessing?"

"Benny Harrington," Alex said.

"The playwright?"

"Dolly died during his play, *The Rogues' Gallery*," Alex explained. "It's the story of a woman whose husband is falsely accused of a crime and she has to trick the guilty party into confessing."

"Poetic justice then?" Barton said. "I like that."

"I want to thank you too, Alex," Regina said, squeezing his arm. "It felt good to take down Dolly's killer." Her smile suddenly faded. "Will that hold up in court?" she asked.

"Virtually ironclad," Barton interjected. "Especially with Captain Rooney as a witness."

"Alex," Danny called. He descended the stairs from the stage and came to meet them in the main aisle. He was carrying a bundle wrapped in butcher paper. "The officers we had searching Nelson's room found this."

He handed Alex the bundle and he peeled back that paper to reveal a stack of neatly typed pages. The first one read: *The Rooster Crowed at Sunset by Margaret LaSalle*.

"It was under a loose floorboard," Danny said. "Now we've got Nelson for Margaret's murder too."

"Good job," he said, handing it back. "I know Iggy will be thrilled to know it's been recovered."

"Well, it's getting late," Barton said as Danny headed back to where the Captain and the Lieutenant stood. "I've got to zap all this furniture back to the *Schubert Theater* and then there's a dozen proposals on my desk."

He bid Alex and Regina good night and headed up to the stage. A moment later he and the borrowed props all disappeared.

Regina shivered as she clung to Alex's arm.

"That gives me the creeps," she said.

Alex chuckled.

"You should try it sometime," he said with no trace of humor in his voice. "It's much worse than it looks."

She laughed and held his arm as they headed back downstairs to the dressing room. He waited for her to change out of the costume dress and back into her regular clothes.

"Would you like me to see you home?" he asked as she gathered up the borrowed dress.

"Have you asked the sorceress where you stand?" she asked, knowing full well he hadn't had the opportunity. "Then I think you can give me a lift to my building."

Alex wasn't excited about that, he'd just helped solve one of New York's most famous unsolved mysteries and he was in the mood to celebrate. Nevertheless, he held out his arm to Regina with a smile.

"It would be my pleasure," he lied.

28

THE LINK

The conclusion of a difficult case always left Alex with a sense of energetic euphoria. Despite its being nearly midnight, he skipped up the steps to the brownstone as if he was walking on air. He'd solved one of the biggest mysteries in New York history and tricked the culprit into confessing. Danny would get his promotion to Lieutenant, something he deserved, and Dolly Anderson would finally get justice. Finding Margaret LaSalle's manuscript in Ethan Nelson's room was just the cherry on top, allowing the police to close Margaret's murder as well.

It had been a good day.

Normally when Alex came home after ten, he had to be quiet, not wanting to disturb Iggy if he'd already gone to bed. As Alex pulled his pocket-watch from the pocket of his jacket, he didn't have to worry about making noise. The stained glass window in the front door had an abstract, art deco pattern that obscured vision, but the glimmer of the kitchen lights shining from the back of the building lit it up, making its colors glow in the darkness of the night.

As he opened the door and passed through the vestibule, Alex became aware of several voices, rumbling quietly in conversation. Since

Iggy almost never had visitors at the brownstone, he assumed it must be Agents Redhorn and Mendes.

"What's all this?" Alex asked, making his way down the little hall that connected the front library with the kitchen. As he approached, he could see Iggy, resplendent in his velvet smoking jacket, puffing on a cigar. Next to him at the table was Sorsha, looking a bit pale, but otherwise all right. She wore a light blue button-up shirt and her right hand was bound against her chest with a wrapping. Mendes and Redhorn were seated on the opposite side of the table, the latter enjoying one of Iggy's fine Cuban cigars. Agent Mendes had untied her kinky hair and it fluffed up around her head like a brown halo.

"There you are, my boy," Iggy said with a prodigious grin. "How did it go at the theater?"

"We got him," he said. Alex didn't think he could feel any better about the night's events, but just saying it out loud sent him walking on air.

"Got who?" Sorsha asked. Clearly Iggy hadn't filled her in on his plan.

"Dolly Anderson's killer," Alex said with a grin he couldn't suppress if he wanted to.

Sorsha raised an eyebrow at that, and Agent Mendes gasped. Redhorn, as usual, was a mask of calculated indifference. The Sorceress must have just come from the sick bed in Iggy's vault, because she wasn't wearing any makeup. Sorsha applied makeup in the same way an Italian master applied paint, with precision and to great effect. That said, there wasn't a thing about her face that required makeup. Any accoutrements were only there to enhance what nature had blessed her with.

"Do tell," she said. Her voice was low, husky even, no doubt a result of her still healing wound. The corner of the sorceress' mouth turned up in a half smile, and Alex felt suddenly warm.

Damn it, Regina, he thought.

Sorsha's expression was one of eager interest, but thanks to the conversation he'd had with Regina, he was starting to attach unintended meaning to Sorsha's actions. The actress had seen something in

Alex's interactions with Sorsha that just wasn't there, but planting the seed of the idea in Alex's head was making him see it, too.

"Sit here, lad," Iggy said, getting up from his seat next to Sorsha. "A success like this calls for a glass or two of my twelve-year-old Scotch."

He hurried to the liquor cabinet in the library while Alex sat down and started to relate the story of Margaret LaSalle's murder and how that led Danny and him to the supposedly accidental death of Dolly Anderson. When Iggy returned with a dram of amber liquid in a tumbler and a thick glass bottle, Alex was relaying the various alibis of the original suspects and how he and Danny had spent days verifying them.

"Wasn't all that stuff in the original police file?" Mendes asked, caught up in the story.

"Danny's lieutenant wouldn't let us look at it," Alex explained. "He said if any of the higher ups got wind of it, they'd take the case."

"Good man," Redhorn commented. "Looking after his people."

"More than that," Alex said. "Danny is Oriental and his lieutenant wants to promote him."

Redhorn nodded.

"Big case like that," he said. "It's a career maker."

Sorsha's raised eyebrow was back, then a sly grin spread over her perfect features.

"You kept your name out of it," she accused him. "Didn't you?"

Alex just shrugged.

"I owe Danny plenty," he said. "Besides, he'll be a great lieutenant."

Alex recited the rest of the story as he sipped the Scotch and the others listened. When he was done, the Scotch was beginning to make him feel warm, and his audience was impressed. They asked questions for a few minutes more, then the conversation lapsed.

"How come you're not that helpful with my cases?" Sorsha said with a mocking smile.

"Why, Sorceress," he said. "Whatever do you mean? Olivia Thatcher won't be making any more Limelight. Arlo Harper is dead, so whatever amount of the drug he took from her is lost forever in his vault. And DuPont will alert you if anyone suspicious tries to buy ytterbium. I'd say your case is pretty well wrapped up, and I was at least a little bit helpful."

"Yes," she admitted, her face becoming serious. "But who gave Olivia the recipe for Limelight? How did they get it from Guy Rushton?"

"And if you're right about it being addictive," Mendes added, "then whoever that is will want more, and soon."

Alex shrugged at that.

"Olivia was a top tier alchemist," he said. "It will take whoever's behind this some time to find another one willing to help him, and they still have to come up with a supply of ytterbium." He looked at Sorsha. "Sooner or later, the guy will come to you."

"Maybe," Sorsha said, sounding unconvinced.

"I don't think we've got all that much time," Redhorn said.

All eyes turned to him as he paused.

"Why not?" Alex asked.

"Arlo Harper," he said. "He wanted money, so when he got some Limelight, he turned a rune that makes harmless fireworks into one that blew the roof off Grand Central Station."

"He's got a point," Iggy said, giving Redhorn an approving nod. "Whoever is behind this won't just want more Limelight, they'll need it. So what magical monstrosities will they concoct to get what they want?"

A pall descended over the table as they all looked at each other, while Iggy puffed his cigar.

"I think we'd better take a look at the box again," Sorsha said at last.

She pointed to the far end of the table, past Redhorn and Mendes, where a cardboard box sat. Alex could see bits of alchemy glass sticking out of the top. Agent Redhorn rose and retrieved the box, setting it in the middle of the group. He began pulling things out and setting them on the table. Mostly it was the notes taken from Olivia Thatcher's ruined lab, and the ones Alex had collected from the Harpers' room at the Carlton Hotel. There were some of the more intact bits of glassware from Olivia's lab and the few packets of Limelight they'd managed to grab. Other than that, the box was empty.

"All right," Sorsha said, picking up the cork to Iggy's Scotch bottle and shoving it in tight. "This is what we have to work with. There's bound to be something in here, we just haven't found it yet. So everybody take something and look again. I don't want to wake up tomorrow to find out that our man has burned down the DuPont warehouse looking for ytterbium."

Alex reached for one of Olivia's notes as everyone else picked up something. It was the same mass of unintelligible scribblings it had been the first time he'd seen it. After struggling to interpret something in the mess of crooked lines, he just let his eyes go out of focus, staring at it.

"Here," Redhorn finally said, shoving Arlo's notebook under Alex's nose. "You'll probably make more sense of this than I will."

Alex accepted the book, dropping Olivia's note on the table. He thumbed through the book without much interest. He'd already been over it a dozen times before Sorsha and the FBI had confiscated it from Detweiler and Nicholson. As he paged through it, Alex found his eyes once again drifting in and out of focus. There wasn't anything to see, just a bunch of unintelligible runes laid out in wavy squiggles.

Just like Olivia's note.

His attention snapping back into sharp focus, Alex sat up and grabbed Olivia's note, holding it up against the book.

"Find something, lad?" Iggy asked.

"Look at this," he said, handing the book and the note to Iggy. "Look how similar the writing is."

Iggy squinted at the page, but then frowned and shrugged.

"These are messy," he admitted, "but they're each done by a different hand, if that's what you were getting at."

Alex looked back at the case debris on the table. After a second, he picked up a piece of the alchemy glass and handed that to Iggy as well.

"Look at this too," he said.

"What are you getting at, Alex?" Sorsha asked, trying to peer around him to see what Iggy was looking at.

Alex pointed to the rune inscribed on the alchemy glass.

"We know that Olivia didn't put these runes on," he said. "And this rune work doesn't match Arlo's runes, but look how similar they are."

"They're all messy," Redhorn said.

"Practically unintelligible," Alex said. "Remember that notebook Guy Rushton was scribbling in?" he said to Sorsha. "His writing looked like this too."

"You think it's the effect of the Limelight," Sorsha guessed. "How does that help us?"

Iggy raised an eyebrow and his mustache bristled.

"For one thing," he said, handing the sorceress the paper and the notebook. "If Alex is right, then once you find a suspect, it should be obvious that he's been using Limelight."

"But that's all," Redhorn said. "It's an interesting idea, but it doesn't help us find out who's behind all of this."

Alex sighed and picked up the alchemy glass from in front of Iggy. He remembered that all of the various jars, beakers, and bottles on Olivia Thatcher's brew table had been enhanced with runes, probably by whoever gave her the Limelight recipe in the first place.

"Stacy," Alex gasped, nearly dropping the bit of alchemy glass he was holding.

"Who?" Sorsha said.

"Nobody cares that you got a new girl, Lockerby," Redhorn growled, turning the note pages upside down while trying to force it to make sense.

"No," Alex said, turning to Sorsha. "Stacy Miller."

"Guy Rushton's boss at Standard Oil," she said, nodding. "What of him?"

"He said that Guy Rushton's Limelight formula required rune enhanced equipment like this in order to work." Alex held up the glass to emphasize his point.

"I don't remember that," she said, still looking perplexed.

"It was when I called him to find out what ingredients Guy Rushton was using," Alex explained. "He was surprised that I knew about rune enhanced alchemy glass."

Sorsha just stared at him, uncomprehending.

"Why?" she asked.

"He said it was a trade secret," Alex explained.

She reached out and took the enhanced beaker from Alex, looking at the rune scratched in its surface. "So who made these for Olivia?"

"The same person who made them for Guy Rushton," Alex said. "That explains how Olivia got the formula, it was given to her by Rushton's missing assistant."

Sorsha was grinning now.

"Buddy," she said, calling Agent Redhorn by his nickname. "Call the night manager over at Standard Oil and find out who Guy Rushton's assistant was. See if they have an address for him on file while you're at it."

Redhorn nodded and excused himself to use the telephone.

While he went, Alex took the beaker back from Sorsha and stared at it. It hadn't really occurred to him that enchanted brewing equipment was a secret. Sure, he'd never seen it anywhere else but Dr. Kellin's place, but Iggy had done those runes, and his rune knowledge was understandably deeper than almost everyone else. Still, the idea of using runes to enhance brewing by better distributing heat and to speed up solubility wasn't a novel idea, and it didn't just work for alchemy. Alex used both of those techniques when he enchanted the brewing pots for Marnie.

"Marnie," he said, his jaw falling open in amazement.

"Another sweetheart," Sorsha said with an unamused look.

"What? No, she makes my coffee," Alex said. He held up the beaker. "I do runes like this one to speed up her brewing equipment."

"I'm not following," Agent Mendes said. "What does that mean?"

"Unless I miss my guess," Sorsha said, reading the grin on Alex's face. "It means he knows where we can find Guy Rushton's missing assistant."

Alex nodded, tapping his nose with his index finger.

"Marnie broke one of the preparation pitchers I made for her," Alex explained. "She works at Empire Station and she tried to get Andrew Barton's new runewright to fix it for her. He turned her down initially, but then offered to do it."

"So?" Mendes said. "Maybe he just didn't have the time."

"That doesn't matter," Alex said.

"He didn't ask what the rune glass was," Sorsha said, understanding. "He didn't have to, because he already knew."

Alex touched the tip of his nose with his index finger again.

"What does this runewright do for Andrew?" Sorsha asked.

Alex's stomach lurched at the question.

"He helped Barton link Empire Tower to his new repeater tower," Alex said, his throat suddenly dry.

"Meaning he could turn off the city's power whenever he wanted?" Iggy said.

"Or use that power to enhance a super rune," Alex said. "When I saw his rune work, I thought he was just sloppy, but now we know it was messy because he's using Limelight. What if he's cooked up something worse than Arlo Harper's blasting rune?"

Sorsha looked into his eyes for a moment and Alex saw fear there. Sorcerers tended to think of themselves as impervious to the dangers regular people lived with, but Sorsha had been mind-controlled and ordered to kill Alex. She knew just how vulnerable a sorcerer could really be.

"Buddy," she said as she stood. "Hang up that phone. Alex, go get your investigation bag. Aissa," she added to Agent Mendes. "Go get my shoes. As soon as everyone's back, I'll teleport us to Empire Tower."

"Sorsha," Andrew Barton's voice boomed through Empire Tower's cavernous lobby less than a minute after they appeared. Alex wondered if his security people had called him or if he just sensed her arrival. Whichever it was, he appeared in the lobby just a few feet away from them.

"To what do I owe the pleasure of your company at this late hour? And what happened to you?" He wore a concerned look that didn't surprise Alex; the sorcerer had always had a soft spot for Sorsha. When he saw Alex and the FBI agents, however, his smile vanished. "Oh," he said, somewhat crestfallen. "It's an official visit, I see."

"Sorry to drag you away from your work, Andrew," Sorsha said, finally getting her stomach under control from the teleport. "But we need to see Mr. Elder right away."

"What do you want with my runewright?" Barton asked. "Especially since you've got one of your own right here," he pointed to Alex. "Brad's good, but he's no Alex."

"He's dangerous," Alex said.

Barton gave Alex a skeptical look, so Alex ran him through the entire Limelight affair, reminding him of the electrocuted couple by the cathedral, then moving on to the suffocated runewright, and finally to the Harper brothers.

"And you think Brad is behind this alchemical drug?" he asked when Alex finished.

"It certainly seems that way," Sorsha said.

"I'd be happy to be wrong," Alex added.

Barton looked at him for a long moment, then shook his head.

"Normally I'd reject such a thing out of hand, but I already watched you solve one of the most famous murders in New York earlier tonight. Now doesn't seem to be a good day to bet against you."

"We should be able to determine if Mr. Elder is our man easily enough, once we talk to him," Sorsha said.

"In that case," Barton said with a shrug, "follow me. Brad should be in his apartments upstairs at this hour."

Alex wasn't surprised at all when Bradley Elder's apartment was empty. Even without Mr. Elder's presence, it spoke volumes. The walls were lined with papers detailing all kinds of runic constructs and the waste basket overflowed with crumpled papers. It reminded Alex of his own vault when he'd been trying to figure out Moriarty's life transference rune. Unlike Alex's notes, however, all the ones in Brad's apartment were drawn with a wavy, unsteady hand.

"What the devil is all this?" Barton exclaimed when he saw the state of the apartment.

Agent Redhorn picked up a paper from the floor and flattened it out.

"I'd say we found the right guy," he said, holding the paper up. It looked exactly like the rambling notes in Arlo's book and on Olivia's notes.

"Where else could Mr. Elder be?" Sorsha asked.

"He must be in his workshop," Barton said, then led the way to the elevator.

He took them up to the lobby of his offices, then through to his private elevator and down to the power generation floor. When they reached the workroom at the end of the catwalk, they found it empty except for the giant, spinning spell that allowed the etherium generators to operate. Looking over the railing of the two-story space, Alex saw the messy linking runes that adorned the lower walls. If he'd remembered them properly, he would have known Brad was using Limelight, since each of them was wavy and badly formed.

"Do you see anything out of place here?" Sorsha asked him as Alex looked around. "Anything you don't recognize?"

Alex shook his head.

"These are standard linking runes," he said, indicating one of the rows that adorned the walls. "I can't be sure, but I'm guessing each one of these connects the big spell," he pointed at the golden spell, spinning slowly in the center of the room, "to one of Mr. Barton's etherium generators here or in the Bronx tower."

Barton nodded.

"That's it," he said. "I don't know where Brad has gone — maybe he has a girl he's seeing — but so far it looks like he's just doing his job."

"Maybe," Alex said, looking up at the high ceiling. "But somehow I doubt that's part of his job."

Everyone followed Alex's finger as he pointed upward. Sprawling across the curved ceiling was the biggest rune construct Alex had ever seen. It took up the entire area and it was so complex Alex could barely follow it. Some of it looked familiar; there were parts of finding runes, transference runes, and even linking runes, but what it all meant was a mystery.

"What is that?" Barton asked Alex. "What's it for?"

Alex could only shake his head.

"I have no idea," he said.

29

LIMELIGHT

Alex rubbed his eyes until he saw green blobs where his palms touched his eyelids. The last time he checked his pocket-watch, it was two in the morning and he still had no idea where Brad Elder was, or what the giant rune he left behind was meant to do.

"Anything?" Sorsha asked, her voice laden with weariness. Alex wasn't surprised. After all, she'd been shot a little over a day ago, and even with her sorcerer's regeneration she wasn't back to full strength.

"No," Alex finally admitted. "It's too complex for me to even guess what most of these symbols mean."

"So it could be a teleportation gate to steal Andrew's technology, or a bomb that will blow up half the city, or something even worse," Sorsha said.

There was a popping sound and Andrew Barton appeared out of thin air. He looked a little green and swayed a bit.

"Bradley Elder isn't in the Bronx relay tower or at the construction site of the new one in Brooklyn," he reported, once he'd steadied himself. "He had an apartment in the mid-ring, but he gave that up when he moved in here. I have no idea where he might be. What about a finding rune?"

"I tried twice," Alex said. "No result, which means either he's out of the city or he's shielding himself."

"And we still have no idea what that is," Andrew pointed at the ceiling. "Right?"

"Sorsha thinks it's there to steal an etherium generator," Alex said, causing Sorsha to kick him. "Well, it's as good an idea as any," he protested.

"So what do we do now?" Barton persisted.

Alex balled his hand into a tight fist then relaxed it, letting out his breath at the same time.

"We need to know what this rune does," he said.

"I know," Sorsha said. "How do you propose we do that?"

"I need a drink," Alex said, turning to Barton. "You got anything good nearby?"

Andrew looked at him as if trying to decide if he was serious, then reached into thin air and pulled out a cherry wood case with art deco designs inlaid in gold. Setting it on the worktable in the corner, he opened it, producing a round bottle with deep red liquid inside. Setting the bottle aside, Barton pulled three glass tumblers out of a space under the box lid and set them aside as well.

"Brandy," he said, filling each tumbler about halfway. Once he was done, he handed a glass each to Sorsha and Alex. "So what do you have in mind after we finish this drink?"

Alex set his glass down and reached into the pocket of his suit coat.

"The only way I'm going to figure that mess out," he said, nodding at the ceiling, "is to get inside Brad Elder's head." He pulled out the packet of Limelight powder Sorsha had given him to show around Runewright Row and held it up.

"No!" Sorsha yelled, grabbing Alex by the wrist more firmly than he would have thought possible. "You know that stuff is addictive," she said. "If you drink it, you'll want more."

Alex shrugged at that.

"Since there isn't any more, I don't see how that's a problem."

"I thought you said the reason you can't read all this," Barton said, pointing up at the complex rune, "was because Bradley was using Limelight. If you take some, how will we understand you?"

Alex thought about that for a moment.

"That's a good point," he said, moving to a bare patch of wall and chalking a door for his vault. Once he had it open, he went to the writing desk in his work area and retrieved a tablet and drawing pencil. He quickly sketched out the basic shape of Brad Elder's rune, then numbered each node.

"What's this for?" Barton asked as Alex drew.

"Come with me," he said, taking the brandy, the drawing, and the packet of Limelight into his vault. Leaving all three on his drawing table, he moved to a shelf with jars of powder for mixing runic inks and took several of them down, then pulled out the wooden panel that made up the back of the shelf. Behind it, set into the smooth gray wall was the door of a medium-sized safe.

"Why do you have a safe inside your vault?" Barton asked, fascinated. Sorsha hadn't said anything since Alex's mention of using the Limelight; she just stood next to Barton with a disapproving look. If her right arm weren't secured to her chest, Alex imagined she would be crossing her arms.

"Because someone might force me to open the vault and, like you, they'd never suspect a safe would be in here." He pulled open the safe and took out a thick accordion-style folio. Making his way back to the desk, he set it down, then put his drawing of Elder's rune in the center of the desk.

"This is my lore book," Alex explained, opening the top of the folio and pulling out a sheet of paper with a rune drawn on it. "Every rune I know is in here along with the instructions that detail how the rune is drawn and cast. I have an actual book, but these are easier to work with. It goes without saying that it's the most valuable thing I own."

"Why are you showing it to us?" Sorsha asked, a note of fear in her voice.

Alex didn't answer, but opened the top drawer of the cabinet by his writing desk and withdrew two large notepads and two normal pencils.

"Here," he said, handing them to the sorcerers. "When I'm under the influence of the Limelight, I'm going to look at each node of Brad's rune." He pointed to the first node on the model he'd drawn, the one labeled with the number one. "I'm going to use the runes pages from my lore book to explain how each node is put together." He pulled a page from the folio and put it down on top of the first node. "The order I put them down is important, so be sure to write down their names as I put them down." He pointed to the large title across the top of the rune page. The one he'd pulled was a minor barrier rune and the label was clear.

"What happens if you don't have the appropriate rune?" Barton asked.

Alex was ready for that, and he turned the rune paper upside down.

"If I put it down like this, it means that the rune is based on the one on the paper." He turned it on its side. "If it's on its side, that means this is the closest rune I have. Hopefully, I'll have what I need. Now I'm going to go node by node, since there will be duplicates, so be sure to get each node down before I start on the next one."

"This is a bad idea, Alex," Sorsha said. "Remember what happened to that runewright who tried to make a better mending rune."

"Redhorn and Mendes won't be back from FBI headquarters anytime soon and I figure you two can handle anything I might do by mistake," Alex said. He gave her a look of absolute confidence...which he didn't feel. Sorsha was right, his idea was insanely dangerous, but what choice did they have?

Alex picked up the Limelight powder and unfolded the paper packet. The powder itself was slightly greenish and he wondered absently if that was where it got its name.

"Only use half," Sorsha said. "If you need more, you can always use the rest later."

Alex nodded. He should have thought of that himself. He carefully tapped about half the powder into the tumbler of brandy. As soon as the powder hit the alcohol it fizzed and disappeared. As it did, the red liquid began to glow green.

"Well, that doesn't look good," Sorsha observed.

Without waiting to lose his nerve, Alex tipped the glass up and drained it.

He stood there for a moment, waiting for something to happen.

"Huh?" he said, putting the glass on top of the cabinet next to his drawing table. "I wonder when it starts to—"

Alex could see everything. It was truly amazing. The lines of magical force that made up the universe ran over every surface in his vault. He could see the makeup of his drawing table and the cabinet and all the various powders and inks he stocked to make runes. They were wholly insufficient, of course. There were so many more runes he would need, so many to be invented, and for that he would need many more ingredients.

As he turned, considering the possibilities, he saw the people, a woman and a man. He knew them, but he simply couldn't be bothered to remember. As he tried to pass them, however, the woman grabbed his arm, pointing out through the door. Alex could feel the presence of powerful runes beyond the door and he was drawn to them.

When he emerged onto the catwalk, the runes on the walls were just simple constructs, and poorly done ones at that. The spell, rotating in the center of the room like a miniature galaxy was impressive, but not the runes. Still, there was something here that he sensed. As he stood, sensing the power, his eyes were drawn up to the ceiling, and he laughed.

The construct was impressive, he'd give whoever wrote it that, but it was so crudely done. Alex could think of half a dozen improvements without even putting effort into it. What he needed to do was make a model of the rune.

Yes, a model.

He hurried back to his writing desk where he discovered that he'd anticipated his need. A rough drawing of the rune sat on his desk along with his lore book.

He let out a laugh.

Lore book? It was a child's primer, a book for simpletons.

He was tempted to sweep it away onto the floor like so much garbage, but something tickled his memory, compelling him to remember.

That's right, in this state his thoughts, all the brilliant thoughts, would be garbled. He couldn't become the most powerful magical being in the universe if he couldn't be understood. That's why the rune book was there. He'd use it to model each construct one at a time, then his two lackeys would write it down for him. It was such a good plan, a plan worthy of a mind like his.

Taking the papers from his lore book, he began laying them down on the first node, building it up so he could recreate it later. It was so simple now that the veil of reality had been lifted from his eyes. He laughed as he worked, delighted by the ease of it all. Once he was done, he'd have to look around to see if there were any more impossible problems for him to solve.

After all, solving impossible problems was the duty of the most powerful magical being in the universe, was it not?

Alex's head was killing him. It was like a hangover, as if he'd been drinking dime store booze all night and then stuffed his head into a beehive. He could tell that his eyes were open because a blinding light seemed to be coming from somewhere, but he couldn't distinguish anything. It was as if he were floating in a vast plain of white light.

For a moment he thought he must have died, but if he was dead, why was his head trying to kill him?

"—ex?" a thunderously loud voice called. "Alex? Can you hear me?"

He groaned and even that sound was oppressive. He tried to say, 'Lay off' but it came out more like, 'Lir-of.'

"Alex," Sorsha voice cut through the fog. His eyes seemed to focus, then the vast plain of light began to condense, squeezing down into the recognizable world.

He was on his back, looking up at the ceiling of his vault. Sorsha's anxious face hovered over him, her ice-blue eyes narrow with worry.

"Alex?" she said again.

"Please stop talking," he groaned, grabbing his splitting head.

"Hangover?" Andrew Barton's voice came from somewhere to his left. "I know just the thing."

Alex tried to sit up, but his head threatened to crack in half.

"I need a minute," he said, his voice barely a whisper.

"Here," Barton said, grabbing his arm and easing Alex into a sitting position. Once Alex was up, Barton pressed a glass into his hand. He tried to focus on it, but his eyes still weren't working properly.

"Don't look at it," Barton said, with mirth in his voice. "Drink it down in one go."

Alex took a deep breath and drained the cup. Two seconds later, he wished he hadn't. His heart raced and the pounding in his head exploded while his stomach muscles contracted hard enough to force the air from his lungs. After a moment that seemed like an eternity, Alex gasped and snapped into full awareness. His headache was still there, but much more manageable and his vision was back to normal.

"How do you feel?" Sorsha asked, the worried look still marring her perfect features.

"Like I've been on a two-week bender," Alex said, gingerly pushing himself up to his feet. "Did it work?"

"You tell us," Barton said. He handed Alex his notepad. Barton had meticulously detailed each node, listing the runes Alex had put down and in what order and orientation. As he went around the construct, examining each rune, he felt a tightness in his bowels that had nothing to do with his hangover.

"Is there more?" he asked, finally looking up from the pad.

"How did you know?" Barton asked.

"On your desk," Sorsha said.

Alex went to the writing desk and found it in shambles. His carefully filed rune masters were all over the place, including the floor and the paper where he'd drawn the rough copy of Brad's rune was covered with unintelligible notes. Interestingly, the cabinet that stood beside the table was clean of debris. It held three items laid out purposefully; the vault key Alex had taken from Arlo Harper, a sheet of flash paper with an unintelligible rune on it, and the hotel key that Arlo had in his pocket when he died.

"What's this?" he asked.

"You said that was for later," Sorsha said. "You weren't very forthcoming."

Alex turned his attention to the writing desk again. On the floor next to the desk was the paper box that held the pack of Tarot cards he'd purchased after Sherry told his fortune. Most of the cards were scattered around on the floor but one had been put on the desk, right in the center of the construct.

"Is there a time when sorcery is more powerful?" Alex asked, picking up the card.

Sorsha and Barton exchanged a long look and then the sorceress shrugged.

"Our power waxes and wanes with the moon," Barton said in a low voice. "We try not to advertise that fact."

"I figured," Alex said, turning the Tarot card around. It had a picture of a large full moon on it. "Whatever Brad is doing, this construct is designed to be used during a full moon."

"Alex," Sorsha said, her complexion going pale. "The moon is full right now."

Alex swore and peered at Barton's note pad again.

"Okay," he said, taking a deep breath. "All we have to do is figure out what he's trying to do and then hopefully we can find him."

"I take it we can't just unravel the rune," Barton said.

"It's attached to all those linking runes sending power to the city," Alex said, scanning the second node on the paper. "If we try to disrupt it, we may break all the runic links."

"That would turn off power to most of Manhattan," Barton said.

"We might also activate it by mistake," Alex continued. "Just let me work."

He moved to the writing desk and tore off the top note page, exposing a blank one beneath. As fast as he could, he began scribbling notes about what each node appeared to do.

"Take it easy," Barton said as Alex broke the tip of his pencil. "The moon is up, but it won't reach its zenith for at least another half hour."

Alex gave him a quizzical look, and Barton just shrugged.

"Sorcerers can sense these things," he explained.

Alex took a breath, then set to work again. Much of Brad's construct seemed familiar, like work he'd seen before, but he couldn't place it. He tried not to worry about that feeling, just let it hover in the back of his mind as he worked. The further he got around, the more it looked like the rune wasn't one single construct, but two that had been woven together.

"I got it," he said as Brad Elder's grand design snapped into focus in his mind. "It's two runes," he explained. "This first one," he pointed to the bottom left side of the construct, "is some kind of conversion rune."

"What's that?" Barton asked.

"Honestly I don't really understand how it works," Alex said. "But as near as I can tell, it changes the electrical energy from your power grid into magical energy."

"That's the reverse of what my etherium generators do," Barton said. "Why does Bradley want to change electricity into magic?"

"That's the second part," Alex said. "This is a transference rune. It can channel energy directly into a person."

Sorsha gasped and her mouth hung open. She looked remarkably like a fish.

"You bastard," she said taking an involuntary step toward Alex. He was sure that if her dominant hand hadn't been tied down, she would have tried to slap him. "That's how you did it," she fumed. "That's why you're still alive. You transferred life energy into yourself."

She was absolutely furious, but her expression was one of relief.

"Very good, sorceress," Alex said with a grin. His mind flashed back to the conversation they'd had in the church cemetery the day they buried Father Harry. She'd kissed him and then told him she didn't want to see him again because she'd lost too many people in her life already. In that moment, he realized that the angry look on her face was because he'd saved his own life, and in an act of absolutely unforgivable betrayal— he hadn't told her.

"Wait," Barton interrupted Alex's thoughts. "You have a rune that lets you refill lost life energy?"

"Apparently," Sorsha growled.

"Does that mean you can live forever?" Barton asked.

Alex shrugged, realizing too late that he'd revealed far too much.

"Is that what Bradley's trying to do then?" Barton guessed. "Become immortal?"

Alex shook his head.

"No," he said, indicating the drawing of the rune. "If I'm reading this right, he's going to infuse himself with magical energy drawn from your power grid."

"So he's trying to become a sorcerer?" Sorsha asked.

"Worse," Alex said. "Depending on how much energy he can absorb, and how long he can keep the construct going, Brad could give himself access to virtually unlimited magical power. He'd be a god."

30

ASCENSION

"Well we can't let my new engineer become a god," Andrew Barton said without any trace of a smile. "How do we stop him?"

Alex turned and pointed to the enormous yellow spell that spun lazily in the center of the room. It was that spell which provided magical energy to the etherium generators that they then turned into electricity.

"Turn it off," he said. "If you remove your spell, Brad's rune won't have anything to draw from."

"He can't," Sorsha said. "The power in that rune is enough to vaporize this building. It probably took weeks to cast."

"Months," Barton said. "I can remove it, of course, but it would take a few days to power it down."

"So we can't turn it off," Alex said.

"Now that you know how the rune is put together, can you destroy it, or sabotage it?" Sorsha asked.

Alex shook his head.

"I'm pretty sure I understand what it does, but the symbols are still gibberish to me," he said. "If I tamper with it, who knows what will happen? It could release all the energy from the spell at once."

Sorsha bit her lip and nodded.

"It sounds like the only point of failure in this chain is Bradley himself," Barton said.

"We need to find him and stop him," Sorsha said. "Preferably before he becomes a god. Where would he go to activate his rune?" This last was directed to Alex.

"I would have thought he'd be here or in the relay tower," Alex said. "That's where the power is."

"That's only where half of the power is," Barton corrected him. "The electricity is generated on site in each tower by my etherium generators. If he's using electricity, he has to wait for it to be generated."

"Why didn't he just tap directly into your spell?" Sorsha asked, looking from the spell to the rune painted on the ceiling above it. "He wouldn't have had to bother with converting magical energy to electricity and back."

She looked at Andrew Barton, but he could only shrug.

"It's because he doesn't know how to measure magical energy," Alex said. "I know it's probably child's play for you, but Brad's not a sorcerer. In order to make his rune work, he would have to precisely control the amount of energy his body is absorbing. The only way to measure the flow is to use electricity because he knows how to measure that."

"So cut the runes that link the spell to the towers," Sorsha said. "That way he'll have to come here."

It wasn't a bad idea, but there was one problem with it.

"Most of those runes are connected to the big one too," Alex said, pointing up at the construct on the ceiling.

"And if we disrupt that, we could incinerate ourselves and the core," Sorsha sighed.

"Time to call in the cavalry," Alex said to the sorceress. "Get your FBI agents looking for Brad on top of a high building, preferably one with line of sight to Empire Tower and the relay tower."

"What are you going to do?" Barton asked.

"Brad isn't going to go down without a fight," Alex said, heading for his vault. "I'm going to need a few specialized runes just in case."

Sorsha returned ten minutes later, just as Alex was rolling a cigarette by hand. Normally he didn't bother, since packaged cigarettes were just as good, but one of his clients had given him a hand rolling kit and a special blend of tobacco as a thank you. He'd told Alex that rolling a good cigarette was one of the vanishing manly arts. Alex didn't feel particularly manly as he licked the rolling paper and secured it in place, but he'd managed the job tolerably well.

"What are you doing?" the sorceress asked, giving him a stern look from the vault door.

"I can't count the ways this thing could go sideways," he said, dropping the three hand-rolled cigarettes into his silver case. "I figured I'm entitled to a final cigarette."

"And you made one for each of us," she said. "You aren't exactly filling me with confidence."

"How'd you do?" Alex asked, as he opened his gun cabinet and took out his shoulder holster.

"Redhorn and Mendes are checking, but so far no one is conducting a magic ritual on any of the buildings in the area."

Alex took off his coat and slipped on the holster, then took out his 1911 pistol and removed the magazine. Putting it back in the cabinet, he withdrew another magazine, one with a white stripe painted across the bottom, sliding it into the gun's handle.

"Just in case," he said, as Sorsha raised an eyebrow. She knew the magazine with the stripe carried Alex's spellbreaker bullets, capable of breaking down a sorcerer's defenses.

"Now all we need is to find Brad Elder," Sorsha said.

Almost before the words were fully out of her mouth, multicolored light bloomed inside the spell room. As Alex pulled the door to his vault shut, Brad's magic transference rune blossomed into full power. Half a second later, the lights flickered. Alex and Sorsha moved out onto the catwalk by the tall glass windows. Outside, the city was dark.

Sorsha said a word that Alex would have sworn she didn't know.

"He's started," Alex said unnecessarily.

The door burst open and Andrew Barton rushed onto the catwalk above them.

"Bradley's begun siphoning power," he said.

"So we gathered," Sorsha said, irritation in her voice. "What do we..."

Her voice trailed off, and she turned toward the wall.

"Do you feel that?" she asked Barton.

"Yes," he said, moving down the spiral stair to the catwalk.

"There," he called, pointing through one of the enormous windows that ran up the side of Empire Tower. "He's on top of the Chrysler building."

Alex looked out toward the northeast and saw a blaze of light shining from one of the upper floors of a distant building. Sorsha ground her teeth so hard, Alex could hear it. Her office was in the Chrysler building, as were Redhorn and Mendes.

"He'll need room for this," Alex said, remembering the setup he and Iggy used at the slaughterhouse. "Is there an observation deck?"

"Not outside," Sorsha said. "It's more of a big room on the seventy-first floor."

Barton moved off the catwalk back into the spell room and looked up at the golden spell.

"Whatever he's doing, it isn't drawing extra power from the spell," he announced.

"Give me your hand," Sorsha said, sticking her good arm out. "I'll teleport us to my office."

Barton reached out — but paused, then pointed to three new runes on the wall. It was obvious that they were new because instead of Brad Elder's cryptic scrawl, they were neat and precise.

"What are those?"

Alex shrugged as he grabbed Sorsha's forearm.

"I thought I might be able to slow down the flow of energy, but I only had the three linking runes prepared. It would take at least a dozen to make a dent."

Barton raised an eyebrow at that, but made no comment as he took Sorsha's hand.

The observation deck of the Chrysler Building was six floors above Sorsha's office and Alex was a little winded when they reached it. To be fair, he'd had a very long and eventful night, but he still resolved to get in some calisthenics from now on.

The door to the observation deck rattled in its frame as if a powerful wind were hammering it from the other side.

"You'd better let me go first," Barton said, stepping up to the door. He tried the handle and a thick spark of electricity leapt between the door and his hand. If Alex had tried that, he'd likely be dead, but the Lightning Lord didn't even react.

"You'll have to do better than that, my friend," he said, then pushed the door open.

"Don't touch the door," Sorsha said, following Barton through and into the observation deck. She didn't need to worry; Alex had no intention of getting anywhere near the door or its metal frame.

As he passed through the opening, Alex understood why Brad had used the Chrysler Building for his magic. The entire top of the building was covered in a steel façade and Brad was using it as a conductor. He must have anchored his linking runes somewhere above, probably attaching them to the massive steel spire that topped the building. Once he activated his construct, it sent the electric energy from Barton's etherium generators here.

The observation deck was a large open room with windows all around the sides. Normally the city would be visible beyond, blazing with light but now only Empire Tower could be seen, shining in the distance. The center had lounge space with couches and chairs, and there was a coffee bar much like the one Marnie ran at Empire Station. A fierce wind blew in the room, rushing around like a hurricane and carrying debris and bits of trash with it.

In the center of the room, Brad Elder had pushed the furniture away and set up his transference rune. It reminded Alex of the one Moriarty had used when he first restored some of Alex's life. Moriarty's rune had three nodes that transferred life energy into Alex's body.

Brad's setup wasn't as elegant. He had three separate constructs surrounding where he stood, each pulsing with purple light. Linking runes blazed beside each of the purple constructs, connecting them to each other and to the façade of the building.

As Alex watched, purple energy flowed up from the runes to Brad. He stood with his arms out and his head back as if a hot wind were buffeting him and his shoes were a few inches off the floor.

"What do you think you're doing, Bradley?" Barton boomed out in a magically enhanced voice to be heard over the wind.

Brad's eyes opened, and purple light shone out from them. Clearly his plan to absorb magical energy was going well. He flicked his hand like he was shooing a fly and a blast of wind slammed into Barton, knocking him off his feet. Before the Lightning Lord hit the ground, however, his body righted itself and hovered in the air. The wind no longer blew his coat and he looked for all the world as if he were standing on a street corner.

"Stop this now, Bradley," he said, his voice mild and earnest. "Before you get hurt."

"No," Brad said, his voice booming just like Barton's. "I'm through taking orders from you." He clenched his fist and Barton threw up a warding hand, repelling whatever magic the young man had thrown at him.

"Enough," Sorsha shouted, her eyes blazing just like Brad's. She stretched out her hand, and Brad was caught up higher in the air. His back arched and his hand stopped moving.

Alex had seen that before — Sorsha's ability to petrify someone like a statue, holding them in place. She staggered as Brad pushed back against her, but she didn't lose her grip.

Barton dropped to the ground and shook his head to clear it.

"We've got to stop this," he said, coming over to stand by Sorsha. "He's getting too powerful."

Sorsha looked at him, then nodded. Alex remembered her telling him that the paralyzing effect could also stop a person from breathing; do that long enough and they'd pass out, longer still and you could kill them.

Sorsha clenched her hand and Brad's eyes burned with purple fire. A moment later the sorceress' spell cracked with a noise like the building was coming apart. Sorsha was flung to the ground as Brad came free.

"You're too late to stop me," he growled, his voice shaking the windows. "I'm the most powerful being in the world."

Barton hit him with a blast of lightning that would have melted a car, but Brad shook it off. He rose in the air and clapped his hands together in Barton's direction. The sorcerer cried out and was flung against one of the large pillars that housed the building's support beams. He struggled, but it was clear whatever force held him there was overwhelming.

Turning, Brad grabbed Sorsha with the same power and pinned her against another of the columns. With his attention diverted, Alex saw his chance. Pulling his pistol, he fired three shots at Brad's hovering body. The first shattered the magical barrier he'd erected to protect himself and the following two hit him in the torso. Alex could see shield runes blaze to life as the bullets bounced off harmlessly.

Clearly Brad was better prepared than Alex gave him credit for. He raised the pistol to shoot again, but he'd lost the element of surprise. Brad flicked his wrist and the gun went sailing out of Alex's hands.

"None of that, Alex," he said with a wolfish smile. "I'm glad you came. I so wanted you to see this."

"You destroying yourself?" Alex asked. "I'd be happy just reading about it in the papers."

Brad laughed at that.

"I know better than to fall for your lies," he said. "You always were a charlatan. Running around getting your name in the paper, associating with sorcerers as if your magic were any good. You thought you were one of them, instead of what you really are."

Alex put on a sardonic smile and shrugged. Maybe if he got Brad talking, Sorsha or Barton would recover enough to take him down.

"And what am I, then?" he asked.

"You're just like the rest of us," Brad said. "Magic's refuse. Only you've fooled enough people that you've forgotten how the world treats us. Little better than palm readers and snake-oil salesmen. You turn a blind eye to your brothers and sisters out there on the streets every day hawking barrier runes in the rain for a nickel apiece, while you live high on the hog. You and your infallible finding rune."

Alex laughed at that.

"You've got to be kidding," he said, reaching into his pocket for his cigarette case. "Mind if I smoke?" he asked, flipping the case open.

Now it was Brad's turn to laugh.

"Whatever you're about to try, it won't work," he said. "In a few more minutes, I will transcend mortality. I will be a god."

"You want a smoke for the road?" Alex said, holding the case out in Brad's direction. When he didn't move, Alex shrugged, selected one of his hand-rolled cigarettes and dropped the case back in his pocket. "Okay," he said, lighting the cigarette with a paper match. "If you think my finding rune works all the time, you don't know much about finding runes."

Brad laughed again.

"See," he said. "I knew you were a fraud."

"And yet somehow I still manage to bring in the bad guys," he said, taking a long drag on the cigarette. "I guess I must just be good at my job."

"Your job as a fraud?" Brad sneered. "It's runewrights like you who give everyone hope, the great Alex Lockerby, the runewright who made good. It keeps them going through the rain and the snow and poverty, the false hope that one day they'll hit it big, just like Alex."

Alex hadn't really thought about that, and he worried that Brad might be right. He'd never lived his life for anyone but himself, but that didn't mean others weren't watching. Obviously Brad had watched, and he hated Alex for his success.

"I never asked to be anybody's role model," he said.

"Oh, is that why you get your name in the papers?" Brad mocked. "So no one would notice you? They practically worship you. Imagine how they'd feel if they could see you now, with nothing in your bag of tricks but a gun with spellbreaker runes on it. Imagine their disappointment that a gun was the best you could do."

"Oh, it's not my best," Alex said, putting on a confident smile. "The gun was just the quick way to stop you. The merciful way."

Brad laughed, throwing his head back with mirth.

"Are you trying to bluff me, you snake-oil salesman? Your lore isn't up to the challenge."

"My lore was good enough to recognize your transference rune," Alex said, feeling a bit irritated. "I knew you were going to change Barton's electrical power into magic energy and then feed it to yourself."

Brad looked shocked at that, then looked down at the purple runes on the ground and smiled.

"You're guessing," he said.

"You had to use electricity because you couldn't measure magical energy; only a sorcerer could do that."

"I can now," he said, purple energy beginning to crackle from his fingertips.

Alex ignored the threat and took another long drag on his cigarette.

"You see, I developed a transference rune over a year ago," he said, grinning in an effort to rub Brad's nose in the fact that he'd done it first.

"Liar!"

"I was dying and I needed it to transfer life energy back into my body," Alex explained. "So I understand how transference runes work. I also know that you needed to measure the energy to keep yourself from absorbing too much too fast."

Brad's eyes narrowed and he lifted his hand, calling a ball of purple fire into his open palm. Before he could throw it and reduce Alex to a stain on the carpet, however, the rune paper Alex had rolled into his cigarette ignited. His cigarette burst in a puff of tobacco and a rune made of two intersecting rhombuses flashed briefly with orange light.

It was an activation rune. Made in pairs, a runewright could cast one on a runic construct, then use the other one when he wanted the construct to activate — hence the name. Alex couldn't see it, but he knew that back in Empire Tower the three linking runes he'd cast had just become active, connecting three additional electric generators to Brad's construct.

Brad hesitated when he saw the rune blaze to life, probably trying to work out what it meant. That hesitation cost him his chance to kill his hated rival as his ascension rune was flooded with new power.

"What?" he screamed, as the purple light from the construct flashed so brightly that Alex had to cover his eyes.

When he could finally see again, Brad was spinning slowly in the air, his eyes blazing like beacons. His hands were pressed against his head and he opened his mouth and screamed.

That was Alex's cue. Breaking into a dead run, he darted across the floor to where Sorsha was still pinned to the support. Moving in front of her, he covered her body with his own. Behind him, the screaming reached a tortured pitch.

Sorsha was looking behind him, her eyes wide in horror.

"Close your eyes," he told her as he touched his forehead to hers, covering her face.

There was a sound like a pumpkin being shattered by a sledgehammer, and the screaming abruptly stopped. Alex felt a warm spray of mist and wet chunks hit his coat and the exposed flesh of his neck and hands. Around him on the pillar, the white paint was stained red and pink bits of brain matter slid slowly down toward the floor.

"Oh dear God," Sorsha gasped, in a nauseated voice. She looked up at him with eyes wide as saucers. "Alex, what did you do?"

"I'll tell you what he didn't do," Barton fumed, approaching them covered head to toe in gore. "He didn't shout a warning." The sorcerer clenched his fist and a wave of electrical energy washed over him, burning away the blood and brain matter without touching his clothes.

"There you go, Barton," Alex said, stepping back from Sorsha, who was visibly trembling. "No harm done."

The Lightning Lord leaned in close and sneered at him.

"My mouth was open," he growled.

That was all Sorsha could take and she dropped to her knees and retched. When she was done, she allowed Alex to help her up, being careful not to look at the now headless remains of Brad Elder.

"Those linking runes you cast," Barton guessed. "They transferred more power into the construct than Bradley could handle. It overloaded his mind and...poof."

Alex nodded.

"I wanted to give him a chance, but..."

"You needed a fail safe," Barton finished, nodding and looking around at the mess. "I may have to drink a gallon of brandy to get this taste out of my mouth, but I'm glad you had one."

As he spoke, the lights in the building came on, and outside the windows, the city was lighting up again as well. In the center of the room, Brad's ascension rune had already faded away to nothing. Alex was glad it was over, but he regretted killing Brad. He kind of felt like he'd failed to save him. The more rational part of his mind realized that there was no way he could have saved Brad; the man was too poisoned by hate and jealousy. Still, Alex wondered if Brad had been right about him.

"Well, Alex," Sorsha said, fully in control of herself again. "I can tell you without reservation that Mr. Elder was wrong about you." She reached out and touched his lapel. As she did, a chill ran over his body, followed by a mist that carried all the bits of offal off his clothes and skin.

"Was he?" Alex asked, giving in to a bit of self-doubt.

"Yes," she said, looking around at the destruction and gore. "Not only are you intelligent, talented, and powerful, but you are, without a doubt, the most dangerous man I've ever met."

Alex chuckled. He remembered the first time he'd met Sorsha, how he'd almost used his escape rune to get away from her. She'd been like a Greek goddess, full of power, fury, and without accountability, in a word, terrifying. To have her think the same of him was a compliment...and a warning.

"Right back at you, doll," he said.

Sorsha's eyebrows went up, and she smirked at him. Taking two steps forward, she moved so close to him that he could feel her breath. He looked down into her pale eyes and she gave him a smile that raised his body temperature a few degrees.

"You don't get to call me doll," she said in a low voice, barely more than a whisper. She suddenly stood up on her tiptoes and kissed him on the cheek. "Not yet, anyway."

With that, she sauntered away in the direction of the stairwell, her hips swaying as she went. Alex watched until she disappeared, then turned to find Barton rolling his eyes at him.

"What is it with you, Lockerby?" he said.

31

VAULTS

An hour later, Alex was dozing in one of the observation deck chairs. Andrew Barton had teleported back to Empire Tower as soon as Alex assured him that Brad's linking runes wouldn't stop working now that he was dead. He had insisted that Alex meet with him in the coming week to discuss having Alex maintaining those runes. Alex wasn't thrilled about that, but as long as he was just helping out from time to time, it would be all right.

Thanks to her role as an FBI consultant, Sorsha was obliged to take control of the scene of Brad's demise. She wanted Alex to stay in case she needed to confirm the events of the evening and how they related to Limelight. He was impressed on how efficiently she woke up a cadre of FBI lackeys to go over the remains of Brad's ascension rune, his rune book, and even his physical remains. Though he couldn't see it, Alex was sure a similar army of dark-suited Agents were going through Brad's apartment in Empire Tower at that very moment.

"We need to talk," Sorsha said, standing over where he sat.

"I thought you needed to keep all these people moving," Alex said, waving his hand around lazily at the bustle in the room.

"Agent Redhorn is handling it," she said. "Why don't you and I go down to my office where it will be quieter?"

Alex opened his eyes and looked up at the sorceress. The expression on her face drifted between concern and fussy librarian. That look meant she didn't want to talk about that peck on the cheek she'd given him. Whatever she did want to talk about, she clearly took it very seriously, and she believed Alex didn't take it seriously enough.

"Fine," he said, getting up out of the comfortable chair. "But I'm tired, I'm hungry, and if you want to talk about something serious, I'm going to need coffee." He reached into his pocket and pulled out the bit of chalk he always carried. "Let's use my vault."

A look of irritation washed over the sorceress' face, but after a moment she rolled her eyes and nodded.

"All right," she said.

Alex led her away to the far side of the room and opened his vault door against the wall. Once inside, he went to the kitchen and used a boiler stone to start heating water for coffee. In the ice box, he had a block of hard cheese, apples, and some milk, all of which he set out on the little table against the wall.

"All right," he said, opening a can of instant coffee. "What do you want to talk about?"

"Why are we doing this here?" Sorsha asked, standing in the doorway with her free hand on her hip. "You have a real percolator at your brownstone."

Alex was about to protest, but her look changed from neutral to mocking.

"You saw that?" Alex asked. He'd been sure that she'd been mostly unconscious when he carried her through his vault from South Brother Island.

She raised an eyebrow expectantly, and Alex took the boiler stone out of the pot of water and returned the food to his icebox.

"Through here," he said, heading back out into the hall and down to the end where the locked door to his room stood.

"When did you figure this out?" she asked as he used his watch to bypass the runes that kept the door closed.

"I used the same technique Malcom Jones used to connect his mind runes together," Alex explained. "Once I figured that out, I realized I could open multiple doors into my vault."

Alex led Sorsha into his bedroom, then down the stairs to the main floor. He went quietly to avoid waking Iggy, but he needn't have bothered, for his mentor was sitting at the kitchen table with a plate of toast, a cup of coffee, and one of his pulp detective novels.

"Well, here you are," he said, setting aside his book. "I note you managed to return without getting shot this time. Both of you," he added, standing as Sorsha came in behind Alex. "Let me get you some coffee and you can tell me all about it."

"Before we do that," Sorsha said, sitting down once Alex pulled out a chair for her, "we need to have a discussion."

Iggy gave her a quizzical look as he set out cups and saucers.

"Ominous," he said.

"You sure you want to bring Iggy into this?" Alex asked as he returned with the coffee pot to fill the cups.

"I don't believe for a minute that Dr. Bell is ignorant of what's been happening," Sorsha said, giving Alex an exasperated look.

"So, what is it you'd like to discuss?" Iggy asked, sitting back down.

"The secrets we keep," she said, sipping her coffee. She closed her eyes and sighed as the warm caffeine revitalized her.

"You'll have to be a bit more specific," Alex said.

"Let's start with your new vault," Sorsha said. "And what about transferring life energy? Are you going to outlive me now?"

"I'm sure Alex would be happy to use the transference rune on you whenever you like," Iggy said.

"That's not the point," Sorsha said. "Over the last few years, we've been accumulating secrets. Secrets like Dr. Kellin's youth serum, mind control runes, and now Limelight."

Alex opened his mouth to respond, but Sorsha kept going.

"And it isn't just Limelight this time, we now know that it's possible to channel power directly into a person to give them magical abilities, not to mention eternal life."

Iggy sighed.

"The ramifications of this are frightening," he admitted. "The kind of power that's being exposed."

"None of that is our fault," Alex said. "What is it you think we can do?"

"We need to work together, Alex," she said. "Who knows how many people the Legion has at their disposal?"

"With a name like the Legion, I'm guessing it's a lot," Iggy said.

"And there's just three of us," Sorsha said. "We've been lucky, but how long is that going to last? How much have we missed?"

"Imagine what might happen if the Legion got their hands on Limelight?" Iggy added, soberly.

"But they didn't," Alex said.

"This time," Sorsha said. "What happens if we're not there next time? Are we going to hope Andrew leaves off studying his grand plans long enough to stop them?"

Alex saw her point, and he exchanged a look with Iggy. After a moment, his mentor gave a barely perceptible shrug.

"Okay," he said. "Are you suggesting I start working with you at the FBI?"

Sorsha shook her head.

"You need to stay independent," she said. "People with magical problems are much more likely to come to you than to the FBI. But when you catch a case with dangerous magical implications, you need to let me know. The Bureau already brings these kinds of cases to me, so when they do, I'll run them by you to make sure we've got our bases covered."

"So what you want is more communication," Iggy said.

"I want more than that," Sorsha said. "Groups like the Legion are out there, working to gain power. If we don't start looking for them, discovering their plans, and countering them — eventually we're going to lose."

"How can we find out what they're up to?" Alex asked.

The sorceress looked at him and shrugged with a sigh.

"I don't know," she said. "But we need to be ready to move when something comes up."

"That sounds fair," Alex said. "We'll share information about potential problem cases."

"There's one more thing," Sorsha said, giving Alex a steady, serious look. "I need to know what you two can do," she said, turning to look at Iggy. "It seems like every time we find one of these cases, you come out of it with new and interesting abilities. I'd be lying if I said that didn't concern me, but I've come to trust you in spite of that feeling."

"And you want us to trust you in return," Iggy said, glancing at Alex.

She held his eyes and then nodded.

Alex sighed and sipped his coffee.

"You realize that however powerful you think we are, you're a sorceress who works for the federal government," he said. "If Iggy and I told you something you didn't like, you could have us locked up, seize this house, or something even worse. It seems like the risk of airing all our secrets only goes one way."

Sorsha nodded, offering no rebuttal.

"I know I'm asking a lot," she said at last. "Just think about it. If I'm right, things are only going to get worse. We're going to need each other."

Alex's mind flashed back to the attic above the slaughterhouse as he lay on the floor, weak as a newborn kitten.

You're going to be my lever, Alex, Moriarty had said. A lever to move the world, to save it from disaster. Sorsha was the second person to tell him the world was about to go to hell, and he was going to be in the middle of it. If this kept up, he was likely to get a complex.

"We'll think about it," he said, intending to go through it with Iggy later. "Right now, it's late, or rather early, and I need some sleep."

Sorsha nodded, looking exhausted herself.

"If you'd like, my dear, you can sleep in my vault," Iggy said. "You don't look like you're up to teleporting home."

Sorsha thanked him and he opened his permanent vault door in the kitchen, leading her through to the bed she'd used after she'd been shot. For his part, Alex went upstairs to his room. The vault door was still open on the Chrysler Building's observation deck from when he and Sorsha had come through, so he went to close it.

Once he was done, he stopped in his workroom. The writing desk was still a mess from his work under the influence of Limelight. He didn't remember what he thought when he was working, but he remembered how it made him feel. Just the thought of it filled him with the desire to try it again.

Turning away from the table, he tried to break the spell. His eyes fell on the folded rune on his side table, the one he'd written under the effect of the Limelight. Arlo Harper's vault key was sitting on top of it, along with the hotel key Alex had pulled from the dead man's pocket.

Picking them up, he realized immediately what he'd been trying to tell himself. He wanted to put it back down and get to it later, but he knew he wouldn't get any sleep until he'd used the strange rune. Taking a deep breath, he put the keys and the rune in his pocket, then headed for the door to his second office.

It was almost ten o'clock when Alex went down to the lobby of the Fillmore Hotel to use the telephone. Picking up the receiver, he dialed the operator at the Central Office of Police. Since it was Sunday, Lieutenant Detweiler and Detective Nicholson weren't likely to be there, so Alex asked for the lieutenant's home number.

"You're a bad penny, Lockerby," Detweiler said once his wife called him to the phone. "Just when I think you're gone, you turn back up."

"What's the matter, Lieutenant?" Alex asked, genuinely confused. "Didn't I help you get all that good press?"

"Yeah," he said. "And then the very next day your buddy Pak solves the case of the decade. Drove all mention of the Brothers Boom off the front page. It guarantees Callahan will be the new Captain."

Alex felt for the guy. He'd done everything right and still came in second.

"You know Captain Rooney can't pick you to succeed him, right?" he asked.

"I know," the lieutenant growled. "It would look bad for his campaign. I just hoped if I got a big enough case, I could force his hand."

"At least Callahan will be a good Captain," Alex said.

"And your friend will be his replacement. No way anybody will object now that he solved the Anderson murder."

"Well, I can't help with the job," Alex said, "but how would you like to get back on the front page?"

There was a pause on the line.

"I'm listening," he said at last.

"Grab Detective Nicholson and half a dozen officers and meet me at the Fillmore Hotel," he said.

"You aren't going to tell me why, are you?" Detweiler sighed.

"You know me so well, Lieutenant."

"Okay, Lockerby," Detweiler said as he strode into the lobby of the Fillmore with Nicholson and five officers in tow. "Why am I here?"

"This is where Arlo Harper was staying before he blew himself up," Alex said.

Detweiler's face brightened.

"Did he leave some of the money in his room?"

"Sadly, no," Alex said, leading the way up the stairs to the room Also had occupied. "That's bound to be in his vault."

"And he's the only one who can open it," the Lieutenant said with a sigh. "So what's so important?"

Alex used the room key and opened the door. The Fillmore was an elegant inner ring hotel and the room reflected that. There was a double bed with a brass rail headboard and footboard. A sumptuous rug covered most of the floor, and a cherry wood roll-top desk stood in the corner. A door led into a small bathroom, and there was a dressing table with a mirror against one wall. The entire room was the picture of style. The only thing out of place was the massive steel door that stood open against one wall.

"Is that your vault?" Detective Nicholson said, as they entered.

"Nope," Alex said, shaking his head.

The vault didn't have magelights inside, but Alex had entered and lit the oil lanterns Arlo Harper used for light. Inside were piles of cash littering the floor.

"He left it open?" Detweiler gasped, looking at the piles of cash.

"Yep," Alex nodded. "Looks like the headline tomorrow will be *Police Recover Stolen Money*."

"Nicholson," Detweiler said, a fierce grin fixed firmly on his face. "Go call in for an armored car and a dozen more officers."

The detective headed back down to the phone in the lobby while Detweiler directed the officers with him to begin bringing the money out of the vault and stacking it on the bed.

"How long will this thing stay open?" he asked.

Alex shrugged. "Until you close it," he said. "Once you do that, whatever's left inside will be gone forever."

Detweiler considered that for a moment, then had two of the officers move the heavy dresser in front of the door to prevent its being closed by accident. As the pile of money on the bed grew bigger and bigger, Detweiler visibly relaxed.

"You did good, scribbler," he said, using the pejorative as a term of affection for the first time. "It's a lucky thing the maid didn't come in and see all that cash laying around."

Luck, of course, had nothing to do with it. The rune Alex had written under the influence of the Limelight had linked Arlo's key to Alex's vault rune. That allowed him to open Arlo's vault as if it were his own. That wasn't supposed to be possible, but Alex was beginning to figure out that when practitioners of magic talked about things being *impossible*, what they really meant was, *not figured out yet*. He didn't know if he'd be able to open the vault again or if the Limelight rune only gave him this one shot, so he'd opened it here in Arlo's room just in case.

Detweiler gave Alex a sly glance, then looked him up and down. "I don't need to search you, do I?" he asked. "Just in case you might have picked up some of that cash, entirely accidentally of course."

Alex laughed at that. He'd been here with the open vault for over an hour. He'd gone through it carefully, looking for any of Arlo's rune lore. It wouldn't do to have something dangerous fall into the hands of the police, after all. He'd removed a few notebooks — and anything else that might be dangerous — to his own vault before he called the lieutenant, but no money.

"No," Alex answered. "I wouldn't mind if you paid me for my time on this case, though."

"You know I can't do that," the lieutenant said. "The Captain would never go for it after the fact."

Alex shrugged. He'd done very well for himself as a detective, so he could afford the occasional pro-bono case. Plus, he'd probably make it up quickly, writing runes for Andrew Barton.

"Of course," Detweiler said with an enigmatic look. "You did find the stolen money, and banks usually post rewards for the return of their currency."

Alex looked at Detweiler, but the big lieutenant was just watching the removal of the cash with intense interest.

"I'll be sure to drop your name to the bank people when we return all this."

"You know something, Lieutenant?" Alex said.

"What?"

"If you tell anyone I said this, I'll deny it...but you're all right."

The door to the room opened and Detective Nicholson came hustling in.

"I called Central," he reported. "They put me through to the Captain when I told them about the money. He's on his way here."

"You'd better make yourself scarce," Detweiler said to Alex.

Alex didn't have to be told twice; he'd only met Rooney on a few occasions and none of them had endeared him to the Captain.

"Alex," Nicholson said as he turned to leave. "Thanks for your help. Would it be okay for me to call on you, if I need any help with magical stuff in the future?"

Alex gave the man one of his cards and headed out. Instead of going for the street, he headed down into the hotel's basement. Finding an empty mechanical room, he chalked a door on a patch of bare wall and went through into his vault, closing it behind him.

A pile of Arlo's notes sat on Alex's writing desk. Most were an unintelligible mess, but there were a few runes Alex could make out. He'd review them later when he was better rested. Moving to the shelf that concealed his safe, Alex took down the jars and removed the back panel. Opening the safe, he picked up the container that he'd taken from Arlo's vault. It was a small jar with a screw-on lid and it was almost full of lime green powder.

Alex's hands trembled as he placed it carefully inside the safe. He grabbed the door to close it, but hesitated, looking back at the pile of unintelligible notes on his desk. He wouldn't need much to interpret them.

"No," he said forcefully. He closed the safe and locked it, then returned the false panel and the jars of components.

Taking a deep, cleansing breath, Alex turned and made his way across the room. As he passed the library with its fireplace and comfortable chair, he noticed a brown file folder sitting on the reading table. Tired as he was, he couldn't remember what it was or where he'd gotten it.

With a resigned sigh, he crossed to the table and picked it up. He thought it was a police folder, but when he opened it, he found details about the museum's missing mummy. He'd forgotten that he'd promised Weldon Swain that he'd look into who stole it.

Alex was about to drop it back where he found it and get some sleep, but the folder was thin with only a few pages. It wouldn't hurt to just look at it.

Sitting in the comfortable chair, Alex opened the folder and read the first page that detailed the museum's acquisition of the mummy. Less than a minute later, he sat back in his chair with his jaw hanging open in shock.

"Son-of-a-bitch."

32

REVELATIONS

It was just after seven-thirty on Monday morning when Alex opened the door to his waiting room. As expected, Sherry was sitting behind the reception desk, but this time she didn't look up when he came in.

As he shut the door, Alex twisted the bolt, locking it behind him. Turning back to the desk, he reached into his coat and pulled out his 1911, holding it down at his side as he approached. The desk was clean of papers, which was unusual, and Sherry had laid out Tarot cards in the center like she had done when she'd done a reading for him. The top card depicted a man in a robe with an infinity symbol over his head, and the text read, The Magician. Below it was the High Priestess, and between them was a card with a tall, shrouded figure bearing a curved scythe.

"Who are you really?" Alex demanded when Sherry didn't look up at him. "Tell me who you work for!"

Sherry flinched under his words, and finally looked up. Her mascara ran in dark tracks down her cheeks and her eyes were red and puffy.

"Please," she said, her voice a hoarse whisper. "Please don't kill me."

Alex hadn't known what to expect when he came in, but he thought he was prepared for anything. Looking at Sherry's miserable, tearstained face, he realized he wasn't. He tried to hold the stern look he'd put on his face, but Sherry looked so morose, he just couldn't.

"Calm down," he said, jamming his pistol back into the holster.

"I'm sorry," Sherry said in a quiet voice. "You wouldn't have believed me," she sobbed. "You know you wouldn't."

Alex held her gaze for a long moment, then turned and opened the door to his office.

"Come in here," he said, his voice softening.

He went in and pulled the bottle of good Scotch out of his desk along with two tumblers. As Sherry came in, he poured two fingers in each glass, passing one to her as she sat in one of the overstuffed chairs that faced Alex's desk.

"How did you find out?" she said, her voice quiet.

Alex pulled a folded paper from his pocket as he sat behind his desk.

"When Danny and I went to look at the telephone that killed Dolly Anderson, the museum curator almost threw us out. Seems he was mad at me because the last time I was there, a mummy and a security guard went missing. I had to promise him I'd look into it."

He unfolded the paper he'd brought, turning it so that Sherry could see.

"This is the information sheet he gave me about the missing mummy," he pointed to a long nearly indecipherable name at the top of the paper.

Ankhesenpaaten Tasherit.

"Now that didn't mean anything to me," Alex said, "but thankfully Mr. Swain provided a handy pronunciation guide."

Alex moved his finger down one line to where the mummy's name had been phonetically written out.

(Anox-en-pay-a-teen Ta-sher-eet)

Taking a pencil from his desk he drew two lines under parts of the phonetic spelling.

(Anox-en-pay-a-teen Ta-sher-eet)

He pointed to the second underlined section first as he read them aloud.

"Sheree Nox. Or rather, Sherry Knox."

"That could be a coincidence," she said, without looking up.

"It could," Alex conceded. "But last year you did a card reading for me. In it you used the Knight of Swords to represent me, then put it between two cards, the Lovers, and the High Priestess. The last card you added to that pile was the Wheel of Fortune, which you said represents great change. Now the only change that involved lovers was the departure of Leslie Tompkins and your replacing her."

Alex paused until Sherry looked up at him.

"Everything in your prediction was precisely accurate," he continued. "But I could never figure out how you related to the High Priestess."

He moved his hand further down the page and pointed to a short line of description.

"According to this, the missing mummy was a priestess of Ra. So now it makes sense why your reading represented you as the High Priestess."

"So you think I'm a three-thousand-year-old mummy?" Sherry said. "Like Boris Karloff in that movie? That sounds crazy, Alex."

She was right, of course. It sounded like the deranged rantings of a madman, but Alex knew better. He'd seen too much to doubt it was possible.

"Three years ago, I'd have said you were right," Alex confirmed. "But not now." He opened his cigarette case, offering one to Sherry before lighting one for himself. "Why don't you tell me how you came to be my secretary," Alex said then. "You can start by telling me what happened to the missing security guard, Paul Crane."

Sherry took a long drag on the cigarette to calm her nerves. Even after she was done, her hands still shook.

"You have to understand, Alex," she said. "I didn't have any choice in the matter."

"What happened to him?" Alex asked, pretty sure he already knew the answer.

"The magic that held my soul intact consumed his body in order to revive me," Sherry said.

Alex remembered the runes that lit up on the jars when he and Iggy examined the mummy. Putting them in order must have activated the construct. They were lucky that it didn't work right away and kill one of them.

"All right," Alex said, keeping a neutral tone.

"It wasn't my fault," Sherry said again, tears welling up in her eyes once more.

"I know," Alex said. "You couldn't have known who would be there when the spell went off. But, of course, you knew someone would be. Someone would have to lose their life to bring you back."

"I didn't make that spell," Sherry said angrily. "I didn't choose to have my body cut apart and buried."

She spoke through clenched teeth, and tears ran freely down her face.

"Who did?"

Sherry took a deep, shuddering breath and mastered herself.

"Someone like you."

Alex chuckled at that. He didn't know if she'd said it to gain sympathy or to try and distract him, but he was pretty sure there weren't any circumstances where he'd order a young woman dismembered and entombed.

"You barely know me at all," he responded.

"I knew who you were long before we met," she said. "The moment I awoke in this world with a new body and Paul Crane's memories in my head, I could feel your presence."

Alex had wondered how Sherry learned to speak English without a foreign accent. Having the dead security guard's memories must have made her transition much easier.

"I doubt you felt anything special about me," he said. "There are hundreds of runewrights in the city, maybe thousands."

Sherry nodded, wiping her eyes with a handkerchief.

"True," she said. "But there are only two who could be Pharaoh," she said. "You, and your mentor."

"Pharaoh? As in king?" Alex chuckled. "We don't have those here. You should know that."

Now it was Sherry's turn to laugh.

"Pharaoh doesn't mean king," she said. "Although many of Egypt's lesser kings assumed the title."

"What is it, then?" Alex asked, more curious than he would care to admit.

"There isn't really a word for it in English," Sherry said. "A Pharaoh is the master of the four magics. I suppose you could say that it means...rune lord."

Alex shook his head as he poured another Scotch for himself.

"I hate to disappoint you, Ms. Knox," he said, moving the bottle toward her. "But there are only three branches of magic, and runewrights are the least of them, not the other way around."

Sherry held out her tumbler and Alex refilled it.

"Give me your pencil and a note pad," she said. When Alex complied, Sherry drew the runewright symbol that was on the office's outer door. It was a simple device that he'd seen every day his office had been in the building, just a triangle inside a hexagon with an inkwell in the exact center.

"This is the symbol of your craft," she said. "But you don't know what it means, do you?"

"Of course I do," Alex scoffed. "The hexagon is for the geometric school of runes, the points of the triangle are the three branches of magic, and the inkwell represents how runes are made."

"No," Sherry said in a mild voice. She used the pencil to point to the tips of the triangle. "These represent sorcery, alchemy, and augury." She moved the point of the pencil into the middle, to the inkwell. "All of them surround, and are contained by, the magic of runes."

"Except there's no such magic as augury," Alex felt compelled to point out.

For the first time since he'd come in, Sherry smiled at him. It wasn't so much a smile but a knowing grin.

"Isn't there?"

"If there were, someone would know about it," Alex said.

"But you do," Sherry pressed. "An augur is someone who can see the future."

Alex felt uncomfortably like someone had just poured ice water down his back. He'd managed to convince himself that Sherry's card reading last year had been accurate because it was vague, and that she'd gotten lucky. Deep down, he'd always doubted it, but he knew there was no such thing as fortune telling or oracles. Now that Sherry said it out loud, however, he had to doubt his conclusion. Too much of Sherry's prediction had been accurate for it to be a coincidence.

Besides, Alex hated coincidence. It was the refuge of lazy thinking.

"If you're telling the truth," he said, trying to keep his voice from breaking nervously, "why aren't there any other augurs? Why doesn't anyone know about them?"

She shook her head and sipped her Scotch.

"I don't know," she said after a moment. "There might be one or two, somewhere in the world, but there aren't any on this continent. I'd know if there were."

Alex shook his head to clear it. There were far too many tantalizing avenues of exploration in what Sherry had said, but she still hadn't answered his central question.

"So why did you come to work for me?" he asked. "I know you orchestrated our meeting. What did you expect to gain?"

"That's a long story," she said. "One filled with loss, pain, and even my death. Suffice it to say that in my former life I served a Pharaoh. He was a hard and cruel man who took whatever he wanted, and his rule was absolute."

Sherry had set her drink down on Alex's desk and was rubbing her hands together as if they were in pain. He wondered what this rune lord had required of Sherry but decided not to dwell on the possibilities.

"I don't understand why you came, then," Alex said. "Especially if you thought I was like him."

She looked up at him and smiled. Before she had been afraid, but now he could tell that fear was gone. Now she was just — sad.

"That's why I came, Alex," she said. "Augury isn't like other magic; the gift comes and goes on its own. I couldn't make the cards tell me about you, about...about whether you were too far gone."

"Too far gone for what?" Alex said, now genuinely confused.

"You have great power, Alex," she said earnestly. "Some of it you've had for a while and some you are just discovering, but soon you will have enough power to..."

"To become the kind of man who takes what he wants because he can?" Alex said in a hard voice.

Sherry looked up and met his eyes, then nodded.

"So you came to see what kind of man I was," he guessed. "Put yourself in a position where you could put a bullet in my back if the situation became necessary, right?"

She held his gaze and nodded again.

Alex felt sick. Not because Sherry intended to murder him, but because she actually thought he could be the kind of man she had described. He didn't dismiss the idea outright, though. He'd seen how some sorcerers acted, secure in their status and assured of their superiority. Some of them treated regular people like stray dogs, or at best, pets. It was a by-product of their power, and Sherry had just told him that he was capable of more power than that. What would that kind of power do to him? Was Sherry right to be scared?

Reaching into his jacket, Alex pulled out his 1911. Sherry tensed but didn't move as he cocked it then reversed it, setting it on the far side of his desk near her.

"Pick it up," he said.

She hesitated for a moment, then reached out and took the gun.

"What do you think now?" he asked.

New tears blossomed in her eyes, and she set the gun back on his desk.

"I'm sorry, boss," she said, smiling through the tears. "I didn't know you then. Honestly, I'm not sure I trusted that I knew 'til right now."

Alex left the gun where it sat and sighed. He was sure of his own mind, but it was nice to have Sherry's confirmation.

"That Pharaoh you worked for," he said, once Sherry got a hold of herself. "What happened with him? Why did he have you mummified?"

Sherry tried hide a sly grin that crept across her face.

"I convinced him that a star would fall from the sky and destroy Egypt," she said. "He and his supporters, his sorcerers and his alchemists came up with the preservation magic to escape it. I knew once they were gone, no one would be in a hurry to bring them back.

Unfortunately, he insisted that I come with him. It was a sacrifice I was...willing to make."

"You little schemer," Alex laughed. "You mounted a coup against him. I don't know whether to fire you or give you a raise."

Alex had to give Sherry credit — she'd taken an enormous risk to stop her Pharaoh, and she'd come to work for him not knowing if she'd have to try it again. That took guts.

"Hey," Alex said, realizing what her story meant. "Does that mean this rune lord guy is out there somewhere, waiting to come back?"

"No," Sherry said, shaking her head. "When I worked at the museum, I found out that his tomb had been raided and his Canopic jars were smashed. Once that happened, the magic was lost."

That made Alex feel better. The thought that someone more powerful than a sorcerer was waiting somewhere to wake up made him shiver.

"Well," Sherry said, after Alex had lapsed into silence. "Which is it going to be? Am I fired or are you giving me a raise?"

Alex considered her for a moment, then shrugged. He wanted to question Sherry extensively about how her power worked and just what an augury could do, but he knew she'd only have to repeat it later for Iggy.

"I guess I'd better give you a raise," he said. "Assuming your cards don't have something else in mind."

"Nope," she said with her usual smile. "The only thing they keep saying is that you aren't seeing what isn't there."

"That doesn't make any sense."

"I know," she said. "That's why I didn't bring it up. Now I'd better go fix my makeup before a client shows up."

"Do you have any plans for dinner, Miss Knox?" he asked as she stood to leave.

"No."

"Good, I'd like you to dine with Dr. Bell and me at the brownstone," Alex said. "Will that be okay?"

"Sure thing, boss," she said, then stepped out into the waiting room.

Alex watched her go, then picked up his pistol, uncocked it, and returned it to his holster. He poured himself another two fingers of Scotch, then put the bottle away.

His conversation with Sherry was a lot to take in. The least amazing thing was that his secretary was a three-thousand-year-old Egyptian priestess. The idea that Alex had the skills necessary to make himself a king worried him. He finally understood how Iggy had felt when he began to master the Archimedean Monograph; it was intoxicating but also terrifying.

Alex had a good mind to just forget his conversation, have a nice dinner with Iggy and Sherry and never mention it again. It was certainly the sensible thing to do.

The thought had barely crossed his mind when Moriarty's cultured British voice suddenly echoed in his brain.

Dark forces are at work, Alex. They seek a war, they desire it. They exist to rule man, or failing that, to destroy him.

Alex felt a chill. Did Moriarty know what Sherry believed about him? Was he referring to Alex?

How do you explain the sudden reappearance of ancient and long forgotten magics, of alchemy turned to a devastating weapon of disease, of science given the power to burn down whole cities at the flick of a switch?

Alex downed the Scotch he'd poured. He immediately wanted another, but he was going to need a clear head. Sorsha had been right, they needed to work together. Between the two of them they were piling up powerful and dangerous enemies, and it was looking very likely that they'd need each other if they were going to live through whatever conflict Moriarty saw coming.

He ground his teeth as he contemplated his next move.

"I really hate it when she's right," he growled to no one.

Alex sighed and picked up the phone on his desk, dialing the number of the brownstone. Iggy wasn't happy to learn that his home would be invaded for dinner, but when Alex explained, he agreed.

"I'll prepare something special," he said and hung up.

Alex's next call was to Danny.

"Did you see the papers this morning?" he asked when the line connected.

"I guess Detweiler knocked you off the front page," Alex said, a bit sheepishly.

"Not that," Danny said. "Margaret LaSalle's publisher already has orders for her book. He thinks it will sell one hundred thousand copies and he's putting me in the Acknowledgments at the front."

"Yeah," Alex said, "about that."

"Why are you using your bad news voice?" Danny asked, suspicion in his.

"I was thinking about that manuscript," Alex went on. "If you'd killed someone years ago and some writer was about to publish a book outing you to the world, that might compel you to kill her, right?"

"I suppose," Danny said. "I mean in your example I already committed one murder, so what's one more?"

"But you'd also have to get rid of the manuscript," Alex said. "You couldn't let that book go to print."

"Right," Danny said, following along. "So what?"

"So after you killed the writer and stole the manuscript, do you hide it in your bedroom?"

There was a long pause, then Danny sighed.

"No," he said. "I'd burn it."

"Me too," Alex said. "I don't think Ethan Nelson killed Margaret LaSalle."

"But he confessed to killing Dolly," Danny protested.

"And I'm sure he did that, but I'm pretty sure someone else killed Margaret."

"Okay, I'll bite," Danny said. "Who do you think killed Margaret?"

"Paul Baxter," Alex said.

"What makes you think Margaret's publisher would kill her?"

"It was something Iggy said last night. He said what you said, the new book would have sold one hundred thousand copies."

"So?"

"So remember Margaret's bank book," Alex pressed. "She only had a couple thousand in it."

"Okay," Danny said, understanding where Alex was going. "If her previous books sold anywhere near a hundred thousand copies, she should have piles of money."

"Baxter was stealing from her," Alex said. "I bet she figured it out and that's why he had to kill her."

"All right," Danny sighed. "I'll get a warrant and seize his records. That way, at least I can prove it if he was stealing."

"You can do better than that," Alex said. "Baxter isn't a criminal mastermind. How much you want to bet he kept the gun he used on Margaret?"

Danny chuckled at that.

"No bet," he said. "I guess I'll go over and search his house for a .38 revolver."

"You can let me know tonight over dinner at the brownstone," Alex said. "Six o'clock?"

"Are you cooking?" Danny asked, trepidation clearly evident in his voice.

"No," Alex laughed. "Iggy will be doing the honors."

"In that case, I'm in."

Alex hung up and sat staring at the phone. He was just reaching for it when his office door opened, and Sherry came in.

"You just got a call from Regina Darling," she said. "She wants to know if you talked with Ms. Kincaid yet? She said to tell you that she'd like to go to dinner with you tonight."

Alex sighed. He'd forgotten about Regina. More to the point, he'd forgotten about Regina's insistence that he talk to Sorsha. After last night, he was pretty sure it was a conversation he didn't need to have.

"Thanks," he said to Sherry. "I'll be sure to call her."

She nodded and withdrew back to her desk as Alex picked up his phone.

"Hello," Sorsha's voice greeted him.

"You were right."

"Alex?" she asked. "Right about what?"

"We need to work together," he said. "More than you know."

"Oh? Has something come up?" There was an edge in her voice that spoke of caution but also energy, as if whatever the danger was, she was ready to run off and face it with him.

"You could say that," he replied. "Meet me at my place at five and I'll explain everything."

She wasn't happy with that cryptic invitation, but she promised to be punctual and hung up.

This time, Alex didn't hesitate. As soon as his call to Sorsha disconnected, he picked up the phone again and dialed Regina's number.

"You were right," he said when she picked up. He didn't mention the sorceress, but Regina knew what he meant.

"Well, I'm sorry about that," she said. "Not for you, but for myself. I guess I'll have to find someone else to take me to dinner tonight."

"Are you angry?"

Regina snickered at the question.

"Maybe a little," she said. "But I'll get over it. The show must go on, after all. Take care of yourself, Alex."

"You too," he said.

33

THE IRREGULARS

Alex took the precaution of visiting Empire Tower before his meeting with Sorsha, so he had a pot of Marnie's excellent coffee waiting for her in his vault's small kitchen. With Iggy preparing dinner in the brownstone's kitchen, Alex wanted to talk where it would be quiet, and they wouldn't disturb him.

"Okay," Sorsha said as she sipped the coffee he'd offered her. "There's no way you made this, where did you get it?"

Alex gave her a knowing smile but said nothing as he poured a cup for himself. Sorsha sat with her legs crossed at the table which was barely big enough for two people. She wore a deep red dress that reminded Alex of the one she had on the night she'd almost killed him while under Malcom Jones' control, only this one wasn't so fancy. Her usually pale legs were covered in dark stockings, and she wore black pumps that gave her enough height that her head almost came up to Alex's nose.

"I guess this meeting is about secrets," Alex said, sitting opposite her at the table. "Maybe I'll tell you later."

Sorsha gave him an exasperated look, then set the coffee cup down and folded her hands in front of her.

"So tell me," she said, a faint trace of uncertainty in her voice. "Last night you weren't big on the idea of working together, but now you're all for it. What happened that changed your mind?"

"Before we go into that," Alex said, reciting a speech he'd rewritten about a dozen times in his head, "I want to know I can trust you to keep anything I might tell you between us."

Sorsha gave him an appraising look, then nodded her assent.

"That's fair," she said. "How about I tell you one of my secrets?"

Alex didn't know what the sorceress might consider an important secret, but the prospect of learning whatever it was had him nodding along.

Sorsha leaned forward across the table, looking left and then right as if she was afraid of being overheard.

"I know that you have the Archimedean Monograph," she said.

Alex opened his mouth to protest, but she went on.

"You blew it when you used those temporal restoration runes last year," she explained. "That's power no runewright ever had. In fact, all the runewrights in the city couldn't manage magic like that if you added their talents together, and you used them like they were nothing. Just another rune in your book." She shook her head. "When I saw that, I figured you must have found the Monograph after I used the truth spell on you. Imagine my shock when I asked around the Central Office of Police and learned that you used one of those runes five years ago, right before you and I met."

Alex remembered. He'd used a temporal restoration rune to restore the remains of a man named Jerry Pemberton who'd been murdered and then burned to hide the evidence.

Sorsha's face suddenly clouded over in anger which snapped Alex back to full attention.

"Somehow you stood there in that dead runewright's workshop and you lied right to my face. You told me you didn't know anything about the Archimedean Monograph's whereabouts."

"To be fair, you were using an illegal truth spell on me at the time," Alex pointed out.

If Sorsha felt any shame about that, it didn't show on her face.

"Now it's obvious that Dr. Bell found the Monograph," Sorsha continued. "Probably years before he became your teacher. Since he'd found it, you technically didn't lie when I asked if you had."

Alex stifled a smirk and nodded.

"Of course when I met you, you'd never heard of the Monograph. I remember how eager you were for me to tell you what it was. So that means that Dr. Bell must have told you about it after you learned of its existence but before I used the truth spell on you."

"Very good, Sorceress," he said. It was an impressive bit of deduction. Iggy would have been proud.

"Don't call me that when we're alone," she said. "I have a name."

Alex apologized and she went on.

"So you see, I've known a secret the FBI, the Army, and the government want to know very dearly, but I've kept your secret, and I promise I'll keep any others you share with me."

Alex hated to admit it, but he was impressed. Sorsha had the power of a sorcerer and dressed in the latest fashions, but she was no empty-headed socialite. Her innate elegance and beauty made it easy to forget that.

Reaching down into his kit bag, Alex pulled out a thin, red-backed leather book and set it on the table.

"I had planned to tell you about this anyway," he said, sliding the book over to her.

Sorsha's hands trembled as she picked up the book and opened it to the first blank page. Even though she didn't understand the runes or the lore, she turned each page with reverence, examining the drawings and the spidery script. Alex didn't interrupt her, he just sat, sipping his coffee and watching the expressions of awe and wonder cross Sorsha's porcelain face as she went.

"It's magnificent," she said finally, closing the book. "I'd like to read some of the notations later," she said, pushing the book back across the table to Alex. "I saw some very interesting names in there."

"As long as you read it here, I don't think Iggy would mind," Alex said, returning the book to his bag.

"I'm glad you showed that to me, Alex," she said. "Now hadn't we better get on to the reason you changed your mind?"

Alex sighed.

"Well, that's a bit of a long story," he admitted.

"Then start at the beginning."

Alex told her the story of how Iggy had come to have the Archimedean Monograph, though he left out Iggy's true identity. After all, that wasn't his secret to share. He related how the former Royal Army runewrights had gone looking for the Monograph and how Iggy had to flee to America.

Sorsha knew some of the story already, but she sat sipping her coffee as Alex spun the tale. When he mentioned Moriarty, she put down her cup, and she gasped at the revelation of a fourth branch of magic. When Alex finished, Sorsha just stared at him for a long moment.

"If I didn't know you, I wouldn't have believed half of that," she said.

"I lived it and I still don't believe parts of it," Alex said with a grin.

"Do you think he's right?" Sorsha asked. "Moriarty."

Alex could only shrug.

"If he's not, then all of this — new magics, secret societies, magical weapons — seems very coincidental."

Sorsha set her jaw in a grim expression and nodded, looking up at him with her pale blue eyes.

"I don't mind telling you," she said at last. "It frightens me."

That was something Alex never thought he'd hear from her. That said, he'd be worried about her if she wasn't at least a little bit afraid. The implications of what Alex had told her in the last twenty minutes were literally world-altering.

"It scares me to death," he admitted. "I've been juggling all of this for a few years now, but I can't go on like this. I need help. We are going to need help," he amended.

"You're right," Sorsha said. "Whoever these enemies are, they're organized. Far more than I'd imagined. We aren't going to be able to fight them by ourselves."

"That's why I've invited Sherry Knox and Danny to join us for dinner."

Sorsha raised an eyebrow in a questioning look.

"Danny knows about Dr. Kellin's youth serum and he's kept quiet,"

Alex said. "We can trust him and, once he's made a lieutenant, he can keep us appraised of cases with a magical element."

Sorsha nodded.

"I'll do the same thing with the FBI," she said. "What about your secretary?"

"I still don't know what her magic is capable of," Alex admitted. "We need to keep her close."

"It's a good start," Sorsha said.

"I figure once we get ourselves organized, we can bring in others. Barton and maybe Lieutenant Callahan; he's about to be made captain over the detectives."

"We need to be careful," Sorsha said. "If anyone official learns about our little group, they'll want to know what we know. There are people in positions of power in the government who could make life very difficult for us if they wanted."

Alex had no doubt of that. He was just a simple private detective and the government already made it hard for him to do his job. If they wanted something from him, they could easily put the screws to him.

They sat in silence as they each considered what had been said. Alex refilled their coffee as the silence stretched into minutes. Finally Sorsha sighed and nodded.

"All right," she said at last. "We're in this together."

"Afraid so," he said with a grin.

Sorsha drained her coffee cup and handed it to Alex.

"I guess we should go help out Dr. Bell, then. After that, we'll have a lovely dinner and you can tell the others what you just told me."

"Then what?" Alex said, taking the cup and putting it into the little sink along with his own.

"Then we start pushing back," Sorsha said. "We go looking for the Legion and anyone else who wants power so they can steal or murder or rule."

"You make it sound easy," he said, offering her his arm.

"It won't be easy," she said, standing. "But I suspect nothing will be impossible for Alex Lockerby and his Arcane Irregulars."

Alex snickered at that, but then stopped suddenly.

"Hey," he protested. "Why am I in charge?" That was a job he definitely didn't want.

"Moriarty thinks you're going to be his lever to move the world," Sorsha said, giving him an amused look. "And Sherry says you could be a rune lord. No matter how you look at it, Alex, you're the person at the center of everything that's happening."

"I think you just don't want to be the one in charge," Alex said as she swept out into the hall.

She turned and patted him on the cheek with a mocking look.

"You're cute when you're feeling put upon," she said, then walked through the open vault door and down the stairs to the kitchen.

Alex followed, unsure of how he felt. When he started out, this little cabal felt like a good idea. Now it was starting to sound like the plan was to paint a bullseye on his back, then try to catch anyone taking a shot at him. Sorsha was right about one thing, though. Everyone seemed to think that he had some destiny laid on him.

He didn't believe in destiny, but then he also didn't believe in coincidence.

"Just keep your eyes open," he muttered to himself. It was the only thing he was sure he could do.

THE END

A Quick Note

Thanks so much for reading my book, it really means a lot to me. This is the part where I ask you to please leave this book a review over on Amazon. It really helps me out since Amazon favors books with lots of reviews. That means I can share these books with more people, and that keeps me writing more books.

. . .

So leave a review by going to the Limelight book page on Amazon. It doesn't have to be anything fancy, just a quick note saying whether or not you liked the book.

Thanks so much. You Rock!

I love talking to my readers, so please drop me a line at dan@danwillisauthor.com — I read every one. Or join the discussion on the Arcane Casebook Facebook Group. Just search for Arcane Casebook and ask to join.

And Look for Alex's continuing adventures in Blood Relation: Arcane Casebook #6. Available now.

ALSO BY DAN WILLIS

Arcane Casebook Series:

Dead Letter - Prequel

Private Detective Alex Lockerby needs a break and it materializes in the form of an ambitious, up-and-coming beat cop, Danny Pack. Alex and Danny team up to unravel a tale murder, jealousy, and revenge stretching back over 30 years. It's a tale that powerful forces don't want to come to light. Now the cop and the private detective must work fast and watch each other's backs if they hope to catch a killer and live to tell about it.

Dead Letter is the prequel novella to the Arcane Casebook series.

Get Dead Letter Free at: danwillisauthor.com

In Plain Sight - Book 1

In 1933, an unwitting thief steals a vial of deadly plague, accidentally releasing it in at a soup kitchen in Manhattan. The police, the FBI, and New York's 'council of Sorcerers' fear the incident is a trial run for something much deadlier. Detective Alex Lockerby, himself under suspicion because of ties to the priest who ran the kitchen, has a book of spells, a pack of matches, and four days to find out where the plague came from, or the authorities will hang the crime squarely on him.

Get In Plain Sight on Amazon

Ghost of a Chance - Book 2

When a bizarre string of locked-room murders terrorize New York, the police have no leads, no suspects, and only one place to turn. Now private detective Alex Lockerby will need every magical trick in his book to catch a killer who can walk through walls and leaves no trace. With the Ghost killer seemingly able to murder at will and the tabloids, the public, and Alex's clients demanding results, Alex will need a miracle to keep himself, his clients, and his reputation alive.

Get Ghost of a Chance on Amazon

The Long Chain - Book 3

In a city the size of New York, things go missing all the time. When New York is blanketed in an unnatural fog, Alex finds himself on the trail of a missing scientist, a stolen military secret, and a merciless killer leaving a trail of bodies in their wake. Now Alex must unravel a tangled web of science, murder, and missing memories before the clues vanish into the ever-present fog.

The Long Chain on Amazon

Mind Games - Book 4

When wealthy socialites hire him to track down their wayward daughter, finding her is easy, but that's just the beginning of Alex's problems. As he's trying to deal with the no-longer-missing heiress and her family, Alex gets another case from a desperate young man who wants Alex to prove his wife is innocent of murder. As Alex investigates he becomes convinced that both of his clients are being manipulated by someone with a bigger agenda.

Mind Games on Amazon

Dragons of the Confederacy Series:

A steampunk Civil War story with NYT Bestseller, Tracy Hickman

Lincoln's Wizard

Washington has fallen! Legions of 'grays' -- dead soldiers reanimated on the battlefield and pressed back into service of the Southern Cause -- have pushed the lines as far north as the Ohio River. Lincoln has moved the government of the United States to New York City. He needs to stop the juggernaught of the Southern undead 'abominations' or the North will ultimately fall. But Allan Pinkerton, his head of security, has a plan...

Get Lincoln's Wizard on Amazon

The Georgia Alchemist

With Air Marshall Sherman's fleet on the run and the Union lines failing, Pinkerton's agents, Hattie Lawton and Braxton Wright make their way into the heart of the south. Pursued by the Confederacy's best agents, time is running out for Hattie and Braxton to locate the man whose twisted genius brings dead soldiers back to fight and find a way to stop the inexorable tide that threatens to engulf the Union.

Forthcoming: 2020

Other books:

The Flux Engine

In a Steampunk Wild West, fifteen-year-old John Porter wants nothing more than to find his missing family. Unfortunately a legendary lawman, a talented thief, and a homicidal madman have other plans, and now John will need his wits, his pistol, and a lot of luck if he's going to survive.

Get The Flux Engine on Amazon

ABOUT THE AUTHOR

Dan Willis wrote for the long-running DragonLance series. He is the author of the Arcane Casebook series and the Dragons of the Confederacy series.

For more information:
www.danwillisauthor.com
dan@danwillisauthor.com

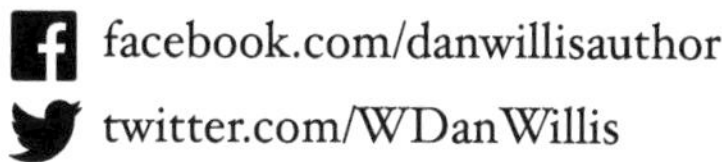
facebook.com/danwillisauthor
twitter.com/WDanWillis

Made in the USA
Middletown, DE
13 September 2021

48194547R00203